"DAV, IT'S YOU? ARE YOU OKAY?"

As she clutched at his jacket, he felt the shaking in her arms, the tremble in her body.

"No, but I'm alive, and thank God you are too," he said with heartfelt relief as her shaking hands raced over him. He could tell she was bound as well, since her hands moved together, tugging at his shirt and his lapels. More than anything, he wanted to crush her to him, hold her tightly, feel her life. "I'm okay." He said it over and over until she began to relax and stop running her hands frantically up and down his chest.

Then he added wryly, "But when we get out of this, Gates is going to kill me." He felt her stiffen, then felt a tremor rock her body. "Carrie, are you okay?"

"Believe it or not, I'm laughing," she said, and her voice quivered. "Although that doesn't seem appropriate. If we get out of this, Gates will probably want to kill me too."

"Oh, Carrie," Dav said, his heart sinking. "I am so sorry."

"Hush, Dav," she said, her voice firm and sharp now. "We're here. We'll figure it out. What is it they say? While there's life, there's hope."

Please, God, let her be right.

More from Jeanne Adams

DARK AND DANGEROUS

DARK AND DEADLY

DEADLY LITTLE SECRETS

Published by Kensington Publishing Corporation

DEADLY LITTLE LIES

Jeanne Adams

ZEBRA BOOKS
KENSINGTON PUBLISHING CORP.
http://www.kensingtonbooks.com

ZEBRA BOOKS are published by

Kensington Publishing Corp.
119 West 40th Street
New York, NY 10018

All Kensington titles, imprints and distributed lines are available at special quantity discounts for bulk purchases for sales promotion, premiums, fund-raising, educational or institutional use.

Special book excerpts or customized printings can also be created to fit specific needs. For details, write or phone the office of the Kensington Special Sales Manager: Attn. Special Sales Department. Kensington Publishing Corp., 119 West 40th Street, New York, NY 10018. Phone: 1-800-221-2647.

Zebra and the Z logo Reg. U.S. Pat. & TM Off.

ISBN-13: 978-1-4201-0883-5
ISBN-10: 1-4201-0883-2

First Printing: September 2011

10 9 8 7 6 5 4 3 2 1

Printed in the United States of America

This book is lovingly dedicated to my family,
especially my husband and sons because,
really,
it's all about love

Acknowledgments

Many thanks, once again, to my dear friend, Vasilia Contos, for her assistance with the Greek, and her patience with me wanting to know "bad words" in another language, so Dav could curse. A huge thank you to fellow Washington Romance Writers member Lisa Arlt for her firsthand knowledge of Central American countries, politics, flora and fauna. Thanks as well to The Avocat Noir group, for plotting help, and as always to the fabulous Romance Bandits (www.RomanceBandits.blogspot.com) for being supportive, brilliant, funny and eager to read Dav and Carrie's story.

Prologue

It's hard to retire when you're an assassin.

Jurgens's latest assignment, a very inconvenient therapist who had learned far too much about certain clients, twitched and died as blood pooled on the highly polished, trendy concrete floor of the office loft. As he slipped out the man's wallet and retrieved an ID—not the driver's license, that was too obvious—he contemplated how best to extricate himself from the job.

"Too many targets," he muttered, "so little time." His beloved Caroline had laughed when he'd said that to her. His German accent faint but still with him after decades of living in the United States.

"There will always be someone willing to kill for hire," Caroline had reminded him as she made him breakfast before they left for Boston to execute this contract. It was true, of course. Many enjoyed killing. Few did it as effectively as he did. Fewer still kept at it as long.

Still, with the boy and Caroline now permanently in his life, and hopefully more children once they wed, it was time to give it up.

He frowned as he covered his tweed jacket with a chunky canvas coat. There was a new call waiting for an answer. A request for services with a very large paycheck attached.

It was one to ponder, however. One did not lightly accept a contract to kill a billionaire, especially when that billionaire was Davros Gianikopolis.

Always keep moving, he reminded himself as he tucked his trousers into work boots and affected a slouching, limping walk. He pulled a cap over his close-cropped hair as he slipped out of the warm brick building through the service entrance. It emptied into an alley with no surveillance, not even a nearby ATM camera.

Boston in March was a bonus on a job like this. The clothes let him blend in with construction workers in the area, returning to various job sites from early breaks. Most people were just arriving at work, so there was a bustle of foot traffic on the sidewalk, despite the wind. Jurgens walked with them, pretending to bob his head in time with music from an MP3 player.

As he crossed the street and turned in a new direction, he changed his gate, striding rather than strolling, head up rather than down, music player tucked away. Within blocks he had tugged his pants from his boots, removed his cap and tucked it inside his coat. Inside a coffee shop, he removed the heavy canvas coat, returning to the slightly rumpled sport coat.

It was cold in Boston. No one batted an eye at his attire.

"You still offer the grounds, for the garden, yes?" he asked the young girl behind the coffee counter as he ordered and paid. She nodded vigorously and called for the manager to fetch coffee grounds. He sipped his latte and thought about Dav, as many called him, and whether or not to take the job.

In a convoluted way, Dav was responsible for his current

happiness, for the chance to court Caroline as if he were a legitimate businessman who had met her through her late husband. No one need ever know that Jurgens was the assassin who'd killed her husband, nor that Caroline had known the plan all along.

As the manager bagged the coffee grounds, she offered a coupon for a free drink. "Sorry you had to wait. That's the second request I had today," she said, handing him the bag.

A short cab ride later, he used his hotel key to enter the back stairwell of the elegant Luxe Inn near Nob Hill. Out of range of the security cameras, he cleaned the rest of the therapist's blood from the gardener's all-purpose knife with the coffee grounds. He was careful to remove all trace of skin and blood from the blade and wiped it once more for prints, even though he'd worn gloves.

Earlier he'd tucked a garden cart into the stairwell; now he dropped the knife and coffee grounds in a bin that held a mix of grounds and soil, which the Luxe used in their atrium lobby. When and if the blade was found, it would be returned to use, with no hint of the assassination Jurgens had performed. Nor was it likely the police would ever find a knife half a city away, buried in coffee grounds in a garden cart.

He moved the cart to the hall so it would quickly be reclaimed for use, then went to his room. He cleaned up and changed, then took a moment to comb and part his hair a different way and add wire-rimmed glasses before leaving with his briefcase. The bed, mussed as if he'd slept there, the dampened towels on the floor as if he'd showered, all said one-night stay for a businessman. The key card he'd used for the outer door and the one he left on the dresser bore no connection to him whatsoever.

Back outside, he changed his walk, his very persona, and joined his beloved at the Boston Children's Museum.

“Caroline,” he breathed her name, spotting her lovely face in the crowd. She saw him as well, and her smile was joyful.

Later, he would get her advice on the matter of killing Dav Gianikopolis.

Chapter 1

"It's about time," Dav Gianikopolis said jokingly as his former security expert and longtime business partner, Gates Bromley, arrived for their meeting. "I was beginning to think Ana had tied you up and chained you to the computer."

"Well, she does have this sexy new program running," Gates said, and grinned. "It's designed to dig out large transfers from accredited U.S. banks to banks in Central America. It's for one of *those* clients." He made air quotes around the word "those" as he said it. Ana, his new wife, had retired from the CIA, but her contacts had drawn four government clients for their new business before the ink on the incorporation papers had dried.

"That's good. Those clients pay the bills better than most. So, how does it feel to be the CEO of your own budding empire?" Dav asked, motioning Gates to a seat. He sat as well and poured coffee for them both.

"Co-CEO," Gates corrected. "It feels good. Surprisingly good. You were right," he said, then stopped when Dav laughed. "Yeah, yeah, you laugh. Go ahead and gloat. I'll say it as many times as you need me to—you were right. I needed to get out on my own again, and I'm glad I did."

"Excellent. Your incentive was quite impressive," Dav

said, referring to Ana. "Not to mention an excellent choice as a business partner. How's the other venture?"

"The one we were working on before I left? It's going well," Gates replied, sipping the coffee appreciatively. "The Colombian government decided they would indeed let us send them two of our colleagues to bring their tax system into the twenty-first century."

"I thought we only promised to get them as far as the twentieth. Didn't we decide the twenty-first would require a second contract?" Dav joked.

"Considering they were operating at about the level of the Sheriff of Nottingham with an abacus, we'll do plenty of work just to get them to the twentieth," Gates replied with a laugh.

"True. Getting them all the way to the twenty-first century would require rewiring their entire capital."

Gates smirked. "I think you offered to arrange that too, for a price."

Dav grinned. "I think you're the one who offered that. Either way, we got the deal. Did the check clear?"

"It did. So I've got two specialists and two guards going down next week." Gates pulled a roster out of his briefcase and they started setting up the rotation of staff.

They spent the next hour discussing the job—the placement of their team and what kind of information and bribes they were going to have to pay to be sure their team was protected. It was still somewhat dangerous to put personnel anywhere in Central or some countries in South America, though most of the governments had stabilized. There were still plenty of desperate people who would risk death to ransom Americans. This was one area where being Greek rather than American worked in Dav's favor. He might not like payoffs, but outside the United States, they were fairly standard procedure, and he knew how to employ them to good effect.

"Good. So, you're coming in when the new security geek starts, right?" Dav asked. He knew, of course, but it was a way to get the unspoken out into the open. It was far harder than he'd imagined not having Gates around. He'd put off replacing his security chief for months, only beginning the hiring process at Gates's actual departure. He'd put off a hiring decision for several more months.

"I'm so easily replaced." Gates pantomimed great sorrow, then laughed. "Don't comment on that. Seriously. Don't." His grin dimmed a little. "I miss being here, you know. Not so much that I want to give up Ana and the new business and come back, but I miss it." He sighed. "And that's not what you asked. Geddey, the new guy, as you so slanderously labeled him, starts next week. And you know that too."

"Yes, but it's good to review it and to have you here," Dav admitted, and saw that Gates understood. As was the way with longtime comrades, no more needed to be said, so Dav changed the subject. "I've sent a request to your assistant, whom you stole from my employ." He put on a frown, though he knew young Alexia was thrilled to be the assistant to the new co-CEOs. "For a quote on several business matters. I've also sent her the dates that the cottage in the Hamptons is available, as well as the place on Maui."

Gates looked surprised. "That's gracious of you."

"The contracts? Oh, you'll earn those."

Gates rolled his eyes. "You know what I mean." A speculative look stole over his face. "Ana would like the Hamptons."

"You would know," Dav said, giving Gates a sly look. He both enjoyed and envied the satisfied smile that lit his friend's face.

"Speaking of Ana, did I tell you that she had a lead on the other culprit in our caper last year? The rogue agent who took out her friend TJ," Gates explained, evidently seeing the puzzlement Dav felt. So much had happened since last year's whirlwind events that he'd forgotten the stray thread that had never been snipped.

"Hines?" Dav pulled the name out of his memory. "Didn't he go to Canada?"

"So we thought, but Ana has a lead on him in Central America, Belize or Guatemala. McGuire's been digging."

"Speaking of rogues," Dav drawled, remembering the retired agent who'd helped solve both the original case and assisted in unraveling the puzzle of the art theft and all the events that cleared Carrie's gallery. Ana had invited him to her wedding to Gates, and to everyone's surprise, McGuire had come.

Gates grinned. "I don't know if he'll go hunting or not, but I've heard the Gold Coast in Central America is nice in spring."

"Hmmm. I've never had any ambitions to visit. Perhaps you and Ana can investigate it and suggest some investments there." Dav waggled his eyebrows, teasing his friend.

"Not a bad idea," Gates said, taking the jibe with ease.

Dav checked his watch. He had an appointment with a beautiful woman, and he wasn't going to miss it, so he said, "Come and walk me out to the car. I've got to go into the city. I'm having several pieces reframed and Ms. McCray has finally agreed to have lunch with me."

He said it casually, knowing the comment wouldn't slip past, but always willing to give it a try.

"Oh-ho!" Gates exclaimed, rising along with Dav. He landed a manly punch on Dav's upper arm. "She finally agreed to go out with you? What did you do, bribe her?"

"Riiiiiight," Dav drawled, slipping into his impeccably tailored jacket. "I do not have to bribe women to go out with me."

"No, not women in general. Just this one," he joked. Dav enjoyed their banter all the way to the car. "Hey—" Gates brought him back to the moment. "Have a good ride in and a good lunch. She's a nice woman. I like her."

"I do too," Dav said, wondering if he should confide how nervous he was. Seeing Gates grinning at him, he decided not to. He knew it was just lunch, but it had the weight and feel of something far more serious. "Maybe I'm reading too much into it."

His concern must have shown because Gates set the teasing aside and shrugged. "You never know," Gates temporized. "It's been nine years for her since the lying, cheating husband died. Then it was all dug up, fresh—no pun intended—last year. Maybe she realized it was time to move on."

"Maybe," was as far as Dav would agree.

Gates smiled, evidently understanding that Dav didn't want to discuss Carrie's motives. "Either way, enjoy it. We'll get you those figures."

Dav pondered the Colombian deal on the drive to the city. It kept him from focusing on his impending lunch with the elusive Carrie McCray. They'd met years before when Carrie and her husband, Luke, had just opened Prometheus, now one of San Francisco's foremost art galleries. Dav had just begun to build his business empire from the ashes of his father's mistakes, choosing to locate his headquarters in San Francisco rather than Athens.

Trying to keep the family together, he'd hired his half brother, but that hadn't worked out. They'd fought over Niko's less savory tendencies and Dav had sent him off to make his amends or die trying. Then their father had died, leaving everything to Dav. At the funeral, Niko swore out his hatred and vowed never to come home again.

Truth be told, Dav still wished the old man had given it all to Niko. Dav had built the foundation of his own businesses by then and didn't want to be dragged back into the dark family dramas his father so enjoyed orchestrating. As an adult, he refused to play the games, but his father fooled them all in the end, dumping everything on Dav.

When Niko had died in Somalia four years ago as part of

a mercenary troop, Dav had genuinely mourned. He still wondered if Niko had gotten the business—the prize—would he still be alive?

Not the way he did business, Dav decided, as he usually did. *He'd have been killed early for some of the stunts he was pulling. Or been jailed in any country that caught him.* Dav had always tried to help Niko, but it never worked.

"Are we picking Ms. McCray up, sir, or are you going in?" Damon's question broke into his murky thoughts as they reached the outskirts of San Francisco. The young man was a superb driver and Dav welcomed the distraction. He shook off memories of the past and focused on how much he was looking forward to lunch with a beautiful, intriguing woman.

"I'll be going in. You'll probably have to circle the block," Dav told the driver, checking the time. He hated to be late, but you never knew how long the trip over the bridge would take.

"Very good. And no worries on the circling. I know a good spot to use as a holding pattern."

Dav eyed the cloud bank over the bay. It didn't look like rain, but this late in the spring, there could be fog. It was warmer than usual this year. The previous spring, he'd been hip deep in the art fraud investigation that brought Ana and her brilliant skills to his door. She'd unraveled the mystery of the missing paintings, and the devious involvement of Carrie McCray's late husband in the case.

Clearing Carrie and her gallery was an unlooked for bonus, and somewhat balanced out Ana's subsequent theft of Gates's heart. It also brought Carrie more closely into Dav's life.

"Always a silver lining," he murmured, checking his watch again. They cleared the bridge and he saw the sun shining on Coit Tower. Good. It would be a nice enough day to walk to the restaurant he had in mind.

Gates and Ana made him realize he needed to pay attention to more than business. He'd done a lot of soul searching in the last few months. He had money, status and the empire he'd built, but none of it mattered. Not really.

Family, though, that was permanent. Family required personal attention, involvement on a human level. People needed tending, especially children. It was time he had children in his life.

"Looks like it's still nice in the city," Damon spoke again, "and we've made good time over the bridge. Will you want to go on to the gallery?"

"Yes, I'll let Ms. McCray know we're earlier than we thought." Pleased at the timing, he called Prometheus.

As the phone rang, he remembered the first time he'd gone into the gallery. It had been a day like this, sunny and bright. He'd been gloomy, however, brooding over his future, over his father's machinations. His father was testing both his sons unmercifully to make them fight for the company, fight to be his heir.

Walking and thinking, he'd seen the sign going up outside the old building that housed the gallery. Their symbol, the Greek demigod who brought fire to mankind, had been portrayed carrying a flame and a paintbrush.

In that moment, desperately homesick for Greece, he'd seen Carrie.

She'd stood, framed in the window, a pale, dark-haired wand in the middle of the huge space, flanked by massive, colorful paintings. He didn't even see the art, though he'd later bought two of the pieces she'd been hanging that day. The image of her, her raven hair pulled away from sharp features and highlighting startlingly blue eyes, was etched on his memory. He'd been instantly captivated, feeling his heart lift at the sight of her slim beauty.

Then Luke had come around the corner and given her an absent pat and a peck on the cheek and he'd seen her smile. His heart had plummeted. He'd known in an instant, by her response to the man, that she was out of his reach. Now

Luke was dead, these nine years, and he and Carrie were both free.

"Prometheus Gallery." A young voice answered the phone, jarring him back to the present. He didn't recognize the female tones, but he knew Carrie frequently employed interns so he paid it no heed.

"This is Davros Gianikopolis, calling for Ms. McCray. Is she in, please?"

"Certainly, sir. If you'll hold a moment, I'll get her."

As the music-on-hold droned in his ear, he continued to remember. The art fraud scandal had nearly broken the gallery. Luke had bailed out on both Prometheus and his wife. He'd run, and died, leaving a cloud of suspicion hanging over Prometheus and Carrie.

A breathless voice came on the line and he smiled. "Dav? Hello?"

"Hello, Carrie," he replied, enjoying the sound of her, the hint of laughter in her voice. That came more easily now, he realized. "I'm afraid I'm a bit early. I hope that's not inconvenient."

"No, no, not at all." He heard the smile in her voice. "I'm ready whenever you are."

"Really?" He grinned, delighted at the opening. They'd been bantering, and enjoying this verbal play for months now, on and off. She'd continued to put him off about a date. Until today.

He needed to determine if she was interested in him as a man or a client.

Today would give him a better idea. Or shoot him down. Not that he would give up, however.

"For lunch, Dav," she said, but he heard her laugh. "Hang on, let me tell Inez. . . ." She paused, then said, "Drat, the girl's on her cell phone. Well, I'll tell her in a minute that the timetable's moved up a bit."

"Inez?" He frowned. He didn't remember an Inez.

"She's moved to working days. I'll tell you all about it when you get here."

"Excellent. We'll arrive in less than ten minutes." He hesitated, wanting to continue the conversation, even though it was commonplace, meaningless. "Well, good-bye for now, then," he finished, clipping the words so his foolish reluctance wouldn't show through. She replied in kind and he cut the call.

"Damon, who's on duty today?"

"Dec, Thompson, Queller, Georgiade. Oh, and me, of course."

Dav smiled at the eager young man. "Of course."

The first thing he noticed when he got out of the car was the new bronze plaque on the building. It listed Luke's birth and death dates. Since Ana had proved Luke's relative innocence in the art scheme and uncovered that he'd been murdered to ensure his silence, Carrie had put up the plaque in memory. It helped, she'd said, that the gallery was in the clear at last, thanks to Ana.

He'd greatly admired that Carrie had held her head high, maintained her equilibrium and had been the epitome of grace under fire. He'd always been attracted to her, but kept his distance. Even so, he never failed to attend an event if she invited him. She never failed to show an artist he recommended.

But she never let him get close, not until Ana came along. The events of last year, the deaths, the danger, put things in perspective for him. Life seemed very short and very precious.

Sometime in the middle of everything, in the chaos, Dav had decided that Carrie was what he wanted. More, she was what he needed.

That decided, he went on the offensive, just as he would in business. He'd sent flowers, arranged meetings, asked Carrie out point-blank.

She'd turned him down on every occasion. He'd persisted.

Now, finally, she'd agreed to lunch. He got out of the car and put his topcoat over his arm in case the afternoon turned cooler. He didn't plan to let her get away with a mere hour or two over a meal. He had an agenda and he was good at getting his way.

The thought made him smile. This—planning, executing the plan—was something at which he excelled. It had built a worldwide network of companies that had weathered every downturn, so far. It could build a mutually beneficial relationship.

"She'll probably try to tell me she's not seeing anyone, not dating, that it isn't me," Dav muttered as he strode alone to the gallery doors, waving off his security detail. "Can't piss off a big buyer, but you have to give him the set-down, tell him to quit bugging you."

He'd decided not to let her get away with that.

In a lightning shift of thought, Dav wondered if thinking about her as much as he did made him a candidate for—he mentally searched for the American term—ah yes, "stalkerdom."

It was yet one more thing to ponder in his campaign to woo Carrie and begin a new stage of his life.

Andras. Husband.

That had a solid sound to it. He'd once thought of marriage as a trap, a shackle created to give a certain type of woman a safety net, a security for which she'd not worked or striven or thought. Usually, the women attracted to men as wealthy as he did not work. They played tennis or ran charities or managed the many properties their husbands owned. And when the inevitable divorce came along, they made everyone pay; the husband, the children, the staff. He'd never wanted that. In fact, he'd avoided it at all costs. Even if a family came with less pain than his father had caused, it seemed pointless.

Seeing Gates and Ana together had proved it could work. Marriage could work. Passion could work. It could work for two people who were smart and equally powerful and equally driven. Even when passion inevitably died, as he assumed it would, they were so well matched in business, Dav could see them spending decades together, driven by their joint fascination with their business skills.

"Terma," he said, smiling. *The decision is final.*

He would make it work. Given that he had great respect and affection for her, Carrie was, in his mind, the best possible candidate for the position of his wife.

He'd never failed at anything before, once he set his mind to it.

This would be no exception.

Dav stepped into the quiet gallery, and another term came to mind as he saw a magnificent oil painting of a man tenderly holding a child, his dark, angular face relaxed in a smile. The artist had captured heart and pride with bold strokes of the brush, and subtle highlights that showed the vulnerability of the sleeping boy in the man's arms.

Patera. Father.

Though it had negative connotations in his own life, he would make sure his children, Carrie's children, didn't suffer what he had suffered.

Yes. He smiled, feeling the rush of adrenaline he usually felt only as a business deal came together.

Excellent.

Eh-la, he thought with anticipation. *The game begins.*

Chapter 2

"Dav." Carrie came out of the shadowy side gallery, heading toward him with every evidence of pleasure, hands outstretched in greeting.

Shoots the theory that she'll turn me down. Another good step.

"Hello, my dear." Dav took her hands and kissed each of her cheeks in the Greek manner. She smelled fresh, like lilies or roses. "Ready for lunch?"

"Absolutely. Let me get my purse," she said, slipping free of his hold. He couldn't tell if she was uncomfortable being close to him or if she was just nervous.

"You won't need it," he called after her.

She stopped and looked over her shoulder and laughed. Once again, he had a snapshot of her in his mind, captured in that moment, with that laugh ringing between them. "A woman always needs her purse."

"That," Dav said quietly to himself, "does not seem like a woman who's going to shut this down."

"I'm sorry, sir, did you need something? May I help you?" a familiar young voice asked, and he pivoted to face Carrie's assistant. He hadn't seen her there and could have kicked himself. He knew better than that. *Always be aware of your surroundings*. The admonition rang in his mind. Of course, with Gates in charge, Dav would never have been in the gallery alone.

Feeling a bit like a naughty schoolboy, he hoped his two security hounds weren't too miffed at his ditching them at the car door. There had been no attacks in six months. It felt good to have a little space. His bodyguards were trying to follow Gates's imperatives, but all of them were in awe of their boss, an ailment Gates had never suffered.

"No, thank you, I'm just waiting for Ms. McCray," he said, remembering to answer the girl's question.

The girl looked surprised, and then unaccountably nervous. "Oh, I'll let her know you're here." She rushed through the words, which made her sound young and unsure. Before Dav could tell her he'd already seen Carrie, she hurried off.

The two women came back together. "Dav, this is Inez, my new daytime assistant. You remember Cal?" Carrie asked, a slight smile curving her lips.

Cal had been integral to the gallery for years. "Of course."

"True love, it seems, called him to New York, so I had the good fortune to get Inez for the daytime hours before anyone else snapped her up. As she's worked some of the gallery events in the evening and has an art degree, it worked out well for both of us." The compliments made Inez blush, making her seem even less confident rather than bolstering her as he assumed Carrie had intended. In fact, the girl was acting like a bashful debutante. "Be sure to lock up the front at one, when the delivery arrives," Carrie instructed, her introductions completed. "It's better to be safe when we have a shipment coming in. Tyra will be in as well to help you get Mr. Kerriat's purchases ready to ship out later this afternoon."

"Yes, ma'am, Carrie," the girl replied, shooting a look at Dav from under her lashes. If she was this self-effacing, he wondered how she managed clients. He'd nearly expected her to bob a curtsy. "Lock up for the shipment, and Tyra will help me with the order going out. Got it?"

"Exactly. Thank you," Carrie said, her tone encouraging. With a slight frown, she turned to him. "Well, Dav, shall we?"

"Of course." He offered her his arm and with a pleased glance, she took it. No, he didn't think she was going to shut him down at all. He smiled. It was a good date already and they'd barely cleared the door of the gallery. Through the glass, he could see Inez watching them as she raised her cell phone to her ear.

Carrie asked him a question, and he forgot Inez entirely.

"So," Dav said as they turned down the sidewalk. "Much to the chagrin of my security, I thought we could walk to Ma Maison. It's only a block or so. Does that suit you or should I have Damon bring the car?"

"Oh, it's such a nice day, walking's fine. Are you sure you should?" Carrie asked, her grip tightening on his arm as she glanced furtively around, presumably looking for his security detail. "I don't want to put you at risk."

He patted her hand, more as an excuse to touch her than for reassurance, though it served for that too. There was that need again. Every move he made was an excuse to touch her or be closer. It bothered him, in a way. He didn't like to need anything or anyone. Need offered leverage and that wasn't wise.

"Dav?"

Jolted back to the moment, he ran the conversation back in his mind. Risk. Yes, that was what she'd been asking about.

"No, no," he denied. "The risk is minimal. Since we closed the art fraud case, there haven't been any more attempts on my life." He smiled at her. In her low heels, they weren't eye to eye as they sometimes were at events. He forgot between those meetings how diminutive she was without her elegant high heels.

"I'm glad," Carrie said, and she tightened her grip on his arm, a brief squeeze. "It was a difficult time."

"More so for you, I think," Dav offered, giving her the opportunity to talk about it if she so chose. To his pleasure, she did.

"It was horrible, in some ways," she admitted. "Digging up all the scandal, having to exhume Luke's body to confirm his murder, finding out everything." Carrie kept her eyes forward as she spoke, looking at the street and the sidewalk, anywhere but at him.

"Silipitiria," he said automatically, knowing it was inadequate in every way to cover his sympathy for her many griefs. Then, realizing he'd spoken in Greek, he added, "Even after this time, I'm sorry for your loss."

"It's okay. In some ways it's like it happened to someone else," she admitted, shooting him a look before continuing to glance in the passing shop windows.

They approached the restaurant and noted a film crew and large barriers cordoning off a nearby side street. It wasn't unusual in San Francisco to see film crews on the streets. It was a popular venue for moviemakers. He scowled at the crew for a moment, realizing that no one had informed him of this. That would have never happened when Gates was in charge.

He hoped the new man, Geddey, was as good.

"I wonder if that's for the new action film being shot here," Carrie said. "Lazaria's directing, I think, but I thought they were shooting over at the Presidio." She looked puzzled.

"Perhaps you're right," he agreed, still pondering the change in security teams. He held the door open for her and she moved forward. He was distracted by the long lovely line of her back as she preceded him in. Her perfume teased his senses, and he lost all thought of security, or films, or even lunch.

"It is hard to remember how things were before the case was reopened last year," he admitted, searching for a conversational gambit that didn't involve her physical attributes.

"You too? Really?" she looked at him, full on now. "That's weird. Why would you feel that way?"

"Everything changed," he said, realizing as he spoke that it was true. He knew she wouldn't let him get away with that answer, but the maître d' gave him a reprieve. As they were led to a table, he checked the restaurant exits, noting the three members of his security detail among the patrons. Damon would be nearby in the car, as would several other team members.

As freeing as it was to not be shot at or threatened for months, he needed to remember that it wasn't just his life in jeopardy. From now on, if things went as he hoped, it would be Carrie's as well. If she was with him, she was a target, should anything happen.

Leverage, again. He wasn't sure he liked that part of the deal.

He forcibly unclenched his jaw. The benefits outweighed the risks in this case. He was not going to worry about it. That's why he *had* a security detail—they would be watching. That's why he paid them.

"Let's sit outside," he said, noting the tables in the sun and the sparsely populated area. It would give them more privacy, in a way, than sitting in the crowded restaurant, but with tall planters and potted trees, they wouldn't be unduly exposed either.

"Oh, that would be nice," Carrie said, smiling at him. "The sunshine's welcome after this winter, isn't it?"

He agreed and let the maître d' lead them to a table along the side of the sheltered, but sunny, patio. Patio heaters improved on the sunshine, making it very comfortable to sit out and enjoy the day.

"So," Carrie said, after they'd ordered and were both sipping their wine, "why did everything change? Is that why you asked me out?"

Dav leaned his elbows on the table, matching her pose.

He decided bluntness might best serve his cause. "I've wanted to ask you out since the first time I saw you, nearly thirteen years ago."

The shock on her face was priceless. "But—"

He shook his head, heading off the question. "You were married, I was involved with someone. It wasn't meant to be and I knew it."

"Then everything went to hell," she said quietly.

He nodded. "Then there were so many terrible things. Luke. The gallery's troubles." He lifted his hands to encompass all she'd gone through. "I couldn't say anything then without seeming—" He paused, unsure of how to say it in English.

"Predatory?"

"Exactly. I wanted to give you time. We were both busy with our lives, you dated some," he said, remembering when he'd come back to the States, intending to court her, only to find that she was already seeing someone.

"Yes, I dated some." She smiled. "So did you. I seem to remember a photograph of you on the French Riviera. A model, wasn't it?" She grinned at him.

"Ah, *ma chère*—" He put on the excessive French accent to amuse, and succeeded. "She meant nothing to me, nothing."

"I'm wounded, Dav. Just wounded that you would prefer a blonde." Her attempt to seem pathetic was totally spoiled by the giggle that escaped to delight him.

"So why, my wounded darling," he continued, only half joking now, "did you turn me down when I did ask? I gave up on the Riviera, you know." He held up three fingers as he'd seen Gates do. "Scout's honor."

"Right." She was still giggling when the waiter set down their orders, offered to refill their glasses.

It wasn't until the young man stepped away, toward the street-side planters to retrieve the water pitcher, that Dav noticed the street noises, and the sound of cars passing. He didn't think anything of it. The sound of an engine gunning down the street didn't bother him either. He was too busy waiting for Carrie to tell him why she'd turned him down.

"It seemed like I was always turning to you for help." She gestured and he followed the graceful movement of her hand. "I guess I wanted to be in a place where I didn't need help before I accepted a date."

"Hmm, I guess that makes some sense." He smiled at her, adding, "In a convoluted sort of way."

A commotion inside the restaurant caught his eye, and he saw Declan, the young redheaded member of his security team, struggling to get through the crowded interior. Dav could see the man's mouth working, shouting, though Dav heard nothing.

He knew what it meant, however.

"Carrie, come with me," he said, standing up and letting the chair fall behind him. "There's something wrong." He tugged her from her seat, pulled her around the small table, and toward the restaurant—toward Declan and the others. Declan's reaction meant an attack of some kind was imminent.

A powerful black Suburban burst through the pots, trees and railings surrounding the patio, sending the young waiter flying. Blood spattered over Dav's face, into his eyes, distracting him for one crucial moment. That moment gave the huge vehicle time to come to a stop.

As the Suburban's doors opened, Declan burst out of the restaurant, screaming, "Dav, hit the deck!"

Dav obeyed instantly, and dragged Carrie down to the ground so he could cover her with his body. Declan whipped out a weapon and took aim. Shots flew from the car behind them and Dav saw Declan stagger, then a second round of ammunition spun him round, sent him careening into the restaurant's glass walls. Already fractured, the glass gave way and fell with a terrific crash of sound.

Carrie screamed as she saw Declan fall, and screamed again as more bullets flew. Two more of his men burst onto the patio. Georgiade got off several shots, but he and Queller were driven back by the rapid spate of return fire.

Dav yelled, started to help her up, make a run for it, but the sound was cut short. He was jerked upward, away from her. He began to fight, driving an elbow into his attacker, hearing a grunt of pain.

Carrie! He must protect Carrie. It was all he could think.

A black-clad man grabbed Carrie around the waist, hauling her up, dragging her toward the Suburban.

OHE!!!NO!!! He screamed the denial in his mind, as he saw them lift her, saw her fighting them.

From behind him, another man pressed the hot barrel of a weapon to Dav's head. "Come," he ordered. "Or she dies."

Dav straightened, hands in the air. The gunfire ceased. Dav prayed his other team was close enough, prayed Declan was alive, that he'd worn his vest. Prayed that Queller and Thompson had found a way to stop this.

A man leaned out into the street around the dirt and debris from the planters, firing at someone or something. Dav heard the squeal of tires, and the sound of crunching metal and shattering glass. People shouted incoherently and Dav heard screams as well. Someone returned fire as he was yanked forward, shoved headfirst into the car. He heard the shriek of metal on metal as bullets hit the car, but nothing slowed the Suburban's retreat as it peeled out of the wreckage of the patio and roared away.

Everything Gates had taught him, all the tactics, raced through his mind, but none of the scenarios had included Carrie.

None had included a hostage other than himself.

A serious oversight.

A heavy canvas bag dropped over his head and a sickly sweet smell filled his nose. He tried in vain to hold his breath, but a blow to his back forced a sharp inhalation.

Everything went black.

Niko rubbed his aching cheek. The blow his brother, Davros Gianikopolis, had landed thirteen years ago today, had cracked his cheekbone. On days like this one, with San Francisco's changeable weather, and with the barometric pressure dropping to herald a storm, he felt it as a bitter echo of the long-ago battle.

It throbbed; thirteen years of pain.

None of the bones he'd broken since, in jail or in his time as a mercenary in South America and Africa, had hurt as much or ached as long. He took it as a sign that this first pain was the deepest, the one that most needed redress.

It was time to take his revenge.

"Time to serve the coldest dish up to *you,* Dav, long past time," he chuckled. None of this would have been possible when Dav's former security team was in charge. No. Only now, in the interregnum, the time between the old and new, could he strike, and strike hard.

The contacts he'd cultivated with little success had suddenly opened up when Bromley was attacked the previous year. Instead of ruining everything he'd planned, the debacle with the woman trying to kill Gates had worked to his advantage. It proved he was on the right track; it was destiny.

Those same contacts now believed him to be part of Dav's organization. It was a beautiful con and he'd profited significantly already. At last, everything was ready for the final steps.

He was ready.

He paused long enough to send a text to his mentor, the man who'd taught him to think cold, to plan, to play the long, hard game. He'd wanted Niko to hire someone for this task, keep it impersonal, but Niko knew he had to handle it himself. Revenge should be personal. Tomorrow the world would change.

Ready to implement, he typed.

"This time, brother," he murmured, lowering the binoculars, but still observing every angle to be sure he was unwatched, "it will be me, taking everything *you* love."

He called the girl, Inez, and kept her talking until he saw Dav and his protective detail round the corner toward the restaurant. He'd waited half an hour, just to be sure they weren't coming back, then dialed again. Everything was in place; it was ready and had been since Inez had gushingly told him about the date Dav had arranged with Carrie McCray. She was his inside "man" and she'd played her part to perfection.

"Hi, honey. Lock the front doors like you're getting that shipment, I'll come to the back, okay? I'll knock—" He let his voice drop to a sexy range. "I know we won't have much time, but I need to see you, to touch you." He tucked the phone in between his shoulder and his ear as he told her what she wanted to hear, that she was beautiful, sexy, desirable.

After parking several blocks away—a lucky break in the popular neighborhood—he walked to the back of the building.

"I'm so excited. This is like clandestine stuff, you know?" she whispered over the phone.

"Uh-huh. Scary sex is great sex, babe."

She gushed and giggled into the phone and he rolled his eyes. Women were all alike. At the edge of the building he stopped long enough to pull on the thin gloves and slip surgical booties over his shoes.

"I'm just at the back door now, babe. Come let me in," he crooned, moving up to the receiving dock, while staying out of range of the camera. "Yeah, that's right," he muttered in answer to some inane question she asked. He hurried up the steps, easing along the wall so the secondary video wouldn't catch the movement.

When he knocked, the door creaked open, offering just a slice of light in the shadowed area under the receiving dock's canopy.

"Hey, handsome," Inez gushed, swinging the door wide. He saw her frown at his shoes, so he swept her into his arms, tugging the heavy door shut behind him, making sure only the back of his head and jacket were visible to the inner door camera.

"Hey, baby," he crooned, kissing her and grabbing her ass. He boosted her up into his arms and she wrapped her legs around his waist. With her clinging to him, he moved quickly down the hall. His body reacted to her sensuality and the kisses she pressed to his neck. It was a pity he didn't have time for sex. She was young, enthusiastic, and flexible. At least screwing her had been a bonus rather than a chore, although he'd have done it, no matter what.

"Hey," she giggled. "What took you so long? They've been gone awhile."

"I know. Trouble parking," he lied, swinging open the door to Carrie McCray's office with his hip. It was good to be in the cramped space, where no cameras peered. He set her on the desk, had her blouse open in a moment, her bra unhooked. She laughed, pulling his head to her for a kiss.

"You're in a hurry," she moaned throatily, then frowned again, noting the gloves on his hands.

It really was too bad. She noticed the little things, lots of little things. It was a shame she was so smart.

He distracted her by flipping up her skirt, fondling her so that she closed her eyes and let her head fall back. He'd counted on that. It was a studied move on her part, designed to make a man feel like he was doing a good job. Every time he touched her below her waist, she did that very move with the head toss and the closed eyes. He grinned, hating that he really didn't have time for a quick fuck.

Too bad.

He eased the long, thin, sharpened palette knife out of his pocket with one hand, keeping her busy with the other.

She was so focused she didn't flinch as he slipped the knife easily between her ribs, hitting the heart in one stroke. One twist opened the wound more, ensuring the incision was lethal. It was a poetic move, he thought, to kill her with an artist's implement.

Her eyes flew open and her head jerked forward, once. To his delight, he saw the betrayal, the shock in her eyes as they dimmed in death.

How very satisfying. Even a bit . . . arousing.

He let her body fall backward and to the side. The blood was oozing around the handle of the blade now and he wanted to be sure he wasn't marked by it. He switched on the desk light, looking at the gloves under the bright white light. Good, no blood, even on the gloves.

"The nice thing about hitting the heart the first time," he told the dead girl, "is that if you do it right, and position the body correctly, the blood all pumps into the body cavity." He remembered the first time he heard the words, delivered in a highly accented voice from his mercenary captain. "You still die," he observed, speaking to the dead as he hooked the desk chair with his foot to pull it over, prop her feet on it so her body wouldn't fall onto the floor. "However, you don't get blood all over your killer. Bad for you, good for me."

With a quick twist, he gathered her blouse in one hand and used it to turn her body to its side, leaving the knife in the wound like a cork. All the blood would now pool inside the body until the cops turned her onto her back.

"Lovely. Just lovely," he said, patting her hip with both affection and care. He'd had a good time with her, but he didn't want to dislodge the weapon or mar his handiwork. "Now," he said cheerfully, "where is your cell phone?"

He dumped her bag on the floor and took her driver's license and the lone credit card in her wallet. As an afterthought, he pocketed the hundred dollars he found there as well. Why not? If the cops thought it a robbery gone bad, all the better.

"Ah, yes, you were talking to me just before you answered the door, weren't you?" Before he retraced his steps to the back door, he turned off the camera. He moved quickly, knowing there might be an alarm on the cameras. If one shut down, it could either trigger a backup or the cops. The cops wouldn't be as much a problem as the backup camera.

Then again, he was well known to be dead already, so it wasn't that much of a problem either way.

He checked his watch. Dav and Carrie would be taken by now. It was all going as he'd planned. He grinned, knowing what awaited his idiot brother.

There, on a pedestal by the locked rear door, was her phone. Excellent. The number she'd used for him was a throwaway phone, but he took no chances. With the phone in his pocket, he used a nearby broom to reach the camera, turn its seeking eye toward the wall. A quick trip back to the office where he jumped the security disk back to just before he came in, set the camera back on and left the building locked up nice and tight. Within minutes, all evidence of him would be taped over and he would be the ghost that killed Inez.

He chuckled at his cleverness and as he walked toward his parked car, he gave the hundred to several bums, a twenty at a time. He stopped a scruffy-looking messenger and handed him the credit card.

"Hey, dude, use this for me, would you? My girlfriend stole it from me, bought a few things, then gave it back. I was about to report it stolen, but there's got to be a bunch more on it or I can't press charges on her." Total bullshit, of course, but the kid wouldn't know that. "Go buy some gas or something. You got an hour before I report it missing." When the boy's eyes turned sly, he knew he'd picked a winner.

The boy snatched the card and sped off. Two blocks later, Niko tossed her driver's license into the gutter. He took a last look at her picture, and smiled.

"A good picture. What a surprise," he told her photo. "Usually look like mug shots. Or worse."

He unlocked the car and as he drove away, he decided it really was too bad she'd been so smart.

Chapter 3

Jurgens disconnected the call, closing the cell phone with a snap of his wrist and a silent snarl. It hadn't been a pleasant conversation. Hardened as he was from years in his profession, he was irritated at the level of venom he'd sensed over his refusal. His annoyance made him more thorough about the methodical destruction of the phone. The largest piece when he was done could have been hidden under a dime.

He had turned down the contract on Davros Gianikopolis, citing both other work and a conflict of interest. He didn't go into details, wouldn't. No questions had been asked.

Frowning, he pondered the repercussions.

"My love," Caroline said, gliding into the brightly lit room, her robe a lush flow of rose silk over her skin. "Come to bed." She came up behind his chair and automatically began to massage his shoulders, easing the tension there with her touch alone.

He turned his face to kiss the hand that eased him so.

"I made the call," he said, knowing she would understand.

"I see." Her hands never stilled, though he felt the brief hesitation, understood it. "What was your decision?"

"I declined."

Her fingers stilled, and then squeezed before resuming their relaxing strokes. "Good."

They stayed connected there, for long silent moments, both thinking their own thoughts as Caroline continued to rub his shoulders, releasing the tension that had taken up residence there when he'd made his decision, notified the potential client. He'd done work for the man before, successfully of course. Perhaps it was that which made the client so angry. Perhaps not.

He was unsure which reaction concerned him more, the lack of respect for their previous relationship or the vicious severing of their business when he'd refused the contract. He knew people, their reactions, their reasoning. It made him good at what he did. Perhaps that was why he knew this would not end here, not with this client.

"Now what? Will you let him know? Will you tell Davros that he's targeted?"

"He knows this, I am sure," he said dismissively, knowing it to be true, but giving her the opening to continue the discussion.

"He doesn't know about this one. You said—" She stopped and he could feel her hesitation.

"Nein." He stopped her kneading hands by spinning in the chair, gripping them in his own. "Do not hide your thoughts from me. We must be clear together, always, *ja*?"

She sighed and kissed him as he pulled her into his lap. She fit there with remarkable ease, something he never failed to appreciate.

"I am sentimental," she said hesitantly. "I know he had nothing to do with our finally being together—you took care of that." When he frowned, she saw it and added, "Yes, I know, we both played our parts. But his situation with the art fraud, the way his people dug it out, gave us a cover and an opportunity that might not have come up for several more years." She smiled and he loved her all the more. Everything about her lit him from within.

"You want me to warn him." He said it matter-of-factly. He knew this was what she did want. It would not be the easiest, or perhaps the wisest course, but for her, for sentiment, he would do it if she asked.

"Yes."

"Hmmm," was all he said, shifting her to lean on his shoulder, enjoying the feel of her lithe body in his arms, on his lap. As always, she waited while he thought it through. No questions, no pleading. This was another thing he loved about her. She was clear, concise. If he asked for reasoning, she would give it, though perhaps in this case she wouldn't since she'd already admitted she was motivated by sentiment, perhaps even superstition.

His decision made, he straightened and she looked him in the eye, a connection that few others would ever make, a looking into his very soul. For that, as much as anything, he would take on the world for her, anyone and anything.

"It will be difficult. I will need to be away, you know this."

"Ja, mein liebchen." She spoke the words with precision and care. She was learning German so she could greet his mother in that tongue, when they met. That trip would be in summer and he was looking forward to it. One step closer to their wedding.

"Gut," he praised. "I will need to think. Go on to sleep, I will come join you soon."

Without another word, but with the warmest of looks, she stood. Bending forward, she kissed him. The connection was strong, powerful and intoxicating. It captured him and blocked out every other thought. When it ended, he felt renewed, alive.

"Make it soon."

He watched her leave, heard her kiss the boy, even caught the faint rustle of the sheets and blankets as she got into bed.

His Caroline.

He could refuse her very little, and since his inclination ran parallel with hers, he wouldn't refuse her this.

Decision made, he began to plan. He would sell this house as soon as they left in the morning. It had been a good bolt-hole in his single days, but it was too dangerous to keep any longer. It was unlikely that anyone would trace it to him, but there were other properties. His corporation would sell it at a loss, he was sure, given the market, but no matter. The proceeds would go to fund a scholarship at a school he'd randomly chosen from a directory. Having made that call from here, he must disconnect himself from it immediately.

He fired off an e-mail to his lawyer that would set a sale in motion. Now, for research. He needed to know who else had been offered the contract on Dav, and which of them had taken the bait, for he knew this party would not have waited to hear from him before taking action.

Dav wasn't dead yet, but he soon could be. His Caroline didn't want that, so Jurgens would be sure it didn't happen.

Ever.

Dav was sick when he woke in the dark. The nausea and pounding headache reminded him of his failings the moment he returned to consciousness. Vibrations thrummed through the metal under his hip and rattled his bound hands. He heard the drone of turbines and the whistle of the wind that told him he was in a plane.

Given the metallic flooring, he was probably in a cargo hold or the back of a small plane, with the seats removed. His hands were tied behind his back, cuffed maybe, but he wasn't sure because he couldn't feel his fingers—the circulation was cut off.

It took him a minute to conquer the fear and anger that rose to choke him. His father had liked to discipline his son by shoving him into the darkest part of the cellar. Dav could still hear the door slamming behind him and his father yelling, "Grow some balls, boy. Can't stand to see any son of mine afraid of the dark."

It hadn't been the dark that frightened him. It had been the closed-in space, the dank walls smelling of old bones and old blood. He knew people had died in that room, and died badly. More than that, it had been the roaches and rats that had sniffed at him or crawled on him, a small boy huddled by the door, praying to survive and get out.

The terror had come from knowing—believing—that he had no control over getting out. Release would come at his father's whim, or not at all.

The shudder was impossible to suppress. All these years later, the fear still haunted him. He drew a deep breath and focused on two very important details. There wouldn't be rats or roaches on a plane.

"Then eeseh enea chronon," he whispered to himself. *I am no longer nine years old.*

Using only small movements, he shifted on the floor. Getting onto his side a bit eased the feeling of illness. He waited a heartbeat to see if anyone noticed him move or was watching him. Facedown as he was, with his head covered, he couldn't tell if he was alone or not.

Struggling to quiet his breathing, he strained to hear any other noise over the engine's roar. Bracing his aching elbows on the floor, he made another shift to the right. He was just getting his balance when the plane banked sharply and threw him over onto his side again. He nearly screamed at the pain in his arms and shoulders, but he worried more when he realized he'd landed on something soft. Something that smelled of flowers and woman.

Carrie.

He wanted to leap up, pull her up with him, but it was impossible. Instead, he struggled to calm his racing heart and mind enough to feel or hear if she was alive. She'd made no sound when he crashed into her, so he feared the worst.

He held his breath and scooted closer, ignoring his aching arms. "Carrie?" he whispered, the bag over his head muffling his voice. "Carrie?"

Leaning toward her, he searched for some sign of life.

In a lightning shift from deathly stillness to action, she burst upward, her elbow pressed into his neck. Her skin was warm. She was alive.

Before he could do more than appreciate the fact, she shifted her weight with a grunt, and knocked him back, pinning him to the floor. Once again, his shoulders and elbows were racked with pain.

"Touch me and I will kill you," she hissed even as she wobbled above him. Shaky as she was, her arm stayed tight on his windpipe.

"It's Dav," he wheezed as her elbow pressed harder. "Carrie, it's Dav."

"Dav?" The pressure eased off and he drew in a lungful of musty air, still catching a faint whiff of the darkly sweet scent of the drug they'd used to knock him out. "Dav, it's you? Are you okay?"

As she clutched at his jacket, he felt the shaking in her arms, the tremble in her body. "No, but I'm alive, and thank God you are too," he said with heartfelt relief as her shaking hands raced over him. He could tell she was bound as well, since her hands moved together, tugging at his shirt and his lapels. More than anything, he wanted to crush her to him, hold her tightly, feel her life. "I'm okay." He said it over and over until she began to relax and stop running her hands frantically up and down his chest.

Then he added wryly, "But when we get out of this, Gates is going to kill me." He felt her stiffen, then felt a tremor rock her body. "Carrie, are you okay?"

"Believe it or not, I'm laughing," she said, and her voice

quivered. "Although that doesn't seem appropriate. If we get out of this, Gates will probably want to kill me too."

"Oh, Carrie," Dav said, his heart sinking. "I am so sorry."

"Hush, Dav," she said, her voice firm and sharp now. "We're here. We'll figure it out. What is it they say? While there's life, there's hope."

Please God, let her be right.

First things first—they had to figure out where they were and where they were going. "Can you see?" he asked.

"Oh, say can you see?" she sang softly, then giggled again, her voice returning to the wavery tremolo it had held before. "I think I'm still drugged up. That was far funnier than it should have been."

He grinned, even as he worried for her. In spite of everything she was magnificent. "Yes, it was."

She sobered a bit and added, "It's a plane, it's dark. No one else is back here with us."

"Good, that's good." He shifted, trying to make sense of it all. Unfortunately, that brought him in more intimate contact with her body, driving anything practical out of his head for a moment. "I wish I could see." He felt his heart rate leap as she moved against him. The race of his blood made his bound hands throb.

"You're too pretty to have a bag over your head," she snickered. "Oh, Lord," she half moaned. "I'm sorry. Don't listen to me. I'm just drugged enough to say stuff and just sober enough to realize I'm being stupid."

Well, at least she thought he was pretty. That was something to take to the grave with him. "It's all right," he said, smiling at the thought of her talking without censor. "Can you use your hands? Can you feel anything around us?"

"Yes, I think so. Can you lift up?" she asked, then hummed another tune. He heard her faintly singing words. Something that sounded like "up, up and away . . ."

Dav struggled to a sitting position, and both felt and heard her rustling around behind him. The bag lifted off his head with a rush, and he could hardly believe it, since he still couldn't see. The fresher air, however, was like sweet wine and he drew in the cold, fuel-tinged air with gratitude.

They were in a cargo plane, as he'd guessed, but it was smaller than he'd thought it would be. There were empty crates and bins strapped down to the grooved floor and walls, their gaping sides showing up as darker squares or rectangles in the gloom.

"How long have we been here? Do you have any idea?" he asked, scanning the space for any telltale markings or anything that could help them. Knowledge was power. In any dangerous situation, you had to assess the weapons available, some of which might be data. Of all the possible kidnap scenarios they'd run, figured out how Dav could survive, nothing had been like this.

"It's dark outside," she said, lifting her hands to point toward the small round window on an exterior door about ten feet away near the narrowing tail section. "We met at noon. It was probably twelve thirty when everything blew up." She spoke with calm lucidity, then snickered again. "I've never had a date blow up."

"I strive to be unique," he answered, matching her humorous tone, though he worried that she still was feeling the effects of the drugs, based on the inappropriate laughter. "I have no idea what they used on us, to drug us. Hopefully it'll wear off."

"Yeah," she said, "I really suck at drugs. Even with the dentist." He heard her gasp, turned toward the sound, but she was just a black shape in the gray void of the space. "Whoa!" she gasped again. "Now I want to cry. That was sudden." Her silhouette swayed and he wished he could move to brace her. "I feel like I'm on a roller coaster."

"Deep breaths," he said, harkening to more of Gates's advice. "It'll clear your head and get your blood moving, which will get the poison out of your system faster."

As she drew in steady, measured breaths, he tried to calculate the time in his head, forcibly ignoring the image of Declan's body flying backward through the glass, the vision of Declan bringing down a waiter and panicked patrons, as blood blossomed scarlet on his blue dress shirt.

Dav vaguely remembered seeing the other members of the team beyond Declan, fighting their way through the narrow spaces between the tables. To block the thoughts, he visualized a map in his mind, tried to calculate, push away the faces of his fallen friends. "I'm guessing it's at least seven. Maybe later. We're either somewhere close to the Mississippi, if we took off right away, or over the Yucatán, or the Pacific Ocean. If we went north, we're well into Canada." He called off the directions and considered the possibilities of each compass point.

"Somehow, I doubt it's Canada," Carrie said, her voice more even now. "I can't see anyone lofting you off to the Northwest Territories and dumping you there. Snowbound Dav. That would be weird." Now the giggle was back. She was having another manic reaction to the drugs, swinging from morose to giggly to normal.

"It would be smart, though," Dav said, thinking it through, trying to ignore the worry that Carrie might have been really sickened by the drugs, or that she'd been given a higher dose than he for some reason. "Who would suspect it?"

"Terrible, but true," Carrie said. "It doesn't feel cold though. The cabin's not pressurized, so we're flying low. If we were over Canada it would be cold. It's only April."

"True. Same goes for the East Coast, probably. We may already be over Texas, or out over the Gulf of Mexico."

"They could be planning to dump us in the ocean," she said, and he heard terror in her voice, the incipient panic.

"No, I don't think so," he said, forcing conviction into his voice. "They want something from me, or I'd be dead already."

"What about me?" Carrie said softly. "What do they want from me?"

He leaned toward her, trying for comfort, though both of them were obviously thinking the worst. "I don't know. You may be leverage to get me to do what they want. I hope that's all it is."

"It's weird," she said, in another lightning change of mood. "I'm scared, terrified really, but it's like this is happening to someone else. The drugs are doing that, I guess," she added. "I need to lie down, or lean on something before I fall down," she said, her voice normal once more. She scooted around to put her back against the side of the plane, and then helped him do the same. "Hey, look. My purse is here, so's your coat." The last was said in an easy, conversational tone. The shift and weave of Carrie's emotional state was almost as disturbing as their current difficulty.

"Really? Where?"

"Over there." She gestured with her bound hands. He wondered if he dared try to get his hands in front of him. He decided not to attempt it yet. There was nowhere to go, no one to fight in the middle of the air, in the dark.

"The plane seems to be flying fast and level," he observed, forcing himself to think about the situation, rather than worry about Carrie. If he kept worrying about her, he wouldn't think, not constructively or logically. If there was any chance of escape he had to be rational to see it, to plan. "We're not close to wherever we're going yet," he said slowly, thinking it through, trying to get past the panic, the fear for Carrie. "If we hear anything though, like the pilot or someone is coming back here, you need to put the bag on my head. I'm guessing they don't want me to see anyone. Let's make sure I don't. If I'm not supposed to see them they may only be out for ransom."

"Then why did they take the bag off my head?" Carrie asked, and there was further panic in her voice. "They don't think I'm worth ransom? They're going to kill me, aren't they." She made it a statement, not a question. "Or worse."

"I don't know, Carrie, but here's what I do know," he said softly, forcing her to listen by the very softness of his voice. He moved closer to comfort her, bumping his shoulder against hers for the human connection. If his hands were free, he would hold her. For now, this was all he could do. "Look at me."

She hesitated, turned his way. He could make out the glint of her frightened eyes. Even in the gloom, he could see that her pupils were so dilated there was barely a rim of the rich blue showing. "What?"

"Carrie, just focus on me, on my voice. You've been drugged, you're scared. Eh-la, you know all that. It may be that they were counting on your still being out, unconscious."

Her eyes flickered away, darting around the dark cargo hold as if searching for answers, or villains. He could see the trembling in her shoulders. Whatever sense she'd made earlier was being subsumed by the fear, and the drugs were making it worse.

"I'm cold. Where are the blankets?" she said fretfully. She was struggling now, struggling to get up, to move. If the plane banked again, she'd fall and hurt herself.

"Here, come sit with me, darling," Dav crooned, coaxing her to sit down again. She'd struggled to her knees, trying to rise. "I'll keep you warm. I've got you."

Encountering an air pocket, the plane dropped briefly. Carrie rocked over from her kneeling position, falling awkwardly onto his chest.

"Ow!" she exclaimed, and he barely managed not to cry out with the pain.

He'd wanted her next to him, imagined her in his arms. It would be nice if her falling into him hadn't hurt so much, but he'd take what he could get.

With her body pressed to his, he realized how cold he

was. The imprint of her warmth was a dramatic contrast. He briefly wished the coat she'd spotted weren't so far away. They could use it for warmth. Even the breath mints in the pocket would help ease the nausea that still lurked in his gut. With grim humor, he wondered how long they could survive on mints and whatever she had in her purse.

The warm silk of her hair brushed his neck, and he realized that for both their sakes, he'd have to get his hands in front of him. He couldn't hold her; nor could they stay warm enough with his hands bound back.

"Here now, sweetheart—" He used the endearment as much to soothe his own fears as hers. "Sit up for a moment and let me get my hands in front of me. Just a minute, okay?"

She nodded and he felt the movement on his body. He hated the deepening gloom in the plane's interior, the yawning, inky black maw of the tail section. Her delusions and fear made it worse. The residual drugs in his system made it harder to fight back the memories, the sensory details of rats and roaches. He shuddered again as he began the agonizing task of getting his hands in front of him.

Sweat ran a damp trail down his spine as he struggled with the twists and turns necessary to pull his bound hands under his hips, and from there, under his knees. It took him forever to get his feet through the circle of his arms. Red fury threatened at several points, his temper unbound by the drug and the situation. The pain in his shoulders and elbows raced fire over all his nerves, even as cold fear rose within him because he couldn't feel his hands.

More than anything, he was castigating himself at the sheer hubris he'd displayed. To have his decision to relax security measures cost him his life was bad enough, but to have it potentially cost Carrie *her* life was almost more than he could bear.

"Dav? Are you okay?" Carrie asked, her voice stronger.

"Yamot ti Panayia mou!" The vulgar curse burst forth

from him as he lost his patience with being helpless, with trying to get his hands from underneath him while balancing against the plane's movements. The only plus was that stress and the steady physical activity brought him momentary warmth in the cold of the cargo area. His hands stung in pain with the banging around generated by his struggles. At least he was feeling the pain; it would be far worse, he knew, if his hands had remained numb.

When he finally got them in front of him, he almost wished he hadn't. Swollen and bluish, his hands were secured together with three heavy-duty plastic zip ties. One on each wrist was linked by the third, not only immobilizing him, but deliberately exacerbating the potential for pain.

After one look, he ignored the ties. He couldn't change the situation right now and Gates had told him to consistently focus on the things he could change. "Here, Carrie," he said when he got his pain under momentary control. "Sit closer. We'll keep each other warm."

She moved immediately under the arch of the arm he painfully lifted, and burrowed into his chest. "Thank you." After a moment, she spoke again. "I'm scared, Dav," she murmured.

"I know. I am too," he admitted, hoping it would help her to know it. "All we can do is wait, and look for opportunities to escape or make a deal." Pain raced over him with every bump of the plane. He blocked it by letting his face caress her glorious hair.

That was in the present moment; that was beautiful. Her skin was soft and sweet on the rasp of his stubble-scratchy face. He could still smell her perfume and he focused on that, ignoring all other smells, all other thoughts. He knew it was a momentary respite, but that separation from fear, that brief, sweet lull let his mind clear.

"We could die here," she muttered, and he heard the fear again. "We could die."

"No." He made it a statement. He would not allow that possibility. She was his future. He would not allow it to be otherwise. He would use the stubborn will that helped him survive his father and countless business rivals and they would survive. "We'll make it out of this. My people, they'll know to get Gates. He has all manner of ways to figure out what's happened. He'll find us. He and Ana are the best."

"But they don't work for you anymore," she said.

"I know, sweetheart," he said, smiling into the dark. "But friends don't worry about little things like that. They'll find us."

"Dav," she murmured, sliding her hands up to touch his face. "Dav, why did we wait?"

Dav was distracted momentarily by the shift in the sound of the engines, the subtle drop in the slant of the cabin. "Wait?" he replied, still thinking about the change in the plane's altitude. "Why did we wait for what?"

He looked down into her eyes, loving the feel of her hands on his face. While he recognized all his reactions were off-kilter from the drugs, though not as badly skewed as Carrie's, just the touch of her, the feel of her in his arms, was inflaming his body, his mind and senses.

"Carrie?" he whispered, seeing the dark of her eyes, feeling every inch of her in new ways.

"We fought it, Dav, both of us," she said, her voice serious. But her eyes were still deeply dilated, the effect of the drugs. "We waited for the right time. We didn't make a move, either of us."

While he was puzzling through what she meant, she shifted closer, whispering, "Don't wait anymore. Kiss me now, just in case. I need to know how it feels, I need . . ." she trailed off, quieting in order to bring her lips to his.

The connection was instant and powerful. Every thought about the plane, their situation, sank out of his mind, replaced by the magnificent roar of triumph in his heart. No pain could compare to the sweetness, the fire, of her mouth moving on his. All hesitancy fled as she pressed into him, wriggling closer, heating his body. Nothing mattered but Carrie. Nothing was real or present but her mouth, her breasts pressed to his chest, her hips bumping his.

His mind leapt forward to her straddling him, taking him into her, rising over him, pleasuring them both. He nearly lost control just thinking the thoughts as her mouth moved frantically on his, driving them to a frenzy of movement, making their bodies mesh as best they could in the situation. The pain in his hands and shoulders throbbed a counterpoint to his body's needs. He ignored the pain and focused on the pleasure.

He might never get another chance.

"Dav, oh, Dav, I . . . I . . ." She stumbled over the words, pressing kisses to his face, her bound hands cradling his jaw.

Whatever else she might have said was lost when the plane banked hard again. Now she fell into him, slamming her head into his chin as the altitude dropped.

"Ouch!" she groaned, and he wished he could speak at all. It was all he could do to hang on to consciousness as the blow reawakened every one of his other pains.

Passion doused, Dav struggled to shift gears from their sensuous connection back to the situation at hand. For several long moments, they just lay still, panting as they tried to recover. He knew this wasn't the time or the place, and that Carrie was reacting to the drugs, but the confirmation that she was interested, attracted, gave him hope despite their dire state of affairs.

While there's life, there's hope.

* * *

"What do you mean you left him alone?" Gates snarled the words into the phone. He and Ana were racing toward the city, Ana taking the curves with the competent speed of a driver trained by the military in evasive maneuvers.

"Not alone. We were there, we were close," explained Jasper Whitney, one of the security team. He'd been first on the scene when Dav's team called in the emergency from the city.

Gates shook his head in frustration. No one was off duty now. And yelling at Whitney didn't matter and didn't help. No excuses could change the fact that Dav's security had been breached and he'd been taken.

"Never mind. What about—" he began.

"We found his locator fifteen miles outside the city," Whitney said. "Along with the getaway car, a Chevy Suburban. Rented with false ID. There was blood, but not much."

"Damn." Without the locator, the chances of recovering Dav and Carrie alive went from unlikely to near impossible. "What about Declan? And Damon?"

"Declan's still in surgery," was the worried reply. "They're not telling us anything, but they've all got that tight-lipped look. Damon took a bullet along the left side of his head, as he tried to block the getaway, but he was treated and released. Georgiade and Queller both have cuts from flying glass, and a lot of bruises from the panicked restaurant patrons stomping on them. Thompson has a through and through in the meat of his shoulder."

"Not good. Damn it. Damon could just as easily be dead. Thank God everyone had on vests. Not good, any of it. We'll be there in—" Gates turned to Ana.

"Twenty minutes, tops."

Gates repeated the time. "Until then, sit tight. Get everyone together and we'll meet in the hospital chapel. That's open twenty-four-seven. Barring someone being in there praying, we can use it as a mini conference room while we wait for news. Two people from the FBI will be meeting us there. Keep an eye out for them."

He hung up without saying good-bye and turned to his wife. "What chance do we have of getting Agency help?"

"A lot, unofficially. I've already sent word. They'll do it for me, and for Dav. He made a lot of friends last year. Not that he didn't already have plenty."

"True." In the silence, he went over the situation again, every step his former team had outlined for him. "Damn," he muttered, considering all the angles. "This was brilliantly executed. They took advantage of the change of command. How did they know? How could they know?"

"How would you have done it?" Ana replied quietly. "You're among the best I've seen at running scenarios and coming up with the least likely and most workable in any given situation. And yes, that was a compliment."

"Thanks," he said, knowing that from Ana it was high praise indeed. He'd been trained in the military, but hadn't taken the classes and courses she'd had. He just knew what it was like to lose the people you loved. It made him sharper when it came to seeing the loopholes or gaps in protection. He'd promised himself never to lose another person he loved. In all the time since his family had been killed, he'd managed to keep that promise.

Until now.

"I just can't find a perp in my head. He'd settled with most of the people who were after him. The business last year turned out to be about me, not him," he muttered. "I don't get it. The Saudis were on board with a bunch of new projects. Colombia just hired us. It does them no good to kidnap him. They've already paid us."

"Keep thinking that way and we won't get him back," Ana cautioned. "Think outside the box."

Anger rushed through him, followed just as quickly by

the realization that she was right. “That’s a pisser, but true. Okay. Unknown origin. Not the usual suspects.”

“We can’t handle alien abduction,” Ana quipped. “Anything else, we’ll figure it out. We’ll find him, Gates.”

“Them,” Gates corrected. “They took Carrie. That’s important. Whitney said they took her first. One thread we need to pull is to see who her enemies are. Can’t do like we did last year and assume it’s about Dav.”

“More likely than Carrie,” Ana said on a huffed out breath as she whipped the SUV around a tight turn. She was slim but strong, and she held the powerful vehicle into the turns like a barrel racer. “Probably she’s going to be leverage, a hostage to force him to do something. We can’t ignore the angle that they wanted Carrie, but it’s probably too expensive an op for someone after her. Four Suburbans, decoy cars peeling off to confuse pursuit, the movie camera setup to gain cooperation from total innocents? That was pure genius.”

“They’re all being held, pending,” Gates said, using shorthand to say the fake film crew and decoy drivers were still in custody until the San Francisco police, the FBI and Gates got some answers.

Ana took a hand off the wheel long enough to squeeze his. “Let’s just get there before we draw conclusions. We need more facts.”

“I know. And we’ll find him,” Gates said, squeezing back, trying desperately to believe it.

“So, you have him on the ground now?” Niko smiled into the phone, delighted. “Take him to the camp and put him where I told you. Yes, down there. It’s a perfect spot for a holding pen. Yes. I’m sure.”

“Sí, Niko,” was the brisk reply, and the line went dead.

Niko leaned back in his opulent leather chair, relaxing for the first time in hours. Anything could have gone wrong between the States and Belize. Anything. Now his brother was in his control and nothing could save him.

It was perfect.

Chapter 4

It was time to think, to plan.

If the plane was correcting or changing course, it meant something was happening. It was time to do anything they could to give themselves an edge.

"Carrie, can you reach our things?" They needed to get anything potentially helpful into their pockets, rather than in his coat or her purse.

"I think so," she said, easing out from under his arm to scoot toward her purse.

"When we land, you must pretend to be asleep. I'll pull the bag back over my head. Much as I want to see what's going on, it's best to leave everything as they left it. Carrie?" he said sharply. He needed to be sure she was focusing on him. When she turned his way, he asked, "Is there anything we can use as leverage to get them to leave you alone? If it's ransom they want, Gates knows I will pay. Is there anyone else they might approach for money? Anyone important?"

"My grandfather," she said, grunting the words as she managed to get to their things. Starting back toward him, she continued, "He was a senator. He still has a lot of political connections."

"Good. Good," he said, his mind circling the possibilities.

"If they separate us, make sure you tell them that Gates will pay a ransom, that your grandfather will. Gates will figure it out about your grandfather, I'm sure, but tell them. Do you understand?"

"Yes, yes, I understand," she said, piling the coat and her purse next to him. He'd gotten himself into a higher sitting position. He'd also found the hood and had it in his lap. There'd been no sound from the cockpit, no indication that there was more than one pilot on the plane. Wherever they were going, there weren't many guards. The plane's cockpit was too small to hold more than a pilot and copilot, so their captors had counted on them staying unconscious or at least docile.

"Do you have anything in your purse that might help us? A knife? A nail file? Anything?"

She surprised him by answering in the affirmative. "I have an all-purpose tool," she said, digging to the bottom. "You know, one of those Leatherman tools? It's great for checking things at tag sales, tightening screws, that sort of thing."

She was peering into her purse so she didn't see his surprise, but he was astounded. She'd be more help than he was. Being in this situation, he realized how much he took for granted now, how many things people handled for him. He didn't even keep keys for any of his homes or cars. Keys would be a good weapon if Carrie had some.

"Do you have keys?" he asked.

"Keys?" She looked up in surprise, then nodded. "Sure. They're right here." She held up a well-laden key ring.

"Put them in the pocket of my jacket," he said, turning as much as he could to give her access. "I'm betting they've already patted us down for weapons, checked your purse and so on."

"Keys won't do much," she said, even as she dropped them in his pocket. "They don't unlock anything we can reach."

"You'd be surprised," Dav said, forcing a smile. "Gates was a good teacher. I can do a lot with keys. Do you have room to put the Leatherman tool and your driver's license in your skirt pocket? Is it deep enough? If not, put them in my pocket too. If they take your purse, we'll still have your ID on us. Gates always told me to plan for survival and rescue. We may need to prove we're American citizens."

"Are you?" she asked, apropos of nothing. "An American citizen, that is?"

"Yes, I hold dual citizenship since my mother was Greek-American."

"She was? Did she—" she began, only to break off as another sharp turn of the plane overbalanced her once more.

"Ssaahh!" Dav managed to hiss out the exclamation rather than scream more curses in agony as she landed on his swollen hands. He didn't want the pilot or copilot to hear, to come back to them before they were armed as well as they could be. It was quieter now, at the lower altitude. With less wind noise to muffle their voices.

Dav couldn't suppress the instant nausea and headache brought on by the blow however. *"Yamoto yamotoyamoto!"* He slurred the curse word together, letting intensity help him disperse some of the pain. *Fuckfuckfuck!*

"Sorry," she said, sitting up, panic etching her face with worry. "What did I hit? Are you bleeding? What happened?"

"It's my hands. They're too tightly bound. You're going to have to help me," he snapped, gulping hastily to maintain control of his rebellious stomach. "You need to rub them, force the circulation." He dreaded even the thought of that, but if he didn't get some circulation in his hands, they would be useless to him. And they might sustain permanent damage if they stayed numb too long.

"But won't that be painful?"

"An understatement, Carrie-*mou,*" Dav agreed, attaching the endearment to her name easily. "But if I want to keep my hands, if I want to ever be able to use them, I can't let the blood settle too much. As it is, I can hardly feel them."

"Oh, my God," she said, jerking her hands away from his, rubbing them on her skirt. "I don't want to hurt you."

"Although it will hurt, you'll be helping me. I'm going to need my hands."

The plane shifted, a softer turn this time. When it leveled out, Dav could tell they were lower, and slower. Whatever their destination, they were closing in on it.

"You must hurry. We'll be landing soon. Put my coat around your shoulders and your purse over your shoulder under the coat. Help me get the hood back on, then lean on me. We'll act like we're still asleep. You can start working on my hands, okay?"

"But the coat, my purse, they'll know, won't they?"

"People accept what they expect to see. They'll see us asleep together. They'll see my coat over you. I would do that if I woke up first, or you might do that if you woke and couldn't wake me."

"No, I would have put it over you," she answered, puzzlement evident in her voice. "You're hurt, you need to stay warm."

He smiled as he realized, once again, why she was the one for him. She would have covered him. *In vino veritas*—in wine, truth—worked for drugs too. She would have thought of him first. Her earlier kisses seemed to be further proof of that.

Short of instantaneous rescue, nothing could please him more. It would make the pain of the next steps, whatever they were, either easier to bear or the worst possible nightmare imaginable. He watched in silence as she maneuvered her license into her pocket, added the bulkier multitool to her other pocket. The slim-fitting skirt showed a bulge, so he had her move the tool to his jacket pocket. Their captors might take the coat away, or leave it in the plane, but they probably wouldn't take his suit jacket.

"Now, you need to rub my hands, get the circulation going," he said, and noticed the horror reflected in her eyes when she saw his swollen fingers, the bluish cast to the skin.

"Oh, Dav," she whispered, and he heard the tears in her voice. He wasn't sure she was going to be able to do what was necessary.

"Just do it, Carrie," he insisted, making it a firm order. "It's the pain now, or possibly losing my hands later."

Without a word, she faced him, braced her feet on the side wall of the plane, and took his hands in hers. With one brisk stroke, she began.

It was all he could do not to moan with the horrific pain every stroke brought to his hands. She hesitated only briefly. He saw her jaw clench, but she kept working, stroking his hands, shifting the blood reluctantly through the engorged tissues. They were so involved, and he was so agonized, they nearly missed the further slowing of the plane, the drop in altitude.

"Stop," he ordered, managing to grip her hands, a minor miracle he didn't take time to appreciate.

"We're landing," she said, realizing instantly what he'd already felt. The hard bump of the wheels threw them together again, but they managed to arrange themselves as he'd suggested, to lead their captors to believe they were still asleep.

"The plane's come to a stop," Dav whispered, feeling the lurch, even though the propellers were still whirring. "Can you see anything out the window?"

Carrie eased off his chest long enough to sneak a peek out the small windows in the cargo area. "No. It's pitch dark. It's clear, there's a little bit of a moon. It looks like there are a lot of trees, but I can't even be sure of that."

"Okay, come back. We must appear to be still asleep."

She put her head back down on him and he let his bound hands circle her once more. The pain still arced through each finger and ran up his arms and shoulders as his circulation fought to clear the pooling blood from his tightly secured hands. They were closer to their normal color now, and it was a small consolation that he could hold her.

The door from the cockpit scraped open and he felt Carrie's body tense. "Shhhhh," he whispered, a thread of sound only she would be able to hear.

There was a rapid spate of Spanish and he heard footsteps approach. He willed himself to be limp, unresponsive, even when the pilot kicked him hard in the leg.

More rapidly spoken words, which he didn't understand. Of all the languages he knew, he hadn't learned more than a smattering of Spanish and nothing sounded familiar. He heard the change in the man's tone, though, and his "Sí, Senor" was understandable.

The man left the plane and hope leaped up in Dav's heart. If they were left alone, even for a few minutes, they might escape. He was pretty sure he could get the plane up into the air, and once there, he could use the radio.

Footsteps returned and he heard a grunt and a slosh. What he wasn't prepared for was the cold blast of a full bucket of water hitting his covered head.

Carrie jerked and gasped, bolting upright and taking him with her, making an agony of his already brutally tender hands. She was spluttering wildly and they were both dripping cold water as well.

"On your feet," a voice snarled in heavily accented English. "No tricks or I shoot you."

Dav lifted his hands and Carrie rose. He struggled to do the same and felt the strength of her hand on his arm steadying him enough to get him to his feet.

"You, woman," the voice ordered. "Keep your eyes down and your mouth shut."

There was a rustling and a sense of movement and Dav felt a rough hand drag at his left elbow. "Come," the voice insisted.

Stumbling sideways, Dav walked blindly with his captor. He could feel Carrie's hand lightly clutching his other arm. He knew where the current players were, but without knowing the situation, or how many other captors there might be, he couldn't formulate a plan. Not to mention that he was still woozy from the drugs. The moment he'd gotten to his feet, his head screamed with pain and pressure, which seemed to throb in time with their footsteps. His body was stiff from the awkward ride in the plane, and every joint ached from being tied at such painful angles.

"Get in," the voice demanded in English, shoving him forward. His shoulder impacted with steel—a vehicle.

"To your left," Carrie whispered. "The Jeep door's open."

"No talking," the voice snarled, and he heard the sound of flesh striking flesh.

Carrie cried out and, propelled by the slap, bumped into him just as he bent forward. Her impetus drove him head-first into the vehicle. He spared a moment to be grateful he didn't rap his head on the door frame. He was at enough of a disadvantage without a concussion. She tumbled in after him and they had no sooner pulled in their feet than the door slammed. Now his head pounded further from hitting the armrest, another strike to add to the myriad pains he already owned. If he'd been able to see through the disgusting bag on his head, he was pretty sure he'd be seeing stars.

On his hand, he felt the lightest touch. A Y, and an O, and a U were drawn, feather light, with exacting care. Then an O and a K. *You okay?*

He flipped her hand over, carefully formed the letters despite the pain in his fingers. Her earlier work on his hands, while excruciating, had helped him regain some flexibility.

Yes. Where?

It took him several tries to make sense of the letters she drew in his palm. Finally, he connected them properly.

Jungle.

How could they be in the jungle? As the vehicle started and pulled away from the airport or airstrip, he visualized the flight path, the possible places they could have gone. Southern Mexico or somewhere in Central America. They hadn't flown long enough, he was pretty sure, to have gone all the way to South America, especially as far as the jungle areas. Nor could they have flown a plane this size to Hawaii or any other Pacific island without refueling.

Carrie was writing again.

Two men. Jeep.

They drove for a short time on smooth roads, carefully signing back and forth to one another. Oddly enough, the two men in the front were silent. Not even the radio broke the hum of the engine and the subtle creak of the leather seats as they twisted and turned. There was an occasional shout or riff of music beyond the windows, but no bustle of real traffic, no city noises.

That wasn't good. It meant a small airport in a remote location.

Without warning the vehicle dropped off the pavement onto dirt. Now the Jeep slowly jumped and bumped on a rutted, jouncing, pockmarked road. No further spelling to one another was possible since they were both desperately trying to stay on the seat and hang on as the car flung them every which way. Dav hit his head again, and this time, even with the bag, he truly saw stars behind his eyelids.

The endless bouncing was made more unpleasant as the angles changed. They were ascending, turning and twisting along a furrowed trace. He heard branches scrape the sides of the Jeep, felt the lurch, sway and groan of the undercarriage as it managed the rocks in the road.

He fought nausea constantly, thanks to the faint odor of

the drugs in the bag, and the incessant movement with no visual horizon on which to focus. It was at least an hour, possibly two, that they traveled. They never slowed, and the road never smoothed out. He was still trying to manage his rebellious stomach when the Jeep lurched to a stop.

He heard the slam of doors, and men's laughter. Voices greeted their captors, who had gotten out. At least two or three more.

"Carrie?" he began, wanting desperately to be sure she was conscious, and okay after the harrowing journey.

Before she could answer, the door beyond his head opened, and fresh, damp, tropical-smelling air rushed in. A new voice demanded, "Come." He felt a rough tugging at his sleeve and shoulder. *"Now."*

Dav did his best to move quickly, while still helping Carrie. At this point, according to Gates, you did your best to cooperate, assessing as you went and figuring out what to do. That meant not antagonizing anyone or getting hit hard enough to do bodily damage or get dead, so Dav dragged himself out of the car and reached back for Carrie.

"Leave the woman," the voice said when Dav made it out of the vehicle and fumbled for Carrie's hands, shoulder, anything. "Leave it!" the voice demanded, and rough hands jerked him away from the vehicle. "*Vámonos,* come, both of you."

Thankfully, within steps, he felt Carrie's hand on his arm. They moved quickly in the wake of their captor. Dav smelled wood smoke and rain, plants and something smoky-sweet—marijuana maybe. Burnt coffee. Bacon.

His stomach clenched with hunger in spite of the ongoing waves of drug and pain-induced nausea. Neither he nor Carrie had eaten lunch and it was now hours upon hours later. His system recognized the scent of sustenance and made its need known.

A hand shoved at him and he stumbled again. He gained his feet, only to have the barrel of a rifle pressed across his belly stop him short. Carrie's hand trembled on his arm; he could feel her grip tighten in fear, as her fingers quivered in a flutter of despair.

"Patrick, take what we need." The smooth voice was new, menacing, amused. It was also at least ten feet away to his right. An unseen hand jerked open the back of the still-damp bag on his head. He felt the cold play of steel on his scalp as some of his hair was cut away. On his arm, Carrie jerked, then froze into place. He guessed she could see the knife cutting her hair, while he had only felt it. The bag was retied, snugly, and the man with the smooth voice spoke again.

"Get the other item as well," smooth-voice said. "We'll need to send that with the hair."

The back of his shirt collar was tugged downward, and he felt the unhoned edge of a blade cold against his skin as it slipped under the chain he wore around his neck. How could they know about that? A memento, his mother's thin gold wedding ring, hung on the chain. He never took it off. It reminded him always of his father's perfidy, and reminded him to beware of the kind of blind, unseeing love she'd bestowed on the old man, the love she'd wasted along with her life.

The chain was whipped to the back, tightening with choking force on his windpipe.

"Got it," the man behind him said, snapping the chain off his neck in one quick tug. Air rasped into his lungs in a rush, but he still heard the clink of the gold chain and ring, felt the absence of the familiar weight along his collar.

Another voice spoke now. "Get in." Nothing happened for a moment, then, "Do it now, pretty lady." Amusement rang in the words. "Or Carlos will shoot you and dump you in. I don't think your gringo millionaire boyfriend would like that."

"Carrie, do it. Follow their directions."

"Dav—" Her voice held panic, but was choked off as someone jerked at her, pulling her away from him, and he felt as much as heard her gasp. Fear resonated in the sound. For a moment, he thought she would refuse, clutching his arm with fierce strength. Then, her hand trailed away and he felt her move forward.

It was hard to locate things by sound, but he could tell she was in front of him. Then she whimpered and the sound retreated, with a faint echo to it. He hoped they weren't being separated. He prayed as quickly and passionately as he could that she would be all right, that they would be held together.

The rifle pressing into him lifted and another weapon shoved at the small of his back. He flinched. This, too, was a rifle, not a handgun; he recognized the imprint of the barrel, the small dangerous impression. If the man fired now, his spine would disappear and Carrie would be alone.

"But . . ." He heard denial in the word, then another gasp as she was either gripped or threatened.

"Do what they say, Carrie," he said as clearly as he could through the rasp of his bruised throat and the muffling bag.

He heard more rustling and grunting, and the sound of her footsteps receded further, but did not disappear. God, it was so brutally frustrating not to be able to see where he was, see what was happening to her.

"Now you, Senor *millionaire*," the amused voice spoke again. "Time to go down."

Down? He scooted a foot forward and felt air under his shoe. He lurched a bit, drawing his foot back from the abyss.

"Turn, and climb down into the hole."

Down. Into a hole.

With a flash of blinding clarity, Dav realized who was behind his kidnapping, as impossible as it seemed.

"Whatever Niko is paying you," he stated, striving for calm, "I'll double it. The woman and I are not of that much importance, but money talks. If you get me out of here, my money can speak my gratitude."

There was a spate of Spanish and raucous laughter resounded in the night. Listening carefully, despite his rising panic, he detected at least three distinct voices, three, maybe four different laughs.

"Not enough money printed, gringo, for us to stop this," the man behind him said. "Besides, there are plans. Climb down or I push you in and you maybe break your leg. No matter to me, long as you don't die."

Realizing that it was futile to argue, Dav knelt and felt for the hole. He caught the edge of the ladder, felt it waver. His guts turned to water as he pivoted in the dirt and fumbled to set his foot on the top rung. More sneering laughter followed his efforts, but the comment about the broken leg forced him to caution. It told him the drop was deep enough that a break was possible.

It also told him they intended to keep him alive, at least for now.

Descending into the earth, in the dark, with his bound hands and covered head, was a thing of nightmare. It took all his considerable willpower to keep moving, to force a dam against the rising tide of his childhood fears. He was unable even to feel his way, or see the ladder in front of him.

Relief flooded through him when his searching foot found solid floor rather than another rickety rung. Carrie's hands reached for him, grasped his arm.

Both of them went flying as the ladder jerked.

"The ladder," Carrie gasped, struggling to rise. He held her in place. It was no use to try to grab the ladder. What could they do with it, even if they had it?

Wood shavings showered them as the ladder was drawn upward, scraping through the metal opening, and that metal clanged in a deep, harsh note as something heavy was flung over the hole. The snick of a lock told him they were now prisoners, locked in a deep, dark hole.

Overwhelmed by the thought, he stayed down on the dirt,

struggling to breathe, struggling to stay in the present, not fly back to the terrible times when he'd been locked away in just such a room. This room too, smelled of old blood and old death. Of fear and pain. Of hopelessness, if such could have a smell.

"Dav," Carrie whispered. "Dav? Where are you?"

He could hear her shuffling nearer, trying to find him, but his throat was frozen on the words. Finally he fought through his panic enough to say, "Here."

"Oh, thank God. I thought you'd been knocked out."

"No," he managed, his teeth chattering on the word.

"You said something up there, I heard you say something new. Something about Niko? Who is that? What did you mean?" she asked as she ran her hands over his head, which made it pound further as she inadvertently jostled the bumps and bruises he'd sustained in their journey. Her searching hand finally found the ties to the bag that still covered his head. Both the pilot and the guy who'd cut his hair had jerked them tight and tied them snugly, making sure he didn't see a thing. The fact that the ties were now wet as well as knotted made undoing them even more challenging.

"I . . . I . . ." He couldn't think, couldn't form a coherent sentence. His thoughts were in chaos, partly battling nightmares, partly racing to figure out how Niko could be alive and desperate enough to orchestrate this.

Thinking of Niko settled his mind, engaged it in something besides old nightmares and that which lurked in the underground dark. He'd carefully followed his half brother's nefarious career in prison and his time with a group of mercenaries fighting in South America and Africa. He'd always kept tabs on Niko, both from the hope of reconciliation, and the knowledge that Niko wanted him dead. But he'd been told that Niko had died fighting in the near-constant conflicts in Somalia. He'd had the rumor checked officially and unofficially; as far as anyone, including Gates, had been able to tell, Niko had indeed perished.

Evidently, they'd all been wrong. Only Niko could have conceived of something like this hole as a punishment and a holding pen. Only Niko would know about the cell under their Athens house, and the horrors it represented for Dav.

"Got it!" Carrie said, her voice briefly excited.

Within seconds, sweet air rushed over his face as the bag fell away. Gasping, Dav felt the chill dampness of the night air, and the sticky smell of dusty age and disuse flooded his nostrils along with the faintest underlying scent of rusting metal, and death.

It was that smell, the smell of spilled blood and the faint, sickly sweet smell of decay, that tied his mind and stomach up in knots yet again. Anger burned along with the fear. Only Niko would know how this affected him. Only Niko would torture him this way. Deliberately.

"Dav? Are you okay? Dav?" There was a frantic note in Carrie's voice as she called his name again. She'd removed the bag, but his lack of response was obviously terrifying her.

He marshaled his fear, forcing it aside. It demanded attention, demanded that he look into the dark and see the monsters that awaited. Coming for him. To kill him.

No.

Gritting his teeth, he forced them back. He would not die, they would not kill him.

Carrie mattered to him. He would not give in to the demons of his past, or these present fears. He must be there for her. No one had helped him in his cell, and he'd come to expect that no one would, but he wasn't his father. Nor his brother. He wouldn't leave Carrie to face this alone while he retreated into some recess of his mind, gibbering in fear.

"Then eeseh enea chronon." He ground out the words between his chattering teeth. Words he'd just said hours

ago as he'd thought about Niko and his father. *I'm not nine anymore.*

How ironic.

"What? Dav?" Carrie's voice was laced with anxiety. He could feel her fear in the trembling hands that raced over his face and neck; the fingers that hurried along his arms to chafe his hands were trembling. "Dav? What are you talking about?" When she spoke again, it was slowly, as if to a young child. "Dav, did you hit your head?"

The shock of pain as she rubbed at his hands brought him further back to himself.

"I said, I'm not nine anymore," he replied. "My half brother and father used to lock me in a dark hole like this." He had to stop there, just for a moment, and beat back the memory once more. "That's why I tried to bargain up there. I understood at once, that if they weren't killing us, merely dumping us underground to wait, they want money. And probably revenge. Niko, my half brother, is behind this." He tried to uncurl his stiff body. "Bastard! I will kill him for this."

"How can that be? Why would he do that?" Carrie's bewilderment didn't stop her from continuing to chafe his hands and her consistent stroking woke fire in his nerves. Oddly enough, the pain somehow calmed his fears as well. It was real, present. The monsters were not. "Why would your own brother try to kill you?"

The words sounded tinny in his ears as he sat up. He had to fight a wave of pain and wicked nausea. He held tight to the litany he'd developed. He wasn't alone. He wasn't nine. He wasn't stupid, as his father had always claimed. He was Davros Gianikopolis. He was his own man.

Determination flared within him. Somehow he would get out of this, get Carrie out too, and when he did, he was going to make sure Niko was dead. For this, Dav would kill him with his bare hands.

"I'm sorry, Carrie." He forced the words out, forced his teeth to unclench, his painfully clenched jaw to relax.

Confusion still rang in Carrie's voice. "You've never mentioned your brother. Why would he do something like this? Why would he or your father put you in a hole?"

"Ah, darling," Dav soothed, feeling more like himself with each exchange, with every moment his brain cleared, with every breath of damp earthy air. "Families are not always very nice. Mine would be the finest example of dysfunction you could imagine. I thought my lamentable brother was dead." He paused to catch his breath and straighten further, letting the pain flow away as best he could. "This is, as you Americans would say, the terrible result of a family feud."

She managed to laugh a little at his wry statement, and it lifted his heart. "There now—" He tried to inject humor into his voice, to soothe her as well. "Let's get untied. Where is that all-purpose tool? Did they search you? Take it?"

"No. They didn't touch me, other than to cut off some of my hair and shove me down here. And I still have my purse. It's under your coat, like you suggested," she said, and he heard the susurration of fabric, the snick of a metal catch. "It's . . . oh, wait, we put the tool in your pocket."

Her hands roamed over his torso, distracting him further from his fears. He'd imagined her hands on him in just that way, but the circumstances had been much more attractive. Hard to believe that he could switch from fear to sex, but both were passionate drivers in the human animal. And truthfully, the lascivious thought was a welcome distraction from the fear tearing at him, tugging at his mind, trying to suck him back into the nightmare of their situation.

"Ah-ha!" Carrie's triumph came with the jangle of keys and a clank of metal. "Here, hold out your hands."

It was agonizing to hold still as she clamped the tool's scissors down on the zip ties, a further agonizing pain when they finally gave way and the blood, pent up and pulsing, poured into his hands once more. He could feel the pounding of his heart, the beat of the blood as it flooded into his hands, making them ache and sting and throb as if he'd plunged them into a hive of stinging wasps.

Letting them lie heavily in his lap, he panted through the pain. "Oh, God. That hurts," he muttered.

"Your hands? Should I rub them again?" Carrie asked. "What can I do to help?"

"Nothing yet," he managed. "Let them be for a bit. Can you get your own hands free or do you need help?"

"I think I can do it," she said. He heard the snap of the plastic, then the clinking of the keys and her sigh of relief as her bonds fell away.

"Can you find the bag, the one from my head? Keep the ties from our hands too. We need to keep anything that might help us get out of here. You never know what will help."

"Really? The cut ties . . ." She let the thought trail away and he heard her moving around at his side, felt the swish of her searching fingers. "Here's the bag," she said. "I'll put the ties in it."

Without warning, there was a flare of light up above them. A blindingly bright flashlight shone down into the cell, the grate rattled and the lock was opened. No one said a word, but a bag dropped down to the floor. The grate fell back into place, the lock snicked shut and the torch disappeared.

The transaction was over so quickly, it barely registered. Instead, all he could think about was what was in the bag.

"Be careful," he said sharply as he felt Carrie move to investigate. "My brother, may he rot in hell, used to put rats and cockroaches in the room with me when we were children. I'm hoping that's food, but it might not be."

"Shit, that's nasty," she cursed, and it surprised a laugh out of him. He'd never heard her use any foul language.

"Carrie?"

"What?" she snapped with a testy tone. "Man, I have a headache. I think I broke the strap on my purse and I lost track of where the bag dropped, thinking about rats. Damn it, why'd you have to say that?" Now she was muttering. "God, I hate drugs, they make me feel like crap. And I hate rats. Dirty nasty things."

He actually found himself chuckling at her indignant tone. "Sorry, but it's true. Food would be good, and they haven't harmed either of us yet, barring that slap to you on the plane"—he recalled she'd been hit twice now and his gut burned—"and at the car. Those, however painful, weren't torture."

"No, just showed disdain for women," she replied, and he could tell by her voice that she was moving toward the middle of their cell, looking for the sack. "Fuckers."

"Carrie!" Now he was shocked into laughing out loud.

"Sorry, but a spade's a spade, and none of them will ever be clients in my gallery so I don't have to mind my reputation or my language for them. Fuckers," she repeated. "Pisses me off."

He chuckled again. It felt good to laugh instead of shiver in fear. "I can tell. And it is better to be angry than despairing so, yes, they are indeed fuckers and should die." He said it lightly, but meant it as well. To change the subject, he asked, "So, did you find the bag?"

"Yes," she said, sounding more like herself. "There's nothing moving inside it, or at least not that I can tell."

He thought about that and repressed a shudder. "Good. Smell it, if you can, and maybe that will tell us something."

Warmth and movement alerted him that she was next to him. In the pitch black of their cell, that was the only warning he had and he fought down memories again, memories of sudden scratching and nibbling as a rat leapt on him in the darkness of his childhood captivity.

He should not have mentioned rats.

"So," she said, oblivious to his mental struggle, "smells

like dust, mold and fruit. Bleech." She sneezed. "That'll teach me to stick my nose right up against it."

"Sorry," Dav managed around a shaky laugh, brought back to the moment by her grounded practicality. "But hard to tell what it might be without being able to see it."

"They say blind people's other senses get very sharp," she said conversationally. "I guess I can understand why."

She sounded so calm that he had to ask, "Carrie, are you okay?"

"No, I'm not," she replied, her voice sounding just as conversational and calm as it had a moment before. "I'm hanging on to my sanity with my teeth, trying not to focus on the fact that I'm cold and wet and exhausted. Oh, and I'm in a hole in some unknown jungle, far away from light and air and people." He heard the hurried pace of her breathing. "Now can we talk about something else? Please?"

"The latest exhibit at Prometheus looked promising," Dav quipped, thinking back to picking her up at the gallery. Was it just a day ago?

"It is," she said, and he heard humor in her voice. "I'm going to make a killing on this one. New artist, brilliant. Not your style," she added, and now his ears caught the underlying panic she was trying to talk herself out of. "Too busy for your taste, I think, but I've got some clients who are going to eat this guy up."

"Not literally, I hope," he said lightly, reaching out to see if he could help. Rising onto his knees, he found her hands, felt her fingers tugging at the ties of the bag. His own fingers were still swollen and painful, but together, they managed to get it open.

"Well, Augustine Shepherd might like to, literally, since he's her type of boy toy, but I think this kid's grounded enough not to go for her lures."

"Ah, then he's smart too. Should I consider him a rival?"

he said, half joking, half serious, since admiration was plain in her tone.

"Oh, no. He's far too young for me," she said, taking his hand as they eased the bag to the ground together.

"You're quite young, my dear," Dav said quickly, remembering her lithe body and elegant carriage, which he so admired. "And lovely."

"Why thank you," she said, and he heard pleasure in her voice. "But dating the artist would definitely put me in cougar country."

He laughed at the thought. "I disagree, but I find myself glad that you think so."

There was silence for a moment, and then Carrie changed the subject. "How do we figure out what's in the bag?"

He dismissed the thought of bugs and snakes. He had to if he wanted to keep his cool. "Reach in and feel around, I guess. I'll do it."

"No, your hands—" she began.

He cut her off. "Carrie, let me do this. I'm the reason you're in this mess. If there's something dangerous or questionable, let me do it. My goal is to get you out of this alive, and back to San Francisco."

"Not without you," she said immediately.

They sat in silence for several heartbeats. He didn't know how to respond. Her safety, her life, were paramount. He'd give his up to save her, in the blink of an eye, as would any man. "Thank you, my dear," he said, "but you are innocent in all this."

Her hands found his face in the darkness with unerring instinct. "Dav, I'm not your 'dear' anything, in that avuncular way you say it. I'm not weak, I'm not stupid and I'm not helpless. We'll get out of this together or not, but don't you treat me like I'm helpless."

The rush of anger behind her words was punctuated by the pressure of her fingers on his face. Following the line of her arms, he found her shoulders in the darkness, let his still throbbing hand slip upward to caress the softness of her cheek.

"Helpless? Never," he said, picturing her lovely face, letting his fingers be his guide as he felt the fullness of her hair, the soft brush of it on his hands. "Strong, beautiful, competent, brilliant," he murmured, losing himself in the feel of her, which did more to push back the dark and the fear than anything he could imagine. "But never helpless. Never that."

There was something building in the dark now, something that was good. Something sensuous and compelling. He couldn't see her face, her features, but he could feel the yielding of her body, the angle of her form moving into him.

Without thought, without hesitation, he moved as well, finding her lips with amazing accuracy. The kiss was better, deeper and truer, than their frenzied passion on the plane. That moment had been motivated by the lack of inhibition brought on by drugs, this was honest attraction, stripped bare of social convention.

This was real. This was powerful.

Her hands moved into his hair and he wanted to growl with delight. Her fingers were cool, caressing his neck, soothing him and exciting him as she leaned further into the kiss.

It was a sound that broke them apart. A deep, roiling rumble.

"Oh, my gosh," Carrie said, and he thought she snickered.

"Carrie?" Dav was having a hard time shifting from passion to humor.

"It's my stomach. It's growling." He could feel the tremor of laughter where he still held her.

He grinned. Then laughed out loud. "Then, by all means, let's explore our dining options," he said, smiling. The dark—both bad and good—receded as her amusement replaced any residual fear.

Together they delved into the bag, finding a mango, some

bananas, and peculiarly, two wax paper–wrapped, thick-sliced ham sandwiches with mayonnaise and cheese on white bread.

"A picnic," Carrie said. "Too bad they didn't think to add some champagne or something fun to drink."

"Ah, but they did," Dav corrected, pulling the last items free of the bag. Two bottles with old-fashioned caps rattled together. "No idea what's in them, but the caps seem to be secure, so we can hope they've not been tampered with."

Dav tried to twist off the cap, but his hands were still too swollen. "You'll have to do the honors, my . . . Carrie." He corrected the "my dear" he'd been about to say. Evidently she didn't like the way he said it, or what it implied, so he'd stop.

They held hands as they ate the scant meal and drank the grape soda. Dav drained every drop of the drink and wished for more. He felt as if he could drink a gallon of water and not be totally satisfied.

"I wish there'd been a second bottle," Carrie echoed his thought. "I'm still thirsty."

"Me too," he said, finishing the sandwich and offering her the mango. "The mango will help though, to quench your thirst."

"We don't have anything to cut it with."

"Doesn't your tool have a blade? Otherwise, I think teeth are going to have to do."

It took them a while, with Dav wielding the knife in short careful strokes to skin the mango. Finally, they were able to eat it all and it did indeed go a long way to quenching their thirst. "You said to save everything," she said, and he heard the doubt in her voice. "Does that include mango rind and pit?"

"No, let's close it all up and put it in the bag. We don't want to attract . . ." He let that thought drift off, not wanting to think about what the smells of food would attract. "Anything."

"No, we don't. Here, put the bottles in the other bag. We'll keep those. We can break them if we need something sharp, or fill them up with water if we get a chance."

"There's no bathroom down here," Dav said, careful to keep his voice level. "We'll need to plan for that situation. The fact that they've fed us leads me to believe they aren't going to kill us right away, but we can't count on them bringing us up for potty breaks either."

"Why did they cut our hair?" she asked, reminding him of the brief incident aboveground.

"Proof of life. That tells me they'll be asking someone for a ransom."

"What makes you think they won't kill us?"

"They haven't yet," Dav replied, and smiled. "That's good for now. And if they are cautious enough to blindfold me, and send someone our hair, they have an agenda."

"Do you really think that means anything?" Carrie sounded dubious. "They could send that and still kill us."

"Yes, but if they'd wanted us dead, why bother with a kidnapping? If they wanted us out of the country before they killed us, then they could have done it when we landed. I'm guessing the landing strip is very remote by the lack of city noise or machinery humming. Or they could have killed us before they dumped us in here. If they were going to kill us tomorrow, why feed us?"

"Which all means what?" He heard the quaver in her voice. She had proven herself to be strong, but his litany of reasons why they were still alive seemed to be making her more afraid rather than reassuring her.

"They want something," he said flatly. "Money, most likely. Or, given that my brother seems to be behind all this, revenge."

"That doesn't sound good."

"It isn't."

Chapter 5

Dawn came early in the tropics. Bright sun lit the inner recesses of the underground cell and outlined the carved rock interior. Lines and traceries revealed by the early morning light showed fanged faces and whorls and patterns of an ancient people whose fear of the gods knew no bounds. Marching around the walls were war gods, people rushing away in fear, serpents with feathers and seated monarchs who levied punishment on the prostrate masses.

"Wow," Carrie said, as they both woke, sitting up in the brightening space. They'd talked long into the night, huddled close together, shivering until their clothes finally dried.

Dav told the story of his brother and their disagreements; she talked about her husband's betrayals and the healing she'd found from the previous year's resolution of the art fraud case.

"Look at the carvings. No wind or rain to wear them away down here. Those are pristine." She called the names of the deities she knew as she walked the perimeter, letting reverent fingers glide over the preserved sculptures. "I think this is Kukulcan—also called Quetzalcoatl—who'd be one of the principle gods for the ancient people in Central America."

She looked over her shoulder at him. "Your guess about our location was probably right, given what's carved here."

When he just nodded, Carrie turned back to the wall. "And this, I think this is Voltan, god of Earth. I don't know all of the Mayan pantheon by any means. It's very complicated. All that pre-Colombian art course info got filed in the "interesting but not immediately useful" section of my brain. I remember just enough to be dangerous," she joked. "But I don't think this is a common jail cell. Not with these kinds of carvings. It might be serving that way now, for these guys, but this is some kind of ceremonial space."

Dav watched her as he stretched to loosen up. He wiggled his fingers, which still ached, and bent forward to flex the kinked muscles in his back, all while watching her move excitedly from wall to wall, carving to carving. Now that it was sunlit, he could see the cell was about eighteen or twenty feet long, by fifteen or sixteen wide. Its shorter ends were the more heavily carved, with the grate-covered entry hole dead in the center of the ceiling.

"Look!" Carrie exclaimed, as the rays of light edged into a new cranny of the space with the rising of the sun. "It's like a sundial," she said, hurrying to gently brush at the floor where the light hit it. "There's stone under here, with markings and everything."

"I hate to confess it," Dav said, and found a smile for her enthusiasm, "but at the moment, I'm slightly more interested in that." He pointed to a portable toilet shoved tight into the far corner. Against that same wall, iron shackles hung. They were obviously of a much newer vintage than the carvings, though not so twenty-first-century as the portable john.

"Oh!" Carrie said, and he saw her eyes light up again. "I thought we'd have to"—she broke off, blushing—"well, you know."

"Yes, I do. Please, go ahead, I'll just be over here." He walked to the farthest end of the cell. It was impossible to ignore the process, but he focused on the carvings instead to give her at least the illusion of privacy. The one he was examining showed the god she'd called Kukulcan stacking up bones, then carrying them away. He moved down the wall to see more, but Carrie interrupted his art appreciation.

"Okay, your turn," she said. "When you're done, we should go through everything we have, figure out what's useful and what isn't. If there's any chance at all that we can get out of here, we need to be ready."

"Now you sound like Gates," he said, trading places with her and taking care of his immediate needs. Hunger rumbled his stomach, but he didn't mention it. It must have been on her mind, however.

"I was thinking I sounded more like you," she said, smiling. She deepened her voice and added the slightest hint of his accent as she mimicked his words, "We must save everything."

"I don't sound like that," he demurred, embarrassed at the portrayal.

"No, you sound much better than I do." She bent to straighten out his coat, smoothing the fabric they'd layered under them to keep the ground's chill from making sleeping any more difficult that it already was.

"I have some protein bars in my purse, if you're hungry," she said, sitting down again.

"I think we should save those for later," Dav cautioned. "You never know what might happen. If they brought us dinner, scant as it was, they may bring breakfast too."

As if the words had summoned them, they heard their captors' voices approaching.

"Turn your faces to the wall," the smooth, amused voice called out. "If I see your faces, I shoot you."

Dav whispered an additional order. "Put your hands in front of you, like you're still tied. We don't want them to know we have any skills or weapons."

He saw her comply as he turned to face the wall. Dav fought down the urge to reach for Carrie's hand. Much as he wanted to reassure her, he didn't want anyone to see just how important she was to him. Doing that might put her in yet more danger.

Dav focused on the carvings as the rattle-clang of the lock and grate echoed in the small space. There were grunting sounds and the slap of metal and fabric as something was lowered down.

"We'll be back for you in two days," smooth-voice said.

"Or not," another voice said. Coarse laughter greeted this statement. "Adios for now, rich man."

The voices receded and both he and Carrie turned to see what had been left for them. Four canteens of water, some fruit, what he presumed were hard-boiled eggs, more sandwiches, crackers, a bunch of bananas, an out-of-place plastic baggie full of bacon, and to his great surprise, a jar of Nutella.

Carrie looked from the provisions to him and back again. "That's a strange breakfast. Strange provisions." A flash of fear crossed her face, but she showed no other sign of concern as she said, "Why do you think they're leaving?"

He considered it as they advanced on the cache of food. "Perhaps to get Niko. Perhaps to contact someone regarding ransom." He looked around the cell, strange as it was, and then up at the locked, metal grate. There would be no escape for them, not from this hole. "Either way, these aren't regular kidnappers. They're not prepared for us to be here for a long time, nor are they thinking too far ahead." He didn't want to go into the ramifications of that, so he asked, "Do you still have your watch? They took mine at some point."

"Well, it was a Rolex," she said, smiling at him. "Easily hocked."

"Yes, too tempting, I guess." He hesitated. Should he tell her the watch had held a locator?

"Look at it this way," she added. "One quick way for Gates to find you, if it turns up in a pawnshop in the States."

"Good thought, since it does have a location device built into it," Dav said, making his decision. He wanted to hit something, knowing it had been taken. How could anyone have known it had the fail-safe locator in it?

This was a problem. As cunning and snakelike as Niko was, he wasn't into tech. He'd either hired that kind of smarts or . . . or what, he didn't know. Either way, it made a grim situation even more desperate. Gates would have no way to know anything about where they were or even what direction they'd gone. "However," he said, softly, "without it we're a needle in a . . ." He paused, searching for the phrase he wanted. "A worldwide haystack."

"I know," she said, glancing away. "But maybe it will lead him to something. Some conclusion that will help. If he finds it."

"Oh, he will." Of that, Dav was sure. Gates would be on the locator like a stooping hawk. Hopefully it would yield something that would direct him their way.

"It's nine A.M., Pacific time," she said, bringing him back to the original question as she handed him an egg. "And I'm an optimist. We'll hope, right?"

"Right."

They pulled the odd assortment of food closer to their sitting area and began peeling the eggs. "Hang on a second," Carrie said, digging into her purse. "I was just wishing I could wash my hands, and I remembered this." With a "ta-da" she pulled a small bottle of waterless hand soap from her purse. "It won't last us long in this situation, but hey, we can pretend we're somewhat civilized."

Laughing, he used the gel sparingly, then went back to peeling the eggs. "I don't know much about food," he admitted, scanning the pile before them. "I'm thinking we should eat anything that would spoil, first. I guess the bacon would be okay for a day or so."

"If the sandwiches have mayonnaise on them, we'll need to eat them. Mustard would keep okay, I think, but the bread will be stale pretty quick."

"Crackers too," he said. "I could never keep crackers fresh, back in my starving student stage," he said idly, turning the box to look for an expiration date. He slipped a finger under the cardboard and opened it to find the interior waxed bag with crackers still sealed.

"I can't picture you as a starving student, somehow," Carrie said, glancing his way. "You've always seemed so polished, so urbane. So," she hesitated, then added, "rich."

"Urbane?" That was an English word he'd not come on before. "Does that mean something good or something bad?"

She laughed and it made her blue eyes twinkle. "You make it so easy to forget that you weren't born here. It means something good."

"Eh-la, well, thank you, then. I'm afraid I was very much the starving student. I wanted to go to university in America, my father was against it. He wanted me closer to home. I wanted to get away from him and from my brother and from all the watching eyes. And frankly, from all the women."

He said it without thinking, because it had been true. Then he winced for it must have sounded pompous, macho and arrogant. Carrie's response told him he was right.

"Oh, really?" Carrie drawled. "That sounds chauvinistic."

"Hmmm, it is," he muttered, struggling to figure out how to explain without sounding even worse. Only this woman could disconcert him so. Perhaps that was why he had always been so intrigued with her. "In the suburb outside Athens where my father kept his estate, he had many families who worked for him. My brother had run through one generation of the daughters, and when one of the young women got pregnant, my father gave her money.

"Unfortunately young women and even young men, everywhere, when they need a job, will do many things they might not otherwise do to secure their future. There were also the daughters, and sometimes the wives, of my father's associates, who would follow me around or seek to come into my room." He felt the heat rise in his face at some of the memories associated with that time. "My father made sure everyone knew that he had pitted my brother and me against one another to prove our worth. What is the old saying? To the victor go the spoils? That was to be the deal."

"Oh, my gosh, that's terrible." Carrie looked shocked, appalled.

Dav nodded. "It was. You never knew who was helping you because they liked you, or thought you would be the winner in the game, or who was helping to actually hurt you." And some had truly, truly hurt him, in those games. Dav tried to make his tone lighter, more upbeat as he finished his story. "He made only one rule. We could not kill one another, for if either of us died, he would give it all away, he said. Neither Niko nor I would inherit if we were rash enough to cause an inconvenient accident." Dav sighed, thinking back to what had started the question. "He also made it known that if we managed to kill one another, he had no compunction about naming a bastard grandson as his heir."

"Which attracted even more women, looking for a chance for a child." She quickly picked up on the ramifications of his father's pronouncements. "What a dangerous, cruel game your father played with you both," she said, and he saw pain in her eyes.

Pain for him. His appreciation for her deepened, something he'd thought impossible.

"True," he said lightly, feeling her caring soothe the old ache of his father's callousness. He leaned forward and kissed her on the mouth. "Thank you for caring about that. At the time, I thought little of it because I had grown up with such treatment. It seemed . . ." he hesitated to say it, but they had already revealed much. He wanted to share more, and if his plans ever came to fruition, she must know the truth anyway. He would not have a wife who did not know the darker side of him, so he must be willing to speak. "It seemed normal."

She nodded. "People can get used to a lot of cruelty, can't they?" He agreed and they both pondered in silence as they ate. Trying, evidently, to change the somber mood the revelations brought, she asked, "So what happened when you came to America?"

"He cut me off," Dav said, shrugging, as if it hadn't hurt, hadn't devastated the young man he had been. "I managed a scholarship, and he deigned to pay for my books; he did that much, but anything else was on me."

Carrie cocked her head to one side, a ghost of a smile playing about her rosy lips. It made him realize he'd never seen her without makeup or lipstick, without her feminine armor.

"I guess he did you a favor, didn't he? You didn't ever count on him, so when the time came to count on yourself, later, you knew you could do it."

That perspective had never occurred to him. "True, very true." Another thought occurred right on the heels of the paradigm shift though. A dark thought to balance the lighter one. "That one decision may be why we're here, however," he added with a snap of anger for Niko's continued treachery. "My brother hated me for leaving, putting myself not only out of his reach, but out of Father's reach as well. For four years, I didn't go home. Not for holidays or for summer. I took jobs in construction, in manufacturing, in management as I got to be older. You can get those jobs with a student visa, though once I took internships in management positions, I began to think about applying for citizenship."

"Bet that pissed your dad off," she said as she wrapped the sandwiches more tightly in their wax paper.

"Yes. It did." An understatement if there ever was one. Dav winced at the memory of the rage that had sizzled through the transatlantic call forbidding him to apply for American citizenship. The fact that his father had been so against it made it all the sweeter when he received it.

Carrie watched him, speculation in her eyes. She was about to ask more, he could sense it, but he decided it was time to talk about something else. Those memories were raw, and dangerous. The anger at his family, never far from the surface, threatened to overwhelm him given their present situation.

"Here, let's figure out what to keep for later," he said, brushing her fingers as he reached for the bundle of eggs. "These will keep, as will the crackers and this." He hefted the Nutella. "The sandwiches"—he pointed at the bundles she'd made of the sandwiches—"we should eat today."

"Good idea. What about—"

"Shhh," Dav said suddenly, catching her arm, straining to hear a repeat of the sound that had caught his attention. "They're leaving. I was not sure they were serious about that."

Fear leaped into her eyes. "Oh, God. Do you think they'll come back?"

"I don't know." He said it as calmly as he could. "Carrie-mou, we're in a terrible position," he admitted, using the endearment because he felt he could, because he knew that they were in so very much danger it didn't matter. Besides, had he not already decided that this woman was who and what he wanted?

He sat still as stone, straining to hear any movement, any sound. The bird noises resumed as did the hum of insects buzzing in the warming sun above them. Underground, shaded, it was still fairly cool, but still warmer than most April mornings in San Francisco. "I have no idea if they'll come back."

He stood, stretched again, trying to ignore the way she was

watching him, the way her gaze roamed over his chest. It made him feel primitive, powerful. It made him want to . . .

He caught the thought before it hatched, stuffing it into the back of his mind. Women always complained that men thought with their libido. Unfortunately, they were far too often right. Time for a change of subject.

What had Gates told him about being held captive? Keep moving. Stay limber. Be ready to run if you get a chance.

Looking around the cell, Dav realized the outlook was bleak and getting bleaker, but he couldn't tell Carrie that. Nor could he think it himself. He had to act as if there were something they could do, some way to effect an escape or to ensure rescue.

"We need to explore this place," he said briskly, assessing the space with a renewed sense of purpose. He forced all the dark thoughts away; he would not let Carrie see his fear. "We should see if we can reach the lock up there. Perhaps, if you stand on my shoulders?"

"On your shoulders?" Carrie echoed, standing now, and looking upward as well.

"Yes, we need to figure out what we're going to do if they don't come back," Dav said, injecting a firm note into his tone. "We must do what we can to help ourselves."

"God helps those who help themselves," she muttered, walking to the center of the cell and staring at the grate. "So," she said, with patently false brightness, "which is worse, if they do come back or if they don't?"

"We have no way to know," Dav admitted, coming to her side. "Come now, Carrie-mou," he soothed, reaching out to smooth down the fabric of her sweater, knowing it was a futile gesture in some ways, since there was nothing he could offer in the way of truly meaningful action. "The most important thing is to keep thinking for ourselves, to keep thinking and looking for options."

"I know, I know. Think positive."

He smiled, running a hand up and down her back, feeling the faint tremble in her body. He moved behind her, slipping his arms around her. For a moment she stiffened.

"Come," he coaxed softly. "Let me hold you. It won't get us out of here, but we'll both feel better for it."

She relaxed in his arms and for a long time they stood that way. He closed his eyes and let his cheek rest on her hair. He was fascinated by the silk of it, regretted that the heavy growth of his beard caught its fine strands.

"What was it you said earlier? While there's life, there's hope, eh? If we're taken out of this hole, we may have chances. We must stay active while they are gone so we can be ready to run, or fight. We need to plan." He was already doing that in his own mind. "But for now," he added, "I like standing here, holding you. I like it very much."

He felt the hum of her agreement through her back. Slowly, she turned to face him, letting her hands slide round him, one pressing his back; the other, at his belt, clutched the leather as if a lifeline. He stroked her back again, let his fingers rest at her waist where the material rode up. He let the heat of her skin warm his hands.

It was irresistible to let the fingers of his other hand slide into her hair, remembering the kisses she'd pressed on his face when she was intoxicated with the drug.

As he stroked, she relaxed, melting into him with a pliancy that made his heart beat faster, made his body fire and respond. Here, finally, was Carrie, in his arms. They were alone at last, together, but there was no magic carpet, no fantastic meal or wine with which to ply her, no theater tickets or stunning gems with which to shower her.

Just the two of them. Alone. There was no past, no future. Nothing but the moment.

Carpe diem. Seize the day. The ancient adage floated into his mind.

Pulling away a bit, he let the hand he had in her hair slip

round to caress her jaw, tilt her face toward his. Her natural compliance encouraged him and he gazed into her gorgeous blue eyes, seeing the desire kindling there.

"Carrie." He whispered her name, saw her lips curve upward in acquiescence. Kissing her was like sipping hot coffee on a cold morning, like the finest brandy at the end of a delicious meal. It made him want. It satisfied him, then drove him higher, fed his hunger in the most fundamental way.

She shifted slightly, changing the angle of the kiss, drawing him in, drawing him deeper to her. Her hands were active now, digging into the heavy muscles of his back, sliding lower to cup his backside and pull him forward. He felt more than heard her reaction to the pounding erection she inspired.

"Mmmmm," she moaned, pulling him away from the light, toward the wall. He followed as best he could, never breaking the connection of their mouths, the impassioned race of his hands. "Come here, please," she implored, turning him to brace his back on the wall. "No one can look in, or see us here. The angles," she explained obliquely. He took her word for it, so distracted by her luscious kisses that he really didn't care if anyone saw them. He found her full breasts with his hands, caressed them, then hesitated, wanting to see her reaction.

"Ohhhh, yes," she moaned, as she clamped his hands there, and arched her hips into his. She'd pulled her mouth away long enough to express her enjoyment, but she was quickly back, a hot, powerful woman, matching him kiss for kiss, caress for caress. When she slid a hand between them to grip him, he nearly exploded. Red passion hazed his vision and he envisioned lifting her up, tearing off her clothes and impaling her, pounding into her until neither of them could take any more.

The thought was almost father to the deed. He lifted her easily, felt her wrap her legs around him. She was tugging at his shirt, unbuttoning it, pulling it open to run her hands through the thick hair on his chest.

Now it was his turn to moan. Her slender fingers were an erotic dance on his fiery skin. He shed his jacket, letting the shock of cooler air add to the passionate play. With her body braced on his hips, her neck was open to him, and he ran hot kisses up the delicate line of her throat.

Her guttural cries were like a match to a fire. He tugged her shirt free and felt himself harden even more at the sight of her lacy bra, and the magnificent breasts it constrained. He let himself feast on them, trying to be mindful of his beard. Her skin was so beautiful he hated to mark it in any way.

"Let me, let me . . ." she said, pulling away to unfasten the garment, let it drop.

Dav was undoing her skirt, with her hands mirroring the action on his belt, when he froze.

"Wait," he panted, desperate to have her, desperate to complete what they'd started. But if that sound were rescue, or their captors' return, he wouldn't leave her vulnerable to them, nearly naked in his arms. He gripped her close, his ears catching the sounds beyond their cell, beyond their passion. "Shhhhh."

"God, don't stop," she growled, shuddering in his arms.

"Do you hear that?" he insisted. As the words left his mouth, the roar of a plane or truck reverberated in the sudden stillness above them. Whatever the vehicle was, it was close. Passion quenched by necessity, they sped to right their clothing, both straining to hear. Dav still wanted her desperately. The press of survival, of danger, made that desire an even sharper need. Though he'd long ago learned to control his body and his mind, this time, both were reluctant.

The light had dimmed only slightly, but the shadow that passed over the grate was fast. A plane.

"A flare gun would be nice," Dav muttered.

"If it's someone friendly," Carrie shot back. "If we're in

Central America, there could be a lot of unfriendly people." She struggled back into her shirt and fastened her skirt, tucking the sweater in as it had been before they'd started at each other. They were both peering up through the grate, straining to see if anything was happening.

Distant voices rang out, shouts and laughter, but they came no closer to where they waited crouched in tense silence. The sound of an engine neared, then died away, along with the voices.

"Do you think . . . ?" Carrie began in a whisper.

"Wait," Dav cautioned.

No sound reached their straining ears. Nothing moved above them, and nothing marred the clear silence of the afternoon, not bird calls or the wind, or the sound of trucks or planes. For at least fifteen minutes they hunkered down, elbow to elbow, out of sight of anyone who might look in, stretching every sense to hear anything that might connote rescue—or more enemies.

"Do you hear anything?" Dav whispered.

"No, and I have to stand up. I'm getting a cramp in my thigh," she said irreverently.

Thinking about her thighs was probably not the best thing, but he couldn't help it. It was true that a man's thinking started first with his body's needs, he decided ruefully.

"Here, let me help you," he said, taking her elbow. He held on when she'd risen, turning her to face him. "Carrie, about our earlier interlude," he began.

She smiled. "Now you're getting formal with your English again. An interlude? What a lovely thing to call it. I would have said, 'About when you nearly jumped me, earlier,'" she said, her voice holding a strange pain.

"Well, since it was mutual and something I've longed for—" he said, stroking her cheek, watching her blue eyes change and darken. He hoped he wasn't exposing himself too much, but he couldn't bear that she might regret the whole situation. "Nothing could have pleased me more. I was sorry to have it interrupted."

At first, she ducked her head, then met his gaze. "Me too." She looked up again, then around the cell, and sighed. "This sucks."

"Tell me about it," he said, following her assessing route. "Shall we try the idea of you standing on my shoulders to reach the grate?"

"No time like the present, I guess." She nodded, sighing. "You've got your jacket off already, so that's one thing. Let me take my shoes back off."

"I have no idea how to get you to my shoulders," Dav admitted. "Not something I've ever needed to do in my life, I confess, but I know it can be done. Do you have any experience with that sort of thing?"

For the first time in hours, she laughed. "Yes, I do. I'll have you know I was a cheerleader."

"Really now," he said, imagining that and feeling his body respond again with the image of a younger Carrie in a short skirt, holding pom-poms. Being around her was a constantly stimulating experience. "So. You will instruct me."

"Okay," she said, motioning him closer to the center of the room. "Here's how it goes. You need to bend your knees and hold one hand here." She positioned his arm to one side. "And one hand up here." She extended his other hand upward. "That way, I can, essentially, use you as a ladder and your hands as a handrail. Once I'm up, you need to brace your hands on the back of my calves, okay?"

"Got it," he said, positioning himself as she directed. He felt foolish, in a way, acting as nothing more than a ladder, with her doing all the work. But the possibility of learning anything about their cage was too great to pass up.

"Ready?"

"Yes, ready," he replied, helping her as she stepped first on his bent thigh, then onto his shoulder. It took them three tries to get their balance and movements coordinated enough for her to mount his shoulders, but they were successful.

The experiment however, was a total failure.

Even with her on his shoulders, the ceiling was at least three feet beyond the reach of her outstretched arms.

"Well, it was worth a try," she muttered, bracing herself on the wall to dust off her feet and slip back into her shoes.

Dav agreed, adding, "We should eat again, while we still have daylight."

"Oh, is it getting dark already?" She looked upward, measuring the sun's path. She looked around the room as if marking the time as she'd done first thing that morning. "Look." She pointed to the wall, her face reflecting hope and a touch of awe.

The path of the sun's rays traced across the floor, bringing the carvings to life with shadow and relief. Demonic faces grimaced from the rock, and deep in their crevices gleamed gems. Dav squinted into the grate, noting that there were clouds skidding across the sky.

"Do you remember anything about the weather, did you see the news or do you remember anything about it?" he asked with some urgency. He couldn't remember if there was a rainy season in this tropical area, but the thought of torrential rains filling the cell was vivid in his mind.

"Not for Central America. It was supposed to be sunny in San Francisco," she added, her smile rueful. "Here, I have no idea."

"I do not either. I'm just wondering what this place is like when it rains. See—" He pointed upward. "The clouds are getting thicker."

"Hmmm. Not the best place to be in a storm."

He continued to stand, staring at the sky, racking his brain to remember anything about the countries in Central America. The geography was easy, thanks to his business dealings. But remembering the weather or other facts? That was hazy.

"Dav," Carrie called. "Let's sit and eat."

He turned to see that she was arranging a picnic, setting out one of the canteens and the sandwiches. Another egg and a piece of fruit joined the feast and when she'd placed them just so, she looked up at him and smiled.

"Very neat," he complimented, dropping cross-legged to the ground. He could feel the stone's dusty chill through the fine wool of his coat, laid out like a picnic blanket, but it wasn't so bad with the warming sun still up. It would be colder by nightfall. Even in this tropical climate, early spring underground was cool.

"So, what have we here?" he drawled, trying to inject some lightness into the situation. "A veritable feast. Something from almost every food group, lovingly prepared by our chef du jour, the divinely beautiful Carrie McCray."

"Thank you, thank you." Carrie took up the play, but he saw the color in her cheeks. "And plated for you this evening by the chef herself. Here, m'sieu," she said, using the French nominative. "Sit, enjoy, please."

Laughing at themselves, they ate. "This is the first picnic I've ever had," Dav admitted, crunching through the dry bread, bacon and cheese.

"You've got to be joking me." Carrie looked at him, astonished. "No childhood picnics?" she began, then her face fell. "No, I guess not. But college? Nothing?"

"I was too busy surviving and working and building my business," he said, wondering what else he'd missed in his search for freedom from his father and brother, for the power to tell them all to go to hell. That gave him another thought. "I thought I would never go back, you know. To Greece."

"Really?" She cocked her head, a listening pose. "Why did you?"

"My mother. I had just graduated. I had decided to say to hell with my father, and I applied for citizenship, as I mentioned." He grinned as she shook imaginary pom-poms.

"Good for you."

"Ah, but the villain of the story had other plans, alas," he said dramatically, lowering his voice to the basso profundo range to make it sound serious and scary.

"Oooh, tell, tell," she played along again.

"I'd found a job with a major investment and shipping firm. I was to start on a Monday. My father's secretary called me the Thursday before. She said he'd told her to call, to tell me that my mother was in the hospital and I should come home."

"And you went," Carrie said, unhesitatingly.

"Yes, I did." The bitter pill of that memory still choked him. "They said she was dying." He sat silent, remembering.

"Dav? She wasn't dying?"

"No," he said, and something in his face must have given away the anguish he'd felt back then. "She wasn't dead, but she'd been desperately ill for six months and they hadn't told me. No, this time it was my father who was in the hospital, but he knew I wouldn't come if I thought it was him."

"He played you," she said, reading the situation perfectly.

"Of course. Then, once he had me, he kept me. He had his ways, his connections with the authorities, and I knew it. I could have left, yes. But I would have had to make a scene in a public place, and he knew I wasn't yet that desperate. I put off my return, but in the end, I had to decline the job in America, stay in Greece. At least I was there when my mother did die."

She laid a warm hand on his arm. "I'm sorry."

He smiled, sorry to have gone back in time to that memory. "Me too. I never got to say good-bye to my mother. She wasn't a strong woman, she never thought to defy him, never understood why I would. She was lost to me though," he said, finally. "She had Alzheimer's. It had come on early for her. There were many hospital stays when I went home. The last one, I chose to meet with my father instead of taking visiting hours one day, and she slipped away. He had dismissed her from his life, of course. Nurses managed her. And finally him too."

"Was that when he died? After he had to have nursing care?" she asked, softly.

"Yes. He called me in a last time. We fought." Dav rose, knowing he couldn't sit still, couldn't bear her sympathy. He walked to stare upward at the grate, still talking.

"We'd had altercations before, but nothing like the row we had over his making me his heir. I told him I didn't want his business, to give it to Niko. He told me I'd won, that Niko wasn't his choice and would never be. I could, he said, fire all the people in the company, turn them out to starve if I wanted to, leave them jobless and alone, or I could take the reins of the company and make it mine. He no longer cared what I, or anyone else, did."

"Did you fall for it?"

"Not at first," Dav said, managing to choke down the last bites of the dry sandwich, using it to give him time to think, to figure out how to explain the dynamic between his dying father, his ruthless brother, and his own desire to be gone from Greece, and free.

She too, was eating, and obviously having just as difficult a time with the dry bread and crusty contents of the sandwich.

"Here, ma'am," he said, seeking to return the mood to the lightness of their earlier banter. "Let me offer you one of our finest vintages, freshly decanted by our own sommelier," he joked, unscrewing the canteen and smelling the contents. Water maybe, something that didn't have a strong scent. "I think it's water."

"Well, let's give it a try." She held out a hand.

"I'll do it," he said, taking a cautious sip. The water was fusty and tasted of the interior of the canteen, but there wasn't a taint or anything foul in it. After another sip to be sure, he passed it her way. "Water. Not too bad, not too good."

"Thanks," she said, and she took a cautious sip. "If it does rain, we should set this out, make sure it gets filled back up."

"Now there's the survivalist," he praised. "Good thinking. That's a good way to begin our conversation about what we're going to do next." And an excellent way to move beyond his ancient family trials.

The dead kept their secrets, and his father was surely dead even if Niko wasn't. There were some things no one else living needed to know.

Chapter 6

"The grate is too high for us to reach," Dav summed up the situation. "I don't think the potty over there"—he pointed toward the aluminum and plastic john—"will support either of our weight for any acrobatics, much less the weight of both of us. We have your multitool, the keys, I have some mints," he said with a smile, reaching down to fish the dented tin out of the topcoat's deep pocket. "Neither my gloves, my wallet nor your purse does us any good here. The chains there"—he pointed to the wall—"are rusty and, again, probably no use since we can't stand on them."

"We might be able to toss them up and climb them to get to the grate," Carrie speculated, glancing from the chains to the grate and back. "I don't know if I have enough upper body strength though, to pull myself up."

Dav walked over and tugged at the heavy manacles, dropping them after a few hard tugs showed them to be firmly planted in the ornate carvings.

"Not easily loosed, and since we don't have bolt cutters, there isn't much to do once we get there."

"True. So," she said, shifting to sit with her back to the wall.

Dav continued, pacing under the grate, assessing it. "We've got the room, a little bit of food and the promise that they'll be back in two days, at which point they may or may not let us out."

"And, if they let us out, they may or may not kill us." Carrie carried that thought to its final conclusion.

"Exactly. Which leaves us with each other, a bit of food and a lot of time on our hands. Too bad we don't have a chess set, eh?"

"I suppose we could make one in the dust," she said, looking over the room. "I didn't know you played."

"I do, yes," he said, surprised that she did. "Do you?"

"Yes, I do too. My father taught me."

"Tomorrow then," he said, pleased at the idea of matching wits with her. "To pass the time, we'll play."

"We should do yoga, to keep us from getting stiff," she said, unexpectedly, then blushed. "I mean . . ."

Laughing, he took the opening she offered to talk about their interrupted passion. "Carrie, it is fine. We can talk about it. The situation is dire. We're attracted to one another." He shrugged. "I've been attracted to you since before I met you." He turned to look at her, face her and show her the truth of his words. "I watched you, from outside the window before I came into Prometheus that first day," he admitted. "You were so vibrant, so alive."

Knowing he would most likely die in the next few days, he decided not to lie to her. "And I've wanted you every day since."

"So, you have him," the older man stated, and then he smiled. Watching from across the room, Niko felt his gut clench. Suddenly, the room seemed colder, the fog beyond the windows more impenetrable. He hated San Francisco, hated the cold.

"You plan for ransom, I presume?" the man continued. "Numbered Swiss account?"

"The Caymans," Niko finally said, chilled by the implied menace in the other man's smile. There was something different now, something . . . off. He'd never seen it before, not in this man.

Niko's confidence faltered, ever so slightly. He knew this man—his mentor in so many things—was dangerous . . . deadly, in fact. Niko also knew that he himself was not the one in control here. He did have something the man wanted and thus he was still useful, which meant he would probably live through this encounter.

Probably.

"We've sent the items for proof of life, with instructions. With the money deposited, we'll give the security geek the coordinates to his location." Niko managed to keep his voice level, professional and without emotion. As when facing a jungle cat or a feral beast, if you showed fear, you would indeed die.

"Good." The neat white mane of hair didn't move as the other man nodded his approval. "Very good. Where have you put him?"

"The team took him and his lady friend to Belize, five miles from the next dig site. Nothing there yet but the basic block building and the initial dig-out. Ecologic Reserve guards don't care what we bring in or out, given the stipends we provide to them. In fact, we've not seen the guards at all this trip. The team pulled out for a two-day hiatus, to let my unlamented brother stew in his cell."

"Left with food, though?"

"As per your suggestion," Niko was quick to reassure. Much as he'd wanted Dav to suffer, along with his woman, he'd followed the guidelines they'd agreed on. So far. "No pain, no starvation."

"Water?"

"Four canteens."

"Good." A faint frown still wrinkled the other man's

brow. That worried Niko. He wanted this man happy, not concerned. Before he could say anything, the older man continued. "Let's talk about the next moves. Come, sit." He motioned Niko to a chair. The guards stationed just inside the office door shifted to behind the desk as Niko sat down, ensuring that he would die before he could pull a gun and make any attempt on their boss. The man had a tendency to inspire mortal fear, blind loyalty or searing antagonism.

Niko was man enough to admit that he came down heartily on the side of mortal fear. As smart and dangerous as he knew himself to be, this man was ten times smarter and at least that much more dangerous. Certainly smarter than their father had ever been, and smarter than Dav in the real ways of the world.

"Here's the plan," Niko began, outlining the next steps, watching for the frown or smile that would signal his direction.

"What's the sit-rep?" Ana snapped out the question before they even cleared the door of San Francisco General's chapel. Inside were gathered ten men and women, six of them Dav's team, four "interested observers" from two federal agencies.

"Declan's out of surgery. He's hangin' in. Damon and Thompson're bandaged up, treated and released, but they're both doped up pretty good. Queller and Georgiade are patched up, they'll be here any minute."

"Good. What else?" Ana knew she'd cry for Declan before the day was over, but for now, she had to focus all her energy, all her attention, on getting Dav back. If they lost Dav—she couldn't even think it. He was Gates's friend, and he'd become hers as well. He'd earned not only her respect, but her loyalty and affection as well.

"No further sign of the small plane we tracked on radar

crossing the border heading south," one of the interested parties chimed in.

"Thank you. Gates, you want to fill them in on the data you pulled up?"

Gates began outlining the division in the Gianikopolis family ranks that had started in Dav's childhood. "Right now, it's the most plausible scenario. I've spoken with our contacts in Colombia. They are waiting for our contract employees, and eager to get started. They are disconcerted"—he made quotes marks in the air—"by Dav's difficulties and will let me know as soon as possible if any informants or troops hear anything about a captive American being held anywhere. Same with—" Gates stopped short, then smiled at the Bureau and Agency suits. He amended whatever he'd been about to say, finishing simply with, "Several of our other colleagues around the world."

"We've always admired your resources," one of the men said. "I'm Sewell, by the way." The man half rose to shake Gates's hand, did the same with Ana's.

The other strangers introduced themselves as well.

"Bickman, FBI," a tallish woman said.

"Trout, Agency," an equally tall, dark-skinned man said, nodding to Ana. "Worked with you in Barcelona."

"I remember," she said. "Great to have you here." Trout had a sharp mind and never said a word that wasn't weighed and measured. If he spoke, you'd better listen.

"Carlisle, Agency." The last brusque introduction came from a gray-haired, round-faced man. His physiology looked jolly until you saw his eyes. Those eyes had seen too much, grieved too many. Ana repressed a grimace. That kind could be either an asset or a liability. They'd had too many ops go bad and tended to be negative. She and Gates couldn't afford any negativity in searching for Dav.

They'd have to see how it went with Carlisle.

"Here's what we know." Gates picked things up as Ana

sat back and watched the dynamics. Dav's security team was feeling defeated, worried and anxious. Already laying blame on their own hearts and playing the "if only" game in their heads. They'd have to shake all of them out of that. The Feebs were alert, attentive. Sewell was taking notes. Trout looked half asleep, but Ana knew he was taking it all in, processing.

A door opened behind them and as one, twelve people pivoted and nearly drew down on the baffled minister who walked in.

"I beg your pardon," he said, wide-eyed and startled. "I . . ." He glanced at the door, at the altar beyond them. "I'm supposed to start service in forty-five minutes. Are you here for a loved one?"

"Sorry to startle you, Reverend." Gates was quick to soothe. "We'll be out of your way in ten minutes if you'd indulge us."

"Certainly, certainly," the man said, backing out the door, letting it fall closed. They heard his footsteps hurrying away.

"Let's wrap this up, then." Gates strode back to his position facing the group, standing in the aisle, leaning on the side of a pew. "Sewell, if you and Bickman would coordinate with the locals, see what they're getting from the dupes hired as distractions? Trout and Carlisle, if you could check in with your sources, anything you find would be helpful."

"Will do." Sewell closed his notebook with a soft snap, tucked it away.

Trout just gave a short nod, saying, "On it."

"Dav's team—" Gates called their wandering attention to him. "This is not your fault. Stop second-guessing or going over it. Leave it. It's done. Focus on what we can find out, where we go from here. It's the only way to save him. Got me?"

So he'd seen it too—the distraction, the self-blame.

A ragged chorus of "Yes, boss," and "Got it" answered

him. It would be a while before they did get it, but they had permission—orders even, from someone they trusted—to let it go and focus on the now.

"Ferguson, go check on Declan's status. Meet us in the waiting room. Ana and I will stay here for a while. You and Callahan will take second watch at around"—he checked his watch—"eight o'clock. We've got permission to have someone here round the clock. We'll set up turn and turn about, so Jenkins, find somebody and take the watch after Ferguson and Callahan. Now, let's get out of here before they throw us out."

Volunteers for watches called out, and there was shuffling and general noise. Ana noted that Ferguson stopped long enough to genuflect and cross himself before leaving. Callahan and Jenkins, looking baffled, followed him out, headed for the cafeteria to eat before their watch.

Within minutes the chapel was empty of all but Ana and Gates.

"Gates," she said, softly bringing his attention her way. "I need to hear you say it, say that you think we can find him. I know the stats, so do you. I'm not some mush-minded, puppy-eyed optimist, but I know I can go on, do this, and do it right, if I hear you say it."

"We can find him," Gates said, taking her into his arms. "We *will* find him."

The door opened again and a San Francisco detective, his badge clipped to the pocket of his sport coat, looked in and spotted Gates and Ana. Kit Baxter didn't smile, although he held out a hand to them both in turn, giving each of them a brisk, strong, professional grip.

"Detective," Ana said, shaking his hand. "I'd say 'good to see you,' but under the circumstances . . ."

"Yeah. Sorry to hear about this," Baxter said. He'd worked with them the previous year, so the detective knew them both well. "And sorry to add more bad news, but there's been a murder at Carrie McCray's gallery. A young woman." He referred to his notes. "Inez Martin, a new clerk."

"New?" Ana questioned sharply, flicking a glance at her husband. "How new?"

"I never figured I'd feel cold in Mexico," Dav murmured into the darkness. Night had fallen with tropical suddenness as they gathered up their meager food and finished sharing out the first canteen. Carrie had said nothing about his declaration. Not yet.

"Do you think that's where we are?"

"Mexico or somewhere south of it, could be Guatemala or Belize, perhaps Honduras. Either way, never thought it would get cold." He smiled at her. "Resorts don't get cold, you know. Not on the gold coast."

"True. It's always bikini weather there." She looked around. "We're underground, which drops the humidity and makes it feel colder," she said. He must have looked quizzical because she laughed and said, "You store art in underground vaults sometimes, because it's cooler and dryer, usually."

"Yes, I have heard that. I'm thinking we may be in the mountains too, which would be cooler. Remember when we were driving in the truck? It was always at an upward angle."

She gave an affirmative grunt. "Unfortunately, I remember."

They sat in silence, listening to the noises beyond their cage. Night-calling birds, the distant roar of some predator, were the music of the night.

"Carrie, about what I said earlier, and what happened—" he began.

"Dav, I think we need to—" she said at the same time.

"Ladies first," he offered, wondering what she was going to say, feeling his gut clench. It was annoying that being in this circumstance made him feel young and inadequate again.

She moved, maybe nodded, but he couldn't be sure in the dark. He heard her sigh. "It's easier to talk about it when I can't see you, and you can't see me."

"Really? So, you don't like seeing me blush?" he said, hoping to lighten her mood. She sounded so serious, so somber.

When she didn't laugh and didn't speak, he reached out, found her hand. "Carrie, there is nothing you could say that would upset me or make me think less of you. Nothing."

"I didn't cheat on Luke," she whispered. "But I wanted to. When he cheated on me with what seemed like every intern, every female artist, I really wanted to. He would come home, give me a brotherly peck on the cheek and say good night. I could smell the sex on him, the other woman's perfume. It was like he was coming home to his mother after a long night playing the prince." Anger rushed out in waves he could almost feel. "I wanted to make him see me, flaunt a lover in his face as he so often did in mine. I kept thinking, what about me? Why not me?"

Dav's anger at Luke was a cold, powerful thing. He wanted to go back in time and kick the man's ass for treating Carrie with so little regard. He was about to speak, but Carrie wasn't done.

Acceptance and a faint note of defeat flavored her tone as she said, "Then I realized he wouldn't care. It wouldn't impact him at all." She paused for a long moment. "You have to care for someone, for them to hurt you, or hurt *for* you, and he just . . . didn't. Not enough, anyway."

"Ahh, my flame, I am so sorry that he hurt you," Dav murmured, squeezing her hand, wanting more than anything to snatch her up, make her forget the terrible blows to her self-confidence.

"Thank you," she whispered. There was a long pause and Dav wondered if he should speak, fill the void with additional reassurance, but when she spoke again, he was glad he'd stayed silent. "I came to realize that he didn't," she said obliquely, pulling her hand free to gesture. He couldn't see it, but he felt the air stir as she gestured.

"That he didn't—?" Dav asked when she was silent. He wasn't following her thought.

Her laugh was strained. "Hurt me," she explained. "He didn't actually hurt me, emotionally or physically. Not really."

"What do you mean?" His concern that she still carried a torch for Luke had bothered him. The man was long dead. However, if he was understanding these words, it was a triumph in some ways. He wouldn't have to compete with a ghost.

She sighed, a gusty, defeated sound in the velvet darkness. "I came to realize that it wasn't him I cared about, that his infidelities weren't what bothered me. His ignoring me was painful, but I came to realize, after he was gone, that it wasn't him, personally, that I missed. It was having someone who was supposed to be there. If you have a husband, you're supposed to have love, passion . . . someone who asks about your day and cares about the answer." She paused again. "And I didn't have that. I was hurt and angry and flat-out pissed that he was there. He was my husband, but he wasn't what I wanted or needed as a husband or a lover." Another sigh, but lighter this time.

"I also came to realize that if everything hadn't happened with the fraud, I would have found my spine eventually. We would have divorced and probably remained business partners."

He considered that before he spoke, and was surprised to feel a huge surge of relief.

"I remember meeting him for the first time," Dav said, grudgingly admitting his reaction that day. "I didn't like him. I seldom spoke to him, because I knew I wouldn't be . . . nice. I wanted what he had," he growled the last. She was right, the dark did allow you to say things you might not say otherwise.

"In some ways I'm glad I didn't know that," she laughed softly. "When we met you, you were so self-assured, so confident. I remember thinking—" She hesitated, and Dav found her hand again, squeezed it in reassurance. "I thought, 'There's a man with confidence. That's the kind of man who wouldn't cheat,'" she declared. "That was just after I'd talked to a divorce lawyer. I was going to file for separation. My second appointment, had I kept it, was scheduled for two days after the authorities showed up at the gallery door."

Dav couldn't believe it. His heart leaped up, knowing that she'd found him attractive, that she'd thought of him at all.

What a woman he had found. The determination to get them out, somehow, someway, rose like magma within him.

"Then everything fell apart." He heard the tears in her voice. She sniffled a bit and he patted his pockets, found his handkerchief, and passed it to her. "Thanks." She pulled her hand free again, and he heard the hiccup in her breathing. "That's done, though. I'm done with that."

"You never really got to move on, did you?" Dav questioned, with the deepest sympathy. Now he understood her reluctance, her distance. As Gates had surmised, her sorrow had all been renewed, this last year. The worry, the betrayal had been unearthed, literally, to solve the dangerous attacks on Ana, Gates and his own estate. "It took you years to get out from under the suspicions, yes? You said so yourself, last year when it all came to a head."

"I can't tell you how much it meant to me that you believed in me." She found his hand again, squeezed his fingers, then brought them to her cheek. "You never wavered, did you?"

"Never," he said, because it was true. He couldn't help it, he had to touch her, hold her and ease her sorrow. Using the anchor of the hand she held, he moved closer, found her face with his other hand. "Carrie, you're like a dark flame to me, with your beautiful black hair, your sapphire eyes and your brilliant mind and wit. I carry a picture of you in my head." He caressed her cheek, felt the dampness of a tear, but didn't let that deter him. "I measure other women against you and they always come up lacking." He admitted it without thought, without worry about how she could use his admission, or the repercussions if she did.

"Dav," she breathed his name in surprise. He laughed, a bit ruefully, knowing how much power he willingly put in her hands.

"Yes, my flame? Was there something you wanted?" He found her mouth with his, murmuring the words as he brushed kisses over her lips. He wanted her to respond to him freely, come to him again, so he kept it light, teasing. "There is little enough I have to provide at the moment, but what I have is yours."

Triumph flooded through him as she rose to meet him, on her knees, bringing them together in a rush of heat. Her mouth was hot on his; her hands raced over the silk of his shirt. As they had before, they came together with the fierceness of a summer storm, all crash and fire.

Within seconds he had her shirt off, and she his. Her hands were like erotic butterflies, flitting over his skin, leaving a raging need for more in their wake. He wanted to devour her, take her in enormous, greedy bites.

Her clothes fell away under his onslaught, as did his. He didn't know how she'd undone his belt, freed him, but when she grasped him as she had earlier, he growled her name and dragged her closer.

"Come here, come closer," he demanded, his hands lifting her into his body, wanting to meld them together.

"Let me—" She wriggled free for a moment, and the cool air swept between them. He reached for her just as she moved into him again. She was naked, her slim body open to him in every way. His triumph nearly undid him. Breathing heavily, he reminded himself to slow down, not to frighten her.

"Carrie, I'm rushing you, I'm—"

"Shut up, Dav, and kiss me again." It was her turn to demand, to devour. She pushed at him, and he followed her direction, lying back on the coat and letting her pull his trousers free. Then she was back, sliding up his body, her smooth skin a delicious tease, a tantalizing note in the resounding symphony of need.

When she moved up, then down over him, his body quivered, rising, pushing, needing her, needing completion.

"Shhhh," she soothed, leaning down to kiss him as she rocked over him, sliding the softness of her breasts and hair over him, but not yet taking him inside. Her kisses were hot, the movement of her body, her breasts along his chest, was agonizingly slow, drawing out the pleasure as she arched away, then brought them together in a long, brilliant sweep along the length of him, legs, hips, belly, chest.

Madness hazed his mind. She was torturing him with her glory, she was . . .

All thought left him, she wiped his brain clean, as she took him in one hand, guided him in, sheathing him fully in her powerful wet heat. He wanted to roar in triumph, to take, to mate with the desperation of the damned. He wanted to make every molecule of her his.

She wasn't having any of it. With the barest sound, the barest movement of her hips and mouth, she checked his blind impulse, without ever saying a word.

The slick, slow movements she began left no room for coherent thought, for any memory of their desperate situation. The feel of her was so exquisite, so all-encompassing, that for several long, delicious moments he lost all sense of time and space and let her have her way.

As her excitement rose and her movements grew faster and less refined, as she began to lose control of her own release, Dav recovered enough to take charge. He let her move, and guided her hips to keep her rhythm as her passion got the better of her. He let her think she was in control until he could no longer breathe for wanting her.

In one swift move, he reversed their positions, easing her to her back as he thrust forward, the motion all one symphony of excitement. Her groan of delight drove him higher, her frantic breathing and the heave of her breasts where they pressed into his chest made him crazier, hotter if it was possible.

"Dav, Dav," she cried, her body arching and shuddering, twisting into him and around him as she climaxed with a fury. "Dav!"

"Here, my flame," he growled. She was his fire, his. Now, she was his in body. Finally.

"Dav, I need you, I need you," she moaned, rising into him, retreating, rising again. He struggled not to move, not to pour himself into her, not to explode. Every movement she made was an exquisite torture, a gratification beyond words. As her reaction eased, he slid out, slowly. "Ahhhh, no, no, don't go," she protested, gripping his hips and pulling him back in.

"No, darling, I'm not going. Let me please you," he said, feeling huge, powerful waves of need, desire and triumph pour through him. *Yes!* his soul roared to the heavens. *Mine!*

"Now, Dav, now," she insisted, tugging at him. He wanted to laugh, to howl, to celebrate his conquest like a wild thing baying at the moon. Instead, he said nothing, just eased out again, carefully, fully, shifting his hips to tantalize her, let her feel all of him, to feel all of her as she clenched in need. "Dav—" His name was a plea.

He gathered himself and powerfully, but gently, stroked in.

"Ahhhhhhh." Her delight was like intoxicating smoke; he breathed in every sound, every reaction. Each moan was more and more a drug, driving him to focus on her alone as his body, his mind, cried out for release. "Daaaaaav," she cried.

It took everything he had, every ounce of control, to hold on, to ride the waves of her erotic writhing as she came a second time. When she arched up, crying his name, each movement of her hips harder, faster, to meet his slow, steady thrusts, his control broke.

He surrendered to the driving pulse of her, pulling her hips to him, meeting her as she rose to him, steadying them both as they came together.

"Nownownow!" she demanded, nearly screamed as she came, her words tearing the last shreds of his long-chained need. He roared her name to the tropical night as he buried himself within her and let his release take him, mind, body and spirit.

It was a long time before either of them moved. Even then, they didn't speak. He eased to the side, shifting his weight off so as not to crush her. She murmured in protest, curling into him, her long silky legs sliding along his, making him stir again. He drew her more tightly into his arms, and she purred, rubbing her face gently on his chest, her hands lazily massaging his back.

"That was . . ." she finally said and her voice rasped. "Magnificent." The heartfelt praise broke the comfortable, velvet silence, but in the best possible way.

"You are the magnificent one, darling Carrie-mou," he replied, kissing her tousled hair, and running a smoothing hand down her elegant back. "So delicate, but strong," he murmured, finding her mouth again. They spent a long time exchanging soft, enticing kisses. Exploring one another with light caresses, warm, spent and delighted with the moment.

They were still prisoners, they were still in an impossible situation, but nothing could change this moment or take it away.

When he felt her skin pebbling up with goose bumps, he pulled his coat over her back, cocooning them together in the dark. They made love again, the banked flames coaxed to life by their constant enjoyment of skin on skin, mouth on mouth. Another blinding climax took every ounce of energy he had left.

Together, they dropped into dreamless, formless sleep.

Chapter 7

"How's Declan?" Ana snapped out the question the minute she and Gates cleared the waiting room doors. Callahan and Ferguson were already there, taking first watch.

Callahan shook her head as she stood. "It's not looking good. Doc told me they had to shock him twice to get him through. They just don't know." She shrugged, looking bleak. "They said stuff like he's not getting perfusion or something. If he makes it, he may have some memory loss."

"I could use a little of that," Ferguson muttered.

"Shut up, Fergs."

"We're heading to Agency headquarters." Gates cut the incipient argument short. "They may have a lead. Let everyone know as they come on watch. I'll call you." He pointed to Ferguson. "Let you know what we find. You disseminate. Got it?"

"Got it."

Callahan looked mutinous, but stayed silent.

Having to use the paddles to restart the heart was never a good thing. Memory loss, even some tissue damage could result, depending on how long the heart stayed silent.

Leaving the pair to their now-silent feud, Ana and Gates headed for the nurses' station. Declan's family was flying in, but hadn't arrived yet, so in lieu of family, Gates felt they should be there.

"Will you let us see him?" They went through the usual bullshit about being family. It only took one call to the hospital administration to clear it, however. Dav's name changed all the rules.

Standing by the hospital bed in critical care, Ana searched for her husband's hand. Declan, usually the jokester, the self-proclaimed "Energizer Bunny" of the crew, lay still and silent in the bed. His cheek, chest and hands were bandaged, monitors tracked him constantly, beeping their notices of heart rate, blood pressure and oxygenation. The drip, drip, drip of the blood and plasma infusing his system made a monotonous undertone, barely heard, but vital.

"The round in the upper chest was the worst." Ana pointed to where the bandages were heaviest. "The lacerations on his cheek, hands and back were from the window glass."

Gates struggled visibly with his emotions, as grief and worry warred in his face. Ana squeezed the hand she still held in silent support. After a moment, he cleared his throat and asked, "Did the two waiters and the other guy, the restaurant patron, make it?"

Ana shook her head, delivering the bad news. "DOS." *Dead on scene.*

"Wrong place, wrong time." Ana heard the pain and anger underlying the clichéd phrase.

They stood for a long time, just holding hands. Ana thought of Declan as his vital, ebullient self. He would hate to be here. When he woke up, she predicted he'd be the worst patient ever. As they were ready to leave, Ana bent down and kissed the young man's cheek.

"I expect to see you dance at more weddings, Declan. And play that stupid saxophone." Declan had been the life of the party at their wedding. No one had known he could play anything other than the ladies, but he'd whipped out a sax and joined the band.

Then he'd gotten thoroughly drunk, made a play for Callahan. She'd refused, but he'd cajoled a song out of her and together they'd sung old Irish ballads after Callahan had tied on a few more drinks. Ana heard he'd slept it off alone, in one of Dav's best guest rooms, and been mortified the next day. She'd also heard that the team had ragged him unmercifully. "We'll set you up with some voice lessons too. A present for getting better," she added.

She kissed his cheek again, and straightened, flushing at the surprised look Gates wore. "What?"

"Nothing. But you know he'll take you up on that. Be prepared."

"Nah," she said, squeezing Declan's bicep. "You're too chicken, aren't you, Dec? Sing? You? Ha! How about I bet this husband of mine a hundred bucks that you won't take me up on the singing lessons, what do you say?" She didn't look at Gates, but knew he understood. They both knew Declan might be able to hear them. Anything, anything at all, that got Dec to focus on survival would be a good thing, even if it was singing lessons.

"You're on," Gates said. He patted the young man's leg. "Go for it, Dec. I could use the hundred. Might have to pay some bribes."

With a last look at their deeply sleeping comrade, they slipped out as quietly as they'd come in.

In the car, heading for the Agency office, Ana fought back tears.

"It's hard. Seeing him like that," Gates voiced her feelings. She nodded.

She took a deep breath. She had to get it together. As they pulled up to the guard gate at the Agency office, she finally felt composed enough to speak.

Before he rolled down the window to present their credentials, she put a hand on his arm to stop him.

"I hope you win the bet."

He smiled, said, "Me too," and checked them in.

"So, you are going down to Belize, Niko? You will be seeing to this personally." The older man's emphasis on "will," made it an order rather than a request. "Ransom is a good thing. Seeing your enemy die, that's even better." Dinner had been brought in as they sat at the desk talking. The older man gestured with his gleaming knife. "You haven't tried the scallops. They're quite good."

"Thank you." Niko served himself some, still uncertain of his place, his fit in the organization, or in this man's plans. He'd risen from occasional, distant hireling to having dinner with the head of one of the most powerful, hidden organizations in the world. It was akin to having dinner with a hungry dragon. As long as the dragon liked the other items on the table, you were safe. If not . . .

"These are good, as is everything else. Thank you for dinner. And yes, I'm going down." The ransom requests had been sent. He was certain they'd be paid quickly. Once the money was banked, he could finish everything. "Dav is my last loose thread to tie up. My team's good, but the end of this is on me."

The older man nodded, still methodically cutting and eating steak and scallops. The elegant table service was delicate china, something Niko's mother might have used. There was music in the background, and a tray of froufrou desserts sat on a rolling cart next to the table.

The opulent elegance, the calm pool of comfort, was a contradiction to what he knew of the ruthless, mysterious man who sat opposite him.

"Good. It is good to take on these things yourself. One

thing I've made a policy of." The man leaned back, dabbed at his cheek with a fine linen napkin. "I get my hands dirty. My people know that I won't send them to do something I wouldn't do, nor will I sit on high, letting them fall for something while I keep my hands clean." He smiled, a crooked, unpleasant smile. "Besides, I like killing. It has such immediacy to it."

"Yes, it does." What the hell else did you say to something like that? When his mentor sat silent, Niko added, "No matter what, though, Dav's my deal, so I have to settle that myself."

The man nodded. "Wise. I have admired the way you run your team. You've done good work for me, all of you. I was glad I could help you with this last little thing. Are you still determined to stay independent?"

"For now, sir," Niko said, hoping the gleam he saw was approval, not aversion. The earlier thought of the dragon sprang back into his mind. The older man had repeatedly urged Niko to come into "the fold" as he'd put it, and work exclusively on his projects rather than staying freelance. Niko and his team had decided it was too risky to go under someone's banner, especially someone as cloaked as this man was. Their profits for working solo were handsome, and under their control. Being on the payroll might not be.

The other, deciding factor, was that Niko couldn't read the old man. He knew his mentor had an ulterior motive for helping him, but as deeply as he dug, he couldn't figure out what it was or why he, or Dav, were important to the old man.

"Very well. You need to know that your venture has had some unexpected benefits for me. With news breaking of Dav's kidnapping, stock in a number of his companies has dropped, allowing me to buy in where I'd not owned before. Also, several other ventures opened up for me. I've wired a token of my appreciation into the usual account. Clear it through to your other accounts before you leave, however."

The dismissal was evident, and actually welcome. The longer he sat, the more he felt the menace, the sheer capacity for destruction inherent in his mentor. As hardened as he was, it made him uneasy.

"Will do, sir. Thank you." Niko rose and started to extend a handshake. The gleam was back, so he didn't.

"I'll be in touch," the older man said, turning back to his plate, and his wine.

With that threat hanging over him, Niko left the dining room, and within the hour he was headed south. He couldn't wait to get to Belize. He'd been like a caged animal, waiting for hours at the old man's compound in Colorado for word that everything had gone without a hitch. When he reconnected with his team, got to Dav, he'd finish it. Finally, it would be over.

A clean break. Sitting at dinner, he'd made his decision. He'd thought to torture Dav, play some cat and mouse. But he was just going to end it, quickly. The more he thought of it, the more he realized that's what he wanted.

Needed.

He'd have the ransom money, the bonus from the old man, and a clean break with the past.

And then, he was going to stay away from his mentor for a while. A return to distant hireling might not be a bad thing.

Watching young Niko go, the older man decided it was time to implement some of his other plans. If Niko were what he'd been looking for, the next forty-eight hours would tell it.

"You know what to do?" he said to the silent man waiting by the door. The room was darkening and the dusty mountains of Colorado were gleaming gold and red with the last rays of the fading day's sun. Snow lay on the ground, but spring was coming. Soon.

"Yessir," the man replied, never moving a muscle until he was so ordered.

"Then go."

The morning sun woke them as it crossed the floor and warmed their faces.

"Mmmm," Carrie murmured, stretching like a cat. She felt better than she had in a long time. Maybe the best she'd ever felt. Odd to think that, since they were trapped in a hole in the ground in some Central American country, naked as the day they were born, with limited food and water and little prospect of rescue. She said as much to Dav. "It should be criminal how good you make me feel."

"I assure you, I keep all my business aboveboard, including my cell-bound liaisons." He smiled, running a long finger along her cheek, slipping a strand of hair behind her ear. "No criminal activity whatsoever."

His smile was slow and sensuous, and just for her. It changed his lean, angular face from shuttered and ascetic to warm and personal. She realized how much she enjoyed the long planes of his jaw, and appreciated his lips when they curved just that way.

Not for the first time she wished to be an artist, a good one, who could capture a moment like this, preserve it for all time. He was like a magnificent Greek statue come to life, right in her arms. His shoulders were broad. She saw scars and wanted to ask about them, but she thought she might know their cause, given what he'd said about his father and brother. Right now, she didn't want that hard look to ice his dark eyes, so she just brushed over them and moved on. His chest was sculpted and strong. She ran her hands over the planes and ripples of it, loving the rumble of pleasure he made. She felt it as much as heard it.

"Mmm. How then, do you explain this?" She ran her hands downward, enjoying the change in his eyes, the intensity of his gaze. His body tensed, his strong, heavily muscled leg hooked over hers, drawing her in. His hands cupped the back of her neck, and he brought her to him, brushing her lips. It was a shimmer of a kiss, a feather of desire that rippled over her whole body. Instantly wet, instantly ready, she needed him with a frightening intensity.

Pushing the swaddling coat aside, she straddled him. This time she would control the pace. She wanted to see him, see his face as they made love.

"Let me," he began, but she put a shushing finger to his lips. He took it gently in his strong white teeth, nibbled. Delight ran through her, a quicksilver shiver, from their erotic play.

"Shhh, I want to see you," she explained. "Watch you." She got her first glimpse of how luscious it was going to be, seeing his eyes droop half closed, with a gleam of a smile playing over his mouth.

"Watch me, my flame? As I do this?" He lifted his hips, rolling them slightly so that he moved within her, setting every nerve afire.

"Ahhhh, that feels . . ."

"What? How?" he whispered. "Tell me what you like, what pleases you."

"It feels like heaven," she managed as he did it again. She leaned forward, her hair screening them in a private curtain as she kissed him. Lifting her hips, she teased him with her hips and tongue simultaneously.

The growl in his chest was feral and hot. "Carrie, let me please you," he groaned, and thrust upward to meet her, seek her.

"You are, Dav." She drew his hands to her breasts. They

were turgid and aroused before he touched them but she couldn't stop the moan of delight when he half raised to flick his tongue over first one nipple, then the other. "Ohhhhh, that feels like heaven too," she managed.

The rolling of his hips and the flick of his tongue were more than enough to send her flying. Dav supported her as she climaxed. Desire and something more, something deeper, reflected in his face as he continued to rock into her, drawing out her orgasm.

"Now," he said, "let me do more."

"No." She recovered as well as she could, gripping his wrists. "My turn," she insisted. "Mine."

He muttered something in Greek, but lay back, not relaxed, but not taking over either. Good.

Mimicking his pace, that slow roll of the hips, had a marvelous effect. She saw the muscles clench in his jaw, his readiness to pounce. She captured his hands in hers, prevented him from taking over, flipping them and ending it with a rush. She knew he still could, he was strong enough and they would both enjoy it, but she wanted more.

It might be all she ever got.

Running her tongue up the side of his neck, she tasted him, male and aroused. Now it was his turn to move with restless excitement beneath her ministering hands and tongue. By the time she'd come again, she had brought him to a fever pitch. His hands were everywhere, racing over her skin to ignite every nerve, every sense.

As she rose over him, it was her turn to watch as he took command, even from his position beneath her, guiding her hips, lifting her as her climax turned her muscles to water, urging her higher, faster.

"Again." He used his velvet voice, that deep resonant growl, to call her to more satisfaction, more pleasure. "Come for me again, my heart. Yes," he murmured. He must have seen it in her face, because he continued to rock her as she crested so powerfully that she brought him with her.

"Ahhhhh!" The shouted praise couldn't have come from her, could it? She had never . . . She decided it didn't matter what she'd done before as she collapsed onto his chest, throbbing and trembling with the intensity of the release.

Their panting breath was loud in the closed space, intimate, reflecting their shared experience. His heart beat under her cheek, steadying now as their breathing leveled too.

"You are a miracle, my flame." He kissed her hair, toying with the strands of it that trailed down her back. He seemed fascinated by her hair. She loved the way he called her his dark flame. When he said it, she felt invincible, impossibly sexy and feminine. She felt powerful.

"I hate to say it," she whispered, and she very much did hate to speak of anything commonplace, hated to break the golden cocoon of pleasure. "But I need to get up, go to the bathroom, such as it is."

"Of course," Dav said, loosing her from his capturing arm, and bracing himself on an elbow as she rose. She knew he watched her as she slipped into her shoes and made her way across the dusty floor. She felt his gaze caress her skin, and shivered, aroused all over again by his watching her.

She knew the moment he turned away to give her privacy. The room felt cooler, darker.

"I'm sorry I couldn't provide a long hot shower too," he said, as he began to retrieve their clothes, sort them into piles of his and hers.

"Don't even talk about it," she groaned. "Really." She desperately wanted a shower. Even a cup of water and a washcloth would be a blessing but they dared not chance wasting what little water they had. She dreaded the thought of getting back into her wrinkled skirt and sweater.

As she watched him, she had to grin. Their things were strewn everywhere, with no regard for how little they had, or the conditions. He was having a hard time separating her jacket from her sweater.

"I guess we really did rip each other's clothes off," she said, pointing at the various items. "I think that's your shirt. Do you see my bra?"

Dav rose and once again a Greek god came to mind. He could be the young, powerful Apollo, she decided, though the more she looked, the more he reminded her of the statue of Poseidon in Copenhagen harbor. His body was strongly muscled, his hips narrow without seeming disproportionate. Broad shoulders and bronzed skin made her want to touch, to taste, to explore.

He held up her lacy demicup bra. "Had I known you wore this under that quiet"—he hesitated—"I think the word is demure? Yes?" he asked. When she nodded, he grinned and continued. "That demure sweater, I might have suggested a different place for lunch."

She smiled as she came over and took the bra, slipping into it with practiced ease, then did the same with her panties, although she'd have preferred not to. Dav was dressing as well.

"Ah, I believe I've done something bad," he murmured, lifting the sweater by the shoulders. Along the asymmetrical neckline, where beads had studded the narrow band of the collar, there was now a tear. The fabric drooped downward, leaving the neckline exposed halfway down to the midline.

"Oh, my." She took the garment from him, turning it to and fro. She pulled it over her head and the rip caught on her breast, then dropped below it.

"Anywhere in the world but here," he said, his smile pained, "I would buy you a dozen to replace it. I'm sorry."

"It's okay." She grinned at the look on his face, not really hearing the words as she tried not to look at his magnificent body. She knew if she did, she'd want him even more. As it was she was sore, wonderfully sore, in wonderful ways, but she wasn't sure how much more she could take in one twenty-four-hour period.

"Here—" He bent down, lifted his dusty undershirt. "Wear this. Much as I love your new look, darling," he drawled, mimicking her former gallery clerk, "it won't do to show too much skin." He kept the smile on his face as she took the shirt, but his eyes changed and she saw the pain there.

"It's okay. It's what it is. We're alive and that's what counts." She turned the shirt around in her hands, brushed off some of the dust. The cotton was heavy and soft. Like everything he owned it was beautifully made, probably incredibly expensive. She sneaked a look at the tag and laughed.

"Dav, you rascal," she accused.

"What? Is there something wrong?" He was all concern, moving quickly to her side. "Is it ripped as well?" He took it from her, examined it. Puzzled, he handed it back. "You don't want to wear it?"

"It's fine. It's a Fruit of the Loom."

"A what?"

She laughed even more. Obviously the words meant nothing to him. "A plain cotton undershirt."

Still puzzled, he pulled the collar, checked the tag. "Yes, it is. I have many of them. My assistant buys them in large packages." He indicated the size of the packaging with his hands. "Why? Is something wrong with it?"

She shook her head. "Your shirt—" She fingered the material. He'd slipped it on, but hadn't buttoned it. She really wanted to run her hands over his skin again, but confined herself to the shirt and remembered to continue the sentence. "Probably cost what, three hundred dollars?"

"A bit less," he confessed. "My tailor likes me."

"Right. The T-shirts are maybe, what, five or seven dollars apiece bought in bulk?" She let her hands measure the same size he'd shown her.

"Ah, I understand now. You are a snob, my flame," he

said, sweeping her into his arms with a laugh and swinging her around. "Eh-la, you would prefer I wear silk underneath as well?"

"No, no." She giggled at his antics and wiggled to be put down. Embarrassed, she ducked her head. "It's just that I had this thought in my head that here I'd be putting on something dearly expensive in such a primitive circumstance. . . ." She trailed off when she saw he was still laughing at her. "Stop laughing at me." She punched his bicep lightly. "Okay, I'm a snob, or I guess I should say that I thought you were. Satisfied?" The last was muffled in the folds of the shirt as she pulled it over her head.

"Evidently not," he murmured as he swooped in for a passionate kiss, banding her in his arms, the crumpled hem of the T-shirt caught between them. "You look beautiful in my shirt, Carrie." He rested his forehead on hers, his breathing quick and his body hard against her hips. "You simply look beautiful. Anywhere. In anything." And now the grin was back in full. "Or nothing."

"Thank you," she said, holding him close, running her hands up his back. She didn't want to move, or think. Why had she waited so long for this, for him? He'd been there. He'd asked. She'd been the one to hold him at bay.

"You are welcome, my flame. My shirt is common, perhaps, but comfortable. It is good quality cotton and heavy. I sweat a great deal." He said it like it was a bad thing, an embarrassment.

"Means your body's healthy," she said, a little breathlessly because his body heat was exciting her again. Much as she wanted to rip the shirt back off, and jump him again, she was sore. And hungry.

"Perhaps, but what is the commercial?" He lifted his head, closing his eyes to call the concept to him. "Ah yes, never let them see you sweat?"

"Right. Well, I won't get it any dirtier or sweatier than it already is. How's that?"

"That's acceptable." He said it with a pompous, condescending air. "I accept those terms."

"I'm hungry," she said, just as her stomach growled loudly as it had the day before.

"Then, my lady, we should eat. I believe we have an amazing menu this morning," he said with a flourishing bow. The fact that he hadn't yet put on pants or fastened his shirt did nothing to detract from the elegance of the bow.

"I think we wrinkled our picnic blanket," she said, pointing at the rumpled coat.

"I'll fix that as soon as I find my pants. Now, where could they be? So much clutter in this space, so many things to search through. Too much mess for me to see them, I guess. We are terrible housekeepers, you and I."

She'd never seen him so light, making fun of everything and laughing with her as if they had no cares. Perhaps they didn't. There were no meetings, no shipments to manage, no temperamental artists to soothe.

Still laughing and bumping one another, they found his pants, straightened the coat and got out the meager supplies. Sitting with their backs to the wall, they ate.

"You know, I keep thinking about the carvings. They mean something, I know they do. If I could just remember. Aaargh," she growled in frustration. "That damn art course was so long ago. I took this course on Mayan art," she explained when he questioned her angst. "I know I've seen some of this"—she waved toward the walls—"before."

"You are doing a great deal better than I, Carrie." He shook his head. "I've learned about art over the years, but nothing compares to your encyclopedic knowledge of obscure but brilliant artists."

"Hmmm—" She turned her head to look at him. "That really doesn't sound like a compliment."

"But it was meant as one," he insisted. "I remember you told me once at one of the openings about that flamboyant artist, Carusia, you'd shown at the gallery. You said his work reminded you of a Matisse, but not just any Matisse, a particular one. Within minutes, you'd remembered the name of the painting and when and where it was painted. You even knew which museum held it in trust. When that annoying man from La Jolla asked you—" he continued, but she interrupted him with the man's name.

"Mr. Collingsworth."

"Yes, him. You deconstructed Carusia's work, painting by painting, referencing the Matisse that I'm sure only you could see in your head. We all nodded sagely, and Collingsworth bobbed, of course, because when he moves, everything bobs." Dav demonstrated and she crowed with laughter.

"Yes, it does," she snickered. "Just like that."

"Just so. I went home and looked the painting up. It is indeed in the Louvre, as you mentioned." He chewed thoughtfully on a cracker before he spoke again. "I looked at the photos of that painting for an hour. I saw everything you'd described." He met her embarrassed gaze. "Now, don't be shy about your brilliance. Never be shy about that. Too many women are." He reached out and tapped a finger on her nose, a gesture she'd seen him use with his cousin, the elegant actress Sophia Contas. "It was amazing."

She absorbed the compliment for a moment, remembering that opening and the odious Mr. Collingsworth.

"I tried to buy it," Dav broke the silence, looking at her again. "The Matisse."

"Buy it? But . . ." She often forgot just how wealthy he was. He seldom made an issue of it, and now, looking rumpled, dusty and with two days' growth of beard rapidly shadowing the lower half of his face, he looked nothing like the suave billionaire she knew him to be.

"Even the Louvre has a price, love," he replied with a shrug.

It boggled the mind. Really. "Did they sell it to you?"

"Not yet," he said, and a predatory, catlike smile curved his lips and crinkled his eyes. "I will wear them down eventually."

That kind of wealth was astounding to her. She couldn't fathom calling the Louvre, offering to buy something from the collection, then waiting until they were ready to deal. Such patience. No wonder he was worth billions.

Thinking about his power made her think about powerful men in general. The gods of commerce. Trade and commerce.

Staring at the wall opposite where they were sitting, her eye lit on a particular whorl in the pattern. Wait . . .

"Hold this." She passed him the canteen she'd just picked up so she could scramble to her feet, hurry to the wall. Following the pattern she'd seen, the glyph for water, she traced it around the space, stepping over his legs when she got to them and moving back almost to the beginning of the glyph. It stopped though, three or four feet short of its beginning.

"The serpent isn't swallowing his tail," she muttered, stepping back to look for another glyph. She found it high, near the ceiling. Pointing at it, to keep her place, trying not to lose the rhythm of it, she traced it all the way to the same juncture, three to four feet from where it began.

"Carrie?" He heard the impatience in his voice, tightly leashed, but there.

"It's a pattern, a regular thing in these ceremonial sites," she explained. "The glyph begins—" She pointed to the wall, reaching up to tap the fat whorl that began one tracery. "The glyph ends." She pivoted, her outstretched arm showing the path of the wave. "But they're supposed to connect. The never-ending circle of the elements."

He could see it, now that she pointed it out. The ending line of the pattern curved back on itself, on its back, then wriggled down the edge of the space. Other lines and whorls and patterns flowed seamlessly across the blank space but not the ones Carrie deemed to be the most important.

With his help, she searched the whole wall. It took them most of the day, but they found the patterns for water and metal and sun. They found at least one more pattern that Carrie couldn't identify that was a continuous line. It was like a winding maze or an Escher drawing, fooling the eye again and again.

All of the main, important lines stopped four feet before they began again.

Hours passed, marked by the sun's path on the floor. They sat again, drinking to clear dusty throats, brushing their hands off as best they could to save water.

"I think the places where the pattern stops, right there," Carrie said, pointing to the area on the wall where the patterns didn't quite meet. "I think it's important." She didn't want to raise his hopes, or hers, but she couldn't help but blurt out her suspicions. "Dav, I think it's a door. I can't be sure," she temporized, "but it could be."

"Where would it lead? Would it lead out?" She heard the hope, quickly suppressed, rise in his voice. "Or just to another chamber?"

"I have no idea. But it's something, it's something." Turning to him, she searched his face. "Isn't it? It's something. Maybe something we can use to get ourselves out of here."

"Yes, it is. You're brilliant, Carrie," he praised, reaching over to caress her cheek the way he had the night before. He was looking at her with admiration, with approval written all over him. It warmed her right to her soul. He was open and smiling and her heart lurched.

Love was such an ass-kicker. How could fate be so cruel to give her, finally, a man like this, a lover, a friend, someone honorable and amazing? Why would love come now, like a terrible nightmare in these conditions, when today might be their last day?

He must have seen her thoughts in her face. "What is it? Carrie?"

"Nothing, it's just . . ." She choked on the words. "We finally get together and you're amazing and, and, and—" She fought for control. Throwing up her hands, she let the tears roll. "Here we are. Stuck. Probably going to die today, or tomorrow. And here you are. Finally."

"Oh, my flame," he said, pulling her into his arms. "Hush now. We'll find a way. We will," he insisted when she shook her head, the gesture lost as she pressed into his chest, wishing the haven of his arms offered more hope. "Carrie? Carrie, listen to me."

He forced her away, not to arm's length, but enough so she had to look at him. Face him.

"Are you listening?"

"Yes." What did he want? She felt angry now. Didn't he see how hopeless it all was?

"Look over there." He pointed to the wall they'd been examining. "You found that. Life and hope, you said, yes?"

Dav stood up, moved to the space where the patterns stopped, stretching to graze his hands over the wall, starting at the top and moving over it to the bottom.

"What are you doing?"

"Finding the edges. If it is a door, and the patterns are stopping in this space, there will be edges. Come help me."

She struggled to her feet and complied, listlessly following his movements. "What are we doing?"

He grinned at her, his face a mask of dust and sweat. "Where there is a door, there is a doorknob, isn't there? At least in Greece there is. I may be just a poor, young Greek businessman, but even I know that."

"You're a funny guy, Davros Gianikopolis." She poked at his bicep again, an excuse to touch him. "Very funny."

"I try, I really do. Now, shall we look for our doorknob?"

Finding her resolve, and feeling a surge of hope, she nodded. "Absolutely."

Chapter 8

When Ana and Gates left the garage, they were silent, but not as grim as they had been going in.

"It's a chance," Gates said, finally breaking the tense quiet.

"If there's any chance, I'm happy," Ana said, steering the vehicle out into busy San Francisco traffic.

"A whiff of a chance is better than none," Gates agreed, tapping keys on his small, high-powered laptop. He was zooming in on the high resolution photos of a small plane crossing the Mexican border at an altitude just below radar, but at a significant airspeed. He quickly ran a vector program comparing rate of speed, direction, and the size and capacity of the plane. Utilizing another program, running simultaneously, he initiated a search on the numbers Ana's former colleagues at the CIA had deciphered on the plane's fuselage.

"What are you running first?"

"Flight vector analysis, registration elimination plan." He grinned with fierce glee, seeing the numbers start to drop into place like slots. "If there's something to find, I'll dig it out."

"I see you grinning," she said, and he heard the lift of hope in her voice. "What do you have?"

"The whiff just became a breeze," he said, his fingers flying over the keys, adjusting the program to run another analysis in conjunction with the first. "This plane's got history. I've got some legitimate landings, and some not so legitimate ones."

"Which ones are giving you that wicked grin?"

"The legitimate ones."

"Where?" she demanded, slipping through traffic like an eel, edging past a semi truck with a whisker of space. He didn't even notice, trusting her implicitly.

"Central America. Punta Gorda. Belmopan, and a wildlife reserve. Puerto Cortés and someplace with no name just outside Tegucigalpa, which is the capital of Honduras. Then there are landings in Argentina, and in Guadalajara and Mexicali, and Villa de Álvarez in Mexico as well."

"I thought Punta Gorda was in Florida," Ana said, frowning. "What country is that? Guatemala? I know the Mexican ones. And I was in Argentina. Once."

He made a buzzing sound. "That's a miss on Punta Gorda. Wanna go for another try, little missy? And by the way, there is a Punta Gorda in Florida."

"Ha-ha," she said, pulling through the gates at the hospital. "Nicaragua?"

"Schools these days," he tsked. "Neglecting geography."

"I sucked at Central America. Now, Europe, name your country, I'll give you chapter and verse."

"We'll try that sometime. For now though, Punta Gorda's in Belize." He shifted to look at her. "The others are Guatemala and Nicaragua. I looked them up."

"Ah. Good, I don't feel so dumb. It's a smaller haystack, I guess, but still a haystack."

They headed into the hospital, going straight to the elevator and up to the intensive care unit without a pause. Once there, Gates sat down in the waiting room, shifting slightly in the chair until he got the best wireless connection.

"Most people can't even get cell service in the hospital," Callahan said, rising and stretching after hours sitting in the same chair.

"He's not most people," Ana said with a smile.

"Well, duh," Callahan said, rolling her shoulders and slipping into her raincoat. "I'm going to take a walk, get some fresh air." She glanced toward the unit where her partner lay. "I'll be back, though."

"Stop in the cafeteria," Ana ordered. "Get something to eat."

Callahan looked at her, looked away. When she looked back, the tough facade had cracked and Ana saw the fear. "I can't eat," she said, and her voice shook.

"Try," Ana insisted, knowing how much harder despair hit you when you were low on fuel.

Callahan swallowed, not meeting her gaze. She stood that way for a bit before saying, "It won't go down."

With that, she hurried away.

Ana felt her own grief rise up to choke her at the words, and watched as Callahan got into the elevator and disappeared. Behind her the clacking of keys hesitated, stopped, resumed.

"What?" She said it without turning. "What did you find?"

"Another tiny piece of the puzzle just fell into place."

"What?"

"The plane hasn't clocked in anywhere else in the last twenty-four hours."

"Private airstrips, then, with no towers," she summed up.

A different beeping pinged in the waiting room and now she did turn. "What now?"

"Sending an orde . . . texting a request to have the yacht go down from Key West to the Gulf of Mexico. If we can find him somewhere down there, we need to have a way to get him out. Carrie too."

"Yeah, they don't have their passports—no plane ride without a passport."

"Well, no public planes. I don't want to alert anyone, though, by flying one of the jets down. Especially since we have no idea where we're going."

"So use an Agency plane," she said, knowing he had a reason not to, but not sure what it might be. Several agencies had offered the use of personnel, equipment, pretty much anything they might ask.

"Too conspicuous. Besides—" He looked up at her now, a frown of frustration on his face. Something wasn't adding up for him and he wasn't happy about it. He'd worn that look a lot when they first met.

That thought almost made her smile.

"Besides what?"

"You're beautiful," he said sincerely, the frown never leaving his face.

She could feel the blush. More than a year of knowing him, months of marriage, and still he made her blush.

"Thank you. Now, spill."

"Even if it is some family thing," he began, shifting in the seat. She could tell he wanted to pace, so she sat down and took the electronics from him, freeing him up to stand. As she had mentally predicted, he began to pace, talking it out. "Like I said, even if it's a family thing behind the abduction, that isn't all it is. There's something else going on here and I can't put my finger on it."

"Fact or hunch?"

"Both."

"Lay it out," she encouraged.

"The pickup was brilliantly planned and executed, right down to the phony film crew and the innocent bystanders supposedly watching an action flick being made. The dupes driving the cars thought it was all part of the camera work. The camera team thought they were really making a film."

"And?"

"That's layers within layers within layers. If someone in Dav's family is working this, it's not anyone I know or have met. I've checked them all out, *all* of them." He said that with emphasis, making her smile. He'd even checked the ones he liked, admired or both. His next words confirmed that thought. "His cousin Sophia? She has the brains and the guts, knows the film people, but she genuinely loves Dav. His cousins from his mother's side?"

"The ones who came over for New Year's?"

"Yeah," he agreed, still pacing. "They're too young."

"Smart enough I think, but I agree. And they're impulsive."

"His brother's supposed to be dead," Gates growled. "We checked, damn it."

Ana's attention sharpened on that note. "Supposed to be?"

"Yeah. Supposed to be. Reported dead. I checked it out, Dav checked it out. I had them do DNA—they had a body."

"If you didn't see it dead, it may not be dead." She stated the obvious just to get it out there in the open. "Payoff, then. DNA can be gathered from the living too, you know. What country?"

"Somalia, but I had it checked. With all associated bribes paid. They said dead."

"Huh. So likely that he really is dead." She wanted to pace with him, but it would only agitate them both. Instead she asked, "But, on the chance that he's not, let's play it out. This brother, he smart enough to pull this off?"

He looked at her, half smiled, but with no humor. "He's Dav's brother."

"Got it. He's smart enough." She took the next steps in her mind. "Smart enough, obviously coldhearted enough if Dav turned against him. Is he bankrolled enough to pull it?"

"Ah, now that's what bothers me. He had a hefty cash flow as a mercenary. His funds flipped quickly out of sight when he died, which was pretty predictable. We didn't think much of it." He kept pacing, a little faster now. "That happens. Partners, brothers-in-arms."

"So are you looking at him, seriously, or someone else who maybe knew him or wants Dav dead and is trying to lead us that way to divert us?"

"Ah, there's the rub, as the Bard would say. It could be any of the above."

"Okay," Ana said, on familiar ground now. Running scenarios was her thing and this tangle meant that they were at least onto something tangible, something that *could* be unraveled. "Let's look at the dead brother. Does he have a name?"

"Real name is Nikolas Gianikopolis, older half brother, cut out of the will by the old man, who pitted them against one another for the right to run the family business. The family biz was half legit, half shady, and Dav didn't want it."

Ana winced at that; she really didn't want to know about the shady stuff. What you didn't know, you couldn't be called on to testify about.

Oblivious to her thoughts, Gates continued. "When the business went to Dav, he brought Niko into the company in a high-level position. He felt Niko had been cheated of what should have been his, at least in part. I think he would have given Niko the business if Niko had proved that he could handle it. Truly, Dav didn't want it. He'd begun to build his fortune here and didn't want his father's shadowy legacy, his leavings."

"But neither he nor the father left it to Niko," Ana said, filling in the blanks immediately.

"Quick rundown," Gates offered. "Niko picked up where his father left off on the shady side of the business dealings. Dav had shut them down, Niko opened them back up. All the while he pretended to be learning the ropes."

"Dav caught on."

Gates smiled. "Give the lady a prize. Dav did, indeed. Altercation ensues, threats made, curses and fists fly." His smile turned feral. "Niko departs in acute pain and disgrace. Six weeks later, the father dies and the empire is Dav's."

"Good reason to hate your younger, smarter, more successful brother. Especially if he beats you up too," she said whimsically, reading between the lines that Dav hadn't lost that fight. "A tale as old as Esau."

Gates looked blank.

"Bible story," Ana said, shaking her head. Amazing how few people knew the old stuff anymore.

"One I missed, obviously."

"Stolen inheritance, and all that."

"Got it. Good analogy then," he complimented, pacing up, then pacing back. "So, moving on to scenario two, Niko really is dead and someone who knew him is out to either gaslight Dav—"

At Ana's puzzled look, he rolled his eyes. "Tit for tat then, on Esau. You know, the movie, *Gaslight*? Where the husband tries to make the wife think she's crazy?"

The light dawned. "Right," Ana said. "Got it. So yes, either that or someone who knew Niko learned enough from him to get to Dav and we'll be getting a ransom request."

"More than thirty-six hours now, closing in on forty-eight. No requests."

Gates's expression turned grim. "I know." He paced a bit more, then continued. "Third option—it's revenge for Niko's death."

"Then why not just kill Dav outright? That scene at the restaurant was tailor made for a killing. And why kill the gallery clerk?" Ana demanded, playing devil's advocate. "She's a loose end I don't like. Something's there too, and we need to tug that lead."

"Not us. That one's for Baxter," Gates insisted.

She nodded, knowing how thin their resources were spread. Not everyone could drop all their tasks to hunt for

Dav. "If anyone can, even with all he's got going on and no help, then Baxter can do it."

"True. So then we have Door Number Four. There's something a whole lot bigger going on here."

Ana thought for a minute, trying to get a broader, bigger view. Obviously Gates had already taken that step. "Rival?"

"Exactly. But who?" Gates questioned, his frustration obvious. "Nobody legit would do this and the black market dealers are just as happy that Dav keeps it on the up and up. Hell, he'd own them, and their businesses, if he wanted to run on the dark side."

Ana gave him a fond smile. Much as she agreed, he made it sound like some kind of competitive sport. "True. So, no one obvious on either side. Hidden rival. Lot of women and men out there with money who'd love to see Dav go down."

"Yeah, but with this kind of push? This took not only guts, but long-term planning and an almost uncanny amount of luck. Anyone willing to leave three dead, and at least ten wounded just to get Dav, that someone wants him really badly."

Ana added that to the mix of thoughts and ideas running circles in her brain. Queller and Thompson had taken the latest watch, despite their injuries. Gates had had to threaten the others to get them to go home and rest. A young woman walked by, her uniform looking crisp and new. Her name tag read *Inez*. The name sparked another thought.

"The clerk," Ana said, remembering where she'd heard the name. "She fits in somehow. I wish she weren't dead."

"Yeah, that's probably why she is," Gates replied. "Wait, clerk. Carrie's former clerk. The one who was there forever. What happened to him, the one who ran the gallery when we met? Whatshisname." Gates snapped his fingers as if that would help him remember. "Cal, yeah, that's it. You remember the last name?"

"Crap, no. We need to find out. Find out why she was

there and he wasn't. Interview all the clerks, make sure we find out who's new, who's not and who knew Inez."

"Another one for Bax," Gates said. "Along with finding Cal. He's important, I know it."

He was probably right. He usually was.

Cal's last name was right on the tip of her tongue, just almost there, when the elevator dinged and a group of harried-looking people all but leapt off the elevator with two of Dav's staff in tow.

She stood up, and Gates whipped around. Before Ana could speak, her text alert signaled and she pulled out her phone. Gates read over her shoulder.

Shit. They'd finally gotten a ransom demand, along with proof of life, and he couldn't focus on it. He had to focus on what was in front of him.

These could only be Declan's parents. Declan had the look of his mother, with her dark red hair and bright eyes, but his father's breadth of shoulder and height.

"Are you Ana? And Gates?" Like homing pigeons, they focused in on Ana and Gates and headed toward them, hands outstretched.

"Oh, please tell us we're in time. We've been driving all night."

"Did you hear that?" When Dav spoke, Carrie paused in her painstaking search for a way to open the wall in their cell. They'd spent the rest of the day searching for the door, but now, in the late-afternoon warmth, his hand closed on her arm in a firm, insistent grip. She stopped and listened.

"I don't hear anything."

"Neither do I," he said. "And that's not good. The birds stopped making noise; so did whatever makes that other sound, the screeching."

"Monkeys, I think."

"Something's disturbing them, scaring them."

"Maybe it's the men, coming back." Carrie didn't want it to be their captors. As hungry as she was, and as tired as she was of crackers and Nutella—the supplies they were down to—she didn't want the time with Dav to end. Their captors' return meant death, most likely. She wanted to be free, to be with him in the light and air.

Fear clenched her belly and her heart. She wasn't ready to face whatever came next.

They stood, motionless and listening, as they heard the crunch of gravel, the hum of an engine. Doors slammed and after a few more silent moments, they heard voices.

"Ramierez, check the perimeter." It was the smooth voice of the leader of their capture team. They were indeed back. "Carlos, go check on our guests."

Footsteps approached and the accented voice said, "Wakey, wakey." He thrust the barrel of an automatic weapon through the grate and rattled it noisily between the bars. "Happy to see us, eh?"

There was a shout and the man, Carlos, looked up.

"Perimeter secure?" The demand in the question was sharp, imperative. "Ramierez? White? Report!"

Carlos was crouching above the grate now, low and watchful.

"Sir, perimeter is compr—" A scream and a distant thud punctuated the sentence.

"Positions!" The leader screamed the order, and the man above them flattened to the ground, his weapon poised to fire. Dav pushed Carrie behind him and shifted along the wall, away from where they'd been, keeping them out of the line of the man's weapon.

Yells and orders were a cacophony after the last two days of silence. "Carlos! Get to cover!"

The man on the grate shifted, started to move, and there was a soft, wet-sounding pop-pop-pop. Carlos spun sideways, keening in pain, but crouched and fired toward the jungle.

The automatic weapon spat shell casings and the biting taste of carbon snapped in the air. Brass jangled through the bars and onto the dirt. Carrie and Dav both covered their ears as Carlos fired again.

He'd paused in his firing, so Carrie uncovered her ears, just in time to hear another sound, deeper this time, like a wet towel slapped on pavement. Splat, splat, splat. Carlos grunted in pain, dropped to his knees, air whistling out of his nose and chest. With a gurgling sigh, he fell forward, over the grate. There were indistinct shouts and the sound of gunfire, all muffled by the body of their captor. The waning daylight now penetrating the cell through his limbs, showed them his dying, staring eyes. Blood dripped onto the stone floor in a steady stream. It was mesmerizing, the stream-drip-drip-stream pattern as Carlos's heart beat its last. The flow of blood slowed and finally stopped, along with the noise from beyond the grate.

Frozen along the wall, Dav held Carrie behind him, shielded by his body, protected by the stone at their back. They both jumped when Carlos's weapon slipped between the bars with a rattle and clang, and hung tantalizingly within reach. Blood dripped from the barrel to the ground, a secondary stream darkening the floor below.

It seemed like hours they waited, pressed together, held up by the stone. After the first barrage of gunfire, silence had returned. Beyond, in the clearing, the birds eventually resumed calling, the screeching monkeys shrieked their insults back and forth once more. Everything returned to normal, except that now, the people who had locked them in, but brought them food, were all wounded or dead.

And there was no way to know if the shooters were friend or foe.

Chapter 9

"Quick, Carrie, up on my shoulders," Dav said, realizing they needed to act. If the shooters had taken up sniper positions, they would wait for a while before coming down. If they came and were not friendly, he and Carrie needed to be ready. "See if you can pull yourself up using the gun strap. Maybe he has the keys. If you can get up there and unlock the grate, maybe we can get out."

"I don't think I'm strong enough to push him off the grate," she protested, hurrying to get her shoes off and climb onto his shoulders as they had before. They were quicker this time, taking only two tries to get her steady.

Carrie could reach the gun, and he felt her weight shift and lift off his shoulders. Triumph warred with the knowledge that she probably couldn't push the dead kidnapper off, not without more leverage than they had. He heard the jingle of keys or change, but dared not look up or alter his balance with just her toes resting on his shoulders.

"I can't do it, Dav." Her weight sagged onto him again and he felt his heart drop. How would they survive? "I can unfasten the gun, but I don't know that it would do us any good."

"Does he have anything on his belt? A sidearm or a rope or anything?"

"Rope would be good," she grunted, pulling up again. "No. Nothing. Wait . . . Oh my God, it's a flashlight. I'm going to work it loose, but can you catch it if I lose my grip on it?"

"You'll do fine." Why would she lose her grip?

"Oh, a canteen too or a flask. If I can get it first, maybe the flashlight will be easier." When that came down to him, dropping into his outstretched hand, he understood her concern. Blood covered its surface, making the smooth metal so slippery he nearly dropped it himself.

"Got it."

"Going for the flashlight."

He could tell she was tiring by the strain in her voice. Rifling through a dead man's pockets, while standing on tiptoe to reach him, by holding on to the man's dangling weapon wasn't a task anyone should have to manage.

But she was doing it and he admired her more every minute for her courage. His heart clenched as she slipped and he reached higher to brace her.

"It's stuck. I think . . . shit!"

The exclamation warned him and he reached out just as a heavy-duty, black metal flashlight passed in front of him. He fumbled it, but managed to grab the bloody haft of the flashlight. He tried to stay steady for her, but it took them both a bit of weaving back and forth to reestablish their balance.

"Did you get it? Dav?"

He looked at it, black and blood-covered in the fast-fading light. Somehow he'd managed to keep the only source of light they might have for days from hitting the stone and shattering the bulb.

"Dav?"

"Yes, I got it. Come down, there's nothing else you can do up there."

"Okay." Relief was evident in her voice and as she eased

her full weight back onto him, he felt the quiver of fatigue in her legs. Between their bouts of lovemaking and this, they'd both had a full day's workout.

The thought made him smile in spite of their dire predicament. He handed her down, then caught her in a bear hug. "Fabulous job, my flame. Fabulous job." He kissed her hair, then bent to kiss her mouth. "You were magnificent."

She shivered, a long, shuddering ripple of distaste. "If I never have to do that again, it will be a hundred years too soon."

It took him a minute to unravel the metaphor. "I agree. Being below you, not knowing if I could catch you if you fell, or catch the light, was a bit nerve-wracking as well. It concerned me that the gun might go off," he said, grinning now with relief that it hadn't.

"I'm sure." Heartfelt sympathy colored her words as she shuddered again. "I'm glad I didn't think about the gun. I don't know about you, but I don't care if it takes all the antibacterial gel we've got left, I have to get the blood off my hands."

"Yes. Absolutely. We'll wipe it off with the wrapping from the food. We don't need it anymore. Then use the gel, yes?"

"Okay. Let's hurry."

They moved back along the wall to where they had set up their makeshift bed. They used the flashlight sparingly, to make sure their hands were clean, to use the facilities, but both agreed they wouldn't waste the battery.

"I can't help thinking of that scene in *Cast Away,* you know the movie with Tom Hanks? He has a flashlight, but he falls asleep with it on?"

"Yes, I remember." He also remembered the sense of despair that came through so poignantly in the movie, the loneliness and hopelessness. At least Hanks had been able to move about in the light and air. Dav had watched the movie only once and had never forgotten it.

Now, the gloom and the coppery smell of blood made him queasy and dizzy, a weakness he abhorred.

"Dav?" Carrie's voice wavered in the dark. "I'm . . . I'm . . ."

"I know," he reassured her, though he felt no security himself. "It's not good." He had to shift his thoughts, steer his mind away from the walls, which seemed to be closing in with the darkness and the despair of their predicament. "Tell me more about the walls, about the carvings."

"The walls? Okay. Okay, I get that," she said, her voice gaining strength. "We have to focus on something else. Something besides . . . him." She gulped a few times. "Can I sit with you, right next to you while we talk?"

"Of course, Carrie-mou, come," he said, thankful that she too craved the warmth of contact. The dead man above them brought the coppery, fecal smell of death to their prison, tainting it even more. Dav did his best to ignore it, and the noises of the night animals that were coming to investigate the blood. He wouldn't mention it to Carrie, but tomorrow, there would be vultures, or worse, to take their turn. It was a jungle and things, especially dead things, didn't stay whole for long. It wouldn't be pretty.

"These symbols, they represent the seasons, the rivers, the crops, even the cycles of the gods in this part of the world. Like the Greek gods, which you know, they had their lovers, their jealousies, their favorites. It's a very different system, of course, and more masculine in its orientation, but very comparable mythology."

"I see." He didn't really, but it kept her going, kept his mind off the dead and the dark.

"Well, they weren't that similar, I guess," she said, and shivered. It wasn't cold in their cell, but the situation was worthy of shivers if anything was. "Anyway, they were a whole lot more bloodthirsty. You think the whole Spartan thing, and the perfection required of their athletes was severe? It wasn't anything to the Toltec, Mayan and Olmec traditions. Their games?" she said rhetorically. "Bloody as hell. People, well, young men, died every time there was a game."

"No bad game days, I guess," Dav mused. "Or at least you only have one."

"Right," she half laughed. "So, these markings show the river in good order, the crops in the fields ready to be harvested, the people praying to the gods."

"Is that good or bad?"

"I don't know, but I think it means that if this is a ritual site, it's for plenty and prosperity. Or . . ." and now her voice held a desperate edge, "it could be a cell showing the occupant all they'll be missing."

"Nice thought. Let's say it's the first. What do you think the door means? Do you think it *is* a door?"

"Oh, yes. I just have no idea how to open it, or if it's booby-trapped or anything."

"Booby-trapped? Shades of *Indiana Jones,*" Dav quipped. "Blow holes and poisoned darts."

"Yes. That sort of thing was used, you know. That's where the writers for Indy got it, I guess. Even the exaggeration has a basis in fact."

He chuckled. "I see. Eh-la. We'll take as many precautions as possible, but we need to open it if we can. There's really no option at this point, yes?"

"True," she said ruefully. "It's that or starve. Or wait for whoever shot those guys to come back." She gestured toward the ceiling and shuddered. He felt it all along his body, and it reminded him of their passion, their desire for one another. There would be none of that tonight with death ever-present in their sight and in their senses.

"Tell me more about the Mayans," Dav said, encouraging her to focus on him, not on the growling and scuffling sounds that had begun above them. He didn't know what kind of wildlife might be around the clearing up above them, but scavengers had been attracted by the blood, and the smell of death. Even with the presence of man, this area was wild and the animals were efficient in the jungle.

Carrie began to talk about the Mayan civilization, distracting them both, but soon her voice drifted into silence and she fell into a doze in his arms, bundled in his jacket. For hours, Dav sat listening to the noises above them, watching as the body on the grate jerked when something tugged at it. He didn't want to waste the flashlight's batteries checking it out.

It was worse, though, sitting in the dark, listening to the rustle and shift of fabric. The renewed dripping of blood woke him much later, while it was still dark. From the dripping and from the wet tearing sounds, he knew that whatever had been after the body had managed to get through the clothes. It made him ill to think about it, so he did his best to shut out the sights and sounds, just as he'd done as a child. He had Carrie to think about now.

He was a grown man.

When she woke in the dark, she could feel Dav shivering next to her. "Dav?" she whispered, the darkness and his tense body making her want to cower in fear. Still, she reached out to him. "Dav?"

"It's like before," he said, and she could tell he was forcing the words out. When she touched his face, she felt the rock-hard tension in his jaw, his stiff posture making him unyielding under her seeking hands.

"Like before?" she coaxed.

"I told you, they locked me in. The bugs. The rats."

Now she was the one shuddering at that thought, and at the thought that Dav was losing it. In the silence she heard it, the gnawing sound above them, the wet smacking, crunching sounds. The bugs. The rats.

No wonder he was reliving the past.

"Oh, God. Carrion feeders," she managed. Her teeth were chattering now. "It'll be worse if we turn on the light, won't it?" she asked, knowing the answer.

With his face in her hands, she felt him nod. "Much worse. The sound is bad, but the sight would be worse, Carrie-mou."

"Tell me, what does that mean? Mou?" It was a distraction, a lame one, but better than nothing. "You call me that. I like it."

"It's like . . . 'sweetheart.' Or 'd-d-darling,'" he stuttered, and she knew he was lost in the dark, back in his terrible childhood. What kind of father pitted his sons against one another? What kind of monster locked his child in the basement to toughen him up?

"So, if I call you Dav-mou, it's like saying 'darling Dav'?"

He laughed, the sound strained and with an edge of wildness to it, but it was a laugh. "It sounds odd with my name, but yes, it is." He turned his face into her hand, pressing a kiss to her palm. "You are so special to me, Carrie-mou. You always have been."

The words, the sentiment, sounded saner, more like the Dav she knew, so she tried to keep that line of conversation going.

"I feel the same way," Carrie admitted, realizing it was true. She'd always compared other men to him, long before she'd lost Luke. There'd always been Dav. "You've been there for me, in so many ways." She leaned in and pressed a gentle kiss to his lips, continuing to tease and taste to her heart's content. It wasn't sexual. It was quiet. Reassuring. Promising.

And the hum in her body and mind as his lips warmed and responded drowned out the disgusting noises above them.

He groaned out her name, banding her in his arms and rocking them both with fierce power. "It's hard to be here, the memory rises to choke me here, memory I thought I had left behind." He squeezed a bit more, then loosened his grip. "I'm glad you're with me, even as I wish you could be a thousand miles away, safe in your beautiful home."

"Better to wish us both away from here," she offered, leaning on him, letting his solid warmth settle her nerves, help her forget the wildlife and their dire situation. "Your estate is exquisite, I hear."

"You've never accepted my offers to visit," he said, a pensive note in his voice, but he no longer sounded lost as he had before. "Why?"

Relief coursed through her as she heard more sanity in his words, more of who he was and less of his fears. "Oh, Dav, I knew that once I said yes to you, about anything, there would be no going back."

To her surprise, he chuckled. "You would have had a choice, Carrie-mou. Always."

"No," she said, shaking her head so that he would feel her denial as well as hear it. "I knew I wouldn't be able to resist being interested in you. I had to be sure I was . . ." She hesitated, then went silent. How did you express that kind of fear? Fear that you'd lose yourself, that you'd become so weak you'd just disappear in the shadow of a strong man?

"Sure you were what? Safe?" he questioned.

"No, I've always felt safe with you. It wasn't that. I needed to be completely myself. Stable. Strong." She sighed. "I had to know that I wasn't weak or pliable, ineffectual."

"Yourself?" He sounded puzzled, and again, stronger now that he was discussing the world outside, the life they'd led. "Why wouldn't you be yourself? You are a strong, capable woman, Carrie-mou."

Her heart clenched at the endearment. How could she explain to this self-assured man that her weakness was her heart?

"Dav, I lost so much of myself with Luke. I just faded, like a painting that's been hung in strong sunlight. The colors were still there, but so muted, so . . . so . . ."

"Pastel?" he offered.

"Exactly."

"Ah, but Carrie-mou, you could never be pastel. Even with that shadow over you, with Luke and the problems, you still were vibrant, alive."

Was that admiration in his voice? Approval?

Whatever it was, it was warm, and reassuring. "I didn't feel that way, though. I couldn't see myself that way. I was so lost. I kept finding myself at the Bay, by the bridge or down at Fisherman's Wharf, looking out at the water, thinking, 'Where is my color? Where is my strength?'"

He snugged her more tightly into his arms, a brief squeeze, then he relaxed his grip so that she could move, escape if she chose. "You have always seemed strong to me. A willow that bends in the wind, but comes back straight and as strong as ever when the wind dies."

She let out a rough half laugh, half sob. "Oh God, Dav, if only I'd known that someone saw me that way. It would have helped." Tears welled up. "I lost so much."

"Tell me, Carrie," he encouraged. "What made you feel so lost?"

"Everything. When Luke would cheat on me, it hurt," she said. Saying it now, here in the dark with him, she could feel the pain, but it was distant, as if she could let it go. How odd. "Then, he would come back, be affectionate, loving."

"He was so wrong, Carrie, so stupid," Dav said, his hands sliding up and down her back, a reassuring caress. "He should have been, what is the word? Horsewhipped."

She smiled in the darkness. "A very old-fashioned punishment."

"The worst betrayal," he countered with strength, "requires a stern reprimand."

"True." She hesitated, knowing she should shut up now. The words wanted to slip around her good sense. She wanted him to know, she wanted all the horrible stuff out of her mind, spewed into this inky, terrible darkness to be swallowed up and sent away. Purged before she met her Maker, since that seemed fairly imminent. "I got pregnant."

He went very still. His hands froze in their caresses, his restless fingers stilled. "Carrie? Little one, what happened?"

"I wasn't very far along when Luke died. I never got to tell him," she said, and the words ran together. She couldn't get them out fast enough. "I fell. At the funeral home, I fell. Later that night, I had to go to the emergency room. I lost the baby the day after I buried Luke."

She broke. Her voice, and her heart, and her reserve all broke, and she wept. She'd cried back then, in her mother's arms, but this was like a catharsis, an emptying of her soul's pain. All the while, she heard his whispered endearments, mostly in Greek, but some in English. His hands, never still now, reassured her on the physical level, holding her tightly, keeping her safe in the darkness as she cried out the last of the hurt from those long-ago days.

"Ah, darling," he crooned, pressing kisses into her hair. "You'll have another chance, my love, if you want it. You'll see the sun again."

They lay together for a long time, and she listened to the deep resonant sound of his heartbeat, the reassuring whoosh of his breathing. Oddly enough, despite their terrible situation, she felt at peace. "You're the only person I've told besides my mother," she finally admitted. "I felt so alone. So useless."

"Ah, Carrie," he whispered. "You are none of that."

"I know that, in my head," she whispered back. "But it took me a long time, maybe till now, to feel it in my heart."

He was quiet for a long while. When he spoke, he said,

"Yes. I understand that. It is in this place, knowing we may die, that we can be truthful, yes?"

Realizing he was right, she agreed. "I guess so."

"What have we got to lose, telling our secrets here? You know mine," he said, and she heard a deep thread of anger underlying his words. "I still live in fear of the dark, of being trapped. So. Eh-la. I must talk of the light and of other things or I will go mad. If I go insane, you will have to tie me down and force me to eat Nutella and crackers while I quibble in fear."

"Quibble?" She hesitated, searching for what he might mean. Unaccountably, a chuckle sneaked out. What the heck could that mean? It was such a strange word to use. "I don't think you mean . . . um—" She stopped, unsure of how to correct his English, worried that he'd be offended by her laughter.

"What does that mean then?" he said impatiently. "Quibble?"

"I think it means to argue."

"No, no, that isn't the right word." He sounded disgusted. His irritation with the language had distracted him from his fear for the moment, so she took advantage of it.

"To quake?"

"Like the earth? To shake?" He paused, then said, "No, that isn't it. It's a word like making noises, animal noises, the talk and noises madmen make."

"Oh," she said, unaccountably delighted to figure it out. "Gibbering."

"Yes!" he said. "That's it. Eh-la, that is it. Gibbering in fear." He laughed. "The point has somewhat lost its impact, however, with this discussion of words."

"It's better than being crazy with fear," she offered. "Let's play a word game."

"Like you did, spelling into my hand?"

"I couldn't believe that worked."

"It was difficult," Dav said, and she heard the chagrin in

his voice. "I had to translate the letters, you see. Speaking, that is different. Writing, if I can see it, yes, that isn't so hard. But that?" She felt him shift, heard the huff of air as he grunted. "That was hard."

"Is it hard to learn another language?" she asked. "I learned French, but not much. I even learned some Norwegian when I worked at a gallery in college with a Norwegian owner."

"That's not something you'd use every day," he said, and she heard the smile in his voice.

"No. I've not learned much Greek, though."

"I'll teach you," he said. "Should we start now?"

"Start with hello," she suggested, and he laughed.

The mercenary's sightless, milky eyes were the first thing Dav saw when he woke. The midnight scavengers, unable to turn Carlos's body off the grate, had torn into him from the back. Dav could see where the clothing was askew because the legs had been shifted and daylight flowed more freely into the cell than it had after the man died.

The gun, crusted now with dried blood, still stared down at them, an accusing empty eye with a drop of dried blood hanging from its barrel. It occurred to him that if they could get the weapon, they could shoot the lock off, but it still wouldn't help them get the body off the grate or give them a way to climb out, so it was a futile idea.

He felt Carrie stirring in his arms and he deliberately shifted forward so the body wouldn't be the first thing she saw. With the night passed, Dav felt more solid, more stable. He despised that the old fears still haunted him, but he had no more control over them than he did his reaction to Carrie.

"Dav?" she murmured, stretching and turning his way. He moved again, blocking her view.

"Good morning, Carrie-mou," he said, smiling at her,

knowing that if he died tomorrow, it had been a sweet joy to have been with her, made love to her. "I believe we'll be checking out of this fine establishment today," he joked, standing now, so her gaze followed him. "Here, let me help you up."

She stood and he pulled her into his arms. "Carrie, you need to keep your eyes down. The view above us is very unpleasant," he murmured in her ear. She shifted and he said, "No, don't look."

Pulling back a bit, she protested. "Dav, I'm in this with you. Don't try to shield me."

He nodded. "Just know that it is ugly, as violent death usually is, and brace yourself before you look, yes? We are going to find our door today." He shook her slightly to ensure that she focused on him. "Yes?"

She smiled. It was a bit shaky, but it was a smile. "Yes. If you say so. We will." The smile grew a bit broader. "You're seldom wrong, so I'll trust that."

"Good," he approved. "Carrie?"

She had looked beyond him now, and he could see the tears standing in her eyes. For a moment, she said nothing, just shuddered once—a quick involuntary movement—then turned away. "Gee, what's for breakfast? Nutella? How yummy," she said with false cheer. "It's been so long since we had Nutella and crackers, I'm sure you're just as excited as I am."

"Sarcasm becomes you, darling," he said, delighted that she was so strong in this situation. What a woman, his Carrie. He had known she was strong, but this? This stirred a deep admiration for her.

It reassured him to know that when they got out of here, as they went through life, as the passion left them, he would have this deep admiration to sustain them. *Yes,* he nodded to himself at the thought. *It was good.* His father had never admired anyone, much less a woman. That Dav could, and did, told him he'd sloughed off that mantle his father had imposed upon him.

Odd that, trapped and desperate, he would finally feel whole. Terrible that, as he might be living his last day, he was at last free of his father.

"Hmmm, yes, well, you might not appreciate that same sarcasm when I have to eat Nutella again tomorrow, but, for today, we'll just go with it."

They did the best they could to wash up, and clean up as they ate a meager breakfast of crackers and the now-sickeningly sweet chocolate nut spread. At least it was filling.

Studiously avoiding looking up, and ignoring the jungle noises beyond the grate, they both approached the wall.

"He's going to start to stink in a few hours," Carrie offered, not looking at him. "And there will be buzzards."

Dav nodded, studying the wall intently. "And insects." He kept his voice calm, but the idea of it, the idea of having to watch as insects devoured the man above them, nearly brought the Nutella back up. "However, we will be gone."

"Right," Carrie said, with finality. She shifted both her eyes and her body away from the noxious sight. "Let's follow the sky line here—" She pointed to the set of carvings that whorled and shifted unpredictably, even as it made its way around the walls. "Sky is freedom in most cultures. I can't remember enough of my Mayan studies to know if it's right, but we've got nothing but time, so we'll try it first."

"Good plan," he agreed, starting with the whorl above her head as she took the one closer to the Earth line, which featured stylized representations of people and plants. The gods were above it all, above the sky, above the plants and the puny worries of man.

There was no one waiting when Niko landed at the airstrip.

Something was wrong. The hackles on his neck prickled and he knew he'd been double-crossed, betrayed. Somehow.

Had his team abandoned him? Had Dav somehow figured out that it was him and gotten to his men? They were loyal, but money spoke volumes.

Who had given in? Whom had he misjudged? Had his inside man given him away?

He slipped his weapon out of its holster, motioned his pilot to pull them close to the hangar.

"Something's not right, compadre," Sam, the pilot, muttered under his breath. "Why is the second Jeep here? It should not be here. Where are they?"

Niko shook his head. "I don't know, but let's lock the plane down and get out of here. We're too exposed. We check the Jeep for explosives, too, before we start it."

"Damn, Skippy," Sam offered, darkly. "And go expecting a trap."

"You got that right." Together they left the plane, checked the hangar and all the remaining vehicles. Nothing seemed out of place. The extra weapons were in their usual hiding places. Niko selected several, plus ammunition, and made sure that both he and Sam had reloads and grenades. If there were something wrong at the site, they needed to go in blazing.

Or slip away to fight another day.

"Let's go," he said, having checked the Jeep one last time from ignition wires to undercarriage. "We're behind. We need to get halfway there before dark. We'll make camp and come in at sunrise. If something's wrong, better to see it from a distance and in daylight."

"Right," Sam agreed as he cranked the car and wheeled out of the hangar, fast and efficient from start to finish. A man of few words, that was the last he spoke until they reached the halfway point.

That was fine with Niko. He had too much to think about and no answers to ease his mind.

Chapter 10

It was midday and the buzz of flies and worse added an annoying accompaniment to their labors. They'd already snapped at one another twice or three times. The growing heat and the omnipresent smell of death wore on the nerves like nothing Carrie had ever experienced.

She ran a ragged, scraped finger over yet another cloud whorl in the stone, feeling despair creeping into her heart.

"Shit!" Dav cursed in English, then let fly with a string of curses in Greek, Italian and what sounded like French. She spun around, to see him shaking his hand, then pressing on his fingers.

"Dav?"

"Set my fingers in a gap in the stone, then moved wrong and caught them there."

"Ouch," she empathized, then jumped as a raucous screech sounded above them. The body shifted violently and the machine gun swung wildly on its strap, spinning around as buzzards or vultures came to rest on the dead man.

"Oh, my God," Dav said, his voice echoing the revulsion she felt. Turning back to the wall, she continued to run her fingers along the carving. She had to focus. She had to find the key so she could get away from the wet tearing sounds, the squabbling squawks and shrieks as more birds came to rest above them.

"Keep looking, Dav," she said sharply, knowing that she was going to go mad, or throw up or something if they didn't get a break soon. She bent down to peer into a deep crevice of a whorl and saw something. "Dav, do you have my all-purpose tool?"

"Yes," he said, but she didn't look at him or at anything but the deep hole in front of her. She couldn't bear it. She wanted to throw her hands over her ears and howl. It was awful.

Instead, she held out her hand. Dav set the tool in it and went back to his side of where they thought the door might be. She opened the longest blade and used it to probe down in the curl of the stone design. She pressed inward, and wiggled the blade. Why was there a hole here, in this design, in this place?

There was the faintest movement. The barest shift in the stone. She'd felt it in her hand, hadn't she?

There! A quiver of movement. Faint and nearly imperceptible.

Had she imagined it? She stuck the blade farther in, pressed harder.

"Carrie?" Dav's breathless use of her name made her look his way. He'd stepped back from the wall. In front of him was the faintest lip of stone, the minutest shift making a vertical line on the wall.

"Dav!" she squealed, "it worked!"

"Whatever you did, keep doing it," he said, striding to her side.

"I put the blade in here, and pushed," she explained, doing it again. Another whisper of sound and movement and the pivot of the door became more obvious. Instead of a typical hinge, it was shifting in the middle, like an upright paddle, spinning on a central pin.

"What if I push here?" he asked, pointing at the back edge of the shifting panel. "Do you think that would work?"

"Can't hurt. Let's do it at the same time," she said, excited enough to grin at him. "Oh, my God, I never thought this could work. It still might not, but—" She stopped, not sure what to say.

"But it might," he said, returning the grin. His white teeth made a startling counterpoint to his warm skin tone and dark, beard-roughened face. "I would love to not be here when my unlamented brother comes to check on us."

Her heart clenched. "You think he's coming?"

"Oh, yes. He was planning to come—they indicated as much when they put us down here. They were waiting for him."

"Then who killed them?" she asked, totally puzzled.

He shook his head. "Who knows? This area—Central America or Mexico—is rife with rival gangs and drug lords in certain parts of it. Much of it is only recently settled into democracy, or semiregular government. There's plenty of greed, graft, corruption and general lawlessness in a lot of the countries. Some are better than others. Let's hope we're in one of those."

He braced his feet, putting his hands firmly on the shifting wall panel. "Ready?"

"Let's do it," she agreed. "On three." She counted it off and pressed in on the blade as he shoved at the panel.

"It moved," he exulted. "Really moved, look." Five inches of the wall panel had shifted outward on the outer edge and inward where Dav had pushed at it. "Let me get the flashlight."

He skirted around the edge of the room to their belongings, taking up the flashlight. She saw him wipe it off on the edge of his coat before he came back to where she stood, studying the wall.

They moved together to the open side, and Dav turned on

the Maglite flashlight, pointing its powerful beam down the dark corridor.

"Ugh." Dav was the first to comment. The view was dusty, dark and cobwebby. At least she hoped the stringy things hanging in the space were cobwebs. Old ones. Unused ones.

"It reminds me of that movie," she whispered. "*The Lord of the Rings,* where Frodo goes into the spider's place."

"Shelob." Dav's voice was terse, sharp.

She looked at him, surprised. Lines of strain were carved into his forehead. She remembered his confession about the locked room, the insects and rats. His fear of the inhabited dark.

Carrie rested a gentle hand on his arm. His elegant shirt, now tattered and dirty, was wet with sweat, but the fine material was still smooth under her fingers.

"Dav." She waited until he looked at her. "We'll do it together."

He looked away, staring into the dark passage for a long time. Finally he nodded. "Thank God you're here."

It was all he said before handing her the flashlight and taking up his position on the back side of the stone again, bracing his feet and shoving with all his might. The door pivoted another six inches.

"Let me brush off the floor here," Carrie said, stuffing the flashlight in the back of her pants, like a gangster would stow a gun. Like Dav, she skirted the edge of the room to get to their belongings. She riffled through them until she found the rough sack their food had been lowered in. Hurrying back, she dropped to her knees to use the sack like a broom or dust mop, brushing at the crackling dirt, moving it from the path of the heavy stone. At least three inches of soil had come up where they'd shoved the stone around, so she used the pliers on the all-purpose tool to dig at the packed earth, jabbing it up and scraping it away.

Once he saw what she was doing, Dav retrieved her purse. "Do you have anything else in here that's strong enough to dig with? I could break one of the bottles, but I'd rather not do that yet."

"I have no idea," she said, squatting on her haunches. "Maybe." Rummaging inside, she pulled out her makeup kit, then set it aside. Nothing in there would help. "Credit card?"

"That would work, but it's small. What else?"

She laid out a bottle of nail polish, her wallet, a small comb, a case that held her business cards, an empty cell phone case, and her iPod. "Wonder why they left me my tunes," she said, baffled.

His gaze sharpened on the item. "That's weird. At least you can put the tunes on, block out the noise while we work," he offered.

"Good idea," she said, "but no. If you have to listen to it, I do too." She surveyed the pile on the floor in front of her. "I may have some matches in one of the zipper pockets."

"Really?" That seemed to excite him. "Those might be useful. Could you see?"

"Sure."

"Meanwhile, I think I will destroy your card case," he said with whimsical humor. "It seems to be the only metal thing here that might be large enough."

He opened the silver case and slid her cards free, tidily tucking them in an inside pocket on her purse. She had opened the zippered part, and he neatly zipped it closed. When she looked at him, he smiled. "You never know, we may need the paper."

Shaking her head, she laughed. "Save everything, right?"

"Right." He was watching her intently, that smile still playing about his firm lips. She saw the change in his eyes, saw the moment he saw her again, as a woman. As Carrie. It was thrilling to see the intensity rise in his features, heat his gaze. With sudden passion, he leaned in, kissed her deeply. "Carrie," he began, but she stopped him, pressing a dusty hand to his cheek.

"Shhhh. Don't say anything you'll regret, Dav."

He shook his head, began to speak. "No," she stopped him again, laying a dusty, gritty finger on his lips. "There's time enough to say whatever you need to say when we're out of here. Deal?"

With another quicksilver turn of emotion, he smiled again. "Deal. Remember," he said as he turned back to his work. "I am very good at deals."

Laughing, she unzipped the innermost pocket and hit paydirt. "Hey, I was right!" she said, pulling out not one, but two books of matches.

"So," he said, using the unfolded card case to chip away at the cement-hard dirt. "You collect matches?"

"No, but sometimes, if I like a restaurant, I'll pick them up so I can remember the name of it, have the number."

"Ah," was his only comment.

She went back to poking into the dirt with her all-purpose tool. "What does that mean?" she asked, copying his inflection and tone, "ah?"

"Nothing, just a response to your explanation."

"Uh-huh."

They worked hard for over an hour, dripping sweat from the humidity and their exertions, to loosen the debris blocking the door. Using their hands, they scooped it aside.

"Ready to try again?" he asked, rising and holding his hand out to help her do the same.

"Yep. Let's. Then we should eat again. Are we going to try to go through this afternoon?"

For the first time in hours, Dav looked toward the grate. Carrie resolutely kept her eyes on the wall. She didn't want to see the vulture's handiwork. As it was, she saw Dav's face change, his eyes go hard and distant.

"It's getting pretty late. I think we worked past noon. I'd guess it's around two or three. Yes?"

She sighed and dug her watch out of her pocket. The strap had broken so she'd stowed it away. She knew he was dreading the tunnel or cave or whatever it was. She was too, but if there was any chance it led out, she was willing to risk it.

"It's three fifteen, California time." She hesitated, then added, "I think we should go for it."

"Go for it?" Dav said, trying to slow the beating of his heart, trying to face the prospect of the endlessly dark tunnel and the potential for freedom that it offered. "Yes. I believe we must."

"Okay. I'll get our stuff."

Dav stayed where he was, gathering his courage just as she was gathering their things. He knew it was weak, but if he was to get through this, whatever *this* was, he was going to need every ounce of energy and fortitude he could muster.

"Ready?"

"No, but if we wait for that, we'll be a hundred years dead, to borrow your phrase from the other day."

She smiled and held out a hand. He took it and stood, but didn't yet move forward. "Okay. So, you know a little about this culture. Will there be booby traps?"

"Ah, *Indiana Jones* again?"

"Well," he said with a wry smile, "better to ask the question now."

"I think we should watch our step; they did do shafts. They weren't necessarily traps. Some people think the shafts were ways to talk to the underworld."

"Not the way I want to meet Hades, thanks," he managed, feeling sweat tracking down his back.

He turned to her. "Okay, let's be as logical as I'm able to be right now."

"I'm sorry this is so hard," she said, sympathy in her eyes.

"The alternative is the gibbering we spoke of. So. I will

take my coat and make a pack of it. You take your purse, wrap it across your body." He studiously ignored the looming shadows of the chamber, the equally dark opening of the tunnel.

They'd miraculously found it. He wouldn't pass up the chance to get Carrie to safety. Nothing was more important, no matter how much he'd like to sit, rocking in a corner as he had when he was a boy. "We'll go slowly. Feel our way, yes?"

"Sounds like a plan."

"Eh-la, good. So, I will lead. If anyone is to fall into a shaft, I will do that. Perhaps Hades will take pity on me, eh?" He knew his accent was getting more pronounced, and his fingers felt thick and clumsy as he made up the pack.

He could do this. He had to do it. Everything he was, everything he believed about himself, would be for naught if he couldn't find the courage to face that tunnel.

"Okay. So. Now," he said, dusting off his filthy hands and taking up the pack and setting it on his shoulders. "We will go."

He held out his hand for hers, but to his surprise, she moved past it and embraced him.

"Thank you," she said, her voice muffled in his shirt.

He held her in his arms, feeling emotion swamp him. It overwhelmed him. His heart hurt with it and he ached even more that he couldn't wave a hand and make this all disappear. For her.

He realized that fear for her outweighed any fear he had for himself. The banked fires of passion were there as well. He'd never felt this way about anyone before.

It was a strange way to begin a perilous journey, with such a revelation. It would probably mean more if he could define what it was he was feeling. Admiration? He knew he admired her. This went deeper than that. Need? That was part of it too.

He felt tears dampen his already wet shirt and he held

her more tightly. "Come, my love. You will be Persephone, the beautiful young thing, and I will play Hades in our little drama, taking you into the dark, only to lead you back out again, eh?"

"Promises, promises," she sniffled, ducking her head and using her sleeve to wipe at her eyes.

"Ah, now, you have made it worse." He smiled down at her. Her face was a mask of dust and sweat. And still, he felt the stirring within him, that alien sense that called him to her. From the depths of his pocket, he pulled out his bedraggled handkerchief. It was much the worse for wear, but it wasn't nearly as dirty as her sleeves. Or his, for that matter. With utmost care, he used the cleanest corner to wipe her cheeks where the tears had tracked through the dirt. "There. It is not good, but it is better than it might have been. Let us go before I lose my nerve, eh?"

"Okay." She offered him a watery smile. It was obvious from her deliberate attempt to square her shoulders and the deep breath that lifted her chest that she was nervous as well. "Okay," she said again, as if to encourage them both. "You have the flashlight?"

"Right here. I think you should take it. I will use my hands and feet to feel the way." He struggled to remember all Gates's lessons, all the little bits of information his friend had dropped along the way about moving in enemy territory, moving with caution among land mines and traps. "If you need to shine the light anywhere but at our feet, we stop, yes?"

"Why?"

"So we don't stumble forward into something when we are distracted. Gates has said that it is the distractions that kill, not the land mines."

"Ooookay," she drawled, taking the flashlight and switching it on. "That's reassuring."

He laughed. "Many things Gates has to say are like that. Informative, but not always easy."

For a moment, he stared into the dark, thinking of Gates. It made him remember the weapon that loomed above them.

"Carrie, I hate to say this, to ask it, but before we go into the tunnel, I think we should try and get the guard's weapon." He knew what he was asking. She would have to stand on his shoulders again, cut the weapon free, since he couldn't reach it himself. She could not bear his weight on her shoulders so he could do it and spare her the sight of the vultures' feasting. "As horrible as it will be, it will be better to be armed than not."

She shuddered, a visible, reflexive expression of revulsion. "I know you're right. I know it. I think it's smart. I just don't want to do it. It's . . . horrible."

"Yes, it is. I do not wish to ask this of you. However, if our tunnel does lead somewhere, and sets us free, to be unarmed against those who hunt us, when we have access to a weapon? That is unwise."

Her tear-streaked face was taut, her lips twisted in anxiety. He wanted to pet and soothe her, to kiss it away, make it better, but he couldn't and that was killing him.

Watching her conquer her disgust, knowing the courage it took to face their choices, made his heart hurt for her. "I will lift you again, yes? You only have to look up enough to find the strap and cut it. If you cut it, one tug should free the weapon."

"It's a machine gun," she said, setting her things aside as she steeled herself to make the climb onto his shoulders. "I'm guessing that we don't want to drop it, right?"

He smiled. Trust her to think of that. "No. The safety is off. He fired as he went down, so it is primed for use. I don't know how many rounds are in the magazine, but there will be some still left or I wouldn't ask this of you."

"Rounds in the magazine? Does that mean bullets?"

He laughed, and it eased the tension for a moment. "Yes, it does. You see? I have been hanging out with bad sorts, like

Gates, to know all that. I don't particularly like guns, but for safety's sake, I learned to use them."

"He taught you a lot," she said, holding her hands out for his, waiting for him to bend his knee and let her climb onto his shoulders. Having done it several times now, they managed it in one smooth maneuver. The edge of the door helped as well, where it had pivoted into the room, giving her a prop to lean on. "Can I just say that I really, really, *really* don't want to do this?"

"Yes, you may. I'm sorry to ask it of you."

"Yeah, yeah. Just because I can't lift you, right? Hand me the snips. I only want to do this once."

He handed her the all-purpose tool with the blades set to scissors. He could hear the crisp *schrrrup* sound as she cut through the canvas strap.

"It's stuck," she said, her voice choked. "I'm trying not to throw up here, but if anything falls off this guy or gets on me when I pull this strap loose, I'm going to hurl." He heard her gulping against nausea. "Fair warning."

"Fairly warned," he replied, struggling to keep her steady.

"Oh, *gross,*" she muttered, and he heard the slither of fabric and her grunt as the weight of the weapon landed in her hands. "It's disgusting. I hope it'll still fire with all this . . . nastiness on it."

"I'm sure it will." He held up a hand, still bracing her with the other, to help her down. Instead, she slapped the gun into his palm.

"Here, you take it. You know how to use it, right? So you get to clean it up." His quads were screaming with strain, but he squatted to lay the weapon on the dirt floor, well clear of the blood pool, so he could help her down.

"Is this like the fishes? I have heard this from other men—if you catch it you have to clean it?"

She leapt down from his knee and turned to bury her face in his chest once more. He held her tightly, savoring the contact, knowing it would help them both just to hang on. His body, always responsive to her nearness, reacted, but he ignored it. Now was not the time. "My brave Carrie-mou," he murmured, laying his beard-roughened cheek on her silky hair. "Thank you."

"Yeah, yeah," she said, and he felt the race of reaction in her body. "If I never have to do that again?"

"Centuries too soon, yes?" he finished the quote.

"Millenniums. Eons too soon. Ugh. And yes, you can clean the fish."

"Oh, no," he quipped. "This would be why I am rich. I will pay people to clean the fish or I will go hungry. Besides, I don't really like fish."

"I like the sound of that. Of course, right now, I think we'd both take fish raw and wiggling if we had it."

"True." He took his disgusting handkerchief, ready to wipe away the worst of the blood and gore off the weapon. "Why don't you go over by the door? I will clean this, yes?"

She nodded, and when she'd moved away, he began. He wiped it as best he could, the blood flaking away where it had caked on. As he'd been taught, he checked the trigger and magazine for blockage, but he couldn't be sure it would fire with all the dampness to which it had been exposed. He flicked the safety on and tied the remains of the strap back to the front D-ring as best he could.

The room was darkening as the sun angled toward the west. Dav finished his grim task, and slung the weapon over his shoulder. Turning, he faced the tunnel. "I suppose it is now or never, my Carrie. Are you with me?"

"Let's do it."

Chapter 11

Dav took a deep breath and started into the tunnel. The light wobbled, then steadied, and he could feel the warmth of Carrie's presence at his back. Two steps in, she wrapped her fingers in the loop of his belt. Somehow, the contact was reassuring, bracing. The palpable connection made the dark less horrifying.

Their progress was agonizingly slow. They moved forward a yard at a time, with Dav clearing cobwebs and possibly worse from their path. He estimated they'd been at it an hour, possibly two, when he felt a touch of cooler air on his sweat-soaked arm. He'd reached out to snag a hanging rope of nasty, dusty creeper—possibly a cobweb, but if it was he didn't want to meet the spider. Carrie's mention of Shelob, the enormous spider from *The Lord of the Rings,* made him shudder in memory.

"Dav?"

"I feel a draft," he said, excusing the shudder.

"Stop then," she said, tugging on his belt. "Let's look around."

They stopped and Dav put one hand on the wall at his right, making sure he was anchored where he stood.

"Okay," he said, feeling her move up next to him. "Flash

it around, baby," he said with false cheer and a Vegas smooth talker's drawl. He hoped it would get a laugh out of her, and it did. A weak one, but a laugh, nevertheless.

"Sure, slick, I'll flash it around," she joked back. He felt her stabilize herself the way they'd discussed, and she moved the flashlight to the floor on the right, then out three or four feet. The dirt was packed down, the wall rough at the base with a smooth line about four feet up the wall as she moved the light up it.

"I guess this is where you run your hand along the wall," she murmured, "as you hurry along the passage."

"Hmmm, yes. Keep going up the wall. I felt the draft when my hand was up."

She ran the flashlight up, and at first it showed only more rough wall and dirt. As the light rose higher, however, there was an empty space that went on, up and up into the dark clarity of the night sky.

"Switch off the light for a moment," Dav said, clenching his gut at the thought of the endless darkness. Nevertheless, it was important to discover if they could see out the shaft.

The inky black was completely unrelieved when she clicked off the light. Faintly, far above, he could discern stars.

"I see stars," she said, moving closer to him, even though her hand was still linked through his belt. He felt her all along his body, a warm, supportive presence.

Had he ever had such support in his life? From anyone?

"It's a hole to the surface," he said, smiling into the dark.

"Good. Holes to the surface are good. One that's a bit more accessible would be better, but we'll take it as a good sign, right?"

"Right. Switch the light back on before the gibbering begins."

"Always with the gibbering." She put on a fake New York accent and punched the button on the flashlight. They both waited to let their eyes adjust. She raised the beam to the edge of the shaft and then moved it on down the ceiling. Nothing but more webs and more darkness beyond them.

"This is slow going, but it is progress, I guess," he commented, beginning the forward process again. Step, feel the way; step, clear the cobwebs and creepers, step again.

"It's a nasty job, but it's better than sitting in the cell waiting to die," Carrie pointed out. "I don't think I could have taken that much longer without doing some gibbering myself."

He smiled, though he knew she couldn't see it. "I'm glad we avoided that. It's so embarrassing for both of us, yes?"

"Exactly," she joked. "Nothing like a little abject terror to put you off your feed for a week or two."

"Off your feed?"

"Farm term," she explained. "If something spooks cows or horses very badly, they stop eating for a bit. If they don't eat, they don't gain weight, and in the case of cows, that's less beef."

"Oh. That makes sense in a mercantile kind of way," he said, trying not to think about the continuing slow pace.

All of a sudden his forward foot met clear air and he shoved backward, knocking them both into the wall.

"What? What is it?" She gasped the words, bobbling the flashlight.

His heart was pounding as if he'd run a mile, but he said, "I believe I found the first of the shafts to hell."

"Oh, crap," she said, angling the light to the floor only to have it disappear into the endless darkness of a deep pit. The shaft was only two feet wide, easily stepped over, but the yawning maw would trap the unwary and a running man or woman, or even one inching along in the darkness would drop down, breaking a leg, or falling in to be wedged there for all eternity.

"I think I need to sit down," Dav managed, his heart racing, and sweat pouring from him as he contemplated the terrible consequences of a foot wrongly placed.

"No," Carrie disagreed. "We have to get past it, then we'll rest. The longer we stay here in the dark with that before us, the worse it will be." He heard the quaver in her voice, and made sense of the words, but it was like a buzzing in his ears, a ringing that wouldn't stop.

"I don't think I can," he said.

"You made your first million before you left college," Carrie insisted. "You can do this."

She tugged at his arm, pulling him upright. He'd bent over, hands on his knees to pant out his fear.

"One step at a time," she said through gritted teeth. "This one's just a bigger step, right?"

He thought his lungs would burst, or his heart would explode with fear of crossing the pit. Only Carrie's insistence that he move prodded him forward and over it.

"Now," she said, and he heard the exhaustion in her voice. "We rest."

Ten feet beyond the pit shaft, they sat down, their backs to the walls, legs touching. He could feel his knees shaking with reaction and thought hers were, as well. "I think we should drink some," she added, digging into the pack he'd set down next to them. "We're using a lot of energy and the dust is just awful. We need to stay hydrated."

"The way I'm sweating, you'll need a bigger canteen than they provided, Carrie-mou," he managed, eyes closed, head back against the cool stone. He could have easily chugged liters of water and still have been thirsty.

"Here, have at least a few sips," she said, pressing the canteen into his slack hands. She was worried about him; he could hear it in her voice, feel it in the trembling of her hands.

"It is the darkness," he said, knowing that he would pay for shoving his fear down into his gut.

"I know. I don't have the experiences you do and it's getting to me too."

They shared the canteen back and forth, each taking judicious sips until it was half empty.

"We should get moving again," he said, wishing with all his heart that it wasn't true, wishing they could stay put or better yet, be miraculously whisked back to San Francisco. "The longer we stay here, the harder it will be to go on."

"You're right," she said, and he heard fear and resignation. Somehow, her despair was a lifeline for him. It made him know that he could not give up.

Carrie had to live, to be free.

"Up we go then," he said, trying to inject a note of energy in the words. "Come, my love. Somewhere around here, we'll find treasures that will make your gallery owner's heart go pitter pat, yes? Gold and masks, weapons and ceremonial tools, pottery and artifacts galore."

"Sure, sure, promise me the moon," she responded to his feeble attempt to raise her spirits. "I'm sure this was looted long ago."

"Not necessarily," he countered. "May I point out the disgusting state of this passageway as possible proof that it hasn't been discovered or mined or whatever you call it when looters make away with the goods."

"I believe it's just called looting, or raiding," she replied, but he heard the smile. She carefully waved the light back and forth across the floor ahead of him, close, then two feet out, then a bit more, before coming back to do the same thing again as he took a step.

"Ah, the technical term. Perhaps we'll find the treasure trove and we can use that space to rest, sleep and get a fresh start in the morning."

Her hand tightened on his belt. "I don't want to stay down here," she confessed.

"Neither do I, believe me. I am, however, running out of steam, as the saying goes. I wonder where that term comes from?" he asked idly, before continuing. "We left in the late afternoon, yes? As the sun was going down?"

"Not going down quite, but it was after four when we started down the tunnel."

"Yes. And we have been working through this for at least several hours. Though I know time will seem different in the darkness like this, I'm fairly sure that we have been going for a while." It was good to talk, to hear her voice. It kept him grounded. Thinking it through helped too, focusing him on the solutions rather than the dark.

The light flashed ahead of him, then back to his feet. Away again, flickering on the stone, then back to his feet.

When it flashed forward again, it didn't reflect on stone.

"Wait. Stop." He put his arm out to the side, blocking her forward motion. "Run the light along the floor. I think there is another pit."

The beam traveled out four feet, then disappeared. They inched forward to the edge, only to find a step down. A wide circular area about the size of a car lay before them. As Carrie outlined its edges with the light, it reminded him of a trampoline in its perfect circularity.

"This is unusual," he commented, for lack of anything more original to say. "You stay here and hold the light. I will step down and explore this area. This may be a place to stop for the night." He smiled at her in the beam of the light. "It is a larger space, just as you requested, my lady."

Her smile was small and tense. "Be careful, Dav."

"I will do that. Come to the edge and shine the beam ahead."

He sat on the stone, easing his feet over the edge and carefully testing the surface with his weight. It stayed stable and there was no sound of grating or crumbling, so he let his entire weight settle onto the stone circle.

Moving to the left, clockwise, he started around the

circle. Halfway around, his questing hand on the wall met nothingness and he staggered sideways.

"Dav?" Carrie's voice was a half shriek as she saw him fight for balance. "Dav, are you okay?"

"Fine, fine," he said, cursing softly under his breath in Greek. "There is a hole in the wall. Let me come on back around to you, then we will explore, yes?"

There were two more holes in the wall around the circle, but the floor was solid. When he returned to Carrie, he helped her to climb down onto the lower level as well.

"I think we should get some sleep, my flame. If we are tired, we will make mistakes. I think these are tunnel branchings. Perhaps, in the day, some light will come from one of the tunnels, give us a direction to take, yes?"

"I want to keep going," she insisted. "What if there's a way out, just beyond this? What if there's another door?" She stopped suddenly and he heard her draw in a shaky breath. "Oh, my God, Dav, what if it's a dead end?"

"Carrie." He kept his voice firm in the face of her rising panic. "I will not allow you to die. I have told you this, yes? We will find a way out. Now. Come, let us sit down on our stone bed and tell one another stories of our childhoods again. You can tell me your secrets and I will tell you mine."

"I don't think I have any more secrets to tell," Carrie said, the quiver in her voice subsiding a bit. "I'm sure you do, though. Maybe you can tell me the secret to getting rich."

He led her to the center of the ring and knelt, easing her down with him. "Ah, now that is a long story, but a good one. Come, I will tell you."

"Can't be that long a story; you're not that old."

"Older than you, my dear, but thank you."

"I like a good story."

"Oh, it's tedious, but that will help you sleep." He stuffed their belongings behind him, tugged her down so her head was on his chest. It was something he'd thought of, to have her this way, with him, trusting him, but he would give it all up to alter the circumstances. "I will tell you a secret now, if you like."

"Okay."

"Turn off the light and close your eyes, Carrie. Let your mind drift, yes? Let me tell you a story."

"Are you serious?"

"Perfectly."

With obvious reluctance, she pressed the button to turn off the flashlight. The inky blackness surrounded them instantly.

"Once upon a time," he began, and she laughed. "Do not laugh, it is a fairy tale, so it must begin this way, I believe."

"Not laughing," she said, though he could feel her doing just that. He smiled in the darkness and closed his own eyes.

Focusing on the story, he continued. "There was a man and he saw a woman he admired, but she was unavailable. He waited a long time, then suddenly she agreed to lunch. Then the man got the woman in lots and lots of trouble."

"Oh, you did not," she protested. "You're not responsible for this; whoever did it is. Your brother or whatever, not you."

"Thank you for leaping to my defense, Carrie-mou, but this *is* because of me."

"Oh, please. Don't be a martyr. We're in it together," she muttered.

"I was wondering, earlier yesterday, or was it the day before? At the gallery."

"Two days, maybe three. I'm losing track. What were you wondering?"

"If you would think I was a stalker or a"—he searched his mind for the English word—"weirdo, for having thought about dating you for nearly ten years, only to finally do it and get you abducted." He sighed, knowing that no matter what she said, it was his fault.

He felt her hand on his chest, pressure as she levered

herself up to loom over him. He couldn't see her, but he could feel her.

"Let me show you what I think of that," she said. The moment of waiting in the dark was a-tingle with suspense. What was she talking about?

Her mouth closed on his and her hands began to roam over his body, leaving no doubt about what she meant.

Sweaty, dirty and scared they might be, but their attraction for one another hadn't waned in the least. Rising up, he pulled her onto his lap and she straddled him, stripping down fast and pulling his hands to her breasts as she ravaged his lips.

"My beard," he protested, between kisses. "I will scratch your beautiful skin."

"I don't care," she growled, her mouth leaping back to his. She yanked his shirt up and ran her hands over his flesh. Every trial and tribulation forgotten, he feasted on her, reveling in the power and glory of her body, the sheer joy of being alive.

Their coming together was fast and furious, a coupling of heart and mind and body in a blinding flash of passion. Panting, with hot tongues and racing hands, they drove one another to the heights of pleasure.

When she arched back in his hands, crying out, and her body clenched around him, he followed her over the edge with a hoarse roar of completion.

"Carrie!" he cried her name, rocketing his hips upward, leaping to fulfillment as they came together in a blinding, furious explosion.

There in the dark, their murmured words and caresses a luscious aftermath, he knew that he would never let her go.

Niko eased the truck up to the hidden gate at the dig site. Everything was quiet and he motioned Sam to open the gate.

"Stay alert," he warned as he, too, got out of the Jeep, covering his man as Sam dragged the iron gate open, hooking the lock into the ring of the post.

"No worries, compadre," Sam muttered, backwalking to the passenger side door. The two men eased into their seats and Niko let off the brake and slowly proceeded through the gate and down the rough track to the camp.

"Niko!" Sam exclaimed, pointing to a rise of vultures from the edge of the trees where a front sentry would have been posted.

"This is not good." They found the first of their team at the edge of the woods. What was left of him after the animals and birds had been at him, that is.

The rest of the team lay where they had fallen. The clouds of birds and insects surrounding the bodies were a noisy testament to the dreadful manner of their deaths and the speed with which the jungle reclaimed everything.

Walking slowly, and covering one another's backs, Niko and Sam reached the pit. Niko turned over Carlos's body and peered down into the dark hole.

"Davros? Are you down there?"

Nothing answered him. Their presence had scared the vultures into the trees, but the birds were still there, lurking noisily, waiting to resume their feasting.

"Look." Sam pointed down into the hole as he spoke. "There's no one in there."

"Do you think they escaped?" Niko examined the ground around the grate, noting the delicate feminine footprints that only pointed toward the grate, not away from it.

Sam shook his head in the negative. "Nah, one way in, just like you wanted."

"Apparently not," Niko said, spotting the doorway. "They found a way out." He scanned the jungle. "This was an ambush, Sam, but whoever it was didn't come for Dav. They just killed the team. They didn't even come into the camp."

"Agreed. You got an enemy, or we got in someone's territory and didn't know it."

"Yeah, that's what I'm afraid of. Let's back on out of here and call this in, eh?"

"Plan." His answer was monosyllabic, and heartfelt as he backed toward the Jeep.

At the Jeep, they reversed course. Miles up the road, at a slightly higher elevation where they could see the entrance to the road, but not the camp itself, Niko pulled out a satellite phone and made a call.

"No, they weren't there," he said, in response to the question. "I'm going to go in and check, yes, after I get some backup here."

He waited as the word came through that backup could be there in a matter of a few hours.

"Good, we'll wait. My whole team's dead. Yes. Okay." Anger filled him at the thought of his men, all of them loyal, all of them veterans of campaigns with him all over the world. Emergency measures were in effect now, and he'd take all the necessary precautions he and his team had agreed upon. "I'll wait on the signal."

He hung up and turned the Jeep, pointing it back down the way they'd come. "We'll wait here for backup. A few hours, supposedly. You okay with that?"

"Better than being at the clearing, yeah?"

"Yeah. Good. Let's get some rest."

When he hung up the phone, leaving Niko expecting backup, he was smiling. Having isolated the man, separating him from his mercenary troop, then disposing of them, he took the next step in exacting his revenge on all the Gianikopolis men. Now, he would be able to step into Davros's place in the world market, and if Niko came through this, he'd have the older brother as his hit man, a fitting end for both sons of the notorious father.

"Good news," he said to the men who guarded him. "Everything went as planned." He frowned. "With one slight exception. Evidently there *is* a way out of that cell, some kind of doorway in the structure itself." Trust Davros to find it, the lucky son of a bitch. He'd always managed to squeak out of every trap set for him. It was infuriating. "Now we'll see if Niko is cut out to be one of us, permanently, or if he too needs to be culled from the herd."

That Davros had somehow escaped continued to annoy him. He wanted to shoot something, or smash something. Just thinking of killing something, tearing someone or something limb from limb, eased his wrath, so he was able to release the tension with the exercises he'd learned, clenching and unclenching his fists as he thought of pounding them into soft flesh.

Yes. That was better.

Davros was of no matter to him now. There would be nothing for him, in the end. When he found his way out, if he ever did, he would find a bullet waiting. His man was still watching the camp where Niko had found his team. He had reported Niko's movements, so Niko's call had been anticlimactic. After all, he'd arranged the carnage, so he'd had to fake his distress at Niko's losses.

As to Davros, if he didn't emerge, well that was good too. Thinking of Davros, dying in the dark in a hole, further eased his wrath.

"Are you ready to move out?" he asked the leader of his second team. The man's coiled strength was legendary, yet he stood at perfect ease by the ornate doors.

"As ever."

"Then execute the plan."

"With pleasure," the man said, giving a half salute as he turned and left. Without a doubt, he would be in place, his sniper rifle at the ready, when Niko—or Davros—turned up again.

"Make sure the jet is stocked as usual. We leave in twenty minutes." He tossed the order to one of the other men over his shoulder as he too left the room. All would be in order and he would see to this final stage personally.

After all, Belize was so much warmer this time of year than Colorado.

Chapter 12

Staring through the scope of the long rifle, Jurgens could see the bodies where they lay, saw the vultures, saw the Jeep as it arrived and then left. When the men in the Jeep had focused on a body on the far side of the clearing, moving it with care to stare downward, beyond it, they gave him the answer to the riddle.

"A rat in a trap," he murmured, thinking of the elegant Davros Gianikopolis down in a hole. Not good. It had been several days now. He and the woman were either dead or close to it. The three men who had killed the returning team from a distance had not gone into camp, nor had they lingered in the area. He had tracked them back down the road toward Belmopan, losing them as they picked up speed heading away from the scene.

Only one remained, on another hillside, watching the camp just as Jurgens did.

It was a puzzle.

He was certain that if Dav had been visible, the newcomers in the Jeep would have shot him. Instead, they checked the hole, discussed briefly, then backed away, to drive a distance and wait. Jurgens slipped off long enough to find them. The run had done him good after lying so still. When he returned to his hidden nest the other watcher was still there, holding his place, evidently unconcerned about other activities. Killing more watchers was not in his orders then. Davros perhaps, should he come out of the hole, but no one else.

That they were waiting said Davros was still captive, or contained somehow.

He narrowed his eyes, thinking. He'd done his research on the Gianikopolis family. In this generation, there were only the two brothers, Davros and Niko. He guessed, from the look of him, that the man in the Jeep had been the older one. Niko.

"Lazarus risen," he muttered, tapping a note into a small device, under the cover of his camouflage. Something had troubled him about the job offer long before he'd discussed it with Caroline and chosen to refuse it. Once they'd refused and he'd set about protecting Davros, both he and Caroline had continued to dig.

Far away from home, on borrowed equipment untraceable to him, Jurgens had begun to track the man who'd wanted Davros dead. That man was an unknown, a cloaked piece on a chessboard littered with deceit and death.

The hidden player had a high stake in this. Worse, he was manipulating the game to an end Jurgens had yet to uncover. Evidence of his deceit lay rotting in the intense sunlight. Niko's presence, his waiting stance said even more, at least to Jurgens.

Play within play. Game within game. And, he believed, for Niko, betrayal.

Everything about the killing in the clearing, Niko's arrival and easy departure said: *setup.*

Someone had positioned the older Gianikopolis brother to capture the younger and was now playing an incredibly dangerous and delicate game of cat and mouse with the older brother. And Niko seemed unaware he was being played.

None of the maneuvering boded well for Davros. Not at all.

When night fell, as it was rapidly doing, he would contact Caroline. She was continuing the search. It was her special gift, research. The information she could find astounded him, every day.

She astounded him.

A flicker of movement caught his attention and he focused through the scope once more. Two men crept through the thick brush, coming up from the road in a shifting, careful pattern. They carried military-style gear and were heavily camouflaged, just as he was. He saw no markings on their clothing, no indication of their loyalties. They worked quickly, laying a trail of land mines on the road into the compound.

If Niko were to return, neither he nor his friend in the Jeep would leave.

This told him they were not Dav's men, nor did they work for Gates Bromley or his woman.

The shadow player, perhaps.

Not good. Too many forces at odds. Too many pieces on the chessboard.

He continued to watch, unwilling to shift the balance yet. He gritted his teeth when the men turned to the hole as well, having finished with their work at the road. They crept over to the same place Niko had, but they were more intent. When they aimed their weapons downward, he could see both night-scopes and suppressors. Shifting to his work, Jurgens sighed, focused and let out a long, slow breath.

Idiots.

He squeezed the trigger, once, then twice. Pivoting fast, he shot again, taking out the sniper who had been watching the camp as intently as he had. The fact that that watcher hadn't shot meant he worked with these men, therefore he had to be taken off the chessboard.

The mines were not in his purview, but he could prevent the direct murder of Dav and his woman, should they still be alive.

The men fell where they stood, crumpling to the ground. He felt the usual rush of elation as he exercised his skills. The shots were perfectly placed; death had been instantaneous. His shots had been exact enough that neither weapon had discharged.

Now, he would contact his Caroline.

She would no doubt shed some light on the shadows. And they could talk about chess.

Gates jerked in surprise as an e-mail pinged his inbox. It was marked URGENT! And it was from the Agency.

He opened it as Ana answered a call on the house phone, directed to her. Perhaps the Agency was doubling their efforts. He heard her murmured conversation as a background lilt, as he shifted over from his running program to the e-mail server.

They had convened the team at Dav's estate. The Agency must have tracked her here.

He opened the e-mail, finished reading it just as Ana set the phone down. In her stillness, she vibrated with tension, distracting him from the e-mail. They'd been waiting for the package to arrive with proof of life. The ransom was ready to transfer from one account to the designated one the kidnappers had given them. They were trying to dig up more leads in the meantime.

"Did you get the same intel?" he demanded. "South America? There's a lead in Argentina."

She shook her head in the negative, a mute disagreement.

Her inability to speak shocked him and Gates leapt to his feet to go to her.

"What? What is it?" he demanded, a hand on her arm. "They're not dead." He knew they weren't dead, but his heart sank anyway at her refusal to answer.

"No. They're not. That was about a location. It was . . . help." Ana said the words slowly, as if feeling her way to them, which was odd.

"Who? Agency? Where? Why?" He shot the questions at her.

"No, not Agency, and not South America. As to the *who,* I'm not sure."

"Not sure? What? A trace," he began.

"No, she anticipated that, and said it wouldn't work."

"She? Who is she and why are you considering this?" He knew she had reasons. She wasn't as good as she was at their business without good reason and without good instincts.

"Short answer is she's helping because Dav helped her pull off something huge." She stopped, looked him in the eye. "I think it's legit. He's in Central America," she said, answering the questions out of order.

"Agency says South America," Gates answered her, tension singing in every fiber of his being. "They have leads. Solid ones."

She nodded, this time in agreement. "I know. They're wrong."

He ran a hand through his hair and paced. Pacing let the frustration out, helped him think. "Okay. Okay. Lay it out. Tell me why you think this is legit."

"She found me," Ana said with a puzzled shrug. "Here. At this number. Unlisted and untraceable. And I don't live here."

"Could be the kidnapper," Gates said at once, calculating the odds. "They have some pretty sick skills to pull this off. Pretty easy to get a phone number, comparatively."

"No. No mention of the ransom demand, nothing about

the account in the Caymans and the money there, no hesitation in her voice. Calm, but quick. Sure." Ana detailed the sense of the call; the very calmness with which the information was delivered had led her to "profile" the person. "She had nothing to hide," Ana continued, "and nothing more to ask or offer. Just a direction."

"A mislead."

"A mislead would give us more, not less," Ana argued.

He thought about it, checked his gut. When his gut agreed with Ana, he slapped his computer shut.

"Pack gear." Gates shouted the order over his shoulder.

Georgiade was coming down the hallway toward them. He pivoted where he stood and started toward the security quarters at a trot.

Another shout from Gates stopped him, momentarily. "Full field outlay, night ops packs and weapons."

Georgiade nodded and hurried on. Gates knew everyone would spring into action and be ready to go before an hour was out. "Where in Central America?" he said, turning back to Ana.

"Belize," Ana snapped out the answer as she snatched the phone back out of its cradle. "I've got to get on the phone to the Agency. We need a smooth path, embassy help. We're gonna need clearance to go in on search and rescue."

"They aren't going to like you disagreeing with their analysis."

"I'm not going to tell them how scanty the lead is," she snapped, defensive because she was going on her gut, asking him and all the team to trust that her instincts were correct.

He waited through the long tense minutes as she contacted the people who could help them. He listened with only partial attention as he simultaneously made mental lists, revising and shifting what gear they should take as he thought of scenarios.

"We're good to go," she said, clicking off the phone. "Let's move."

"Dogs?" he asked as they hurried down the hall after Georgiade.

"Yes," she said, then saved her breath to run.

They got to the security area within minutes. The team was gearing up with an efficiency that made him proud. When he saw them, Franklin left his pack, coming to them.

"We takin' the dogs?"

"Yes," he said, and Franklin grinned.

Ana panted out a further order. "Make sure they've got that stuff on them, the flea stuff. That's all the Belize people asked for."

"Done," Franklin replied, heading out of the room at a run. He'd gather his best dogs and be back, Gates knew, probably before the others had time to figure out which boots to wear. Franklin had been on this kind of op before and kept a bag packed and the dogs ready.

Ana turned and left the room as well, and Gates knew she'd be sorting through their gear in the car, making up packs that would go with them.

"Who's staying here?" Callahan asked. Her hard gaze dared him to say it was her.

"New guy, Geddey. He's coming in early. He'll keep things tight here while we go hunting."

"Ana?" Royce asked. He was by his locker, and never looked up from the task of strapping a clutch piece on his leg.

"Arming up and loading the plane."

"Feebs comin'?" Damon wanted to know. He wasn't going, with his injuries still healing. He'd get Geddey whatever he needed, and keep watch on Declan.

"Clearing the path for us, but they won't be on the plane," Gates answered for Ana, his hands busy zipping a pack as one of the new members of the team, Holden, zipped another.

"Landscape with Apaches," Holden muttered.

"What's that mean, Holden?" Callahan demanded.

"Like that old painting. They'll be there, probably," Holden said, shifting to face her. "But nobody'll see 'em where they're hiding."

"Agency too, but we won't see them, either," Royce muttered.

They all looked at Gates and he nodded. He didn't say a word. They were right, but he couldn't and wouldn't confirm. With this late knowledge, all of the agencies would have difficulty keeping up with them, but they had people in place inside most of the Central American countries. Someone would be there unofficially.

"Let's keep moving," he said curtly. "We need to head out."

Gates hauled gear and arranged it in the SUV. He was still waiting to find out about Ana's contact. But with that, and his own equipment now humming with various searches and algorithms, he was digging out a web of transactions. The flights and the country had begun to hint not only to Belize but to a man.

A mastermind.

A shadow.

He'd begun forwarding data, and the Agency was interested, but only if they could be sure there was no blowback on them. They had little or nothing on the man in question, and nothing that pointed to a grudge of this magnitude against Dav.

With so little data to go on, they were unwilling to act overtly.

Gates had no such compunction. If there was a chance, even the slimmest, slightest chance that Dav was in Belize, he was going. If Ana's contact—and he still needed to hear more about that phone call—was to be trusted, Belize was the place. He'd sent the yacht to the Gulf already. Now, with more intel, he shot off an e-mail that would have the yacht meeting them in Punta Gorda. He wanted a haven for Dav and Carrie if they found them alive. They couldn't be taken to a hospital in Belize. The media would be all over that, and so would Niko if he was their kidnapper.

To bring them home safely, private transportation was the only way, so he made sure it was available.

If they were right about this shadow enemy, then they were flying blind. Not knowing left them unprepared for matching any subsequent actions if they got Dav out alive in the first place.

Meanwhile the private lab with the ransom materials, including the hair and the gold chain and locket, would forward results to Gates, Geddey and the various agencies as soon as they came through. The lab was being paid handsomely for putting everything through immediately, and it had promised results. He hoped that something in the box, on the hair or materials or the letter, would lead back to the mastermind, to someone who could be held accountable. He seriously wanted someone to pay, and pay dearly for taking his friend.

"Fifteen minutes, be ready to roll," he said, sticking his head into the team's locker room. He didn't wait for an assent before leaving the room to pack the last of his own gear. There was enough on the estate that he could utilize; he'd bought it for Dav and the team, after all. Ana already had their personal gear sorted, he'd add some extra firepower to it.

When they landed at Goldson International Airport in Belize City, there were two cars waiting for them, along with three large black SUVs, their windows tinted both for privacy and to ward off the tropical sun. It was barely into April and he could feel the humidity weighting the air. Off to the side, Gates spotted the two motorcycles he'd requested. As the jet taxied to a stop near general aviation, a man stepped out of a dark blue Mercedes sedan. Ana's CIA contact.

Gates watched as Ana went down the plane's steps and approached him. They shook hands. Even watching for the exchange, Gates nearly missed it. He knew there would be keys, but whatever other items were passed over put a look of intense excitement on his wife's face.

She hustled back onto the plane and demanded a laptop.

"Quick, quick," she said, waiting impatiently for the computer to boot up. She inserted a portable thumb drive and began flicking keys.

Maps, satellite images, road markers, and a series of codes marked with cryptic names popped up on the screen as she opened the files.

"Printer?"

"Check the list, should be *EleniOne,* for this jet."

"Got it," she said, and was already printing files before they finished the exchange. Gathering the packets, she pulled the drive and strung it on one of the key rings. She passed that one to Gates. "Anything happens to me, make sure that disappears."

"Right. Where are we headed?" Gates asked, snagging a gear bag as he followed her out to the tarmac.

"Small airport, south and west of Belmopan. That's the capital," she replied, pulling open the door to the Suburban.

Two of their team stepped up, strapping on motorcycle helmets. Gates gave them their direction, and Ana walked with them to the bikes, her animated hand motions indicative of whatever plan she was imparting.

"I thought Belize City was the capital." Callahan put on her shades, got into the backseat of the same vehicle. "It's the only city I know the name of, and isn't the major airport usually in the capital?"

"'Was' being the operative word in terms of the capital,"

Holden said as he got in the backseat on the other side, behind Gates. "A hurricane wiped most of the city off the map in nineteen sixty-one. They retired the name of Hurricane Hattie after that one. Relocated the capital inland, named it Belmopan."

"And you know this because?" Callahan asked the question, but Gates was listening. It was always good to know about your team. Even if they weren't your team anymore.

"I'm a weather nerd," Holden answered with a sunny smile. "Used to chase tornadoes in high school."

Callahan slumped down in the seat, getting comfortable. She'd once told Gates she could sleep anywhere at any time, and did, knowing that in their line of work you sometimes had to go without it for long stretches.

"Explains a lot," she muttered.

"What?" Holden stared at her. When she didn't answer he looked toward the front, meeting Gates's eyes in the rearview mirror. To Gates's surprise, he grinned. "Hey, it was something to do."

Grinning back, Gates nodded, then focused on the road. It was going to be a long drive on roads that weren't as well maintained as U.S. roads, nor as wide.

"Let's do it," Ana said impatiently, giving him a pointed look. He could tell she was amused by the discussions as well, but her anxiety won out.

"Right. On it," he said, gunning the engine.

"We're disgustingly dirty," Carrie muttered, hours later when they woke. "And I do mean disgusting."

Since he felt grimy and sweaty, he didn't disagree. He was used to hot showers and clean clothes, like most, and having to live in the same clothes for days on end did qualify as disgusting.

"I think showers would be a great improvement to a place

like this, underground palace that it is. We must speak to the management," he said, struggling to wake up and force himself to get moving. He loved having her there, spooned next to him, small and flexible and beautiful, even in the dark.

"Hmmm, yes, if they weren't so long-dead, it would be a good complaint. However, since I don't think showers were invented when people were last here, I'm guessing they wouldn't care to hear it. Besides, I think they beheaded trespassers."

"Unpleasant thought," he muttered, pressing a kiss to the back of her neck. "I know we should get moving, but I'm not eager to get up. My body is saying we just went to sleep a minute ago."

"Mine too, but that can't be right. I can see a little bit of light, way up above us."

Now that she mentioned it, he could see it too, a small round, bright spot. When he looked across the floor of the open area, he spied a soccer ball–sized circle of golden light. Not enough to illuminate the area, just enough to alleviate the unremitting blackness.

"It's nice to see it," he said, "but it doesn't help us much."

"No, not really. But maybe this will." She sat up, though she still stayed next to him. He heard the rustling of their belongings and a snick of sound as she opened something. She tilted the mirror this way and that until she got the right angle, then, using the mirror to spread the light, she illuminated a section of the wall.

Slowly turning the mirror, she played the light along the curve, stopping at the first doorway. It was more of a hole, a broad, black hole. He could probably squeeze his shoulders through it, but not by much.

Carrie resumed her turning, only to stop when the reflected light hit the second hole. When the light penetrated the opening, they immediately spotted rubble. At some point, that path had caved in. He immediately found himself praying that it wasn't the only way out.

"Oh, God, I hope that wasn't the exit," Carrie echoed his thought as she continued the turn. The third hole was just as dark and narrow as the first, but it was taller, more like a door than a window.

"I think we should try that way first," Dav said, hoping it was the right path. He was having enough trouble with the dark. Squeezing through tight spaces made the journey even more unpleasant.

"That seems logical," Carrie agreed. "Let's get moving. I think some of our sluggishness is due to hunger and thirst. The sooner we go, the sooner we get out."

"From your mouth to God's ear." He muttered the old saying, just as popular in Greece as it was in America.

Carrie stood, and so did he. "I think I will have to carry our makeshift knapsack by hand, rather than on my back. The passage looked very narrow to me."

"I think you're right. I'm going to turn on the flashlight, okay?"

"Good. Let's go."

Two hours of scraping and crawling and pressing through narrowing tunnel walls found them at a dead end. The tunnel's terminus was as round as the area in which they'd spent the night, but littered with old, small bones, like those of rodents or small animals.

"Oh, Dav." Carrie wept his name as she sat down on the bone-littered floor with a thump. "Are we mad? Are we going to wander in here until we just fall down and die?"

He wanted to slump down with her. He even wondered the same thing, but if they both gave in to the despair, they *would* die. So he continued to stand, determined that he would find a way to get them out.

"No. We are going to go back to the round, and take the other tunnel. We will see where it leads."

"I don't think I can make it." She said it flatly, with

the calm that came from sheer exhaustion and the dejection that failure brought in its wake.

"You can and you will. As will I. What was it you said? About life and hope?"

"While there's life, there's hope," she answered wearily.

"Then let us drink the other half of the canteen and go back. We know there are no pits in the tunnel, so we will use the light sparingly."

"Feel our way?" She shuddered. "I'm not sure I can do that either."

"Better than wasting the light." Dav was certain that if the light failed, he would not be able to move a muscle. Even if they could find materials for a torch, use the matches they had, he still might not make it. He wondered if he should tell her that.

No. They were both too close to the end of their physical and emotional resources as it was. He didn't want to think about the light failing. At all.

"Okay," she sighed, and got up, fumbling through the pack he'd laid down for the last canteen. When they'd shared it out, they started back. The return trip seemed longer, darker and narrower than it had before. Only the knowledge that Carrie was behind him, and that her survival was his highest desire, kept Dav moving.

As it was, he was so distracted by the sound of her panting breath and worrying about her that he fell out of the tunnel when they reached the end.

"Aaaahhhh," he cried, trying to turn the fall into a roll, trying to protect his hands and face. He was only partly successful.

His ears rang as his head hit the stone, and he heard the crack as one of his fingers bent back when he landed on it incorrectly. He felt the hot tear of flesh and the wet pulse of blood as the bone sliced through the skin.

Chapter 13

"Sir?" The flight attendant knew the penalty for waking her boss, but the penalty for his missing a call from an associate was usually worse.

Usually.

She waited a heartbeat and spoke again, a bit louder. "Sir, you have a call from your specialist."

He sat up so abruptly she gasped. Regaining her equilibrium as quickly as she could, she presented the satellite phone on a tray.

He glared at her, but evidently this was one of those times when missing the call was the worse choice. He took up the phone and spoke.

"You're in place?"

"Yessir."

"Have you seen anyone?"

"The older one, his pal. No sign of the younger, or the girl."

A simple code, but effective. They both knew who they were talking about. "Then stay on wait-and-watch. If it looks like he's pulling out, going under—you know what to do."

"Yessir. And the woman and her man?"

"Same goes." *Kill them all.*

"Understood."

He hung up and handed the phone to the flight attendant. "Thank you, Marjorie. Please bring me something light to eat, perhaps a glass of white wine. A mineral water."

"Of course, sir. Would you like the *Wall Street Journal* as well? We picked it up before we left."

"That would be lovely. Thank you." He turned and looked out the window, studying the clouds, thinking how wonderful it felt to see long-term plans coming to fruition. Interestingly enough, it wasn't as much of an issue now, if either of the men died. They had been stripped of their status.

Their humanity, their ethos—one disgustingly honest, the other determinedly criminal—was broken. The thought of Davros stuck in a cell or a cave with the woman he'd lusted after for so long but wouldn't touch . . . ahhhh, priceless.

"It's better, really. Knowing they're doomed," he murmured to the clouds. "It's been a long time coming, waiting for them to grow up, doomed children of a bastard father."

"Beg pardon, sir?" Marjorie was back, her tray holding a light salad, an elegant quiche on china with a beautiful golden wine in a crystal goblet.

"Nothing, nothing." He smiled at her, thinking she would never understand the joke, the sheer deliciousness of it. "Just appreciating the view. This looks good. Thank you. Ah, and the *Journal* as well. Good. Well done."

She soaked up his praise like a dry sponge; he could see her cheeks flush and her eyes sparkle. "Thank you, sir. If there's anything else?" she asked hopefully.

He waved her away. "No, no. Just peace and quiet to read the *Journal* you've so efficiently procured me."

"Very good, sir. Ring if you need me."

He waved her away, but with a smile. It was always good to acknowledge superb service. Marjorie was excellent at her job.

He worked solidly through the meal, smiling the entire

time, thinking of Dav, trapped with his frigid female, pining for her, but unable to break through. It was such a terrible torture that he chuckled out loud. They were making his revenge so easy, so thrilling, he was almost sorry to end it.

Almost.

The curses flew in four languages as he huddled on the floor cradling his hand. He covered it, gripping it hard to clamp the pain and bleeding. He didn't want Carrie to see the sheared end protruding through his flesh. It was severely broken, that was obvious. A compound fracture. Carrie was calling out to him, but he didn't want her to see the break, so he followed his first impulse and with one strong jerk, he pulled the finger straight.

Agonizing pain shot through him and blurred his vision to black. His sight wavered in and out as he gripped his fingers, pressing them together to apply pressure. Nausea threatened to choke him.

"Dav? Dav? Are you bleeding? Where are you hurt?" Carrie's hands were a flash over his body, and he moaned when she touched the side of his head.

"Oh, my God, did you hit your head?"

"Yes, a bit, but I broke my finger when I landed." He ground out the words, fighting back the blackness and the pain. "It is all right, Carrie-mou. I am not bleeding badly, nor am I likely to die from these stupid mistakes." He might not die, but he surely was in pain. The grating when he'd straightened the finger told him that he'd probably fractured other pieces of the bone as well.

She huffed out a breath, but he couldn't tell if it was pique or relief. "What the hell were you doing?"

"Finding the end of the tunnel," he managed, blocking out the waves of blackness as he shifted his jaw, ran his tongue over his teeth, and gingerly stretched his neck to one side and then the other, checking for other injuries. When no sharp pains or twinges followed the action, he sighed with relief. Stupid he had been, but not mortally so, he hoped.

"You felt you needed to find the end of the tunnel with your head?" she demanded, her voice both scared and irritated.

"Not the best choice, I agree," he answered. "I must be more careful, yes?"

Another huff, and then she answered in a lighter tone. "Yes, you must. I'm going to turn the light on it now, and see what's up."

He closed his eyes, knowing that they would be blinded by the beam.

"Wow, that's bright," she muttered, and then she gasped. "Oh, my God, your head is bleeding."

"Really?" He felt no blood, no warmth or trickle. Then again, his hand was screaming so much, he wasn't sure he'd have felt anything else.

"Not much, but it's in your hair, and on your face."

Now, he thought he detected a laugh. Was she hysterical? He opened his eyes, just a slit of vision so he could see her.

"You are laughing at me," he accused. "Why?"

"I've never seen you look so terrible," she giggled, and he could hear the edge of hysteria in her voice. "Oh, Lord, Dav, you should see yourself. You're bloody and filthy and you have nearly a full beard. I've never seen you with a beard."

He narrowed his eyes, squinted almost to see her. "I have marked your skin terribly," he growled, reaching with his uninjured hand to run a finger down the soft, reddened skin of her neck. "I have hurt you."

"No." He could see the faint gleam of her smile, and some of the calm and sanity returned to her eyes. "You haven't hurt me. But your beard looks . . ."

"Yes?" He gritted his teeth on the word, still gripping his finger to staunch the bleeding and dull the pain.

"Piratical."

He frowned, trying to make sense of the word in his befuddled, pain-riddled state. "Like a pirate?" he guessed.

"Yes, with your skin and your beard and the blood on your forehead, you look like a pirate."

"I feel like a wrecked ship," he managed, shifting off his legs and onto his rear. He moved his head in the wrong way, making pain shoot along his arm once more. His knees were protesting all the crawling, and his back hurt from stooping. More than anything, however, he needed to get comfortable so he could wrap his hand. He hoped wrapping it would prevent further injury and keep it from bleeding more. "I think I'm going to need to tie up my hand, bandage the fingers together. Otherwise I will hurt it more."

She frowned. She hadn't asked to see his hand yet, and he decided she hadn't heard him say he'd hurt it. She'd seen the head wound and focused on that.

"Your hand?" she asked, confirming his guess. "What did you do? Let me see."

"I broke the little finger."

"What? How? Let me see," she demanded.

"I broke it when I fell, and it is badly broken. I have pulled it straight, and the bleeding is stopping," he said, seeing her eyes widen in the light of the flashlight. "But it is not a good thing."

She gulped and nodded. "No. No injury is. Okay." She seemed to gather herself, collect her wits. "Hang on. Here—" She handed him the flashlight, which he took in his good hand as she delved into the coat-pack. She used her tool to cut a wide, long strip out of the lining of his coat. He had wanted to leave the heavier coat behind, but she had argued against it. Now he was glad. "Let me see it now."

Reluctantly, he held out his hand. With the pressure off, it began to bleed again, but more slowly this time.

"Oh, my God," she said, staring as she took his hand with

gingerly care. "This looks really scary, Dav. I'm going to use the last of this hand-wash stuff to try and clean it off, but it's bad," she said.

All laughter had fled now.

He gritted his teeth and agreed. The gel stung in the wound, but if the gel prevented infection, the pain would have been worth it. With a great deal of tender care, she wrapped his last two fingers together, tying the wrapping with another strip cut from the bag.

"It's swelling a lot," she said. "I hope that wrapping it tight may help, but it could make it worse. I have no idea. I don't know anything about broken bones or medicine."

Dav was white-lipped and sweating profusely again by the time she finished. Carrie could see the pain written all over his face.

"Here." She thrust the light at him again. She'd taken it and held it under her arm as she worked, but now she needed him to take it, shine it away from himself so she didn't see his pain. "Hold this while I get you some aspirin."

"Aspirin? You have that?" he asked with a note of relief in his voice.

"In my purse. You have no idea how much of a headache the gallery can be sometimes," she said, trying to lighten the mood. "I always have aspirin."

She made him use more of the water to swallow three of the pills, though he claimed he could do it dry. She'd seen the sheen of sweat, felt it dampening his arms as she bandaged him. He was losing far more liquid than she was. She was perspiring, but he was truly sweating. With his fear of the dark, and now an injury, she could certainly understand. She wished there was more she could do for him, more ways to help.

"We need to keep moving," he said, grunting as he shifted to his knees. He stayed there, panting for a moment before struggling to his feet. "If I sit much longer, I will be like those who die in the snow—I will not get up."

"Okay," she said, feeling panic in her gut. The thought of him sitting there, unmoving and comatose, flashed into her mind. The image was far too real for comfort.

"Let's see how tight the squeeze is."

"Don't say that," he ground out. "Just show me where the tunnel is."

"Right. Got it." She wanted to scream. She wanted to pound on the floor and tell him to make it all go away. It was one of the things he did best. He liked to fix things, make them better. She realized it must be killing him to not be able to do anything. To have to depend on her, and the lone flashlight, to lead the way.

Hell, it was killing her and she wasn't afraid of the dark. She probably would be from here on out, if they ever got out of this hellhole.

"I will go first." He said it tersely, a sharp clipped order.

Even as she understood his need to maintain control, she snapped back, "Yessir, your majesty."

"Huh," he growled. "I am exalted now? I am king of dirt and tunnels. Yes." He grunted again, pulling himself into the narrow, round tunnel opening. "Ahh, that hurt," he cursed again. The Greek was flowing more rapidly now, and she suspected the curses were getting nastier and more foul.

"What does that mean?" Asking about it kept her from thinking about another dead end and another long, dark tunnel.

He didn't answer for a long time.

"Dav?"

"I was going to say, it is not for a woman to hear, but that doesn't seem like a nice thing to say to you, in these circumstances. You have more courage than I, Carrie. Yet I guess saying these things in English would be—" he hesitated, stopping his forward motion.

"Crude? Rude? Lewd? Socially unacceptable?"

"All that and more."

"Keep moving, Dav. Please," she begged, knowing they couldn't stop or she would die. Just die.

"Ah." Again he hesitated. "I am trying to decide if I can get through."

Tears sprang into her eyes and she closed them against the horrible thought of going back to the cell, waiting to die. No. This couldn't be happening. She heard him grunt and the sound of tearing cloth. Her eyes flew open, and she saw that he was five feet farther down the tunnel, but lying on his stomach.

"Dav? Dav?"

"I am okay, Carrie-mou, but my back is now marked as well. Keep your head down as you come through; there is a sharp place in the middle of this part of the tunnel."

"Oh, no, your back," she murmured, seeing the split in his shirt and a welling line of blood along the rent in the fabric, as she flashed the beam of the flashlight on him, rather than beyond him.

"I am through, though, so come on and let us keep moving."

She squeezed down the narrow space on hands and knees, knowing her smaller frame made it a hundred times easier for her to navigate.

"I think the builders must have been a lot smaller than you, or me."

He grunted in response and kept moving. She didn't know whether to talk or not, or ask again about the curses.

Crawling along, she pondered it, but forgot the issue when he cried out again.

"Yamato!"

"What?" She nearly shrieked the word, her nerves strung so tautly that she wanted to scream.

"Yamatoyamatoyamato!" He ran the exclamation to-

gether the way another man might say *"shitshitshit!"* "There is another drop. I caught my hand, the fingers bent again. Ahhhhh." He moaned the last, but she saw his uninjured hand reaching back. "Hand me the light. Let me see if we are going to meet Hades or if it is another way station en route to this particular version of hell."

She passed the light into his open palm and waited, shivering a bit in the deep darkness as he flicked the beam out into space. With his body in the way, she couldn't see what he was seeing and it was maddening. Every part of her body hurt, or itched, or felt scummy and filthy. Closing her eyes, she imagined a shower. A hot one. Hell, a cold one—she wasn't picky.

She could almost feel the water coursing over her body, washing away the tiredness, the sweat and dirt. She was so deep in her imagining of it, it was so real that she heard the water splashing, felt the cooler air on her face.

"Carrie?" Dav's questioning voice broke the moment and her eyes popped open.

She couldn't see him now, though the glow of the light was still in front of her. "Dav? Where are you?"

"Crawl forward, you must see this." There was excitement in his voice. Relief. Hope. What had he found? Scrambling in the dust, she squeezed past the rough rocks.

She reached the end of the tunnel and in the puny beam of the flashlight, saw a wonder before her.

A long, drawn-out and nearly inarticulate "Ohhhhhh," was all she could manage.

"Is it cold?" Carrie asked, even though she didn't care. She just started stripping off her clothes as she walked toward the long, narrow ribbon of water pouring from somewhere high above them and splashing on a round, tablelike stone. The water pooled only slightly in a wide shallow basin in the stone before draining away somewhere below the rock.

"I don't know and I don't care." Dav echoed her thoughts as he too stripped down.

It was an almost orgasmic experience to have the cool water running over her, sluicing away the days of sweat and grime. She tilted her face to the spray and let the water rinse the blood, tears and dirt from her face. Next to her, Dav was doing the same. The wide blade of the waterfall was just enough for both of them to stand under as long as they were close. In the faint light from above them, she saw Dav's expression. He looked like a cat with cream. Or catnip.

"That feels . . . divine," he managed.

"Yes, it does. Turn around, let me see if I can wash out the cut on your back."

He complied and she let her hands trace the muscled contours of his shoulders, and along his spine, washing the dirt away, making sure the long scrape was clear of dust and debris from the cave roof.

"If you keep that up," he said, and she felt the words echo in his chest under her seeking fingers, "we may end up in a compromising position, Carrie-mou."

The thought of being clean, the sensual delight of it, was heating her blood. His hot skin under her hands was turning that sensation up a hundredfold.

"And if I put you in a compromising position?" She moved closer, pressing her body, her breasts, to his back, sliding her hands around to caress his chest and belly.

"I will protest, but I think it will be in vain as you've already—" He stopped talking when her hands cruised lower, finding him hard and ready.

"What, no words? No banter?" She kissed his back, bent her knees so she could press a line of approval down his spine.

"I'm without words," he managed, and she felt his body clench as she carefully tightened her grip on him. Polishing the dirt from his skin was as sensual an experience as she could ever remember. When he turned to her, lifting her wet hair to kiss her neck, his big hands glided down her shoulders, down her arms, around her back to pull her closer.

The water splashed and danced on them and around them, its cool embrace making their caresses hotter, making his skin and his body feel like the flame he'd named her.

When he drew her closer, fitting her body to his, she wanted to purr, to shout with delight. She pulled her mouth away, denying him, but only briefly. Instead, she used her lips to mark a path down the front of his body this time, kneeling before him to enjoy the taste and shape of him. His groan of pleasure made her want more, more of everything, more of him, more feelings, more sensations.

She let him pull her upward, enjoyed the powerful sense of him taking her in a deep, plundering kiss, letting him lift her, helping her wrap her legs around him as she slid over him, onto him.

When they connected, flesh to flesh and body to body, they both cried out. It was an exquisite pleasure to feel him fill her, feel her own body heat to a flash point and envelop him.

"Carrie-mou." He cried her name, lifting her slightly as he drove upward, into her, giving her all that she wanted and more.

"The wall," she said, meeting his powerful thrusts, needing more.

"Your back," he began, and she could have screamed in frustration.

"I'm not fragile." She growled the words, fisting her hands in his hair. "I want you to take me. Now. Up against the wall." When he hesitated, she insisted. "*Now, now, now,* Dav."

"Your wish," he muttered, into her throat where he was devastating her with his tongue and mouth, "is my command."

She felt the solid, slick stone behind her and braced against it, using the unyielding surface to lever herself up, then come down to meet his thrusting hips. It felt better than anything she'd ever felt, better than any other time they'd made love, even.

"Nownownownownow!" she demanded, using everything she had to bring him to the brink with her, to fuel his need with her own and release the nearly unbearable pleasure that was building between them.

"Yes, now," he agreed, his hands underneath her, driving her in closer even as she pulled away and came back. "Now, Carrie. Mine," he cried as he closed his eyes and threw back his head, powering her upward with his complete abandon to their passion.

"Ahhhh . . ." She felt the waves swamp her, the pulsating, amazing delight of a blinding surrender.

It was as if she could feel everything, and nothing. The sound of their harsh breathing echoed around the chamber, but she also felt deafened, stunned by the depth and power of their lovemaking.

He rested his head on her breast, his shoulders heaving as he panted. She felt the heat of his breath, shivering her sensitive skin and nearly sending her into another orgasm.

"You," he said, and his voice was a rasp of sound, "are spectacular."

She bent to kiss his beautiful hair, jet black and slicked to his head from the water. She traced along his hairline, enjoyed the faintest hint of silver at the temples. She loved the look of him, the heavy muscle, the broad shoulders.

"I'd say the same of you," she said, struggling suddenly to form the words, to get them past the realization that lodged in her chest that she was deeply, irrevocably in love with him.

"What?" he said, raising his head to meet her gaze, feeling the change in her, somehow. "What is it?"

"I," she began, and had to swallow against a dry throat. How had he sensed that change, her shift of emotion? His dark eyes were watchful, waiting. "I just realized I must be getting heavy," she said. It was lame, and she knew it.

He smiled, lifting her enough to help her slide down and set her feet on the wet floor, holding her steady as she found her balance.

"Never too heavy, my flame." With a searing tenderness, he framed her face and kissed her—a deep, passionate, lingering kiss. A lover's kiss.

She wanted to make a joke, break the moment, do something to shift the focus from her, from what they were doing. Looking in his eyes, the need passed. He drew her in and held her, his honest and obvious tenderness stripping her of the ability to speak. She couldn't dismiss it, or him. Not when he looked at her that way.

"You will not put me off this time, my love," he murmured. "I care for you. You need to know this. This passion between us is not just the heat of the moment. There was much I had wanted to say to you, even before."

"I know," she managed, closing her eyes. "I know."

As if sensing her conflicted emotions, he tucked her head under his chin, banded his arms around her in the most wonderful hug she'd ever felt. In one moment, one contact, he made her feel safe, and whole. She felt secure and sexy and magnificent, despite the conditions, despite the desperation of their situation.

For that moment, that one moment, nothing else mattered. Filled with a sense of well-being, she drifted off to sleep in his arms.

Chapter 14

"Where are we?" Ana asked, sitting up in the passenger seat. The sun was setting and they were on a long stretch of tarmac. There weren't any other cars visible.

"Wildlife sanctuary. Local contact said it was the fastest way to get to where we need to go that wouldn't break the suspension on the cars."

"Ah, that would explain the lack of lights or other cars."

"Not tourist season right now either."

"What is?"

"December through February, mostly," Callahan answered from the backseat. "I looked it up."

"Any other intel?" Ana looked at Gates, noting the strain in his face. It showed in the fine lines around his eyes, the tightness in his jaw. It wouldn't be obvious to anyone else.

Well, she amended the thought, *Dav would have noticed.*

"Not yet. We're out of range of most of the cell towers and Geddey is going to call on the satellite phone if he can't get us by cell." Gates indicated the larger phone plugged into the dash cigarette lighter. In this older model GMC vehicle, it was a lighter rather than a port.

"Good. How far are we from the airstrip we're headed for?"

"Another fifty miles, maybe forty minutes under these conditions."

"You want me to drive so you can get thirty minutes shut-eye?" she asked, eyes straight ahead. She didn't want the others to think he was less than sharp, nor did she want him to think she was questioning his readiness. She did know, however, that she was fresher for the nap.

"Probably a good idea," he admitted, to her surprise, "but I won't be able to sleep."

"Hmm," she agreed, knowing he was right. She was surprised she'd been able to. "Holden, you have your kit?"

"In the back. Ready to rock. If Mr. Gianikopolis was at that airstrip, I can find traces of him."

"Did you have time to get the stuff from Detective Baxter?" Gates asked.

"The sample?" Holden sat forward and Ana could see the eagerness in his eyes. He was so new to Dav's team, he hadn't developed the familiarity the others had. "Yes. I'll be able to identify Ms. McCray as well."

"Good. Callahan? You have your kit?"

"Got it. No matter where that plane's been, I'll be able to trace its path, and any communications they've made."

"It's just a matter of getting there, then," Ana said with a sigh. She watched the road before them, wishing it would pass more quickly. There wasn't much to see but trees and jungle-y, vine-y thickets on either side of the road. None of the trees were terribly tall. She was about to comment when Holden beat her to it.

"Pretty low trees. I guess that's the hurricane's work. They've not had a really bad one since Hazel, but they've had enough tropical storms to knock down trees, keep things on the regeneration curve."

"Thanks, Willard Scott," Callahan muttered.

Holden gave her a questioning look. "Who's Willard Scott?"

Ana snickered. "Showing your age, Callahan," she teased.

Callahan looked mortified. "Am not. When my great-gramma turned a hundred, he came to see her. I looked him up on the Internet."

"So, he's a meteorologist?" Holden was now delighted. "Cool. Why'd he come see your great-gramma?" His puzzlement amused her, so Ana answered.

"It was his schtick," she replied, laughing. "He always did a thing on octogenarians. He'd have a picture or a memento or something every day, wish two or three of them happy birthday. Used to amaze me that there were so many."

"I always wondered about that too," Gates admitted. "We're rising," he added. "Altitude."

"Time to check in." She inserted an earpiece into her ear, tuned a radio at her belt. "Advance team, you're on."

A quiet voice replied. "Glad you're in range. No activity at the site. We came in from separate directions, swept clockwise. Nothing moving. Thermal scan shows nothing but some animals."

"Gut feeling?" Ana asked.

"It's clear. There's a bolt on the swing-bar gate. You'll need cutters," came a second quiet voice. Both men on the advance team were undercover and in full stealth mode. Going into this kind of situation, it was best to have several days of advance scouting, Ana knew, but since they'd only found out a location today, it was the best they could do.

"Stay alert, Bromley-two out," she said. The sharp intake of breath over the earpiece and the flash of a grin on Gates's face amused her. He was inordinately pleased that she'd taken his name.

Filling the rest of the team in on the report ate up some of the time, but it still seemed interminable, waiting for action, waiting to get there.

The landscape changed again as they continued to climb. Belize was mostly flat and tropical with a ridge of stony plateaus close to the border with Guatemala. All the Mayan ruins were in the mountainous areas, as well as some of the most popular tourist sites. Ana focused on the road in front of them, and as they passed one of the infrequent markers, she consulted the map she held.

"We've got a turn coming up."

It was like electricity. Everyone in the vehicle came to attention, like hunting dogs on scent. From the rustling she heard in her earpiece, she was sure it was the same in the following vehicle.

Ana picked up the walkie-talkie. "Ears in, everyone. And check." Everyone checked their mics and earpieces in record time.

The turn was plainly marked as private property, and the road was well maintained, the gate recently painted. Ana checked her weapon as they made the turn, heard more than saw Holden do the same. The second vehicle would provide covering fire if there was someone at the airstrip that the advance team had missed.

She saw Gates's snarky grin. "Private, my ass. Callahan, you got cutters back there?"

"Ready as soon as you stop, boss."

"Go," he said as the heavy car slowed, its tires kicking up dust into the late-afternoon sunshine. Callahan was out and at the bar, clipping the padlock with an obvious effort before anyone could say another word. She swung the gate open and motioned them through, putting a foot on the running board and grabbing a handhold on the roof rack as the car rolled past. Gates powered down the back window and Callahan passed the bolt cutters in to Holden.

In the sideview mirror, Ana could see that she, too, had her weapon at the ready.

"She climbing in?" Holden asked.

"No," Ana said. "She's outrider. She'll drop before we stop, cover us."

"Oh." Holden swallowed nervously. "Right."

"You checked on that weapon?" Gates said calmly.

"Yessir, but not in this kind of situation."

"Got it," Gates said. "Hang back then, make sure we're clear before you get out. You're too important to the op to lose to a stray bullet."

Ana saw Holden straighten, his protest dying on his lips. Somehow, Gates had managed, with tone, body language and a few simple words, to help a young guy feel like an essential part of the team rather than someone who couldn't handle a weapon.

"We can't afford to lose anyone, everyone's vital," Ana added, sliding her hand across the seat to squeeze Gates's arm, trying to convey approval, respect and love in one quick caress.

His brief smile said he understood what she was saying with the contact. And that he appreciated it.

Amazing how easy it was. With Gates.

Without missing a beat, he reached down and caught her hand in a fast grip and released it. "Look sharp, people," he said.

"Car two, hang back, let us go in first so we don't get boxed," Ana instructed. "As soon as we're out, loose the hounds."

"Let me guess," Gates said, without ever losing one iota of watchfulness, "you've always wanted to say that."

"Yeah—" she grinned. "Yeah, I have." He knew her so well.

The narrow drive widened out to a cleared space where a small building sat. Beyond it was a ramshackle hangar. Two planes sat inside in plain view, but other than that there was no sign the small airport was in use. No indication of life, no other vehicles other than the planes. The runway, beyond the shack, was dark, its scant lighting visible only as wires and metal rails, but not functioning. There wasn't even a wind sock.

"Callahan?"

"Nothing, boss," she said.

Ana contacted the two first-in scouts. "Brixton? Daniels?"

"Still quiet."

"Dogs?"

"At the ready," came the reply from Franklin.

"Go," Ana instructed. She saw the four dogs streak across the clearing. The scent hounds stopped in front of the building, bayed once and dropped their noses to the ground. The outliers, the guards, flew into the hangar, but were back out again in seconds, heading for the building. Another few minutes and both of the big shepherds were in front of the building in the "all clear" sit-stay they'd been taught. The two scent hounds were in the hangar sounding off. Wherever the trail originated—probably one of the planes—it ended at the building and started at the hangar.

"They won't mess up the plane, will they?" Holden asked.

"No opposable thumbs," Callahan said, returning to the open window. Ana laughed and Holden looked blank.

Gates pulled the vehicle into the clearing, stopping close beside the hut.

"She's being annoying." Ana smirked. "The doors are most likely shut. There are monkeys and other curious wildlife here. You want the plane to stay clean, you shut the doors. The dogs can't get in."

"Ah, got it," Holden said, laughing. "Opposable thumbs. Good one, Callahan."

"Hostiles!" The shout rang in her earpiece, and everyone dropped, Holden included. Ana noted that his weapon was in his hand and it was steady.

Nothing and no one moved. Callahan was on the roof with a scoped rifle within a second of the shout.

"Get down," Gates snapped. "He's gone. Guarantee it, now that he knows we spotted him. Daniels, clear sight?"

"Clear sight, boss," Daniels's voice was crisp on the connection, but she heard the adrenaline excitement in his reply. "Scope showed heat signature and a weapon. About four hundred yards up and to the left, down the runway. He wasn't there an hour ago, I'll lay money on it. Ducked and covered, though, at the shout."

"We didn't have the drop on him anyway," Gates said. "Let's get our work done here and move out. Full alert, people."

Ana followed Brixton and Franklin into the hangar. The four dogs, one Plott hound, one black and tan coonhound, and two German shepherd dogs, swarmed their handler, barking their mournful bark, and dancing between him and the plane. Holden was right behind her, kit in hand. Two minutes later, Callahan was there too.

"Check it out," Ana snapped the order.

"Right, I'll follow Holden," Callahan replied. "He's liftin' prints, right?"

"Right."

Holden dusted the rail on the plane's stairs and lifted five or six prints before going inside. Ana followed. The Cessna was fitted out for cargo, with permanent bins bolted to the floor.

"He was here," she said, spotting a mark on the wall.

Holden spun in place, his jaw dropping. "What do you mean? How can you tell?" He was looking everywhere, trying to see what she saw.

Ana pointed. "His mark. A series of initials." She could see them from where she stood, at the angle. She didn't want to move lest she lose sight of them, so she directed Holden to them.

Holden hurried over to the wall of the plane, crouched and stared. He looked at her, his face a study in disbelief. "SSDM? That supposed to mean something?"

Callahan snickered. "Really? That's the code?"

Ana laughed too, but added, "It's not what you think."

Holden looked at them, asked Callahan, "What did you think it was?"

Callahan shot Ana a "can he be that naive?" kind of look. "Same shit, different millennium."

"Close, but no cigar," Ana said, using her tone to remind Callahan that they were working to save Dav. "The S'es are the last letter of his first and last name, and the D and M are his mother's first initial and the initial of her maiden name. A lot less obvious than DG would be, and no one but us would connect it with him."

"Interesting."

"I've got blood," Holden said suddenly. He jerked open his kit, swabbed something on the plane's floor and checked it with a small test strip on which he'd dabbed the swab.

"Human." He offered the test flat for them to see the instant results. "But there isn't much of it. Not enough for a bullet wound or anything life threatening."

"Any other initials?" Ana asked, moving toward them, looking along the same wall where Dav's initials had been scratched.

Holden whipped out a penlight, leaning into the wall where the marks were scratched. "Got some," he said in eager triumph. "EY."

"Is it scratched through?" Ana demanded, leaning in as well, straining to see the marks. "Or defaced in any way?"

"No." Holden was looking at her as if he'd done something wrong. "Should it be?"

"EY equals Carrie McCray," Callahan supplied, understanding dawning on her face even as the worry eased off her features. "I'm guessing no scratch through means they were both still alive when they landed."

"Right," Ana said, feeling the pressure in her chest lighten, just a fraction.

They were in the right place. On the right trail. And Dav and Carrie had been alive when they'd landed here in this plane. Her mysterious informant had been on the mark, and there were no blood pools or bodies on the property, or the dogs would have alerted them. "You hearing this, Gates?"

"Yeah," he said, and his relief was palpable. "We're on the right lead."

Holden didn't wait for that; he busied himself pulling prints and samples, scanning all the data into a portable as he went. Dav could afford the latest and best technology, and for once it was getting a workout. Holden moved from place to place, efficiently dusting, swabbing and pulling prints wherever he found them, following the beeping, morphing trail all over the plane.

"Perimeter secure, boss," she heard the stations report in. She and Holden left Callahan pulling the comm data and moved to the other plane.

"Uh, Mrs. Bromley?"

"Ana," Ana corrected, noting that he'd covered his mic. She did the same.

"Yes. Um, Ana, is Callahan always this . . ." he hesitated.

"Temperamental?"

"I was gonna say hostile, but yeah, I guess you could call it that."

She smiled. "No. She's feeling guilty about Declan."

Understanding and disappointment flashed one right after the other over Holden's boyish features. "Got it. They together?"

"Not yet, maybe not at all. But she thinks she'd have kept them both safe if she'd been on duty."

"Don't we all," he said, and dropped his hand off the mic. They moved to the other plane, leaving Callahan to do her work. Ana wondered how Damon, Queller, Thompson and Georgiade were doing. They'd all been hurt badly enough that they'd had to stay behind. She hoped they were on the mend. At last word, Declan had still not come out of his coma.

She also wondered about Cal, Carrie's former gallery manager. When they left, he'd yet to be located. Bax had given them a brief update on his search for Inez's killer when he called to say he hadn't located the gallery's former manager. Most of his leads were turning out to be one dead end after another.

"This plane is passenger," Holden noted, interrupting her thoughts. "Gonna be lots more prints on this one."

"I'll leave you to it."

Gates met her at the bottom of the steps. "Passenger plane came in second. That means someone followed after they took Dav and Carrie out of here in the cargo. Dav's using every trick he and I practiced, but Carrie is a wild card for him. We ran a lot of simulations, but none of the sims included another hostage, especially not a woman he cared about." He grimly looked around the small compound. She read frustration and something else in his gaze. "This is off, somehow, including the watcher. I'm still feeling like we're playing more than one game here and it's really, *really* pissing me off."

Ana couldn't have agreed more. "It's not standard mercenary practice to throw away a chance for ransom. First, we haven't heard anything else after the initial contact with proof of life." she said, holding up her index finger to indicate that point. "Second, the ransom's in the holding account, but not collected. We know that if it's Niko, he's not the thinker behind this op but he'd collect, I think, shift it and send us looking somewhere for Dav." She ticked off a third finger. "Third, mercenaries don't leave watchers at a place they're not coming back to." She balled her fist. "Last but not least, our anonymous tipster was a woman, and said she was unconnected to whatever's going on here."

Ana glanced around and suppressed an atavistic shudder. "You're right, Gates. This is way off."

He was about to reply when his sat-comm beeped. His shoulders straightened a bit as he read the incoming message, but his frown deepened. "The ransom's rolling from the holding account to an account in the Caymans. We got info back on the proof of life. Initial tests say it's Dav's and Carrie's hair, but the gold ring on the gold chain has more than Dav's DNA on it. They're working on that. There's a coat button too. Queller said he recognized the button as Dav's," Gates said, then drew in a breath. "The ring, if it's what I think it is, was his mother's. He never takes it off the chain around his neck."

Ana took that in, wondering about the ring, and the fact Gates's body language said there was one long painful story behind it. "Why'd they wait three days, Gates?" She frowned. The "off" vibe increased in her mind, and her frustration rose. Real kidnappers got their demands in early, kept hope alive to ensure cooperation and payment.

"More skewed activities. We're getting too many options and too many leads." He shot her a sharp look. "Too many leads. That means either too many hands in this, or a deliberate distraction. Smart as they've been so far, it could be either. Long-term planning is written all over this deal." He said it as a complaint, but there was a dark degree of admiration as well. Whoever had designed this op and carried it out knew their stuff.

Ana admired it too, in a way, but put that out of her mind. They had immediate work. "No vehicle here." She pointed out the absence. "That means they're probably still in-country or leaving another way." She glanced toward the runway. "The watcher says they're in-country and coming back here."

"Does it? I don't know." Gates rubbed at his faintly bearded cheek. "None of this makes sense for mercs."

"Good point. So, if there's a watcher from some other source and they know it, they won't be back. If they think they're safe, they may. We should set a watch of our own." She looked around to be sure Franklin couldn't hear her. He was sensitive about his dogs. "So, how come the dogs didn't give us an alert on the guy?"

"Downwind." Gates paused, scanning the lush green surrounding the small compound. "Whoever it is, they're good."

"Interesting. And weird. Why would they leave a watcher behind? They couldn't know we were coming. Given that, the watcher was here to see if they came back, or who else might show," Ana remarked. "If the watcher is working for the opposition, whoever that is, with the mercs in the middle, we may have just screwed everything."

"I don't think this can get much more screwed up," Gates replied, and Ana winced.

"Don't say that. There's always another way to screw something up, especially this sort of deal."

"You going to tell me about that phone call? Obviously it sent us on the right track and to the right place." Gates watched her closely, and she could tell he was waiting—had been waiting for a while now—for an answer. She also knew that what she was about to tell him was really going to sound like she'd taken them on the wildest of goose chases. If it hadn't panned out . . .

But it had, so she told him.

"The woman said she knew Dav, knew us. She said she'd known about the deal last year and had been involved, in a peripheral way." When Gates started to speak, she headed him off by continuing. "Hear me out, and remember, we got here and it's the right place."

The mutinous look on his face shifted to thoughtfulness as she went on. "She said that she'd gained word of an active contract out on Dav, one that was turned down. There were reasons why it was declined, she said, but that I didn't need to know them. What I did need to know was that Dav had been flown to Belize, and he'd been dumped at a site in the mountains, near a ruin. She said that she would send me a text, sometime today, with the latitude and longitude."

"That's it? That's all you had?" He looked incredulous now, and shook his head. "So between that and the plane sightings, you pinpointed the airstrip."

"Yep," she said, knowing how idiotic it sounded.

"Holy hell," he said, rubbing his eyes. "No wonder it feels like there are more irons in this fire than we can account for."

"There's more," she admitted.

"Oh, crap. More? What?"

"Hines. He's down here somewhere too. Remember, McGuire was tracking him here. If he knows we're here, or has someone tracking our movements in and out of California, he may be here, gunning for both of us as well. Given that, McGuire may be down here too."

"Jeez, just what we need. More ex-Agency help and hindrance than we can shake a palm tree over." He slapped at his legs with the gloves he'd been wearing. "Something's biting me."

"Me too," she agreed, but she'd put on bug spray, so it wasn't too annoying yet. "I've got some spray in the car.

The locals said we'd need it. Some kind of local and very bloodthirsty gnat."

He sighed. "What now?"

"Gather data and wait for someone to direct us, I think." She hated every word she said, hated knowing that they were completely dependent on an outside, unknown source for intelligence and direction. Knowing too, that there was some larger game to which they weren't privy. It made her feel like a chess piece and she hated that.

Frustrated, she turned from watching the swaying trees to looking at the planes. She saw Callahan coming out of the cargo plane. She looked pissed.

Fear and anger curled in Ana's gut. She could tell Callahan had found something that was going to twist things up more than they already were.

"Looks like it's getting weirder by the minute," she muttered to Gates, drawing his attention to Callahan, whose angry strides brought her to them within seconds.

"Crap," Gates muttered.

Callahan strode up. Her headset was off, her mic dangling. She covered it with one hand and motioned them to do the same.

Holding up an electronic reader, she said, "I think we got a mole."

Carrie had no idea how much time had passed when they awoke. "There is no way in hell I'm putting those clothes back on until they've been rinsed out," she declared, looking beyond Dav to their scattered garments.

"You are right about that," he muttered, distaste written on his face. "I fear my trousers will never be the same."

"When we get out of here, I'm burning all of it."

"I will get you a match to light the fire," he offered, bending to gather up their clothes. "Until then, I guess we will wash things, yes?"

"Yes. Better wet than filthy, I think."

"I think the pants will not stand the water," he said, holding up the beautifully tailored wool. "As dirty as they are, they fit now. If they—" He stopped, obviously searching for the word.

"Shrink?"

"Yes, thank you. If they shrink, even a little, they will not fit me."

"True. Mine might not either," she realized, plucking her underwear and his T-shirt from the pile. "Let's set those aside, and my sweater such as it is." She held up the torn garment, but smiled at it. He'd torn it when they made love and that made it precious. She decided she wouldn't burn that, if they got out alive.

She saw his grimace and peered at him, trying to make out, in the gloom, what was bothering him.

"Your hand," she said. "How bad is it?"

He shrugged, but she didn't let him get away with it. "Give me the clothes," she said, holding out her hand for them, brooking no argument. "I'll get them rinsed out, then we'll take a look at your hand."

All the while she rinsed their things, she worried. He'd favored the hand a lot, but then, when they'd made love, he'd held her up, used it as if it were uninjured. Was that why it was paining him now?

If his condition was really serious, what should they do? What could they do?

All the unanswered questions plagued her as she laid out underwear and shirts on the rock ledge to dry a bit. The cave was moist near the waterfall, but really, only there.

Shivering a bit, she knelt next to him. He'd watched her, his hands in his lap, as she worked. Now, the sight of him, nude, with five days' growth of beard, stirred her blood, but she pushed the desire back for the moment, focused on his hand. He'd taken the rag off it so she could see it.

"It isn't good, Carrie-mou. There is much bruising and blood under the skin." He held the hand up and she turned on the flashlight so she could examine it. In the harsh, bright light, it looked nightmarish. Purple and angry red, it was lumpy and had to be massively painful. She could see the torn skin where the bone had protruded. It oozed blood, now that the bandaging was off, and everything about the hand looked wrong.

"It's bad, Dav."

"It is, yes," he agreed. "But there is nothing to be done right now. We should get dressed, even if we are wet, and keep moving. If this goes from bad to worse"—he indicated his hand—"I could get feverish and maybe delirious."

"That would be worse," she said, recognizing the vast understatement the words implied.

"Yes. It could be fatal, in these caves, and I will not allow my brother's jealousy, these games"—he spat the words in angry frustration—"this family idiocy to cost you your life. What happens to me is not nearly as important."

She felt her own anger rise. How dare he? "What makes you think you get to be all martyrlike and put me up on a pedestal? I think you're just as damn important as I am, you idiot."

"Not to me," he snarled back. "Nothing is more important than you."

The words of caring, delivered in such irritation, took a few minutes to register.

Dav had already said he cared about her, but she'd heard that before. Her late husband had been quick to say he loved her, always. He'd been especially free with tossing the words around when he'd been successful wooing some intern or another artist.

This irritable declaration that she was important somehow meant more than any declaration of love.

Rocking back on her heels, she stared at him.

"What?" He scowled at her. "Why are you looking at me like that?"

"You mean that, don't you?" His irritated statement was so absurd, she had to laugh.

"Of course. I do not say anything I don't mean. I don't have to." He smiled a bit. "Unless I'm negotiating; then perhaps I will not be so truthful."

"This isn't a negotiation."

"No, Carrie-mou, it isn't. It's merely the truth and I find it annoying that you don't believe me. I have been attracted to you for years. You are important to me." He used his uninjured hand to tuck her drying hair behind her ear. "Life is too short to lie about that sort of thing. And our lives, right now? They may be very short indeed, so why be false, eh?"

She looked away from the intensity of his gaze, his sincere smile.

He was right.

Something within her crumbled and fell away, a barrier, a fearful wall that kept her trapped in the past, so sure that anyone, everyone she trusted would betray her. Dav hadn't lied to her, he hadn't said he loved her, just that she was important to him, that he was attracted to her.

She let the smile blossom in the gloom, but not where he could see. It was fairly obvious that they were attracted to one another. God, she felt so good. Her body ached from the unaccustomed exercise, both desperate and sexual, but somehow, unaccountably, she felt . . . good.

She caught his hand, pressed a kiss into his palm. "You're right."

"Right? Yes." He leaned in, caught her face, kissed her softly. "And will you believe me, later, when I tell you that you are important to me? When we are free? Or will you doubt it all again?"

She had to laugh. He'd caught her there. "I don't know. I think," she said, feeling her way, exploring the new, free sensation in her chest, in her gut, "that I can try to open my mind enough to consider it."

His brilliant smile lit the darkness. "Good. We will work from there. Now, let us pick another tunnel and keep moving. Somewhere out there, Gates is looking for us." His smile faded. "And so is my brother."

She nodded, and pulled on her underthings. They were still wet, but as clammy as they felt, they were at least moderately clean. The T-shirt he'd given her was stained, but again, still cleaner than it had been, so she pulled it over her head. She'd shaken out her sweater, doing her best to get as much of the dirt and dust out of it as possible.

Dav had done the same and they were both trying to get the worst dirt off his pants and her skirt.

"I think this is an impossible task," he said, giving it up and tugging the pants over his legs. "These are just horrible, I must say," he commented as he fastened the hook and the belt. His look of fastidious distaste was amusing, but since she was experiencing the same thing, she empathized.

"Considering the conditions, I'm glad it isn't worse." She repressed a shudder as she too put on her skirt and slid her feet into her clammy, dirty shoes.

They gathered everything and rolled it up into a more compact bundle. They'd finished the last of the Nutella and crackers the previous night. All that was left was half a canteen of water.

"Let's fill up the other canteens," he said, reading her mind. "We don't know when or if we'll find water again."

"Okay, here—" She handed him the canteens and he went to fill them. "Let's finish this other one now and fill it too."

"Good, you go ahead."

She uncapped it and drank it down, the cool water soothing her throat. She was grateful for the surge of energy it brought. Even without food, they could manage if there was water. She worried about Dav though; his hand looked terrible. At worst, if infection set in, he would get a fever, and if they couldn't get out, he could get gangrene and die from it. At best, he might lose the finger even if they couldn't get to medical help quickly.

"So, shall we toss a euro, to pick a tunnel?"

"You have one?"

"Yes, I do. And a drachma as well."

"Luck piece?"

"You could say that," he said with a smile, and held it out to her. It was shiny and well rubbed, but obviously old.

She examined it, then handed it back, but he declined. "You keep it. We'll share the luck, yes?"

Tucking it in her pocket, she nodded, touched it. "Deal."

They faced the walls together, looking at the various tunnels. "Last time, the tall, accessible one was the dead end," she said. "The rounded, smaller one, led us here."

"Would they repeat or mix it up?"

"My money's on repeat," she said. "What do you think?"

"Since I feel better, and I'm relatively clean, I will be willing to try that. If it comes to it, and it's another dead end, then I feel like we won't fall apart—well, I won't fall apart," he said, with a sheepish smile.

"I'll do my best not to, too."

"Then let us proceed," he said. "Flashlight on?"

She flicked the switch and followed him into the tunnel. They proceeded fairly quickly, even though Dav had to wrestle his way through narrow openings on several occasions.

They had been traveling steadily to the right, which

surprised her since most of the tunnels so far had been straight.

Dav abruptly stopped and she nearly ran into him.

"What is it?" she asked, trying to see around him. The light shone through, but she couldn't see anything.

"You will not believe it," was all he said before he disappeared.

Chapter 15

"It's a dead end?"

"Yes, but look." Dav shone the beam of the light around the chamber they'd come into. A shaft of sunlight, small and faint, shone from above them, but not enough to show what the flashlight did.

Carrie's jaw dropped. Literally. And Dav laughed.

"Yes, I feel the same way," he said. "As if I've wandered into that *Indiana Jones* movie we were discussing."

"Good Lord, how many niches?" she asked, counting as Dav moved the light over the crypts. The light caught the flash of gold and beading and weaponry. The artifacts glinted in the light, despite the dust of centuries.

"All the riches in the world and nowhere to spend them," he said, feeling unaccountably sad. What good was wealth if you had no way to utilize it, and no one upon whom to lavish the beauty of gold or gems? Hadn't he already been thinking that, thinking about a family and why he wanted a daughter or son to carry on his legacy? Had he not already decided on Carrie, he would have now. His admiration and desire for her soared once more as he watched her, eyes alight with curiosity at their find.

Hungry, tired and facing a return down the difficult

passage, she was still appreciative of the beauty, of the history that lay before them. She moved along the niches, her artistic interest outweighing any fear or revulsion when it came to the skeletons. Then again, he had to admit they looked more like Halloween props than real people.

He felt a wave of weakness. It could be hunger, or it could be infection. Either one was potentially debilitating. He knew his strength was waning. "Much as I hate to say it, we should go back."

"Yes, I know," she said, still looking at the niches.

"I hate to say this too," he added, "but we should take a gem or a link of gold or a coin. It may be our only way to barter ourselves to freedom, or get help."

When she turned to him, her face wore a mutinous expression in the flashlight's crisp beam. "The site shouldn't be disturbed."

"No, it shouldn't. But if we can get free, and we have to use whatever we take, I'll buy it back and we'll see that this find is put into the right hands."

She hesitated.

"I promise I will get it back if I can, return it here, Carrie-mou. Do you doubt my word?"

She huffed out a breath. "No, I know you'll do it. It's just . . ."

He nodded. "I know. I feel bad, but I also wish to survive, to get you home."

She nodded as well, and directed him to shine the light more closely into one niche. A beautifully carved bowl was held in the hands of the niche's occupant. It held gems and links of gold, some hammered, some smoothed. She pulled out three items, and spoke, directing her words toward the occupant of the niche: "We'll bring them back. Thank you for the loan."

He said nothing about her promise to the dead. He would

have done the same, said the same. Some superstitions crossed cultures, he decided.

She pocketed the gold and gems and they began the onerous return journey.

When they got back to the waterfall, no light could be seen. The orb of sunshine was gone.

"Do we stop, or try the other path?" she said, wearily.

He felt himself waver again, felt the flush of heat that washed over him, then receded.

Fever. Exactly what they'd been dreading.

"I do not wish to go on," he admitted. "But I have begun to feel feverish, Carrie-mou. I think we must keep moving. If there is any hope that this last tunnel leads out, we must try."

Fear made a mask of her features. "You need more aspirin, and rest."

He shook his head. "No resting. If I get worse, you cannot carry me, my flame. The aspirin, I will take, however." Every ache, scrape and pain in his body made itself known as he spoke. The aspirin would be most welcome.

He took two with a gulp of the water, and they set out down the second tunnel. It ran straight, and even when it narrowed at several points, Dav could still squeeze through. They crossed two more pits as well.

Dav was beginning to believe the tunnel would never end in anything, other than more tunnels, when the light showed them yet another dead end. This time, however, instead of a rounded room or platform, a stacked wall of flat, regular, worked stone blocked the way. He heard Carrie's moan of despair.

"It is not a cave, Carrie-mou," he said, holding on to that thought with everything he had. "It is something we have not yet seen, therefore it could be a way out, even when it does not seem to be."

As they neared the wall, Dav thought he smelled fresher

air. He stopped her. "I feel a breeze again. Check with the light," he ordered. If she resented his terse command, she said nothing.

Together they braced themselves and she began to play the light along the floor leading to the wall, then up the left side, over the ceiling and down the right side. She had just begun to slide the beam down toward the floor when Dav noticed the discrepancy.

"Wait. We have to get closer."

They moved closer, step by step, until they were at the wall. The light disappeared into a narrow margin between the stacked stone and the wall of the tunnel. Beyond the crevice, the light bounced off rocks and dirt. The stone and earth were damp—he could see that in the narrow beam.

"Wait, go back to the right," he said, peering into the darkness. The light played back and he saw green. Leaves. Vines, of some kind.

"What is it?" Carrie demanded, gripping his belt tightly as she moved the light at his direction.

"Leaves. Something grows in there. I think that means it's close to the light, to the surface." He was excited now. If there was a way out, they were saved. "What time is it? How close to daylight?" He was fairly sure they wouldn't be able to assess things with just the flashlight, not from here, through the eight-inch-wide opening.

She passed him the light, her hands shaking, and dug out her broken watch. "It's after midnight," she said, her earlier excitement giving way to sudden weariness as she realized how long they'd been lost in the tunnels.

"Then we will sit here and rest until the sun rises," he decided.

"Good plan," she said. "Or as good as any," she added as they slid down the wall, sitting with their backs to the heavy bricks so the faint breeze could play over their sweaty faces.

"Do you feel that?" she added, lifting her face and turning it toward the crevasse.

"The breeze? Yes, it feels good." It felt more than good. It felt heavenly. The stir of air made him realize how hot he was. Before he'd completed the thought, however, he shivered. The fever was making itself known.

She must have felt the shiver, because, to his surprise, her hand touched him gently, resting on his forehead. "I'm not sure how high your fever is, Dav, but even with the aspirin, you're burning up."

"Yes, I know, my Carrie-mou."

"Is there anything I can do?" she said, kneeling now at his side. "More aspirin? Or is it too soon?"

"Yes, to the aspirin. And no, I don't think it's too soon. It has been several hours." He gratefully took the canteen and drained it, knowing they had the other three left. "And then, we sleep."

"Okay," she said, and she seemed to appreciate that he'd set an agenda. In fact, she sounded weary and discouraged. "That sounds like a plan." She busied herself for a few moments, finding the canteen and the aspirin. She also got out a power bar and split it between them. "I forgot I had these, but we need the energy and the calories."

"We have burned energy today, haven't we?" he said lightly, thinking of their lovemaking as well as their travels.

"Yes, we have," she said, and in the radiance of the upturned light, he saw her smile.

It was her smile that made the decision for him. Tomorrow, when they woke, he would tell her that he planned to ask her to marry him. In fact, he decided, leaning back and closing his eyes, he *would* ask her.

She turned off the light and he pulled her securely under his arm so that he could hold her and they could be close. Although they'd been hot from all their exertions, and he even hotter from the fever, the night breeze was chilling them both. It felt good now, but would be colder by morning, especially if his fever did not abate.

With his battered coat around his shoulders, and around Carrie's back, he sat awake thinking. His mind circled and circled long after she'd fallen asleep, her head pillowed on his chest.

He would ask her to marry him. He wanted to—needed to. Nothing about his feelings for her had changed. He rubbed at his chest, and whispered, *"Andras." Husband.* What kind of husband would he be? Would he be what she wanted? Needed? On one hand, he felt sure she would agree to marry him. But his knowledge of himself was less solid, less quantifiable. There was the cry of a wild animal beyond the wall, and he felt his heart leap in both hope and fear.

The cry of an animal that close meant freedom might be near. But it also meant danger. Carrie shifted in her sleep.

"Shhhh, darling," he soothed, and she murmured something unintelligible and settled once more. He didn't think anything could get through the narrow opening to harm them, but he would watch. And listen. Whatever it was would get to him first, so at least he could protect her.

Another thought occurred to him. Unless she was protected with the pills women took, she could also be pregnant. Not likely, he realized, but stranger things had happened.

He fell asleep dreaming of daughters who looked like Carrie and his mother, and sons that were sturdy and strong, dark-haired and blue-eyed, and calling him father.

"Sir?" Marjorie called to him as he was about to exit the plane. Her brow was creased in a frown, so he presumed that she was worried yet again about disturbing him. He sighed, but smiled.

"Yes, my dear?"

"There is another call for you," she said, sounding a bit

breathless. "Would you like to take it here on the plane, or should I have it routed to the car?" She hesitated and he began to see the issue. Routing to the car, here in Guatemala, might be slightly more challenging than it was in the United States.

"I'll take it here. José!" he called down the steps, catching the attention of his local driver. "Stow the bags; I'll be there in a moment."

José nodded, not attempting to speak over the noise of local air traffic.

He accepted the receiver. "Yes?"

"Sir, there's been an issue." It was the man he'd sent to watch Niko.

"Yes, go on." Irritation rose within him. He didn't like it when things went awry.

"Two hunters of ours were tracking that high-value animal and its mate."

"As we discussed," he said, irritated that they were covering the same ground.

"I'm afraid the hunters suffered a mishap. They're going to have to turn in their hunting licenses."

Dead, then. Hmmm. Not good, and not part of the plan.

Fury singed him, then receded. His man was right to report in; it wouldn't do to take the irritation out on him. "Do we know what caused the mishap?"

"No, not at this time," the man replied tersely. "I'm checking options and possible sources. It may be there were snakes in the grass, but nothing points to a snakebite."

"I see." Had Davros bought one of Niko's men? Had Gates Bromley figured out where Niko had stashed Dav? He wondered how he could shift these new developments to his advantage. It might be an opportunity to pursue, to give Davros's people a lead and be the rescuer this time. Give him more time to live now, and kill him later when things were clearer. "Has there been any sign of the rare beast, or has it escaped its containment?"

"No, sir."

"Interesting. Thank you for letting me know. I will consider our next move. Stand by for more . . ." He hesitated, not wanting to say "orders" or "instructions" on an unsecured network. "Communications."

"Will do." He detected relief in the man's voice, and let a wry smile twist his lips. They were always so surprised when he didn't yell. "Thank you, sir."

He pondered the new development. Was there a third player in the field? He had been sure he'd tied up all the loose ends. No one in Niko's sphere, now that he'd eliminated Niko's team, had the skills to effectively take out three of his men without leaving a trace his man could find. The fact that the grate was still locked, with Davros apparently still inside, puzzled him as well. It would be interesting to see what Niko reported when *he* called in.

Ana and Gates had holed up in the small hotel at the game reserve where they'd secured space. Here in the off-season, the rates were ridiculously low and the proprietors were thrilled to have the team take more than half the available rooms. They were going to fan out from here, having come to the hotel straight from the hangar. Holden and Callahan would process everything, see if they could get a further direction from this point.

"What if we really have an inside breach?" Ana asked her pacing husband. "What do we do?"

"It would explain some things."

"Things?" she said. "What things?"

"Little things that went wrong last year, things that could have been chance and could have been interference, but

I couldn't ever pinpoint the source and I knew they hadn't come from outside or from our known enemies."

He looked grim and Ana didn't blame him. When and if they could catch their mole, she decided she would leave discipline to Gates. It wouldn't be pretty, and she'd bet there would be both personal retribution as well as lawyers involved in a great deal of it.

That brought her back to thinking about Dav. "It's been nearly five days, Gates. What are the chances?"

"The ransom note was delivered three days in," he said, instead of answering. "We can't judge by timing on this one."

"Gates." All the compassion she had for him and her own fear made the one word come out like a combination plea and question.

"I know, I know," he said, raking a hand through his dark hair in frustration. His thick hair was darkened to nearly black with perspiration and his fingers left grooves in the heavy layers. The rooms were stuffy and closed in, and yet it wasn't warm enough to want the air-conditioning on. "There are so many factors here. We have kidnappers who are well organized, well supplied and funded. We have the death at Carrie's gallery, which is connected. Presumably the girl there—"

"Inez." Ana supplied the girl's name. "Art student, part-time employee for events, moves up to full-time when Cal leaves."

"Yes, Inez," he continued. "Presumably she was their connection to be sure that the date between Carrie and Dav went off as scheduled. She was probably instructed to let someone know when they left, keep the timetable right up to par. She probably wasn't aware that she was doing it, Baxter says she had a new man in her life, according to her friends. One about whom she was secretive. Obviously, it's not good to keep those kind of secrets," he added grimly. "That said, she wasn't *our* inside leak; she wasn't even there last year."

"And yet she died because she knew someone's face. Did Bax get anything off the security tapes?"

"Man, wearing a hoodie, enters and sweeps the girl off her feet. This is, we presume, the new mystery boyfriend. They suck face on the way to Carrie's office, making it obvious he knew her and had a relationship with her, probably for some time, since she let him in without hesitation. For five minutes, the camera shows an empty hallway, then goes off."

"No camera in Carrie's office?"

"No. Then again, I don't want one in mine either," Gates acknowledged. "Next thing the camera shows is the wall of the corridor, so the guy went and moved the camera so it wouldn't show him leaving. It wasn't off long enough to trigger the backup alarms. He knew what he was doing."

"No doubt." She said nothing else, knowing that he had to walk through the crime scene in his mind, feel the pattern if there was one. They hadn't had the luxury of walking through it in person. Now they had to think it through in order to find a next step.

"So," Gates continued, oblivious to her thoughts. "Then, as the whole restaurant deal goes down, with this guy at the gallery doing the deed with the gi—Inez." Gates caught himself and used her name. "Is he a dupe, a cog? Or is he a major player? I have no idea. The restaurant op went essentially without a hitch on their part. Sure," he said, waving a hand to indicate their opponent's negligent attitude toward life, "they would probably have preferred not to kill anyone, but hey, collateral damage, right?" He ran his hands into his hair again. "So they're not amateur operators. We know that."

"Professionals all the way. They were in and out of that restaurant with Dav, with decoys flying in all directions, within four minutes. Police response couldn't get past the camera barriers and they were slow anyway because there were legitimate permits for filming and mock gunfire. Cops thought the calls were just neighbors who hadn't known they were filming there. The security guards were real hires as well. They slowed everything down because they thought they were protecting the set."

"Mass confusion," Gates snapped, but Ana heard the renewed admiration in his voice. "Brilliant, really. And in the middle of the chaos, our real snatch-and-grab vehicle, full of our real friends, gets away clean. I'd bet they made a transfer within blocks to a van or another SUV that had nothing to do with the set."

"Another lead for Bax to tug." Ana made a note to e-mail him that potential directive. Who knew if it was the way it had gone down, but if Gates thought it a reasonable scenario, you could bet it was a good thing to check.

"Exactly. But not anything that helps us now," Gates growled in frustration.

"Keep playing it out," she encouraged. "Anything we can figure about the scenario may help. Laying it out this way may give us more keys."

He nodded, paced some more. "Okay, so we've got a nondescript vehicle heading to general aviation at the airport, maybe even to one of the smaller outlying airports for smaller planes, maybe to a private strip."

"Plenty of those around San Fran and Oakland, in the outlying areas. Wouldn't have to drive far. Palo Alto, San Jose, San Martin, any of those would do it."

"Right. No matter what, though, you get them on a plane and head them south. We have the planes here, so we know they left the States pretty soon after they nabbed Dav and Carrie."

"That evening at the latest," she added, thinking of the time line he was presenting.

"Which leads me to believe they cut Dav's and Carrie's hair here, in Belize, for proof of life, rather than in the

States. The FedEx box came from a drop box in Texas, but according to the lab, the box had traces of an adhesive only used on the boxes in the Central American countries."

"That would explain some of the time lag," Ana mused, counting the hours. "And can I say that it's a strange day when adhesives take us in the right direction."

"Tell me about it."

She managed a grin at his appreciative tone. Criminalistics rocked. "So, we're postulating that either someone brought it back to the States to send it to us, or they sent it from here, but through an American account so there was no question that the return addy and account number was San Fran."

"Exactly. And the sender's address has no connection to anything or anyone in Texas, Central America, South America or the like. They make custom doll clothes. I'm sure it was sent back to the States before it was shipped to us," Gates said with conviction. "No question that FedEx gave us real tracking numbers and listings from their origin point in Texas. That means we can be ninety percent sure it was shipped from where the label indicated it shipped from."

"And we won't discuss or mention the hacking you did to confirm that," Ana said without a blink. "Okay, so they get them here to Belize, tag 'em for the hair and the ring. Do they then kill them?" She hated to ask it, hated to think it, hated to think that this was a wild-goose chase or a fruitless search to recover only bodies.

"No, not yet. If they only wanted Dav dead, they could have killed him at that restaurant. He wasn't under cover, didn't have on a vest, and his detail wasn't close enough to stop a bullet. If they knew that, they knew they could take him out right then."

Ana frowned, thinking it through. Her heart clenched. "He wanted private time with Carrie," she said, knowing that had to be why the normally cautious Dav had ditched his detail, kept them contained inside while he and Carrie went outside.

"Yeah," Gates agreed. "He was nervous about the date. He wanted to really talk to her, get to know her on more than a social level."

"He's in love with her, isn't he?" Ana asked, and her husband looked surprised.

"In love? Dav?" He looked shocked, as if that hadn't ever occurred to him.

"Duh, of course," Ana said, rolling her eyes. Men just didn't get that sort of thing the way women did. For the first time in days both she and Gates laughed. "Why else would he want to have lunch out? Why else was he so nervous? Why else would he ditch his detail and walk to the restaurant, make them stay inside? It's not Dav's usual style. You taught him to be übercautious, and last year only reinforced the lesson."

She added up the pieces in her head and came out with a new theory. "That's got to be it. She's the bait because someone saw that it was more than just interest. Someone who knows him really well saw something between them that Dav hasn't admitted to himself, or to you or anyone. All they had to do was wait for him to make his move, let himself be vulnerable to her."

Now it was her turn to pace, to think it out. "He's always with women. He's dated beautiful women, smart women, businesswomen. He works with women. Hell," she exclaimed, "half his business divisions are run by women. Who would have seen that Carrie was different? Who on our team knows him that well?"

"I would have said me," Gates admitted ruefully, "and I knew he was interested in her, but I didn't catch on that it was love."

"Maybe Dav didn't either." Ana narrowed her eyes, thinking hard. "Another woman might recognize it, or a family member."

"It isn't Sophia, or the other side of the family either, the ones with the artist son. They're not sly enough, connected enough."

"I wasn't thinking about them," Ana said. "I'm thinking about the dead brother. You said we couldn't be sure he was dead, right?"

"We're as sure as we can be," Gates said, looking frustrated again. "Without seeing his body."

Ana shook her head. "I'm thinking we need to go in that direction. Let's get the Agency to find out what the scuttlebutt is here in Belize about Niko. And in Somalia for that matter."

Ana began making notes from Gates's comments about Niko's death and their investigation into it. If Niko was alive, who better to be working this deal?

She had a gut sense that she was on the right track. This smacked of something personal, really, really personal. Family-hate personal. There wasn't anyone other than Niko, that they knew of, who would have such a deep and ugly grudge against Dav.

Scribbling notes, she added scorned lovers from youth and his mother's people to the list. She was about to go back a generation and ask Gates about Dav's unlamented father, uncles, and so on, when there was a knock on the door. Hand on his weapon, Gates stepped to the side of the door.

"Gates? It's Franklin."

Ana nodded, recognizing the voice. Gates opened the door. Franklin stood there with one of his dogs on a lead.

"Yeah?"

"Manager asked me to tell you there's a fax for you at the desk. The new guy, Geddey, also called Callahan, looking for you. Wants you to call in."

"Thanks," Gates said, then motioned Ana ahead of him as they left together to get the fax.

Franklin walked around the compound with another of the dogs heeling off-lead as he kept the younger one on the lead. He watched them as they went into the office and Ana wondered if he was their leak.

She wondered if the mole was with them. Who could it be?

The fax was simple. It was a number. The only other information on the sheet was one word, and a time: *Info. 10:00 am EST.*

They got back to the room and Gates fired up his computer to run the number, to reverse-directory list it and check it with the phone company. Meanwhile, Ana called Geddey.

"Mrs. Bromley," Geddey answered on the first ring. "Glad you got the message."

"You didn't call direct," she stated. "Why?"

"I wanted your team to know you needed to call me. You said there was a mole, and I thought it might help us flush him or her out if I was known to be calling you. I have some new info on the extra prints."

Ana's pen was poised to take the information down when Gates grunted a curse.

"Hang on, Geddey." She turned to Gates. "What?"

"Number's a cell. A throwaway," he growled, tension radiating from every muscle. "It's on, but it's bouncing even as I tune into it. San Fran. Oakland. LA. Seattle. All West Coast, but bouncing like a rubber ball."

"Watcha got?" Geddey demanded in her ear.

"Bouncing throwaway cell. Someone faxed us here, saying they had info."

"How the hell did someone know you were there?" Geddey demanded. "Hell, I don't even have the fax number for the damn place."

"I've stopped asking," Ana said wearily. "This is more complicated than a plate of Silly String. Too many loose ends, too many colors, too many sticky parts." She took a deep breath, trying not to take her frustration out on "the new guy." "We flush that mole we discussed, we may figure that out. If we call this number, when they say, we may get the mole or we may get more gooses to chase."

"Let me know." It was a demand, not a request.

She suppressed the irritation she immediately felt. Geddey had the tough job. He was waiting. And if Dav was dead, he had no job. Pretty much sucked all the way around.

"Will do," she finally acknowledged.

Geddey had a parting shot of his own. "Oh, by the way, Declan woke up."

Chapter 16

Dav woke to the sound of chirping birds. He smiled. He hadn't heard that sound outside his bedroom window since he was little. Before she'd become ill, before she'd lost his little sister, Dav's mother had loved to open the windows at night, let the soft air of evening in to cool the house. In Athens, the nights would cool down enough to open the house in the spring and fall. She would come in sometimes, he remembered now, and tell him which of the birds were singing. Their Latin names would roll musically off her tongue, along with their names in Greek and English. He still remembered some of them, but even as he tried to remember, he felt Carrie stir.

Carrie.

Birds.

Freedom.

He abruptly sat up, and Carrie jumped. "What?" she said, peering at him.

His eyes open, with the morning upon them, he realized he could see without the flashlight. "Carrie, the light. The birds."

She looked startled, listening, and turned toward the light. Together they peered into the gap. Old bones lay beyond them, but they looked like animal bones, well gnawed. A musky odor wafted their way in the warming air. Cat, maybe. A big one.

Carrie scrambled to her feet and, turning sideways, tried to get through the gap. It took her three tries, and on the last attempt, sucking in her breath, she managed to squeeze through. He heard the tearing sound of cloth and as she stumbled into the other cave, he could see that even though she wore his T-shirt, wrinkly and crumpled from wear and sleep, it now had a huge rent in the back of it.

She went to her knees and he reached out. "Carrie? Darling? Are you okay?"

He saw her nod.

"I'm just catching my breath. That was a tight squeeze and the ground here is uneven." She turned back and he saw anguish in her eyes. "Dav, there's a way out."

"Yes!" he exulted as she moved forward, toward the vines and the light. "Excellent." He said with fierce delight. "Can you see anything? Can you see a village?"

She shook her head. "I can't see anything but jungle. Dav," she said, moving back to him. "I barely got through. There's no way you'll be able to squeeze out."

He had already realized this, when he saw the tear on the T-shirt. But she would escape. That was the important thing.

"I know this, Carrie-mou," he reassured her, reaching through the gap to touch her face. "I will wait here for you. You will find help, come back for me."

She shook her head, her cheek soft against his rough palm. "It's too risky, trying to find this place, this opening. I think . . ." She hesitated, then plowed on with what she obviously found hard to say. "I think you should go back to the cell."

"Back?" The thought of traversing the tunnels, returning

to the cell, was not only unpalatable, he wasn't sure he could make it with a fever-clouded mind, and alone in the dark.

Before he could protest aloud, she barreled on. "I think I can find the clearing, following the way we came down the tunnels and . . . and . . ." She could tell he wasn't happy, but she continued, his brave Carrie. "If you can get to the cell and I can get to the clearing, then I can shoot off the lock, put down the ladder and get you out that way."

When he started to protest, she overrode the words. "Dav, if this is Mexico or Guatemala or any of the Central American countries, no one will listen to a woman, especially an American woman, and it won't be safe for me to go try and find help. You can say that's all changed and it's the twenty-first century, but not out in the countryside or boonies or wherever the hell we are."

He realized that her point was well taken. It was very possible that harm would come to her as she attempted to get help.

"You may be right," he conceded, and he saw her shoulders slump in relief at his agreement. "You believe you can find the clearing?"

"I think so. If I can get out of the cave going straight up, then I think I can just return to where the center cave was, then turn a little left, then go straight to the clearing."

"I hate to be grim, but you will probably be able to follow the buzzards as well."

"Nasty, but true," she said, her features wreathed in distaste.

"Let us think this through," he cautioned. "Too many things can go wrong. First, you should go to the cave mouth again, see if you can actually get out. Go and see what you see. I will wait until you come back to tell me, yes?"

"That sounds good. It sounds smart," she said, giving

him a small smile. "I can't believe I'm out. I want you out too." She stood up, brushing at her clothes. "Sit tight, okay?"

"I will do this," he said, watching her go. She pushed through the vines and he saw her stumble, then right herself and begin to climb up out of the narrow opening. When he saw the sun glinting on her dark hair, he knew she was going to be free, she would make it. A huge weight lifted off his heart, knowing that she would survive, even if he did not. She was so strong, so determined.

She would make it. He must tell her, he thought, trying to organize his tired thoughts, that he wanted to marry her.

He couldn't judge the time, but it didn't seem long before she was back, scrambling into the cave on her hands and knees. Her smile was excited and positive.

"Ah, there you are, my flame," he said with a smile, standing up to greet her. "Returned from your jaunt, have you?" he joked.

"I can see the buzzards circling, and I think I saw the roof of the building. There isn't a lot of tall vegetation up there." She used one foot to scratch the opposite ankle. "There's some kind of biting bug though. Really itchy."

"I'm glad you could see the way. If I am to go through these dratted tunnels without you, it will help me to know that you will be there, when I find my way." He said it as if he were sure he could make it, although he wasn't entirely confident.

"Here—" She held out her hand for her purse. "Take some more aspirin before you start out, and drink the rest of the water. I didn't see a stream or anything up there," she pointed upward. "But you can refill in the water cave as you go by. Drink lots of water as you go. That fever is dangerous."

"I feel better," he lied, but took the proffered pills and unscrewed the canteen. "But still not well," he admitted when she gave him a look that patently said she didn't believe him.

As he raised his injured hand, holding the canteen, he felt the broken finger throb. At rest, it hadn't hurt, but now it throbbed like he'd hit it over and over with a hammer.

When he had drunk his fill, he handed the second, full canteen through the gap. When she'd set the cord that held it over her shoulder, he handed through her purse, and the all-purpose tool. Then he handed her the weapon. He'd been able to clean it a bit more, but he was still unsure whether it would fire properly.

"Come close, Carrie, and let me show you the safety and the things you need to know about this weapon," he said, holding it up, testing the strap with both hands to be sure it would hold as she climbed.

He pointed out the small safety lever and the gap where the magazine connected. It was loose, so he told her to make sure it was snugly seated before she fired.

"I hope the only time I have to fire it is to shoot off the lock and get you out."

"I do too," he reassured her. "I do too."

He knew he still needed to say his piece to Carrie. So many things could happen between this point and getting back to the cell. He could fall again, or miss a step and meet Hades as he'd joked earlier.

"Carrie, I must tell you some things," he said, slipping her hand through the gap to press a kiss on her bruised and skinned knuckles. "I had planned to ask you to be my wife," he blurted out, knowing he needed to do it before she could say anything else.

Shock suffused her face. "Your wife?" Her voice rose on the second word. "Me?"

He didn't know whether to be amused or hurt by the shock. "Yes. We have known one another for a long time now, and I think we have proven that we are attracted to one another." He sighed. "Carrie, I had not thought to mention it for some time. I have, however, thought it for quite a while now. Of course, I had not thought to end up in the jungle, in a series of tunnels with traps, with dead mercenaries above us, and impassable entrances and exits before us at every step."

"But, Dav, you're . . . you're . . ." she stopped, at a loss for words. He had no idea what she had decided he was, but she was obviously not interested. His gut burned with pain. Perhaps he should have continued to date the models and seekers of safe harbors. Apparently, he should not have attempted to find a wife who understood him.

"I am a man, Carrie-mou. Nothing more. Especially now." He let go of her hand, eased back. "I will work my way through the tunnels and meet you at the cell."

"Dav, I just meant—" she said, then stopped. She didn't reach out, try to regain his touch, and that spoke volumes to him. "I just meant that I'm not marriage material. And I don't think I would ever want to be second place in anyone's life again." Her voice was pleading, quiet.

"I would not put you second," he stated, knowing it was true.

She shook her head. "You wouldn't be able to help yourself. You haven't said you love me," she said softly. "Work would be your wife and mistress and what would I be?"

"I would be faithful, I would treat you with care and respect," he defended, feeling the burn in his gut spread.

He could see the tears in her eyes. They made his stomach burn harder, deeper.

"I know you would, Dav." She shifted the weapon, looked at the ground. Evidently she didn't have anything else to say.

"Then it is settled," he said heavily, striving for some semblance of decorum. He would not beg any woman, or man, for anything. "I will go back through the tunnels." The smile was difficult to muster, but he managed it. "I will race you there."

She smiled as well, and her tear-streaked face would live in his memory forever, along with all the other snapshots of her that he carried there. "Ready, set, go," she said, turning away, the weapon still cradled in her arms.

Dav waited until she had crawled out of the cave once more before he gathered the few other things they'd been carrying and turned to his own journey. Nothing would test him more than this.

"God," he said, addressing the deity he believed in, but had not spoken with very often. "See that she gets home alive."

It was all he would say. For now.

Niko stirred when the phone rang. It was barely dawn, but he had slept only fitfully, so it didn't matter.

"Yes?"

"You will wait until a new team arrives." The order was clear, and it was his mentor; he recognized the voice. If anyone could make sense of this, make sure he got his revenge and got out of Belize to enjoy it, it would be this man.

"Done. Where?"

"Where you are. Longitude and latitude?"

He checked his map, estimated, and gave the coordinates.

Sam watched him, a wary look in his eyes. When he hung up he addressed it. "What? We got no backup."

Niko nodded and said, "Yeah, there's backup coming. A new team." He hesitated, but Sam was the only member of his own team still alive. If he didn't trust Sam . . . "Here's the deal, though. We don't work for this guy, not payroll. We're hired guns."

"Exactly," Sam said, jabbing a finger toward the phone. "How do we know we're not sitting ducks for whoever did that?" He jerked his head in the direction of the now-distant campsite, the massacre. "Som'thin' ain't right here, compadre. And it isn't our team comin'. They had our backs, right down the line. We don't know these people."

Niko stopped the hot denial that sprang to his lips. Sam might not be the sharpest knife in the drawer, but he wasn't stupid either. His common sense had saved them, time and time again.

"You may be right," Niko said. "The more I think about it, the more I don't like it." He scanned the dark jungle, wondering who was watching, who might be listening.

If it was a double cross, why? If it was a rescue mission, why have them stay put?

"We'll move out, get somewhere with a little distance."

Sam started the car, but didn't turn on the lights. "Up or down?"

"Up, toward Guatemala. We've got some contacts there if this goes to hell."

Sam nodded at the directions, but muttered, "Don't know how much farther toward hell it's gotta get, 'fore we bail," as he whipped the Jeep around in the road. Only when he'd eased a few feet down the tarmac did he turn on the running lights, not turning on the full headlights until he'd crept on for at least a mile.

It made sense. If someone was watching them, the Jeep starting might not be deemed unusual; it was still cool at night. The lights going on was a dead giveaway that they were moving out.

From atop his hillside, Jurgens watched the Jeep creep off into the night. The fact that Niko was moving didn't bode well. Jurgens would lay odds that he'd received instructions to stay put. That made him a target. It meant Niko was smart enough to realize that and might be turning on whoever held his leash.

Either way, it didn't bode well for Dav and his lady. With practiced care, Jurgens packed up his meager watching post and shifted back to the position above camp. As the sun crept over the horizon, Jurgens could see that nothing but nearly stripped bones and fragments of clothes were left of the ambushed men. His nightscope had showed animal activity, but nothing moving on two legs, and now the dawn light revealed that even the bodies were being consumed by the jungle. Within a few days, most of the evidence of the mercenaries' bodies would be gone as well, devoured or carried off with the bones.

The sun rose in hot glory and he chewed a bland ration bar, welcoming the energy that flooded through him as the food hit his system. The bugs were unpleasant, but losing sleep was worse. Each night away from his Caroline was an agony.

As if his thought had summoned her, his phone vibrated. The Guatemalan phone, traceable only to the capital city, was being called with a phone card from a disposable phone in Los Angeles. Caroline had gone there on business, his business, and now hers. The legitimate sidelines were growing enough that he would be fully able to replace his excellent income from his freelance work. When that finally occurred, they could be married. That was the benchmark he had set, and to which she had agreed.

"Liebchen," he answered with that one word.

"My love," she replied, infusing the words with such desire that he felt himself harden at the mere sound of her voice.

"The data?"

"Delivered. And some for you. There are two dealers, both old grudges. Both related to your main product." *Two hit men, hired to settle old grudges, and both of the hits were hired by relatives.*

"Strange," he replied, obliquely asking for more information. "That product," he said, meaning Dav. "Is one of a kind, I believe. It stands alone."

"So we—and he—thought." He heard the rustle of papers, the click of keys. "Genealogical Web sites are amazing things. You find out a great deal about who is related to whom."

"Really?" She was amazing, his Caroline, he thought again, as he had many times, even long before he discovered she felt the same way about him.

"Yes, but enough about my hobby," she said, letting him know that she was sure about her data, had sourced, tracked and confirmed it.

"I like hearing about your hobby, love." He couldn't help adding the endearment. "Are these relatives in the mix as well?"

"Why, yes," She feigned surprise. "They are." *So, two relatives after Davros, and two hired killers as well.*

"Perhaps . . ." He let the word draw out as he considered the two men he had killed the day before. "I may have met one of the . . ." Ah, what was the word for it?

"Collateral relatives?"

"Exactly. I met two people yesterday who fit the description."

"Yes, they work as a team, I understand." *The two he had killed in the act of planting mines were a hired team then. Good. That left only three in play.*

"Gut." He felt the satisfaction warm him, as she warmed him. "That leaves only three cousins to meet."

"Any sign of the product you were searching for?"

"There is good hope of finding that product, today," he said, hearing the concern in her voice, knowing that it was about more than the situation. She cared. About him, about their lives together. And about Davros and his woman.

It was more than enough to cement his decision to see if he could free Davros and his lady. Caroline wanted it, which meant he, too, wanted it.

Off in the distance, a movement in the clearing he'd been watching caught his eye. He made a minute adjustment to the scope and saw a woman creep into the open. She wore dress clothes, a dusty skirt and a tattered, wrinkled and dusty T-shirt and sweater. That attire, along with her limping gate told him this was most likely Carrie McCray. To his surprise, he could see she carried a weapon.

"Do you know, my love," he asked Caroline softly as he adjusted the scope, set up the shot should he need it, "what color the top is on the secondary product?" He hoped she would understand his reference.

"I do know, yes. It has a black top, like a raven. The other accessory is blue, and it is a five-six model."

Black hair, blue eyes and five-feet-six-inches tall. The disheveled woman he could see in his scope fit that description.

"You should give your friends the coordinates. I think that product is about to come loose from its packaging."

"Oh!" she exclaimed. "Well, then I will get right on that. Will you be all right?"

The last was as straightforward a question as either of them would dare.

"*Ja,* all is well. I will deal with this."

"Okay. See you soon?" She made it a question, and he heard the longing in her voice that matched the need in his heart.

"*Ja.* Soon."

They disconnected and he checked the time of the call. One minute and thirty seconds. Too short to trace, but possibly long enough to pinpoint location. He needed to move, and quickly.

The scope showed the woman edging around to the grate, weapon at the ready. From the way she held it, she did not seem to know much about it. Her finger was not on the trigger. He squinted into the lens, adjusted, shifted. The safety was on—he would put money on it.

This then, was Carrie McCray. How had she escaped, and where was Davros?

He kept his eye to the scope as he gathered himself to relocate, keeping his movements small and random. A pinpoint from a satellite tracker could give his location too closely, but there wasn't anything quite close enough yet to get to him, or he would have heard it. It was imperative he see what Ms. McCray was doing, so he would have to risk staying put just a bit longer.

Like a frightened animal, she scanned the clearing, hesitating at every step. The buzzards were swooping back in and every time one called out in its harsh screech, or another one landed, she winced and averted her gaze. From the trees, more buzzards croaked, evidently wanting to land where she was, but not bold enough to do so with her there. The remains of one of the mercs lay not too far from the grate and she edged around it, giving it and the other bodies a wide berth. Several vultures left their prizes as she approached, but they too waited in nearby trees, continually calling their harsh disapproval of this intruder.

She disappeared into the small block building, but stayed only a short time. When she reemerged, she was eating something, and drinking from a bottle. She had several more bottles with her and set them down a goodly distance from the bodies.

To his disgust, and surprise, she laid the weapon down as well.

"Stupid," he muttered, thinking she was crazy. This

woman was going to get herself killed. Did she not know how hunted she was?

"Evidently not," he answered his own question in a soft whisper.

He quickly scanned the area. Nothing else moved, but that didn't mean someone else wasn't watching, or that they wouldn't arrive before she completed whatever task she was about.

Now he watched as, with shaky, jerky movements, she heaved and dragged one of the assassin team's bodies from the grate. He smiled to remember the perfect shot he'd made, which took that one out without a whisper. There were times when he loved his job very much.

This body, of course, was not as picked over as the original team's corpses. Through the scope he could see that the underlying corpse, mostly dismembered by the birds, still covered the opening.

With rough sympathy he noted that she had to stop and retch before she got that body moved. Whatever she had eaten in haste had come up in the same fashion. He softly tsked to himself. It was a rookie-recruit thing to do, reminding him that Carrie McCray was a stranger to these operations. A pawn in someone's game, which brought him back around to all that Caroline had revealed. Multiple players. Multiple family members, several of whom Dav was unaware of.

The woman had not yet recovered from handling the bodies, was still bent over at the edge of the brushy clearing, heaving.

He must move. With his target still incapacitated, he took his eye from the scope to survey the surrounding terrain. They were odd, spiky things, these mountains. Not like his mountains in Germany, all strong, sturdy peaks. This terrain was disjointed and covered in scrubby, unpleasant low growth. It offered little cover and even that was a haven for biting insects.

Nothing about it was conducive to his mission, but this was no reason to fail.

He pivoted the scope slightly, getting a fix on a new location from which to keep an eye on the clearing. It would take him at least half an hour to get there, moving steadily, covering his tracks. He would prefer a longer time frame, but moving and seeing were both equally important.

Marking the spot in his mind, he sighted in on Carrie again.

She had moved. Now she was kneeling by the grate, the lock in her hands, trying key after key from a gore-covered ring she held as if it were a live snake. None seemed to fit the lock. As he watched, she stopped and went into the building again. Even from this great distance he could see the gleam of the newly washed keys, the drip of water from her hands as she returned to her work.

Within minutes, she had found the key and opened the lock. When he looked last, she was busily struggling to heave the grate out of the way.

He took this to mean that Davros was still in the cell, or somewhere underground. She had escaped by another way, obviously. Perhaps Davros was injured, or, as a smaller person, she had been able to use an escape route unavailable to the larger man.

With an economy of motion, he secured his weapon and set out. Carrie hadn't been speaking to Davros through the grate. Despite her flurry of activity, she wasn't going down into the cell, nor was she leaving. At his last look, she'd been sitting, weapon in hand, waiting.

Jurgens decided she was waiting for Davros to appear. This would give him the best opportunity to move.

He must also now consider what to do about those land mines.

Everyone was waiting for the go sign from Gates and Ana. Most had slept a little, but everyone was on edge and Ana knew it. But before they did anything, Ana was going to follow her gut again and make the call she'd been instructed to make in the fax.

She dialed the number and the phone rang twice in her ear before the same woman picked it up.

"You have information?" Ana demanded.

"A latitude and longitude," the woman said, rattling off the numbers. Ana repeated them and they were confirmed.

"Why are you involved?" Ana asked with blunt directness.

"Love."

The single word rang with sincerity.

"Dav?" That could pose a further complication, knowing what she now knew about Dav and Carrie.

A musical laugh rang through the line.

"No." That denial was equally sincere, and sincerely amused. "But he was helpful in getting my love and me our chance at happiness. That's all I'll say as I know your husband is busily attempting to trace this call."

"Of course," Ana admitted, glancing at her husband, who was indeed pounding the keyboard, honing in on the signal. From his expression, he wasn't having any more luck tracing the actual call than he had tracing just the number.

"You have three enemies," the woman said, snapping Ana back to the moment. "Two of them are related to your Davros."

"What? Who?"

The woman ignored her interruption and continued, her words coming more quickly. "They are hunting him right now, from opposite directions. One is supposed to be dead."

"Niko." Ana made it a statement.

"Yes." Approval rang through the line along with the confirmation.

"The other?" Ana was frantically writing on her pad. *Other relatives? Who? Where?*

"Is unknown to Dav or Niko. Look him up on Athens GenePool.com. You can find the information there. I did."

"And the third?" Ana scribbled that down, then waited tensely, praying that this mysterious contact would be willing to share a last bit of vital information.

A breath of silence greeted her, then, "The third is someone looking for you."

The line went dead.

Chapter 17

With efficient movements, despite the swaying of the luxury vehicle on the less-than-stellar roads, he snapped the Internet device into his small computer. He pulled up an urgent e-mail and opened it.

The insider is seeking asylum.

He considered it. A man of those qualities would be useful. However, after a few moments, he shook his head. *No.* Once a turncoat, always a turncoat.

He positioned his fingers on the keyboard and responded.

No asylum granted. I suggest Siberia.

He awaited a reply, knowing that his man would be at the controls, waiting for a response from him. He trained his people to act with alacrity, and with independence where it was warranted. However, they also were bright enough to know when to get his approval.

He didn't wait long.

Immediate train or convenient arrangement?

He smiled. If he knew his man, there was probably someone with the turncoat in his gunsights, just waiting to be given the signal to fire. It was a delicious thought and he took time to savor it. Life and death, hanging on an e-mail. How wonderful.

Immediate train. He typed the reply and hesitated, thinking it through, his finger hovering over the Send button.

If Davros's team were not onto the inside man, there was a bit of time. Even if they suspected him, the security geek, his woman and their team had flown the coop and were, presumably, chasing some of the false leads he had strewn about. With any luck, they were about to go on a scouring hunt through South America. They would still be there, chasing the trail he'd laid as Davros breathed his last.

As an added fillip, the security team had already agreed to the ransom, offering an additional sum for Davros's woman and the word of her senatorial grandfather that it would be paid.

He smiled. Perhaps he would save the woman, return her to her grandfather and collect the favor there. He opened another window on his screen to see with which committees her grandfather might have influence.

Yes, he thought, surveying the list. That might be profitable. He made a mental note to have his men cull Carrie McCray from the melee before he let Niko kill Davros. Then, if he were lucky, the two men would kill one another and save him the trouble of executing Niko. He'd already gotten word that Niko had drawn back, left the post he'd been assigned.

That would never do.

He pressed Send.

As he considered the ramifications, the reply came through.

Done.

* * *

The waiting was the worst.

It was killing her to look down into the hole, praying for a glimpse of Dav or even a hint of sound that would tell her he was near. It was worse than fighting through the brush and scrub to get back to the camp, constantly watching on the circling buzzards. Coming on the camp where they'd first been shoved down into their cell was a relief in one way, a nightmare in another.

Carrie scratched at the viciously itching bites on her lower legs. She was sure that she'd received more bug bites in the two hours it had taken her to get back than she'd ever received in her life.

She was hot, tired, sweaty and terrified. What if he didn't make it? What if she had to go *back* through the brush and figure out where the hole was? What if she had to go back through the tunnels without the flashlight?

But no. She'd found the keys. She had the ladder. She could go in through the cell. . . .

The thought of climbing down again, alone, with no one keeping watch for someone who might come and lock the grate again was enough to turn her stomach to jelly.

That fear just redoubled the pain in her heart.

Dav wanted to marry her. How could she bear it?

After all the secrets they'd shared in the darkness, he didn't understand that he couldn't marry her. Not her. She wasn't marriage material. Hadn't she told him that? Shown him that? She couldn't have children; the doctors had told her so after her miscarriage. She was damaged goods. How could he not see that?

More than anything, however, her soul, her spirit, wasn't big enough to live with him, love him when he didn't love her. She couldn't do that again. It would be worse, with Dav.

Unlike Luke, who had cheated again, and again, Dav *would* be loyal. A marriage to her would doom him to marriage with someone he didn't love, with no chance for a family. How could she do that to him? She had been there, lived that way. She wouldn't ask anyone she loved to do it for her.

She felt the tears threatening and fought them back. This was no time to be weepy and sentimental. She had to be firm, strong.

She could do that. She *had* done that. She'd turned him down.

"Oh, God, where are you?" she moaned, staring down into the cell, willing him to appear. She'd found the keys on the mutilated guard's body. After she'd vomited up everything she'd ever eaten in her life—the way it felt—she managed to drag the other body away as well and unlock the grate. It had taken her try after try to get the grate out of the way. She'd heaved and heaved, but it was too heavy. She could put the ladder down without moving the grate though, so maybe he could help her push from underneath.

"Come on, Dav," she said again, straining to hear anything.

Off in the distance, a flock of birds rose into the air, squawking and calling. The vultures in the nearby trees shifted and croaked in response, but didn't leave their watching posts. The ready meal just below their feet was too enticing. With only one puny human blocking them, they seemed content to wait her out.

His first obstacle was the narrow crack of the tunnel leading back into the final cave. He had managed to traverse the corridor without missing a step, or dropping himself down a pit shaft. Now, he was having difficulty getting into the cave mouth from this direction, just as he had when they'd come through the first time.

He managed it, but barely. The long scrapes on his back that Carrie had so painstakingly cleaned in the waterfall burned like fire as they were reopened. New lacerations joined them in a symphony of pain, low notes from the old wounds, higher notes from the new and the underlying bass throb of his swollen, infected and very broken finger.

"Shitdammithell." He ran the American curse words together as he'd heard Gates do so many times. The circular cave was dark, as it had been before, but for the one golden beam of light. It was on a different part of the circle, he decided. He was coming through earlier than he and Carrie had. The light had changed.

That was okay, but the fever he was beginning to feel again was not. The aspirin wasn't battling it back anymore, not as it had before. He didn't dare look at the hand. The dull throbbing was enough to tell him that it was damaged, perhaps beyond repair. It did scare him that he couldn't actually feel the broken finger.

He filled the water bottles and strapped them back on. Stepping under the fall, he let it sluice away the sweat and blood from his back. Cold and wet was better; even that modicum of cleanliness lifted his spirits.

Ready to move on, he stopped. He hadn't realized that there were several tunnels leading in. He walked to the black hole of the opening of the center tunnel and turned back, looking at the perspective on the scene.

No. The angle was wrong.

He moved to the right, turned again. Yes, this was it, this was the tunnel from which he'd spotted the waterfall.

Good.

The sound of the waterfall followed him down the tunnel. He could hear the musical cascade as it pounded on the rock.

It reminded him of Carrie, of making love to her under the waterfall. Her sensual smile, her intensity and her sheer, unadulterated passion—all of them spoke to who she was, and what he felt about her.

What did he feel about her?

Everything.

"It doesn't matter. It cannot matter," he stated, moving to the lone tunnel from which they'd come. He must put it from his mind. She had refused him. For now.

The middle leg of the journey was the worst in terms of watching for the pits in the floor. He climbed into the mouth of the tunnel, then looked back. How lowering to think that a fall into this chamber, a simple fall and a simple broken finger, might lead to his death from infection.

"But not yet," he said aloud. "Not yet." Survival was paramount. "While there is life, there is hope," he reminded himself. Carrie had said that over and over, and if she truly believed it, perhaps he could change her mind. A marriage between them could work.

With renewed determination, he turned his back on the orb of light, on the circular space and the other tunnels and headed into the dark.

To his dismay, the flashlight began to weaken as he walked. The bulb dimmed, then strengthened, then dimmed again. He picked up his pace, trying to remember if there were two shafts or three in this tunnel. It was all blurring together as his head grew hotter and hotter. He should have taken the aspirin bottle with him, rather than leaving it with Carrie. How could he have missed that vital step?

Angry with himself, he picked up the pace, racing the failing light. He made it over another pit, and hurried on.

When he'd crossed the last circular area where they had slept, he turned off the light, using the books of matches instead. Every few feet he would strike a match and hurry forward until the flame burned to its barest nub. Then he'd walk on as far as he thought he could, given what he'd seen ahead of him in the flickering flame. He had to trust himself, even though the fever made him doubt. There were three pits in this last section, but they were closer to the cell, closer to the beginning of the journey.

If he traveled this part of the tunnel in darkness and walked for a while without the light or matches, he could preserve the batteries in the lamp and the rest of the matches. He'd need the steadier light of the flashlight for the last part of the journey to avoid the pitfalls at that point and he couldn't afford to waste it now.

The instant, impenetrable darkness as he let a match burn out made him suck in a startled breath. The old fears rushed through him in a hot flash.

"Then eeseh enea chronon," he whispered to himself. *I am no longer nine years old.*

He chanted the words, trailing his good hand along the smooth line Carrie had discovered on the side of the tunnel. The stone was cool and slick, worn away by countless hands, hands that hadn't touched it for more than a century at least, and perhaps closer to four centuries.

The walls were narrowing.

He stopped. *Trust yourself.* The fever, Carrie's refusal, they made him doubt, but he couldn't afford that. He had to focus, to trust his instincts. They would save him, even as he felt blurred by pain and fever.

He forced his breathing to settle. Standing there, he knew the narrowing wasn't just his imagination, his fear of the dark. He closed his eyes, flicked on the light. Giving himself a moment to adjust, he opened them.

"Ah," he murmured, crouching down. He was glad now that he'd stopped. He was at the tunnel turning and if he'd kept walking he'd have run smack into the wall. He switched off the light again, but lit a match and tossed it forward through the passageway.

He faced the hole, knowing it would require more of his skin and blood to get through. Kneeling, he set both pack and flashlight into the narrow opening and pushed them in front of him as he twisted and turned, trying to slip through with the least effort possible.

"Eh-la, new skin I can grow," he declared, shoving into the tightest part of the space. "I cannot and will not," he grunted as he managed to move himself forward, "stand up a woman, even one who turned me down." He shoved farther through, feeling more of his shirt rip free on the rough ceiling. He heaved, pushing with his legs as much as he could, sliding his shoulders farther in. As he did, he felt the last of the tough, smooth fabric catch on the ceiling. It parted at the center of his back, along with his skin. The stinging heat of blood welling in his wound lent impetus to his movements. "I will not leave her waiting." He shoved again.

"For."

Shove.

"Me."

The flashlight clanked onto the stone at the end of the passage and without thinking he caught himself with both hands before he too fell onto the rough floor.

"Ahhhhh," he gasped in pain. Without Carrie to witness his agony at further injury to his finger, and his abused back, he groaned, let himself rock back and forth on the floor, cradling his injured hand.

The new scrapes on his back added to his pain. His shirt hung in tatters down his back now, but he didn't care. Although the lacerations on his back made him feel as if he'd been whipped, his hand screamed in pain. Bracing with both hands as he fell forward had jolted the injury unbearably. He'd tried to be careful, but it had been impossible.

"It is just pain," he told himself. "Eh-la, will you give up then? Hands hurt, back hurts. They do not kill you." He grunted as he shifted on the floor. "Lying here, that will kill you, Davros. You will use your body as much as you have to, to get out. Business you can do, without a finger or even a hand. But not if you die down here, idiot." He cursed again as the throbbing continued.

For now, he had to absorb the pain, then shunt it aside so he could keep moving.

Grunting again, he shifted to his knees, struggled to rise. It took him four tries, but he managed to get to his feet. Because she'd ordered him to, he drank his fill, draining off half the water in the canteen. Because he was sweating, he sluiced some of the water over his head. His clothes had dried, such as they were.

"So. This I can do," he mumbled, shaking the water and sweat from his eyes. His head hurt and he could tell that his fever was getting worse. The water felt colder than it was, but he was grateful for the effect. He needed more of Carrie's aspirin and it was at the end of the tunnel.

"That is where I will go then." The sound of his voice echoed in the tunnel in a strange way, soft and sibilant. Part of his wandering mind focused on that. The sound. The other part focused on the journey and its end.

Carrie.

He needed more of Carrie, but that was not to be. She had turned him down.

But why had she turned him down? He hadn't asked, just reacted. He'd never proposed to anyone else, ever. He'd never had anyone that he'd wanted to ask. He frowned as he squinted into the darkness.

He switched on the light and stood again, wincing in renewed pain.

"Yamoto," he cursed softly, crouching his way through the next section. When he could stand upright, he stretched, feeling the blood ooze on his back once more. "Eh-la, it is a walk in the park. It will go easily. I will do this."

He turned off the light again, remembering this section of the tunnel better. There was only the one gap left and it was closer to the front of the tunnel. For a moment, it seemed as if the walls were closing in. It was the fever this time, he was sure, rather than actuality. To combat it, he focused on Carrie, waiting for him at the end, at the cell. He would not leave her alone, and she would be there when he made it.

She might not wish to be his wife, but she was not indifferent.

What if it was all a lie? What if she's part of this? Those were the deadliest lies, the ones told by your family, those you thought were your friends. The intrusive, insidious thought slithered into his mind, like a black snake in the inkier blackness of the tunnels.

"No," he insisted, telling the shadows what he believed. What he knew. "Not Carrie. Not her."

She doesn't want you. Not you, or your money. Not your children. Not you, the darkness whispered at him.

"Go to hell," he growled in English, and again in Greek for good measure. "No matter, she is my friend, and she has become my lover. That does not change."

He moved on. The darkness said nothing more, and he was grateful.

"Here." Ana thrust the coordinates at Gates. "Don't worry about the trace. She got us here and here was right. Find this—" She pointed to the numbers. "And let's move out and get there. That's where Dav is. If we'd gone with the Agency lead, we'd be in Ecuador or something. We're close now and we can't be wrong. Or late."

"Argentina," Gates corrected, taking the paper. "We'd have gone to Argentina. What does the rest of this mean?" he asked, even as his fingers flew over the keys and screen after screen shot up, disappeared, and reformed on his machine.

"It means that she also gave us a lead on who did this, and who else's after him." She whipped open her own laptop, booted it up and began a series of searches.

"And this last bit?" He held up the paper, pointed to where she'd written *Me?*

He waited, an expectant silence that she couldn't ignore. She reluctantly admitted the truth.

"A complication. A big one," she confirmed. "She said there's someone down here who knows I'm here and he's hunting me."

"Hines." Gates made the obvious leap. She'd made it too, when the woman told her. Ex-CIA Special Agent Hines had been one of the wild cards in their art fraud case, the case that introduced Ana to Gates, and had nearly gotten them all killed. He'd profited from the sales, covered up the connections, and murdered other agents to silence them. He'd tried to kill his former partner, but McGuire had managed to not only evade him, but hold his own against the thugs Hines had sent to do his dirty work.

It had meant lots of red tape and paperwork, but McGuire was in the clear for killing several of the men sent against him. Meanwhile, Hines had disappeared. From Hines's perspective, Ana and McGuire were his last two loose ends.

Not good, since Hines was an expert marksman.

"Yes. And I think McGuire's here too, tracking him." She could see the fury and fear on Gates's face. "I have no control over him, you know that," she defended. "He's a free agent as far as both the Agency and our company are concerned."

Gates visibly struggled with his anger. "Idiot. Mucking up the works," he growled.

"Yep," she agreed, frowning over her data. "But if he can keep Hines off our collective asses, he'll be an asset."

The unintelligible noise Gates made in response was a mixture of a grunt and some foreign-sounding expletive. He hadn't been idle as they talked, either.

"Got it," he exclaimed, leaping to his feet. "We're moving out."

"Satellite photos?" she demanded, following him.

"Downloading."

They hurried out, laptops in hand, knocking on doors.

Within minutes they were in the cars, checked out and heading out.

"How far away?"

"Thirty miles. Rough terrain, looks like. We're too far south. We have to come up the highway, hang a left and then go on a . . ." He squinted at the screen. "Looks like either a gravel or dirt road."

"The actual coordinates?"

"Looks like a hut, or a small building with a small open field. Not sure what else is there. There's a pattern on the ground that's probably only visible from the air, but I can't tell what it is."

Ana held her phone out to him. "Dial McGuire. I have to keep my eyes on the road."

He did and she fitted her earpiece to her ear. When he answered, she said, "McGuire, where the hell are you?"

"Same place you are." When she didn't respond, he said, "Damn it, girl. I'm in Belize. Is that what you wanted to hear? I told you I was going to go hunting."

"Shit," she cursed, knowing he wasn't going to stop on

her say-so. His grudge against Hines was too deep and too personal.

"We're knee deep in shit," McGuire said. "Got a lead, followed it. I'm betting I'm fairly close to you, since he's after you and he's after me, and some-the-hell-how, he's figured out what I'm doing down here."

She glanced at Gates, mouthed the words "mute it."

He did, and she said, "He's tracking Hines, thinks he's pretty close to us because he said Hines is hunting me."

Gates's reply was succinct. "Fuck."

"Perfect response," she said, signaling him to unmute. "Hey, McGuire, think you can keep Hines off me? We're headed toward a reserve; we have a lead on Dav's location."

"Excellent." The muffled version of McGuire's gruff voice came through the small speaker. "Hope to hell you find him alive and well and all that. I know what you look like now, missy, and most of your team. Don't think I'll shoot anyone by mistake," he drawled. "I've got your back. Go get 'em, girl."

"Will do." They clicked off.

"Damn it, I need him not to be here," she growled, irked that he was, that she was worried about him running around in the jungle. He wasn't exactly young. She'd come to think of him as sort of an honorary uncle, and she didn't want anything to happen to him.

"We need Hines not to be here," Gates corrected. "McGuire's always useful."

"Okay, that's true." She shot him a glance, sighed. "He's on it, he says."

Gates glanced down at his computer, then back to her. "Then he's on it and we'll have to trust him. We're approaching the turnoff. If the road is bad it's going to slow us down."

"I know," she said, knowing too that every moment counted now. Every single one. "Can you get enough of a signal to check that ancestor Web site? Maybe that can give us something on who we're dealing with."

"Yeah, I can do that." He busily punched keys. Without looking up, he added, "I want to check on Declan before we go in, so I may stop on this to call."

"Call now."

"This is running anyway," he said, and pulled out his phone. He clipped on the satellite attachment. The local towers could handle Ana's phone to McGuire's; they were in the same country. To call the United States, they'd have to be sure they got the boost.

It was several long minutes before the phone connected. Georgiade answered on the third ring, and Gates put it on speaker.

"Hey, boss!" Georgiade sounded thrilled to hear from them. They exchanged glances. Was he the mole?

"Hey," Gates replied. "How's Dec? And Thompson, Queller and Damon? How're you feeling?" he rattled off the questions before Georgiade could reply.

"I'm good, Thompson's still sore. Queller's acting like his dog got shot because he didn't get to go with ya'll. Damon's doing good, though he won't be handling the big car for a while, till he heals up. Thompson's mopin' too."

"Dec?" Gates said, hoping that Georgiade's order of information wasn't best news to worst news.

"Improving," Georgiade said, and his voice took on a note of caution. "He's awake, and eating, but he doesn't recognize us. Doc says he thinks he may have hit his head really hard going down, temporary memory loss." Georgiade paused, added, "He recognized his folks though. That was good."

"That is good. Tell him we're thinking about him, okay?"

"Okay. I'm takin' my shift at the hospital in a little while. Thompson's over there now, with the new guy, Geddey."

Ana heard a slight squeaking noise from the backseat and

glanced in the rearview to see Callahan's white face. She'd forgotten that Callahan knew there was a mole. Like Gates, whose expression was troubled, Callahan seemed to be worried that Thompson or even Geddey might be their leak.

Since he hadn't heard anything to make him stop, Georgiade went on. "Geddey is hangin' tough. Doing pretty good getting the hang, you know? He's checking in with Dec a lot, makin' sure he's okay." Georgiade paused, then added, "He's a stand-up guy."

"Good to know it," Ana said, feeling like she had to say something. She still felt odd, knowing that Geddey would be looking after Dav. If they found him alive, that is.

"Who's taking next shift?" Gates asked.

"Damon and Queller. With ya'll gone, we're a bit short, not to mention gimpy, all 'round." He chuckled at his own joke. "They're headin' out in about thirty. You want to talk to either of 'em?"

"No, not right now," Gates answered when Ana shook her head. "Have Geddey call me when he gets back."

"Will do, boss. Ya'll be careful."

"We will."

Gates disconnected the call and, without glancing at Callahan, said, "It's good that he's awake. And it may be good that he can't remember. That may make him less of a target."

"He's not our mole," Callahan said, staunchly.

From the other seat, Holden met Gates's gaze with steady regard. Holden didn't look like he wanted it to be Declan, but he didn't look like he thought Declan was innocent either. They'd taken Holden into their confidence when he too had come to them with evidence that something wasn't right on the plane, or with their data.

Ana watched all the silent byplay in the rearview mirror. They were like momentary snapshots as she shifted from looking at the road to checking out the players.

"Do you think it's Declan, Mr. Holden?" Ana asked softly. When Callahan made a noise of denial, Ana held up a hand. "Let him speak. He's one of the newest to our team. He's observant. He hasn't been with us long enough for it to *be* him, so he's a good one to ask."

"I don't think it's him, but I can't rule him out. Someone made the transmission Callahan found, and it came from inside our compound. That means it could be anyone there, from one of the security team to one of the staff.

"He's a low probability, though," Holden added. "You don't shoot up your inside man. And if you're the inside man, you don't shoot to kill. From what I hear, Georgiade thinks Dec actually got a kill shot. Maybe two." When Gates raised an eyebrow, looking doubtful, Holden crossed his arms defensively. "Just because we haven't found the bodies, doesn't mean they're not there."

Callahan looked belligerent too, that anyone, especially Gates, would question Declan's loyalty.

"Bax is on the lookout for gunshot victims at the local hospitals," Ana commented, trying to find neutral ground.

"Wouldn't go there, you know that," Gates interjected.

"Would if they were dying, or dead," Ana stated.

Before Gates could answer, his laptop beeped a response.

"Let's see what the Mystery Lady was talking about." He scanned the site, which had finally loaded in English. "Athens, birth records, data needed," he said, tapping keys and inputting Dav's birth date and his mother's and father's names.

Lines of script filled the pages and one showed an official-looking document. "Birth certificate," Gates said, scrolling past it to search for information they didn't know.

"There's Niko," he said, pointing to another line of text, another birth certificate.

"Go further back," Ana urged. "Look at his father, or his mother."

"Or Niko's mother." Callahan spoke for the first time.

"Right," Gates said. Without looking up, he said, "Your turn's in fifteen minutes or so, give or take. Holden, watch the time."

"Yessir."

"What year are you on?" Ana asked.

"I'm in the sixties, and there's noth—" Gates stopped in midword.

"What?" Three voices chorused the word.

Chapter 18

The final part of the tunnel seemed to last an eternity. He had managed to walk in the dark for several hours, switching on the light every once in awhile to be sure he could find the last drop shaft.

The beam of light was even weaker and wavered in the darkness. He shone it forward, just as he took a step.

"Ahhh, *shit*!" he exclaimed, and turned the step into a leap as he found empty space beneath his feet. Off balance, he landed on his left leg, with the right slipping on the edge of the abyss.

He threw himself forward, landing hard on elbows and hands.

The pain was excruciating. Every bone in his body rattled, every bruise and slice reawakened to vibrant, throbbing pain. His ankle was twisted and he could only pray he hadn't broken that, too.

Cursing and groaning, he groped for the flashlight. Its fading beam showed his trousers torn at the knees, but the other effects were mere pain rather than the bloody mess he'd expected.

"More bruises. Soon I will be able to connect the dots of my bruises," he said aloud, needing to hear something besides the endless silence and his own thoughts. "I should talk to myself more often," he decided. "At least when I'm not complaining."

He'd often wondered about people who talked to themselves. Now he understood. At least in this situation, it kept fear at bay.

"Get up, Davros," he ordered. "Keep moving. Pain or no pain, you don't keep the lady waiting."

He struggled to his feet, remembering to watch his head in this part of the tunnel. It narrowed again here, briefly.

"It is good that you have a memory for places, otherwise you would be explaining to God why you were stupid enough to get dead and leave Carrie up there all alone." He grunted as he wavered into the wall, bouncing his shoulder off it again. "I do not think God would approve."

He stopped and uncapped the canteen. "Carrie said to keep drinking water." He thought of her as he drank. "I need some of her aspirin. I really do." He winced as he raised the container up, draining it. The motion had pulled loose the tatters of his shirt and reopened the cuts. He felt the warmth of blood on his back, slipping down to soak his belt and pants.

"At this rate, I'll leave a blood trail everywhere I go." He opened the second canteen, drained most of it as well. "Not much farther though."

As he stumbled on in the darkness, he prayed she had made it to the campsite, prayed she would be there.

Be there, be there, betherebetherebetherebethere. The words became a mantra in his mind and he put one foot in front of the other to the rhythm they created. He was so intent on putting his head down and staying upright, that he didn't notice the light.

When he realized he could see his dusty, ruined loafers, he stopped. For a moment he simply stared at them. They were disgraceful, dirty, with warped edges and twisted, shrunken tassels.

Then it occurred to him. He could see them.

His slowed thought processes took a second longer to compute the sight, correlate it with the fact that there was light enough by which to see.

Dav looked up. Ahead, perhaps a hundred yards, lay the entrance to the cell.

"I made it," he whispered. *But would she be there? Had Carrie made it?*

He had to know. Now.

Breaking into a stumbling run, he wheezed down the corridor. The wheezing worried him in an abstract sort of way. Had he broken a rib? Perhaps the dust.

It didn't matter. There was light.

At the last minute, he stopped himself before he burst into the open cell. The movement, the adrenaline of his short run, had cleared his thinking somewhat. Enemies could lie above, anything could have happened while he traversed the interminable dark.

He stopped cold as he got to the end of the tunnel, squinting as the intense light made his eyes water.

The pivoting door was cool against his heated skin. He peered around the back edge of it and saw that the grate was clear. Squinting through the dust and sweat in his eyes, he realized that the lock was gone.

Someone had moved the body off the grate and removed the lock. His heart leaped up.

He had to take a chance.

"Carrie-mou?" he called softly. "Carrie? Are you out there?" He tried again, louder. Then a third time, at a near shout.

Despair hit him like a sledgehammer when she didn't answer. He moved into the cell, noting the blackened, curdled dirt where the kidnapper's blood and other things had dropped and pooled. The grate was heavily encrusted with gore as well, and though it had dried and blackened, the smell was enormous. Evidently, the body, what was left of it, had been pulled off the grate and into the dirt.

"Carrie?" he said it again, yelling this time. What did he have to lose? "Carrie!"

From above, rustling, the pounding sound of running feet.

"Dav? Dav, is that you?" her frantic voice called, and her shadow fell over him as she knelt by the grate. Squinting against the light, he raised a hand to block the glare.

Part of him nearly wept. He had thought he might never hear her voice again, see her again.

As that thought hit, so did the words in the darkness come back to him. *She could be part of it, in on it.*

It really didn't matter. He would trust his gut, and trust her. And if he died for it, so be it.

"Oh, Dav," she sighed his name. "You made it. I knew you could do it."

A grin split his face, causing him to wince as hitherto unknown injuries made themselves known. Evidently, at some point, he'd split his lip because the scabbed wound reopened now, and he felt the sting of salt and blood.

"It's me," he replied, belatedly realizing she would want an answer. "I made it."

"Oh, thank God!" Her heartfelt words were accompanied by a dragging, grating sound. "I have the ladder. I'm going to try to lift the grate again, but even if I can't, I can get the ladder down to you. Then you can push and I can pull to get the grate open."

"Good. Thank you," he added. "Are you all right? Not hurt?" He grimaced at the question. Of course she was hurt. "I should say, no further injuries, I hope."

Her laughter held an edge of tears to it, but it was laughter. "No. I'm eaten up with bug bites and scratched, and if I never see whatever this country is again, I'll be happy. Otherwise, I'm okay. There's food in the building here. Even some cold drinks, because there's power in the damn place, believe it or not. I've been saving you some."

The thought of cold water, a cold drink of any kind, and something to eat made him unaccountably want to weep again. When her beautiful face appeared above him, over the grate, he conversely wanted to whoop with joy.

"You look beautiful," he said without thinking. "You are beautiful, Carrie-mou. Thank God you're alive."

She smiled down at him, her hair falling around her face. Her tears fell through the bars, though her face was wreathed in happiness. One dripped down onto his cheek and he touched it with a finger, capturing it on the tip and looking at the perfection of that tear on his torn and bloody hand.

His heart, his gut, which had burned so desperately when she turned him down, felt like it was flipping over. Could he be . . . in *love* with her? Was this what it felt like?

He had no answers and no one to ask but the woman who had declared him to be unacceptable. He would have to wait to find out.

"Hang on. I'll have this down to you in a minute," she said, and with an oomph of effort, she positioned the ladder by the grate. It took four tries to get it through and resting securely on the ground. She tried to heft the grate again, but it rose only a few inches, before she dropped it. "Damn it!" she exclaimed, frustration making her voice raspy and taut.

"You will need something to brace it, Carrie-mou. Then raise it, and brace again. I will climb up and help you."

"Okay, okay," she panted, letting the grate slip back into position. "A brace. I can do that. Be right back."

She disappeared, and he began to climb. It was slow going, even though he wanted to race up the ladder. His hand couldn't grip the side; it was stiff, swollen and he could smell the infection brewing under the bandages. They would have to deal with that as soon as possible.

He got to the top of the ladder and, with his good hand, pushed at the grate. His hand slipped in the dried blood, and he gagged at the stench that arose.

He retreated several rungs to regain control of his empty, but rebellious stomach. It was an agony to wait for her to come back, but the relief when she did was palpable. He felt even more light-headed to see her glorious blue eyes and smudged and dirty face.

To his surprise, she carried a length of pipe.

"Okay, Dav, you push and I'll pull, and I'll shove this under as we go, okay?"

"Good," he grunted, and climbed up the remaining rungs to set his good hand on the filthy bars. "Ready?"

"On three." She counted and as she hefted the grate, he pushed and she shoved the pipe in with her foot. The grate was opening, even if it was slow. Thank God.

"This is heavy," she groaned, shoving again on the count of three. It took them one more try, and finally the iron bars fell away into the grass. Luckily, he had leaned forward against the ladder as he shoved, so he wasn't directly under the hole. With a terrific clatter and clang, the bracing pipe fell in. The reverberant sound sent the nearby buzzards skyward with a squawking chorus that could have woken the very dead they feasted on.

"Oh, my God, Dav, are you okay?" she demanded, her face white, her voice breathless and scared, as she dropped to the dusty ground, reaching for him. "I'm so sorry."

"Not to worry, Carrie-mou," he panted, both with exertion and pain. "The ladder is remarkably steady. I'm glad you found it, since I do not think I could have climbed a rope." Before she could answer, he forced his feet to move, stepping up one more rung. "On second thought," he grunted, managing another even though his hand, ankle and back were screaming. "To get out of here, I would have climbed barbed wire if necessary."

She managed a laugh. "I get that, but you're almost out." She braced her feet on the side of the hole and reached for his good hand.

His other hand screamed in pain as he wrapped it around the rungs, but he didn't care. He was climbing to freedom, to Carrie and sunlight. The all-but-forgotten clothing pack and the rattling canteens hindered him, but he reached the top and as his head and shoulders cleared the cell, he drew a deep breath.

At the moment, freedom smelled of dirt and blood, carnage and the sweat of their exertion, but it didn't matter. It was sweeter than roses. Carrie helped him out, pulling him over the edge. He rolled clear and lay in the clearing's sparse grass for a moment, savoring the feel of sunlight on his skin, and the release from the imprisoning stone.

The smell of death was still pungent, however, so he didn't lie there for long.

"We need to get moving," Dav said, levering himself up with his good hand. Carrie sat next to him, looking at him. There was something in the way she was looking at him, but he couldn't decipher it.

"There's another Jeep. The keys are still in it." She hesitated and then said, "I think the driver died right by the car door, when he got out. There's blood all over the inside of the door."

Dav prayed that the door had shut, otherwise the battery would be dead and the car would be useless unless they could roll-start it on the road. With his hand the way it was, he wasn't sure he could push the vehicle that far.

"Carrie, I believe I could use some more of that aspirin if you still have it," he said, realizing that he now had access to help. The momentary relief of release and being free were overwhelmed by the headache and heat, which were making his thinking slower than normal.

"Of course. Hang on, I'll get it for you." She jumped up and then froze where she stood.

Dav pivoted on the ground, sensing her fear and coming to his feet in a rush. He moved to stand in front of her, putting himself between her and the apparition that stood before him.

Standing between them and the road was a man. At least he thought it was a man.

"Dav?" Carrie whispered.

"Stay put," he urged. The man hadn't said anything yet.

They stood, staring at one another for a few moments. Dav was unwilling to break the silence. In negotiating, he never spoke first.

This was a negotiation.

The man watched them with hooded eyes. His face was smudged with camouflage paint, his clothes were akin to tatters, but strategically placed to help him blend in with the terrain. The cap he wore was also shaggy and hid his hair. The bill shaded his eyes, as did dark sunglasses.

Dav moved more fully in front of Carrie, his only concession to the silent negotiation. When he shifted to cover her, he saw the man smile. For a moment longer, the man seemed inclined to wait him out, but then shrugged his shoulders.

"There is little time," he said, shifting his weapon in front of him. "You cannot use the road."

Dav frowned at the weapon, recognizing it from Gates's lessons as a sniper rifle.

"Who are you and why are you telling us this?" he demanded.

"I'm . . . a friend," the man said, and let the smile show fully on his beard-roughened face. Between the stubble and the paint, Dav couldn't tell what color his hair was. "You have a number of enemies and all of them are converging on you. You should be gone when they get here."

"What do you know about it?" Dav felt his defensive instincts rise up and snarl.

"This"—the shooter shifted the barrel to indicate the

clearing—"is your brother's doing." He seemed amused when Dav tensed, then nodded briskly.

Carrie's hands braced at his belt. As the man gestured with the weapon, Dav realized that a round from it would go through both of them. The shooter seemed to know the direction of his thoughts and smiled.

"What about you?" Dav said, nodding toward the weapon. "What's your part in all this?"

"As I said, I'm a friend." Although the man kept his voice carefully neutral, Dav caught a trace of an accent. Scandinavian, perhaps. German? He couldn't tell.

"Why can we not use the road?"

"It's mined. The second set of enemies." The shooter pointed toward the bodies lying where the woman had dragged them. "They did that. I believe they were targeting your brother."

"And you shot them." Dav made it a statement, not a question. His gorge rose at the thought. He felt faint and sweaty at the same time, but he forced his face to remain blank, knowing that this man was a cold-blooded killer. A sniper, casually mentioning the deaths of others with no emotion whatsoever, would be unimpressed by his fever.

The rest of the sentence penetrated his fever-clouded brain. "Wait. I know Niko is after me, but someone is after him?"

"Yes."

Dav waited for him to say something more, but he remained silent. Thinking was like slogging through mud. His usually speedy grasp of situations was agonizingly slow.

"So. Eh-la, how can we get past the mines?"

The shooter shrugged. "You set them off, take your chances that you have gotten them all." He paused a moment, then said, "When you do, go south. North will take you into Guatemala—you do not want that."

"What country are we in?" Carrie spoke for the first time.

"Belize."

With that, he turned and left, fading into the trees and grasses along the entry road with barely a whisper of movement to betray his passing.

It took them a long time to move. "Was he really here, or is the fever affecting my mind?" Dav seriously wanted to know the answer to this question.

Carrie gave a shaky half laugh. "Are we back to the gibbering again? Because I think I might be ready to join you." Her voice trembled with anxiety and he slipped his good arm around her shoulders, squeezing her tightly. It was the first time he'd touched her since he came out of the hole.

Sheer pleasure and relief flooded through him at the contact. The warmth of her, the delicate balance of muscle and fragility brought a flood of images into his mind.

Carrie rising above him. Her wild abandon in the waterfall. Hundreds of memories, images and thoughts shot through his mind on fast-forward.

His certainty that he might be in love with her strengthened.

"Yes, gibbering can be arranged," he replied, his face pressed into her hair, knowing she was waiting for his reply.

"It's getting dark," she said, looking around. He heard the rustling of the leaves and wind, noted the darkening skies. Somehow he must move from the heaven of her arms, the solid reality of freedom.

That concept jarred him enough to let go. Much as he hated to move apart, make decisions and focus, he had to. They weren't free yet.

"You go and get whatever food might be in the building. I will begin clearing the road."

Her nod, pressed into his chest, was quick and decisive. "I'll get you aspirin first."

He smiled. "That would be good, Carrie-mou."

She kissed him then, her hands pressed to his face, her body leaning into him. It was a moment that stood in stark contrast to the danger and death surrounding them. For a moment, nothing mattered, no one else mattered but her.

Then she broke the kiss and hurried away.

His newly discovered heart wrenched in his chest and he staggered. He could read nothing into her action, good or bad. Was it a farewell-I'm-sorry kind of kiss? Or a ohmy-GodIreallyloveyou kiss?

He had no basis on which to judge.

Carrie rummaged in the scant cupboards. Her motions were more of a cover for her tears than a real effort toward finding anything. How could he make her feel this way? How could he be so incredibly alive, make her feel so alive, when he didn't love her?

She wanted to cry. She wanted to go home. She wanted . . .

"Stop it," she remonstrated with herself. "You have to get out of here first, and unless you want to die today, you need to go help Dav. Now."

The words, ringing in the small confines of the hut, were almost a shock. The quiet clearing, devoid of all but watching, inimical animal life, was the last place she wanted to stay, much less die.

She pulled two drinks from the tiny icebox, which had been hooked to a battery. They were lukewarm by American standards, but their intact caps and Spanish labels made them seem the ultimate in civilized beverages. She heard the car start and hurried to the door.

Dav pulled the car near to the building and got out. Pain etched his features and Carrie remembered the aspirin. Hurrying to her purse, she found the bottle and got the pills for him. With a quick twist she opened the cap and held it out, dropping four aspirin into his waiting hand.

"I know you're not supposed to take more than three, but I think you should have them," she said, and put her hand to his forehead. "You're really hot."

Dav laughed as he tossed the little pills into his mouth,

draining the soda before he spoke. He was still grinning as he said, "Why thank you. It is good to know I have not lost my suave presence, even under these conditions."

"Suave . . . ?" It took her tired brain a moment to catch up. "You—" She grinned, then laughed. Within moments, they were both laughing so hard they could barely stop.

"I don't think it was that funny," she snickered, "but thanks, I needed that."

"Good. So did I." His expression fell into somber lines. "We must act quickly, Carrie, if our strange protector is to be believed." He glanced at her from under hooded eyes. "He really was real, yes?"

He waited for her nod before he continued. He must be more worried about the fever than she guessed.

"Once we believe we have cleared the road, it will be difficult to drive out with the holes the mines will make. Despite that, we must go, and again, if our friend is to be believed, we must do it fast. The explosions will alert everyone from here to . . . to wherever—" He waved his good hand in a sweeping gesture. "We must be gone when anyone comes to search for the cause of the explosions."

"All right. What do I do?"

"Take this." He offered a weapon and extra clips, which he'd obviously taken from one of the bodies. "Get in the building. I will use the Jeep as cover. I have gathered enough things to throw that hopefully I can set off the mines. If they are personnel mines, they blow upward, which will not leave a huge crater." He stared toward the road, as if willing this to be the case. "The man said there were six."

"He did?"

Dav smiled. Perhaps he was delirious, but when the man mentioned the mines, Dav had seen his hands release the weapon, flash three fingers with a gloved hand once, and then again, before he regripped the weapon.

"I think so. Quickly now." Dav urged her toward the concrete building, always thinking of her safety.

With obvious pain, he climbed back into the driver's seat. Before he could put the car in gear, she made her decision. She ran to the Jeep and jerked open the passenger door.

"Wait," she said, climbing in, dumping the gun and extra clips on the seat. "We'll do it together and then leave. I'm not waiting for you again. It nearly killed me when I thought you weren't coming." She sucked in a breath. "Together," she declared stubbornly, when she saw the protest forming on his lips. "Or not at all, deal?"

She held out a hand and for a moment he just stared at it, and at her. A brilliant smile blossomed through the growth of the beard he sported, startling in its white contrast to the dark hair.

He took her hand and kissed it, then shifted his one-handed grip to her shoulder and pulled her close to kiss her hard on the mouth.

"It is a deal, yes."

"Wait here, then." She ran into the hut and grabbed everything she'd found, snatched up her purse from the tiny, rickety table and got back in. "Let's do it."

"My action hero," he said, smiling, as she dumped the odd collection of gleanings over the seat to be sorted later.

"Wonder Woman, that's me," she said with gritted teeth as the Jeep bounced over the rough ground of the clearing. She studiously avoided looking at the bodies strewn about. There was nothing she could do about them, and any one of those men would have killed them both.

"It is, indeed," was all he said as he fought the steering wheel. She saw the lines of pain return and saw him wince with each jouncing, jarring bump.

He whipped the car across the mouth of the road and got out.

"Now comes the interesting part," he said, flexing the fingers of his good hand. He looked at her now, a keen assessment. "How well do you throw?"

"Pretty well, why?"

"Time to clear the road," he said simply, offering her a softball-sized rock.

From behind the wall of the car, Dav cocked his arm back and lobbed a fragment of stone toward the road. The chunk rolled in the dust and stilled. No explosion.

"Farther up, then," Dav muttered. "Come, get back in."

They crept forward on the road, and he stopped again. They got out.

Another toss, another blank response.

He handed her a fat chunk of charred wood. "You try."

She hefted it, then rose up from behind the car to throw it, overhand as she'd seen in countless war movies.

The explosion was louder than anything she'd imagined. Dav grabbed her, yanking her down below to relative safety behind the bulk of the car. Dirt pinged on the metal, but other than the squawking of the birds behind them, there was no other sound.

"Again."

He threw, then she threw—odd pieces of equipment, pieces of wood, the chunks of stone he'd originally thrown. He counted six explosions.

"Now we must see if we have succeeded. Stand back a ways, Carrie-mou. I will drive through."

The road was a Swiss-cheese-shred of massive potholes now. Some were only inches deep. Another looked as if someone were ready to plant a good-sized tree in a readied hole in the dusty soil.

"No. Together," she insisted. She wasn't going to stand on the road and watch him either blow up or disappear again.

They argued, briefly, but she won. He was either too tired, or in too much pain, but he gave in.

"I do not like it," he muttered. "If we missed any—" he started.

"Six explosions. Six holes. If you're right, we're home free."

He whipped toward her in the seat. "And if I'm wrong?"

A sense of fatalism seemed to have settled into her bones. "We'll die together," she said, with a shrug.

For long moments, he just stared. Something of her determination must have shown on her face, however, because he finally nodded and restarted the car.

"Fast or slow?" he wondered, scanning the ugly mess before them.

"Go for it," she urged. "As fast as you can. Get us out of here." She recognized the hysterical edge to her own voice, but the tantalizing view of freedom, symbolized by the road, beckoned. "God, Dav, just go."

"Eh-la," he said, with more strength. "We go."

Chapter 19

Way in the distance, a flock of birds rose into the sky. Niko trained his high-powered binoculars that way, but saw nothing but sky and dusty trees as the birds disappeared. Had they come from the clearing? Why would the birds have left?

Frowning, he was about to tell Sam when the phone rang. They exchanged glances as Niko picked it up.

"You are still in place?" His mentor's smooth voice rang in his ear. They'd been without contact for hours. He and Sam had decided to head for Guatemala and had turned the car, just before he'd done one last scan of the area.

"I am," he lied, keeping his voice level, unemotional.

"There is a change of plans. I have created a . . . haven where the main roads join. Go, check on your guest, then join me. Once you arrive we will head for home. I believe the ransom has cleared, so you will be well paid. My jet is waiting."

He clicked off. The whole scenario was beginning to smell like rotten eggs. He ran it by Sam.

"It'll get us out of the country," the other man reasoned, voting for the plane. "We can scatter from there and stay out of this guy's way from now on. Guatemala's too hot for me," he added with a wolfish grin. Sam had outstanding warrants in several countries. Apparently Guatemala was one of them. "Be better if I got out another way."

They debated it a bit more, but decided to go for it. A scan of the clearing would give them more information anyway.

When they arrived twenty minutes later, they got a surprise.

"Mines," Sam said, whipping a weapon out and going on full alert to cover the road, actively scanning back and forth.

"I'll go in. Wait for me." It was an order, not a request, but Sam nodded.

"Ain't goin' nowhere."

Niko hopped out, crouching by the cover of the Jeep's front fender. He moved down the road, right at the edge, lest there be additional mines. In the clearing, he saw more damage than what he and Sam had first surveyed.

Pressed against the wall of the hut, he scanned everything, cataloging it. Two more men lay in the shadowy area. He could tell from where he crouched that they weren't his men, and he didn't know them, or he didn't think he did. They were shorter, stockier than his mentor's minions. The man hired tall people, taller than he was, Niko had noticed.

"Tall poppy loses its head." He muttered the old saying, thinking that his mentor made sure everyone around him was a higher target than he was.

These two weren't of that ilk. They were neat, though, and had been clean shaven and well kitted out. He saw the packaging for another mine lying by the second man's side. It had fallen out of his satchel when he'd been dragged.

These were the mine-layers, then.

Niko scuttled to the hole, where the open grate gave mute testimony to the fact that Dav and his woman were gone.

He frowned at the signs below him. The fat angle of stone was ancient, a sharp contrast to the metal facing of the grate.

Without time to explore it, he couldn't be sure, but it seemed as if even the past had conspired with Davros to aid his escape.

When he got back to the road, the car was there, but Sam was gone.

"Carrie." Dav said the word through gritted teeth as they made their way down the steep, rutted road.

"Yes?" She stuttered out the word. The trip back down was better than it had been when they had ridden up the road, bound and blindfolded in the backseat, but it was still unpleasant.

"I think you must drive now," he managed, slowing to a stop. The adrenaline rush of exploding the mines and the sheer tension of making their way out to the road had carried him thus far, but his scant reserves of energy were eroded by the pain and the fever. It was getting dark and his vision was blurring from fatigue and constant pain.

"Okay," she said, unfastening her seat belt. "Just put it in park, we'll switch."

He did, unfolding himself from the seat, using his good hand to unclench the injured one from the steering wheel. The fingers were stiff and unyielding, cramped by the tightness of his grip.

He stumbled round the front as Carrie rounded the back, efficiently switching seats as if they'd rehearsed it innumerable times.

He sank into the passenger side, feeling every scrape, every bruise, every cut on his body. With as much aspirin as he had in his system, he was sure his blood had thinned and he would bleed to death if he were cut now.

The thought was just another in a long line of rambling, unpleasant images rattling his brain. Exhaustion pulled at his consciousness, begging for sleep, for surcease from thought and decision and constant threat.

Carrie belted herself in, primly checked the rearview mirror and the side-view mirrors, and then gingerly put the Jeep in gear. In the middle of everything, despite the pain, he had enough humanity left that it amused him.

"You do not drive?" he asked, wondering at this first show of timidity. She'd been brave as a lion up until now; this checking and rechecking spoke of fear.

"I'm a city girl. I haven't driven for . . . years."

"You can make few mistakes out here, my love," he said, closing his eyes, trusting her to get them going again. The darkness called to him, beckoning his consciousness.

"Dav," she said, and he heard real fear in her voice again. "Please, you have to stay awake if you can. I don't think I can do this alone."

Her soft plea had him adjusting the seat back upward once more, struggling to return to full alertness. It was challenging. Everything in him wanted the healing that unconsiousness would bring. Snatched hours in the cave, waiting for morning, had not been enough. The endless day, traversing the dark caves, had taken every erg of energy he possessed, and more. Pushing past that boundary, they had faced down the unknown sniper and escaped.

Everything within him cried out for rest.

"Eh-la, what shall we talk about, on our Sunday drive?" he managed, sitting forward so his back didn't connect with the leather at every jolt, and spacing the words between jouncing shifts. It was hard to focus, but he thought the rough road had widened a bit in the beam of the headlights.

A nervous laugh was her first answer. "How long have we been here?"

The question set off a cascade of queries in his mind, none of which he had the answers to. "I don't know. I think—"

He hesitated, counting what he could remember of the days. "Seven days, perhaps?"

"They didn't find us." She didn't turn his way, but he saw the white knuckles, the tighter grip on the wheel as she spoke. It took him a moment to unravel the non sequitur. "What if we'd waited, hoping for rescue?" She glanced at him, then resolutely stared back at the road.

He nodded, using his good hand cross-body to hold on to the handle above the door, doing everything he could not to jostle his back, his finger or his aching head. With his hand pressed into his chest—the most stable place for it—he could smell the faint sickly sweet smell of decay. Either the bloody bandages were beginning to stink, or his hand was. He didn't want to contemplate which.

"We would still be there, then, waiting," he said, barely suppressing a groan as the car hit a particularly difficult stretch of the road. "Or dead from one of the killers who came for us."

In the cool light of the dash, he saw her shudder.

They rode in silence for a while and he tried to make conversation. They managed it in stilted sections, between hanging on and trying to see the margins of the road.

The road straightened out for a bit and they could breathe more freely.

"Dav, I don't think I can go on. I'm exhausted and I'm falling asleep at the wheel. I . . . I . . . don't think I can do it."

As she said it, the beams of the headlights showed another road turning off to the right.

"Wait," he said, startling her into hitting the brakes hard. They were both thrown forward into their seat belts, but he waved away her apologies. "Turn in here."

She backed up a few feet and managed to crank the wheel around enough to make the turn. As they rolled down the smoother, planed, but overgrown road, he told her to slow down, switch to the parking lights.

"Take it easy," he urged her. The lights showed mining equipment neatly parked in a fenced-in area. The gate had a padlock, held by a rusted chain. A paved, covered area outside the gate was currently empty of vehicles, but appeared to be a place to park. "There," he pointed. "Back in."

Her skills were obviously rusty, but she turned the Jeep and backed it under the canopy. When she cut the engine and the lights, silence enveloped them. Nothing moved in the darkness but the wind.

There were creaks and pings from the cooling engine, and he felt as much as heard her deep sigh.

"Water?" Carrie croaked the word. "Can you reach it?"

"Not with my good hand," he said, wishing it were otherwise. She grunted and turned in the seat, nearly falling into the back in her attempt to reach the refilled canteens.

"Here." She pressed a canteen into his working hand. "Drink as much of this as you can. We have to get that fever down. Since we don't have antibiotics, you need fluids and aspirin."

"Antibiotics would be good, I'm sure," he quipped, between long draughts of the stale-tasting water. He didn't care though. The wet, cool liquid felt like heaven as it slid down his parched throat.

"They would. We have to get you to medical help as soon as we can," she fretted, twisting the other canteen round and round in her hands. "Maybe we should keep driving."

"No." He reinforced the word with his voice, firm and final. "We are in no shape to go on. Either of us. We are stumbling blindly on a dark road in a country we do not know. We are exhausted, and I am weak and feverish. With this—" He lifted his hand but realized she couldn't see it. "With my hand going bad, you are carrying us both for the moment." He turned toward her, reaching awkwardly to grip the hand now lying limp in her lap. "You must be able to drive, and keep your wits about you. This you cannot do if you are falling into sleep."

"I feel so useless," she admitted. "I feel like I should be able to go on."

"As do I, but I cannot." He thought for a minute before giving her an admission of his own. "It was not easy to ask you to drive. I want to carry you away from this, win your freedom." He squeezed her hand, and felt her turn her palm to his, interlace their fingers. It gave him a ray of hope. "I too have this sense of failure, that I cannot push my body further, get you, tonight, to a place of safety."

She was silent for a moment, then squeezed his hand again. "I get that. I really do." He couldn't see her, but heard the rueful amusement in her voice. "We're both white knights, I guess, trying to do the right thing."

"We are, indeed. Now, come, rest your head on my shoulder, and let us sleep."

She scooted over, and leaned carefully on him, relaxing finally with a deep sigh. They sat like that for long moments and Dav felt the lassitude that preceded sleep beginning to overtake him.

"Dav," she said softly. "Thank you."

"You are welcome, my flame. But do not thank me so soon. We are not, how you say, out of the woods yet."

"No, but thank you anyway." She hesitated and he felt the tension in her shoulders.

"What is it, Carrie-mou?"

"I need you to understand why I can't marry you," she said, surprising him. With succinct phrases, she laid it out. Her dissection was calm, and clinical, and he heard the finality of her decision in her words and tone. For a man long used to reading those things in business, he knew she meant everything she said. There would be no negotiation, he thought, his tired, feverish mind running answers and arguments to every one of her statements. For her infertility, her refusal to settle for less than love, her sure knowledge that he didn't love her and her desire that they remain friends, he could see an argument, but each time he tried to grasp it in his mind, put it forth to break down the walls she had built, it slipped away in a haze of pain.

"I don't want to lose that, Dav," she finished earnestly. "Please tell me that we will still be friends."

"After all we have been through, my flame? You would doubt this?" Somehow he managed to say that, although the words seemed thick and foreign as he struggled to get them out.

"I . . . I . . . yes," she admitted. "I saw your face when I said—"

"Shhhh." He hushed her, grimacing in the dark at the memory. She had said no. Her answer remained no. He would not embarrass either one of them by pressing an unwanted suit upon her.

But his heart ached, still. That long-dormant and elusive sense of love would have to find its way without her.

"We will be friends still, as we have always been. And lovers if you so choose." He added the second bit, but felt her shift in his arms. "Carrie-mou, I will not take it amiss if you do not want that."

"It's not that I don't want it," she began, then stopped. She was about to speak again when he saw the lights.

"Shhh." He silenced her. "Look."

Passing on the road, a set of headlights flashed, then disappeared going downhill from their position.

"Dav?"

"Yes, I know. But we don't know who it is. We must sleep, and find help tomorrow."

"But," she started to protest, then stopped. "You're right."

"Yes. So—" He softened that adamant rejoinder with a laugh. "Will you sing me a lullaby, my friend?"

He felt her snicker, as much as he heard it and smiled.

"No. It would attract wolves or coyotes. It's that much like howling."

"Ah, well then, we will just have to do without."

"Hmmmm," she murmured, relaxing.

Within minutes they were both asleep.

In the early dawn hours, Ana, Gates and the team bounced up the rock-strewn road, heading for the coordinates they'd been given. Ana leaned forward in the passenger seat, as if to urge the car to move faster.

"I can't go any faster," Gates murmured, wishing he could.

"I know."

In the rearview, he saw Callahan and Holden, having taken their now-accustomed spots in the backseats, exchange glances. Evidently they felt the same way.

Hurryhurryhurry! Even knowing it was unsafe, Gates increased his speed. They'd sent the two front men on the noisier motorcycles back toward civilization. With luck, they would get to the yacht in Punta Gorda and report in. When they found Dav, everything would be ready for their departure the minute Ana and Gates got there with Dav and Carrie.

Provided they found them alive.

"Coming up on coordinates," Holden said, managing to read his GPS. "Ahead one mile and on the right."

Ana cued in her mic. "Look sharp, everybody."

They slowed to let two of the men drop off at the half-mile point, taking the "scenic route" as Franklin described it, through the brush. The dogs were with him, in the hopes that they would alert the team to sentries or outposts before they got to the clearing.

"Holy shit!" Ana gasped as she saw the road before them. The deep potholes were raw and new, and evidence of explosives lay in the sprays of dirt that browned the ridges on either side of the road.

"On foot," Gates ordered, and the team piled out, armed and ready. "Stay off the road. Watch for any sign of disturbed soil. Look before you step, people."

Using the throat mic, Ana informed the others about the mined road, then asked, "Team two, any sign of sentries?"

"Negative. I've got signs of a sniper nest though. Tree spikes on some kind of hardwood. Only thing around here you could use."

"Dogs, Franklin?"

"On alert, but not flagging."

No signs of life yet.

Creeping on the upper verge of the road, several feet above where the mines had been laid, they came to the end of the lead-in road and the trees and scrub opened onto a scene of carnage.

Bodies lay strewn about, obviously days old from the bloating and animal activity. Two newer bodies lay where they'd been dragged, mere feet from an open, iron grate.

"Franklin, send the dogs out, locate on Dav."

"Roger that."

With Callahan and Holden covering them from the cement block hut, which they'd cleared, Gates and Ana made their cautious way between the bodies to the hole.

"Niko is a bastard," Gates snarled. "He knew Dav hated being underground."

Surprised, Ana looked at him, before scanning the woods and trees. "Why?"

"His dad used to lock him in this kind of dungeon. A cell-like room in the lower basement. He hates dark, underground places."

"I'm guessing we're in the right place again, then," Ana said. "He's not here, and there's no second vehicle, though I saw tracks in the displaced dirt. That means someone left alive and driving. Either someone moved them, or there was a survivor and they blew the road, then drove out over it."

"I saw that too. Let's drop back to cover, wait for the dogs."

They'd barely reached the hut when the dogs burst through the covering scrub. The Plott hound, a scent tracker, bayed once, then dropped his nose down, ignoring the blood, flies and other noxiousness to follow a trail to the hole.

Next to him, he felt Ana tense, only to feel a second sigh of relief as the hound woofed and began tracking toward them, weaving through the corpses, and stopping for a long moment in the middle of the clearing. He kept coming their way, and stopped in front of them.

Looking down, Gates saw tire tracks marking the silty soil. "They reversed here, drove to the road."

"Dav and Carrie, or Dav and a captor?"

"No way to tell."

"Boss?" Callahan said, pointing. "Those two are newer kills." Her voice was even and steady, but her skin had a slightly greenish cast to it. He looked at the two body armor–clad dead guys, immediately noticing the difference in equipment, and the difference in how much of the flesh the predators had stripped off the bones.

"Second team, report in." They waited as Ferguson and the others relayed positions relative to center of camp.

"Personnel mine wrappings next to one of the newer guys," Holden added, pointing. "These guys came in secondary."

"Shooters?"

"Not snipers." Franklin came huffing up. He hardly glanced at the bodies. "No rifles. And they're not nearly as dead as the other guys. Probably, what?" He turned to Parker. "Dead about two days, maybe? The others have been dead longer. Maybe four days."

"Ugh."

"Yeah, well. Better them than Dav, or us," Gates said.

"Franklin, can you have one of the dogs track for Carrie? We need to know if she's with him."

"Will do." He whipped out a sealed bag containing a piece of clothing they'd been given for Carrie's scent, and set the dog to work. Meanwhile, he set the first dog crossing, checking for other places where Dav's scent might be.

The dog tracking Carrie followed the same paths as the first dog, but went into the building and out again several times, before sitting down in the road. When Franklin set that hound coursing for another scent, the dog bayed and set off downhill, away from them.

Franklin called him back. His face looked pained. "At some point, Ms. McCray was off in those woods, but came back here."

"How do you know?" Ana demanded.

"He picked up the freshest scent first, here at the building, over there by that hole. The trail down the hill's older, but it's there, so when I sent him out again, he went for that, thinking I wanted a track-back."

"Does that mean . . ." She trailed off, obviously thinking of the dire possibilities of Carrie being separated from Dav, even for a while.

"No way to know. No blood though, or the dog would have alerted on that."

"You said the freshest scent was here, though?" Gates said, pointing at the ground where they stood, by the hut. They were all crouched in its shadow, with Callahan and Reed keeping watch. Reed hadn't left the tree line, keeping the clearing under cover, but not showing himself.

"Don't know that yet," Franklin began, when his first dog bayed and sat, right by the same spot the first dog had sounded on in the rutted road.

"That's freshest." Franklin pointed, and hurried to his dog before Gates could caution him to keep his head down.

"Idiot," Ana muttered. "What's he thinking going out

there without evasive?" Franklin had run straight, no zigzagging or evasive maneuvers at all.

"Getting to the dog, that's what matters to him," Gates said, gritting his teeth at the thought that Franklin was so exposed.

He cued his own mic and ordered everyone to fall back to the main road. They'd have to see if they could figure out which direction the vehicle had gone. Since someone was driving it, and the dog had alerted on both Carrie and Dav, he had hopes that they were still alive.

It would take a miracle, but sometimes that was all you had to go on.

Carrie and Dav woke when the sun had risen well into the sky. The air in the Jeep was stuffy and hot, in spite of the overhanging cover and the slightly lowered windows.

"God, I want a shower so badly," Carrie muttered, brushing at her clothes. Dav saw the dried blood staining them and felt fear clench in his belly.

"Carrie, you are covered in blood. Are you hurt? Are you injured? I did not ask," he said, whipping himself in his mind for the oversight.

"No, no, it isn't my blood," she quickly reassured him. "I had to drag that man," she began, gulped, and tried to go on. "The one that fell over the grate. I had to . . . had to . . ." She gulped again. Then, forcibly shoving herself upright, she flung open the door and stumbled out to retch in the long grass at the back of the covered area.

As he neared her, he heard her muttering, "Oh, God, the blood. Oh, God."

He brought the canteen and a towel he'd seen in the backseat. Wetting it, he handed it to her to wipe her face and mouth. He put an arm around her shoulders, and awkwardly used the uninjured fingers of his broken hand to tuck her tangled hair behind her ear.

"Here you are, Carrie-mou. Use this now and wipe your face," he urged. "It is cleaner than my handkerchief could ever be, no matter the origin."

He was rewarded by a weak chuckle. "That handkerchief needs to be burned, along with everything else," she muttered.

"True, but if we survive this, I may keep it, for sentimental reasons."

Her only reply was a grunted, "Ugh."

"Oh, God, I'm going to throw up again," she wailed, and did so.

By the time she'd gotten her rebellious stomach under control, the humidity was beginning to build and the heat as well. "And now, we must go," Dav said, wishing he could help her more.

"I know. Maybe some crackers or something, to settle my stomach."

"We have those. The finest jungle crackers, just for you," he joked, rummaging in the supplies she'd gathered to find an oval sleeve of Town House crackers. "Are you well enough to drive?"

"I think so. There's no other choice. We have to get out of here, so I'm well enough."

"Good, because the fever is making me feel hot and cold," he confessed. "And there is dizziness with it. Driving is probably best left to you, for now."

He took more aspirin, drank more water, but stopped before draining the canteen. They didn't have a map, or a source for supplies. It needed to last.

They crept forward in the car, inching toward the main road. Before they turned into it, Dav got unsteadily out, and peered up and down before he allowed her to come close to the mouth of the overgrown drive.

He was about to get back in when he heard it.

"Quick," he ordered her, slamming into the car and grabbing for the seat belt. "Move it. I hear cars coming from up the road. In the daylight, they will see where we stopped and turned in. We can't be trapped here."

He barely clicked the metal buckle into place before she peeled out onto the bumpy surface and headed south.

Dav gritted his teeth against his wavering vision and hung on to consciousness with every ounce of will he had.

It was about survival now, and that meant speed.

"Go faster if you can," he said, and hung on.

Chapter 20

"Hurry," Ana urged as they made their way back to the road. "They're ahead of us again, but maybe not by much."

"A day," Franklin said, coming up even with her, his dogs trailing at his heels. "Maybe less."

"That's good news," Gates said, throwing a warning glance at his wife. Both he and she knew what could happen in a day, but there was no need to demoralize any of the team, not when they were this close. They each had experience with the heartbreak of arriving moments too late to help or save a friend or colleague.

Still on watch, they arrived at the road, quickly followed by their outliers, Reed and Callahan. When those two arrived, Franklin loaded his restless dogs and climbed into the SUV to reassure them.

They carefully turned the big vehicles back the way they had come, beginning the trek down the steep, rock-strewn road.

They'd barely started when a form stepped into the middle of the road, a weapon pointed right at them. Gates skidded to a halt, the heavy SUV shuddering as he stood on the brakes.

The man was a sniper, dressed to blend in with the surrounding hillsides, his rifle painted the same dusty greenish brown hues as the grasses and brush. But there, standing in the brightly lit road, he didn't blend. Rather, he stood in sharp contrast with the sunlit morning.

He held up a hand in the universal sign for them to stop.

"You, driver," he called. "Gates Bromley. Step out."

Ana put a hand on his arm, but he murmured, "No, it's okay. If he wanted us dead, we'd be dead. And he knows who I am."

"True. Be careful," she said as if she couldn't help saying the words. She eased her Kahr K9 from its holster, slipped off the safety and readied herself to fire.

"Roger that," he replied, without glancing at the weapon. He slipped down from seat to running board and to the ground before raising his hands. Arms still raised, he moved in front of the vehicle, but deliberately stayed to the left.

With the heat of the large engine at his back, Gates positioned himself so that Ana, Callahan or Holden could get a shot at the sniper. He didn't hold out much hope that the man would give them the opportunity, but he positioned himself properly anyway.

"Your friends are alive," the man stated. "The man, Davros, is hurt. I do not know how badly."

"Who are you and how do you know that?" Gates snapped back, masking his surge of hope with flat calm.

A smile curved the other man's lips. "My partner led you here because the man and his woman are alive."

The phrasing reminded him of Dav. A sure sign the speaker wasn't born in America.

"Your partner. Yes." He paused a moment, then added, "Thank you for that." They would never have gotten this far without the woman's help.

The other man offered a brisk nod of acknowledgment. "Go south. I've been down the road, but lost them. There are many players here. Davros's brother is not far behind him. And the third player has arrived in the country. I do not know what reception your man will get, but you must find him first, yes?"

"Yes," Gates answered. The man smiled again, and flicked his wrist, sending something spiraling into the brush. He knew better, but Gates's involuntary response was to look.

In that flash of a moment, the man was gone.

"Damn it," Gates cursed, flying back around the driver's side door to jump behind the wheel. He should have seen that coming.

Then again, he wouldn't have pursued; his focus was Dav, not some crazy sniper informant with twisted ideas of loyalty.

"What did he say? I couldn't hear him," Ana demanded, impatience written in every line of her body. Her weapon at the ready, she quickly resnapped her safety belt but not the safety on the weapon, as he threw it in gear and headed out.

"In a minute. Tell the second team to stay close and push the limit."

The bone-rattling ride wasn't conducive to handling firearms, so Ana ordered everything safetied and stowed, and with obvious reluctance, she holstered her own weapon.

"Spill it," she ordered, grabbing the "oh-shit" handle well above her head to keep herself steady on the bone-shaking descent.

"He's the woman's partner. He's been the source of the info."

"Why didn't he just save Dav?" she snarled. "What's with all this fucking cat and mouse?"

"He said he lost the pursuit down the mountain. He also said Niko's between Dav and us. And the third player's in-country. The uncle."

"What uncle?" This was from Callahan, bouncing around like a rag doll in the backseat. Her shorter stature made it hard for her to brace herself and hang on, but she wasn't complaining.

"That's the search we did. The genealogy thing." Gates spat the words. "Shit!" he said, then flicked Ana a glance as a deep rut nearly wrenched the wheel from his hands. "You tell it."

"Whoever our little helper is, she dug out the data that Dav has an uncle. A bastard uncle, raised in the United States."

"How old would this guy be?" Callahan squeaked, looking mortified that she had gone airborne for a moment.

"Late seventies, probably, maybe eighty. The site says he's older than Dav's father, and I don't remember how old he was when he died, but it's been twenty years," Ana explained.

"Did the boss know this guy?" Holden managed as he too flopped to and fro with the sharp corrections Gates was making as he pushed the limits of both road and vehicle.

"Don't think so," Gates added. "Never mentioned it. And he would have."

The SUV slewed sideways, and Gates corrected. "He could be anywhere, waiting for them."

"I know."

Ana struggled to reach her phone, and he took a hand off the wheel just long enough to steady her.

"Thanks."

She pulled up the number and called Geddey. "Hey, it's Ana. Don't talk, listen," she said when he answered. "We're in pursuit. We've been told both Dav and Carrie are alive. The dead brother arisen, Niko, is between us and Dav. The third player I e-mailed you about is in-country too, but we have no way to know where he is or what he's planning."

"Got it."

"Make sure the yacht staff is ready and the Agency's

alerted. If we can get out of here, we'll need to make tracks, fast. They'll have to cover us with the locals."

"Done."

Ana heard the fast scratch of a pen on paper.

"As soon as we hit international waters, figure out how fast you can get a chopper or seaplane to us and have that ready to rock. Word is, Dav's hurt. We don't know how badly, or if Carrie's hurt too, but we can't take any chances. We get 'em both to medical attention as soon as possible."

"On it," he snapped. More scratching of the pen.

"We'll keep you posted as soon as we know something."

"He's alive, though?"

"Yes. So far as we know."

There was a significant pause, then: "Want the sit-rep here or do you need to go?"

"Hit it," Ana replied, bracing herself for the jolt she could see coming from a pothole. "Shit!" She scooted back onto the seat. "Sorry. Go ahead."

"Sit-rep is Queller and Damon were on the way to the hospital and there was an accident. Queller's dead."

"Aw, hell." Her brain caught up with the words. "Wait. Accident? Really?"

"Don't think so."

Shitshitshit. It kept going from bad to worse. "Damon?"

"Critical."

"Declan?"

"Improving."

"Thompson and Georgiade?"

"Under watch."

"Good. Good work." She didn't know what else to say, so she wrapped up with, "I'll call."

"Do that."

The lightning fast exchange had taken less than two minutes. Ana clicked off and used the hand holding the phone to brace herself for a particularly sharp turn.

"What's up?"

"Either Queller or Damon was our mole. Someone tried to take 'em out."

"Fuck," was Callahan's soft response. Holden didn't speak. He hadn't known either man for long.

"Yeah, I agree," Ana managed, thinking of the eager, soft-spoken Damon.

Queller was harder to pinpoint, personality wise, and that clued her in. "It's got to be Queller," she said. The uncle was tying up loose ends, and doing it fast.

That didn't bode well for Dav and Carrie.

Carrie drove like a maniac down the rutted road. Her lips set in a tight line, she navigated every turn with the latent skill of a veteran race car driver. Her lament that she'd not driven in years proved that the skill, when combined with the threat of imminent death, could be recovered in an instant.

"You have missed your calling, Carrie-mou," Dav said, feeling weaker and more feverish by the moment. He coughed and she looked over. "Keep your eyes on the road," he said, more sharply than he'd intended.

"My calling?"

"NASCAR, or the Indy 500, would be glad to have you." He coughed again and couldn't suppress the groan at the pain in his head and hand.

"Are you okay?" she asked, her voice sharp and high with tension.

"No, but I am alive and so are you," he replied with force. "I will be thankful for that for now."

"It's the hand, isn't it?" She dared to look again, despite his order. "It's infected."

"I think so, yes. It was very badly broken and the conditions were—" He hesitated, struggling to think of the proper American term.

"Barbaric?"

He laughed. "Yes, that will do. I was going to say, less than . . ." Bump, rut, bump, pain, pain, pain sang through him like a pattern.

"Less than?"

"Sanitary." He finally managed the word, over the roar of the road. "It has not been tended to in several days. I did not stop to wash the wound, thinking only to get back to the cell, and out, with you." He grunted in pain as they swerved suddenly.

"Sorry, sorry," she muttered. "Damn road. Doesn't anyone in whereeverthehellweare believe in paving?"

"Belize, the nice man in camouflage said," he offered, and realized that the laugh bubbling inside him was vastly inappropriate to the setting. "And I'm guessing that no, they do not pave things here."

As he said it, she gasped. "Oh, my God, paved road!"

"Efaristo, Cristos." Thank God. He knew he'd lapsed into Greek, but the words were wavering a bit in his mind, along with the need to burst into laughter.

The smoother ride was like a miracle. He sat up, feeling the grating of his ribs. He was fairly sure that he had cracked at least one rib, perhaps several in his many falls in the tunnels. The long, albeit shallow, wounds on his back stung with his sweat and he knew he was bleeding on the scant remains of his shirt and into the leather of the seat.

It didn't matter though, if Carrie got out alive. He would like to live too, he decided blearily, but she mattered more.

"Which way?" she asked, peering ahead into the distance. He could see now that the road joined another in a T formation. They would have to choose a direction.

"We will flip a drachma," he managed, coughing again, feeling the pain in his ribs, chest and back. "Ahhh, that hurts."

"Oh, God, Dav, look," she moaned, as four men stepped

into the road, weapons drawn. She slowed. "I'll put it in reverse, we'll go back." She started to do so and he heard the despair in her indrawn breath. Painfully, he turned to see. Racing up behind them was another Jeep, much like their own. It skidded to a spinning stop, blocking their retreat.

They were boxed in.

"Drive forward," one of the men yelled. "Don't try anything or we'll shoot her."

Dav knew what that meant, even in his delirious state. "Carrie. Stop."

"Oh, my God, Dav, what do we do?"

"We do what they want." He forced the words out, but his tongue felt thick and tangled. "For now, we are free, and we are alive. If we can stay that way, we will. I am so very sorry, Carrie-mou."

"Shut up," she fired back. "Just shut up. This is not your fault. And by God, where there's life there's fucking hope, okay? We're not dead yet."

"That's my Carrie-mou," he said, at once both stung and proud of her spirit.

She followed the gunmen's directions, pulling off the road again onto yet another rutted track. In a smaller clearing there was some kind of building. It looked like a park service facility, with road machines and a small compound with official-looking vehicles.

They were pulled roughly out of the car and marched inside as the second Jeep followed them in.

"Ah, welcome, welcome," an older, white-haired gentleman called, standing to greet them. The genial comments were accompanied by the waving direction to chairs, given via a gun barrel, appointing locations for them to sit.

Adrenaline gave a rush of clarity and as Dav's vision sharpened, he saw that someone else sat before the old man. There was a two-second delay before recognition sizzled into his mind. With a roar, he leapt forward, fury suffusing his veins, driving him forward in a mindless rush. The blind anger obliterated thought as surely as the fever had.

"You son of a bitch, you fucking bastard," he shouted, reaching for Niko with both hands, determined to wrap even his damaged hand around his brother's throat and choke the life out of him.

"Stop him," the older man said quietly, his words barely discernable over the curses as Dav stumbled forward, bent on destruction.

Hands immediately jerked him to a stop, pinioning his arms and banding around his chest. The agony of his ribs and back were a dash of sanity in his madness, stopping his headlong sprint for his brother.

The older man clucked with disapproval. "Now, now, is that any way to greet your long-lost brother, eh? No love for the risen dead, the prodigal son?" He tut-tutted again. "And such language. Why would you greet him with these hateful epithets?" The faint disapproving smile dropped away, replaced by cold indifference. "If you cannot be civil, be silent," he ordered coldly. To the men holding Dav, he said, "Put him there, in that chair. Tie him well. The woman too."

They were both bundled into their chairs and bound, arms to sides, then arms to chairs. Dav's only consolation was that Niko was also bound.

This then, was the real threat, this man. He stared at him, searching his mind for any shred of recognition, any glimpse of who he was or why he was doing this.

While something about him was familiar, he couldn't place him.

Carrie had no such problem. "Mr. Kerriat, why are you doing this? What have we ever done to you? You're my client, you know me. Why would you hurt Dav, or me?"

The older man smiled and it was a bitter, knowing smile. "Yes, yes. Your gallery was quite the pivot point in my plans over the years, my dear. You see, I saw young Dav here, mooning after you, years ago. I was already cultivating my long-term strategy, considering how to hurt him before I eliminated him. Then you got in trouble." He frowned. "I had thought you useless to achieving my ends."

"Why?" Dav could not fathom this. "What have I done that you should want my death?"

"Ah, that is the question, isn't it?" the man drawled, uncorking a bottle of red wine that sat on a nearby table and pouring himself a glass. He swirled it, sniffed, and drank with a deep appreciation before answering.

"There are so many reasons," he allowed with a teasing smile.

"Sir?" one of the men from the road came in, interrupting.

Anger crawled over their captor's features before he schooled them. "What?" He lashed the man with the word.

The man winced but continued. "We have more company. Two SUVs. It seems to be his security team." The man pointed Dav's way and despite the fact that these newcomers, too, were under the gun, Dav felt hope lift his heart. Gates. Could it be Gates?

"Bring them in. I might as well deal with them all at once."

Within minutes there was the sound of additional vehicles and their captor smiled as he sipped his wine, at ease in the hard wooden chair he'd chosen.

Slamming doors and the thud of feet heralded company. The door opened and Gates, Ana, and five of their team were prodded in at gunpoint.

"Hello, Gates," Dav said, almost merrily, knowing he sounded like an idiot. He couldn't help himself.

"Hey, Dav. I thought you were going to let Ana and me check out this part of the world for you, before you bought up the whole thing."

"You know I am frequently hasty." A patent falsehood,

but it made a good comeback. Dav smiled, pleased at the thought. "I'm a bit feverish, so please forgive my . . . repartee."

"It's just good to hear your voice," Ana added.

"Be quiet, all of you," the older man ordered, evidently tired of the banter.

"Hello, Mr. Gianikopolis," Gates drawled, turning to the older man. "Dav, meet your uncle. I don't know what name he goes by now, but his birth certificate says his name is Miklos Gianikopolis. He's your father's bastard brother."

Dav stared, astounded. Now that he knew, he could see why the man seemed familiar. There was the same tilt to the head, the same arrogant set to the shoulders. A similar look in the dark eyes.

It all made a sick kind of sense now. His father's pitting of him against Niko.

"He fought you for the family business and you lost," Dav guessed.

The man spun his way, menace in every feature. "I did *not* lose. I won, but our father still chose him."

"Just as my father initially chose Niko," Dav said, nodding. For the first time, Niko spoke.

"What are you talking about? What are you saying?"

"You had won, Niko, until you got Theresa pregnant and her family had to be bought off. Father didn't want any more bastards mucking up the works, no matter what he told you." Dav said the words mockingly, knowing they would twist in his brother's gut. A little payback for all Niko had done.

Niko struggled to rise up, to come after Dav, since the old man was long dead and beyond his reach.

The older man sighed and turned to him. "This is why you fail, Niko," he said with false sorrow. Stepping closer, he slapped Niko hard enough to whip his head back. "Hasty action leads to mistakes." Slap. "Stupid folly, misplaced trust." Slap, slap, slap. "Foolish risks." With a last vicious slap the old man stepped back, shaking his hand. The anger cleared from his face like a storm cloud flying across the sky. "Nothing that leads to success in the end," he said sententiously. He tsked once more, and shot Niko, point-blank, in the head.

Everything stopped, every breath, every movement—even sound.

They all watched in horror as Niko slumped forward, dead in an instant as the bullet pierced his brain.

"He was so tiresome toward the end," the older man said, conversationally. "I had hoped he would shape up to be my heir. I even eliminated his previous connections to bind him more closely to me, but"—sadness now colored his tone—"alas, it was not to be. He got too wary, too concerned for his own safety. It really was too bad."

He patted Niko's bowed head with a look of distant affection, or as one might pat a dead dog one would miss somewhat.

"Now, who is it that managed to kill my assassins? Niko here told me that my second set of watchdogs, who were supposed to kill you"—now he walked around behind Dav, leaning down to hiss the words in his ear—"the very ones who killed Niko's team so efficiently, were also taken down."

There was a moment of silence; then he shouted. "Who was it! Tell me!"

There was total silence for a moment, and then Holden spoke. "I did, sir. I was the first-in scout," he said. "When I saw they were going to fire down into the, uh, the holding pen, I took action."

Aghast, Dav looked at Gates and saw that Holden was lying. No one else might know, but Gates's eyes were furious. He, Dav and Ana knew that Dav's newfound uncle might treat Holden to the same fate as Niko.

The man stood up smoothly, with just a brief cuff to the back of Dav's head. Turning, he eyed Holden with interest.

"Good shot, I hear," the man complimented, setting down his weapon to pick up his wine.

"Thank you, sir."

Another interruption from outside had him snarling again. "What?"

The armed man blanched, but his voice was steady as he said, "We've turned back a motorist, but we shouldn't stay more than another hour, sir. Also, there's been some disturbance up the hill. I've dispatched men to check it out."

"Yes, yes, don't bother me with these details." He glared at the man. "And I will be finished when I am finished."

As closely as he was watching Gates, Dav could tell there was something either amiss with this new information, or unexpected. The barest quirk of the lips, the narrowing of his eyes gave him away. Hyperaware of everything, Dav knew he would pay for the stress on his body. Regardless, he forced himself to think.

Gates was straining against the need to look at Ana. Deliberately *not* looking. Interesting. He knew it meant something but even with adrenaline-sharpened senses, he couldn't make his brain con out what that elusive meaning might be.

The thought of life and hope flitted into his mind again, as another wave of heat flowed over him, diverting what focus he'd achieved. Sweat broke out on his neck and shoulders, burning its way down his back once again. He lost all notion of what Gates or Carrie or anyone was doing, for a moment.

"So, Davros." The now-hated voice filled his ears, closer. He opened his eyes, wondering when he'd closed them. He was losing time to the fever now, which was dangerous.

"Yes, Uncle," he accorded the old man the title, in Greek. "You said something?"

"Did you ever suspect? Ever know that I was there?"

Dav shook his head, probably not the wisest move as his senses whirled. "No. I never knew."

It seemed to be the right thing to say, because the man nodded and turned back to his wine.

"Just as well. If you had no idea, then you left no evidence linking me to anything. What about you, Mr. and Mrs. Bromley. Whom have you told about me? Eh?"

Gates smiled. "No one. Who would we tell? We've been following the trail to Dav."

"Ah, yes, the trail to Davros," he repeated agreeably. "You should not have been able to find him." The man smiled and cocked his head to one side, as if he were just giving them a gentle reprimand before letting them off for good behavior.

"It is too bad. You are better than I thought, but that means you will have to die too. Such a waste. Especially you, Mrs. Bromley. Before I kill you, let me say *bravissimo* on your brilliant handiwork last year. Very keen intelligence work." He sighed. "Although I suppose I have you to thank for this debacle." He waved his hand at Dav's team, lined up with their hands linked on top of their heads, a gunman behind them to keep it that way. "Your ability to find information is legendary."

Dav saw the twitch in Ana's shoulders. There it was again. Through sheer force of will, Ana had managed not to look at Gates. There was a smile in her voice as she answered. "Thank you, but I can't take all the credit. There are just so many wonderful databases, you know."

The man nodded. "Quite true. So. We must move on," he said with a determined note entering his voice as he poured himself some more wine, and picked up his weapon.

"Ms. McCray, your grandfather still has influence on the Ways and Means Committee in Congress. I would be willing to let you go, if you will assist me in persuading your grandfather to make some recommendations."

"Do it, Carrie," Dav hissed, praying that she would, praying she would survive.

"I don't think so," she answered, firmly, with conviction.

Then Dav heard the old man's chuckle. It even sounded like his father.

How strange he thought as he fought off yet another wave of sick heat and cold.

"What is it you want?" Dav croaked, thinking he could buy the man off. Probably not, given all that his uncle had done to bring them to this point, but worth a try. "If it is money," he began, but the man cut him off.

"Oh no, young Davros. It has nothing to do with money. I have plenty of that. It seems—" He used the gun to lift Dav's chin, force him to meet the hard, cold and bitter old gaze. "That our family has a knack for making money. And a lot of it. Who do you think financed the interesting operation that brought you here, eh? Niko?" He spat the name with disgust. "I don't think so. My brother, curse his name, was right about one thing. Niko was definitely the weaker son, unworthy to inherit."

There was a sound outside and the man looked up, annoyed, but left the gun under Dav's chin. Oddly, the cool barrel felt good on his hot face. If he was going to die, at least the gun was cool.

The bleak thought snapped him back to reality for a moment. He didn't want to die. Not now. Not with Carrie unrescued, unsafe.

"You." The barrel lifted away, to gesture at one of the armed men. "Todd, go see what that's about."

"Yessir."

Another of their guards left. Dav flicked the barest glance at Gates. His friend was frowning and resolutely not looking at any of his team. Dav managed to count them.

Not enough. As his gaze passed over Callahan, he smiled at the fiery woman. She looked mutinous, but was holding steady. He recognized the others as well, but couldn't find all their names in his bleary brain. He managed to catch each of their gazes, however, give them a tiny nod and a smile.

They were there for him. How sad. And how strong.

There was another sound outside, but they heard someone call out, "All clear."

"About time," Dav's uncle declared, twitching the barrel of the gun back under Dav's chin so that his head bobbed a bit with the forceful shift. "Now, to business, young Davros."

His open hand cracked forcefully into Dav's cheek, rocking his head to the side and wrenching his neck. A fresh wave of sweat, pain and nausea exploded within him as every nerve registered the pain and echoed it in a thousand sensory shouts.

"Ms. McCray." He distantly heard the hated voice addressing Carrie. He had to concentrate. He had to save Carrie. He loved Carrie, and that was very important for some reason. More important than anything. "I'm sorry, but you are being very uncooperative. It is a shame to kill you, but I'm afraid I must." He turned the gun her way and Dav, as blackness threatened to overwhelm him, rose up, chair and all, to thrust his shoulder under the man's gun arm.

The room exploded in gunfire. Bodies spun and fell, and for Dav, everything blurred but the need to get between Carrie and the man with the gun.

Dav landed heavily on his uncle, but that wasn't enough to stop the spry, older man, who shifted under him, taking aim at Carrie once more.

When he fired, however, his howl of frustration blended with Dav's scream of denial.

"Nooooo!"

"Oheeeee!"

The Greek and the English slurred together, as Dav wrenched the arm of the chair out of its mooring, using the freed arm, with its wooden attachment, like a club.

Grappling with him, the other man took hold of his bandaged hand and squeezed with wrenching force.

Agony blinded Dav, and he retched in instinctive reaction. But he could not let Carrie die.

Would.

Not.

Hardly cognizant of his actions, he braced his legs, kicking upward as his uncle brought the gun to bear again. The shot went wide and hit one of the old man's henchmen square in the chest. The look of surprise on the other man's face was the last thing Dav saw before the fearsome darkness swallowed him up.

Chapter 21

"What the hell?"

Dav heard the voices swimming in his mind, but couldn't identify them as he faltered in and out of consiousness. That had been Gates. What was Gates doing here?

"McGuire?" Now Ana. Was she here too? Where were they?

"Cover those two."

He didn't know that voice, he decided as he sagged into the arms of sleep again.

There was rustling and chaos in his mind even as he sank deeper into his agonized stupor, but he was jerked back to the moment when someone cut his bonds.

"Ahhhhhhhhhhh," he moaned, struggling to hold onto consciousness he'd so forcefully regained. Urgency filled him with sudden fear.

He had to know. Had to. "Carrie? Carrie?"

"Hang on, Dav. We're checking her."

Who was checking her? Where was she? He couldn't clear the blurriness from his vision. He heard the sounds, but they made no sense. He tried to move, felt something within him tear anew, and pain engulfed him from head to toe like a blaze of fire.

His last thought was of Carrie.

* * *

"We have to get him out of here. He needs a hospital, now."

"I'll handle this fuckup here. I can wait for the cavalry as well as anyone," McGuire grunted.

"Hurry," Ana urged.

The team improvised gurneys, and lifted the unconscious Carrie and the equally unconscious Dav into them for the short journey to the back of the waiting SUVs. Thank God they were now on smooth road.

"How'd you find us?" she asked McGuire as the injured pair were loaded up.

"Shot Hines, back up a ways," he said casually, waving off in the distance. "Ran into this fella who said he knew where you were." McGuire paused long enough to turn and spit a stream of tobacco juice from the chaw in his cheek. Ana tried not to wince. "Wasn't sure it was legit, but I checked it out and saw your mark." He nodded at Ana.

"You left a mark?" Gates said as he lifted the end of their makeshift stretcher, settling it gently into the cargo area, where the seats had been flipped down. Gear and blankets were packed around their patients for stability.

"Habit," Ana managed, trying not to think about the damage to both Carrie and Dav.

"So, I ran into this guy again up here, before I got to this locale," McGuire drawled. "And he said you were in fat trouble. Since we both had our sniper gear"—he lifted the sleek, scoped weapon off his hip in salute to the unknown assistant—"we figured we'd help out."

Ana gave McGuire a look. His khaki shorts and Hawaiian print shirt weren't exactly unobtrusive. "He took point," McGuire said innocently, defending his see-it-a-mile-away attire.

"Ready, boss," Holden said, jumping into the driver's seat.

Ana hugged McGuire. "The cavalry's already on its way, but we'll give them the exact coordinates."

"Young Franklin and I can handle it," he said cheerily. "You get going."

She could see him waving in the side-view mirror as they pulled out, for all the world like a happy grandparent seeing "those kids" off on their way home.

"He's a piece of work," Gates muttered, bracing himself against the sway and speed of the SUV as he started cataloging the injuries to his friend, and to Carrie.

"The best."

He grinned, but it quickly faded as they looked back. They'd brought emergency medical supplies, of course, and Holden had hooked both Carrie and Dav up to IV fluids, but said he didn't dare do anything else without knowing the extent of their injuries.

"We're going to have to risk a local hospital."

The phone rang, startling them both.

Ana answered it and all the others could hear was her, "Yes. Yes. Perfect. We'll be there. Yes."

"That was enlightening," Gates said, with heavy sarcasm.

"There's a helicopter waiting at Punta Gorda. There's a Coast Guard hospital ship just off shore, redirected from a stop in Mazatlán. They have full supplies now, thanks to Geddey, and are ready for Dav and Carrie."

Gates turned to Holden. "Drive faster."

"Yessir." Their speed increased to a smooth ninety miles an hour, and Holden never wavered in his focus from the paved road.

It was forever before they saw the outskirts of the port. They saw flashing lights and Holden groaned, until the police vehicle whipped out in front of them, clearing the way to the docks. Along the path, other police blocked traffic.

"How'd he manage this?" Ana wondered aloud.

"Geddey knows his stuff," Gates said.

Within minutes they were loaded into the helicopter and flying to meet the ship.

The narrow corridors of the hospital ship made a terrible waiting room as the medics worked on both Dav and Carrie.

"I know they're doing everything they can," Gates said tersely. Ana could see he wanted to pace, but the confined space made it a futile desire. "I just wish I knew something, anything, we could do."

"Me too, love, me too," Ana said, moving into his arms, striving to reassure both herself and him with the connection.

"We need to check in," he said, after a moment. Listening to his pounding heartbeat, she agreed. Maybe that would settle him, give them both something constructive to do.

"Yes, but should we—" She hesitated, raising her head to meet his gaze, then blurted it out. "Shouldn't we be here, in case?"

Gates understood. "They know where to find us. Let's go make some calls."

Their first call was to McGuire, who let them know his "buddy" in camouflage was nowhere to be found. Not that they had expected anything different, but Ana felt a wave of disappointment.

"That figures," Gates said, remembering how easily the man had slipped away, lost himself in the jungle.

McGuire regaled him with the arrival of the locals and how much fun they'd had getting Franklin's dogs to stop growling at the old man's bound guards. According to McGuire, Franklin had let the more menacing shepherd walk up and down behind the seated men, growling like he was going to attack at any moment. McGuire had heartily approved.

"Did he make it?" Gates asked, sure that McGuire would understand. Ana watched him, waiting for the response.

"Nah," McGuire said, unrepentant. "That blow to the head, along with the shot Callahan got off with the other guard's gun, did him in. Can't say I'm sorry, if he's the cause of all this."

"He is, and I'm not sorry either." Gates heard Ana's sigh of relief.

Ana's phone rang, and she flipped it open. "It's Bax," she mouthed.

"Okay, McGuire, we'll see you back in San Francisco, you hear?" Gates made that firm; he wanted to be sure McGuire filled them all in. "You've got a debrief to give."

"Pronto," McGuire drawled. "You give that fireball wife of yours a hug for me. Didn't get to say good-bye."

"I will." Gates smiled as Ana grabbed a pen from where she'd stuck it in her ponytail.

"Righty-o," and with that he was gone. Gates moved behind his wife and wrapped his arms around her as she talked to the San Francisco detective.

"Got it," she said into the phone, noting down a series of numbers, circling one that held four digits. Her call with Baxter was brief, and her notes singularly frustrating in their lack of readable information. "They found Cal," she relayed, leaning back into his embrace with a burdened sigh. "He'd been beaten and was in the hospital, that's why we couldn't find him. His friend, the one he went to New York for, is dead. Break-in, they say."

"Break-in," Gates snapped sarcastically. "Is that what they're calling it these days?"

"Of course." She smiled at his tone, adding wearily, "Violence on the rise, everywhere, you know?"

"Geddey found evidence of Niko all over Inez's apartment, so he could have proved Niko did it, if we'd needed to," Gates said, relating the other bit of news that had come in via text from Geddey.

"Helpful, if he wasn't already dead and we wanted to

keep him alive and rotting in jail somewhere. But at least her parents can know for sure," Ana said on a sigh. "It won't help, but . . ."

Gates rubbed a hand down her back. "I know. What is the word, closure?"

"Yeah. Maybe all this insanity will give some of that closure to Dav. What else?"

"Geddey found enough to link Queller to Niko and the uncle both." Anger tugged at him, but he quashed it. Nothing to be done now but track back and plug whatever leaks Queller had caused. "He was feeding everyone information."

"But why?" Ana wondered, and he heard the plaint of betrayal in her voice.

Since he was still stinging over Queller's betrayal himself, with no more clue, he just cursed. "Geddey doesn't know that yet, but he's working on it."

This time is was her soothing him, but he could tell she was equally injured by the young man's murky allegiance. "Whatever the reasons, he didn't profit from it," she finally managed. "And I can quit looking over my shoulder too."

"Hines?"

Ana smiled now, on surer footing. "According to McGuire's briefing to me, Hines is toast. What did McGuire tell you?"

"That our mystery couple was instrumental in our rescue once again. He didn't seem to be shocked that sniper guy was gone." And here Gates put on McGuires's New Orleans drawl. "Hell, when the dust cleared and the shootin' stopped, ol' McGuire couldn't find that feller anywhere, *cher*."

"Big surprise," she muttered. "Who was that masked man?"

"I have no idea, but I'm glad he and his girlfriend were on our side."

"Me too."

They continued to talk, and more calls came in updating them on Damon—he was conscious and would recover—

and on Declan. To everyone's relief, Declan's memory had returned, up to and including the offer of singing lessons.

As they finished their respective news, a young ensign arrived in the office they were using, and they were shown to quarters with the reassurance that Dav and Carrie were still in the hands of the doctors.

After a shower and a meal, they put on scrubs the Coast Guard provided while their clothes were washed. They talked. They sent texts and asked questions.

But mostly, they waited.

Finally, hours later, as night fell and dinner was being cleared, one of the doctors came to find them.

They both jumped to their feet. "Dav? Carrie?" They called the names with one voice.

The doctor smiled, but he didn't look like everything was peachy-keen, Gates thought.

"Holding their own, both of them," he said wearily, sitting down at the table and motioning them to do the same. "They were both severely dehydrated, and hadn't eaten for several days. Ms. McCray's injuries are less serious, of course, but she has a concussion and is reacting oddly to some of the medications. We're going to monitor her closely, run some tests." He pulled off the cap that matched his scrubs to wearily run his hands over his bald pate.

"And Dav?" Gates asked softly.

"I need some coffee," the doctor procrastinated, rising to get a cup from a pot nearby. "Do you want any?"

Ana and Gates exchanged glances. Not good. They demurred.

"Just spit it out, Doctor," Ana urged. "Please."

"Mr. Gianikopolis isn't in good shape. He's got two broken ribs, and two others are cracked. One of them punctured his lung. We've got that situation under control and have reinflated the lung, dealt with the ribs. Being dehydrated is a severe handicap here because he's not going to fight infection as easily and he's got a whopper of an infection from the injury to his hand. He's running an extremely high fever." The doctor looked solemn. "It's a miracle he was even coherent over the last twenty-four hours, much less doing what you claim he did to save his friend."

"He's strong," Ana managed, groping for Gates's hand. It was going to get worse, she could tell.

"He's going to need to be. We had to remove the little finger on his left hand. He had a compound fracture and the wound had gone septic. We couldn't save it, I'm afraid."

"But he'll live?" Ana insisted, feeling hope rise. Was that the worst? What was a finger, among friends? "He'll be okay?"

"I hope so, if the infection and fever can be brought under control. We've got him on IV antibiotics, fluids, you name it. The conditions"—the doctor shrugged—"were terrible and these injuries would have been bad even if he'd gotten medical help right away. As it is, he's had two to three days with the infection gaining a foothold in his body. He's responding to the treatment so far, but that's right now. We'll be monitoring him around the clock and we're going to all pray the infection isn't a resistant strain, that there are no other injuries internally or externally, and that he's still strong enough to fight."

Gates looked determined on Dav's behalf. "Oh, he'll fight. When can we see him?"

"Couple hours," the doctor said, looking at his watch. "Get some sleep. I'll have somebody wake you."

The hours passed, and finally an orderly came for them. The ship's sickroom was empty now, except for Dav and

Carrie. Both lay still, with monitors beeping around them, and nurses and corpsmen hovering nearby.

They went to Dav first.

"Hey, buddy," Gates said. "It's Gates. We got you out," he said. "You and Carrie both. You're safe, okay?"

Ana squeezed Dav's unbandaged hand, and as she had with Declan, she gently stroked Dav's arm. "Hey, dude," she drawled. "You've been loafing long enough. Time to wake up and say hello. We've come a long way to see you, you know. Least you could do is open your eyes and give us a word.

"I will give you a word," came the faint, raspy reply.

Delighted, Ana gasped and leaned closer. "Hey, you. Welcome back. I'll read you the riot act later. What's the word?"

"Carrie?" The whisper was stronger, but he didn't open his eyes.

"Alive. Concussed, but alive."

"Ahhhhhhh." The sound was a pleased sigh, and a smile bowed his lips. "Good. Love her. Going to marrrrrrry herrrrr," he slurred, and slipped back into sleep.

"Did he say what I think he said?" Gates was leaning close as well, from the other side of the bed.

"That he loves her and is going to marry her?"

"Yep," Gates agreed, grinning now, as well.

"Excellent," Ana crowed softly. "Now, he'll get well."

The nurse peered around the curtain. "You should let him rest."

"We will," Ana said, straightening. "We'll just look in on Ms. McCray, then let them both rest."

"Good," the nurse approved, obviously protective of her patients.

"Hey, Carrie," Ana said, as they entered the curtained space. Carrie's cuts and bruises stood in stark contrast to her fair skin, and her dark hair hadn't yet been washed.

It lay in lank strands on the pillow, striking still, in spite of everything. Ana could see why Dav had fallen for this interesting, gorgeous and obviously strong woman.

"Who is it?" she managed blearily, struggling and failing to open her eyes.

"It's Ana and Gates. We won't stay long, but we wanted to tell you that you're safe. We're on a hospital ship."

"Dav?"

The question made Ana smile and Gates reached out a hand to his wife. She took it as she answered Carrie's question, tears in her voice. "He's alive. It's going to be tough for him, but he said to tell you he loves you."

Carrie's eyes flew open at that, focused on Ana for a moment, then unfocused again. She groaned. "Hurts to open my eyes."

"You've got a concussion."

There was a throat-clearing noise from the nurse.

"We have to go," Ana whispered, "but it's real, Carrie. He loves you." She flicked a glance at Gates before she continued. Her inner sense told her there was something amiss between the two of them, so she added, "He's never said it to anyone else, Carrie. He's never asked anyone to marry him before. He wants to ask you, when you'll let him."

Gates frowned at her words, and she could tell he was puzzled, but it was a woman's intuition thing. He wouldn't understand even if she could find the words to explain it to him.

"Give him a chance, Carrie. Give him a chance."

Another "Ahem" had them standing, moving away from the bed. "We'll be here, Carrie, if you need us," Gates added as a parting shot, before they left the room.

In the bed, Carrie heard them leave, felt the nurse's presence at the bedside.

"It hurts when I open my eyes," she complained, hating

the whine in her voice even as she seemed to be powerless to stop it.

"Concussion, ma'am." The woman hesitated. "And you've thrown up twice."

"I did it before, in the jungle," Carrie managed to tell her, worried now that she had some dread jungle disease that would take her away from Dav, just when she might have found the courage to love him.

The last thing she'd seen before her chair was knocked down and her head connected with the leg of the table was Dav shoving forward, chair and all, to deflect the shot aimed at her. He had been willing to give his life for hers.

How could she not believe in that? How could she not believe that there was a chance he could love her, if he was willing to do that?

"Get some rest, ma'am," the nurse advised, and she felt the woman pat her arm. "We'll do some more tests in the morning, see what else needs to be done."

"Okay," Carrie whispered, and the words seemed loud in her ears. She was fading into sleep, but the warm knowledge of Ana's words followed her in, and sang in her dreams.

Hours later, she awoke in the semidark. The room had been dimmed so that both she and Dav could sleep. When she stirred, the nurse padded over on quiet feet.

"Hey," the woman whispered, "how're you feeling?"

"Better," Carrie admitted, after a brief internal assessment. "But I have to—" She hesitated.

"Use the facilities," the nurse supplied with a smile. "Perfectly normal after two bags of fluids. Do you think you can walk, or should I get a bedpan?"

"Walk," Carrie said, determined to at least see Dav on the way to or from the bathroom.

They made it to the small ship's lavatory and back without incident.

"Could I sit with him?" Carrie asked, motioning toward Dav's still, sleeping form in the next bed.

The nurse frowned, but nodded. "Not for long, though. You need to sleep more yourself. Sleep heals," she murmured.

"I'll sleep, but I need to sit with him, just for a bit."

The nurse fussed over the chair and over Carrie until she wanted to scream at the woman to go away, let her have some space and peace. She didn't do it, but she let out a sigh of relief when the woman finally moved back to her nearby desk with the parting shot that she'd be back in a few minutes.

Carrie waited until she could hear the woman shuffling papers and tapping keys before she turned to Dav. He looked strange, lying so still. He was so vital and brilliantly alive, but this was shocking in a way, this unnatural stillness.

"Dav?" she whispered. "Dav-mou?"

For some reason that seemed to get through to him, the endearment.

"Carrie?" The faintest breath of a word, although he didn't open his eyes at all.

"Right here," she said, pressing his large hand between her own smaller palms.

"It's dark. Are we still in the cave? I can't move." He stirred restlessly on the bed. "Why can't I move? Carrie?"

"Shhhhhh," she soothed hastily, shooting a worried glance toward the nurse's station. "We're on the hospital ship, Dav. We're safe."

He was quiet so long, she thought he'd gone back to sleep, but finally, when she'd made the reluctant decision to call the nurse, get up, and let him rest, he spoke again. She had to lean in to hear him.

"You were right, you know. To turn me down," he rasped, still not opening his eyes.

"No, no, Dav, I wasn't," she protested, her voice urgent. He had to understand. . . .

It was his turn to shush her. "No, you were. I didn't understand," he whispered softly, his voice fading out for a moment. "But I do now," he hurried on, as if the words must come out immediately with no interruption. "I understand."

He managed to turn his head toward her and she saw the gleam of his glorious dark eyes as he managed to fight off the drugs, his injuries and even the sleep that he so desperately needed to open his eyes and look at her. His dark gaze thrilled her and he smiled. "You're so beautiful," he said, and a smile curved his beautiful lips. He drew a deep breath, still smiling though his eyes were drifting shut again. "I love you, Carrie-mou."

"Oh, Dav." The words she'd longed to hear, real, heartfelt words of love, shook her to the depths of her soul.

His strength was visibly fading, but he smiled again and squeezed the hands she'd wrapped around his. He tried to raise them to his lips, but didn't have the strength. "Marry me, Carrie-mou," he said, his voice dropping back to a whisper. "Do not turn me down again. I could not bear to live without you now."

"I won't," she breathed. "I won't turn you down," she corrected, seeing the beginnings of his frown, realizing how she'd phrased her reply.

"Ahhh." He smiled again and his eyes drifted all the way closed. "Good. Eh-la, this is good. I love you." He squeezed her hand, and his eyelids fluttered, trying to open. Trying to communicate more. "It is good to say it," was all he managed.

"It is," she whispered, rising to press a kiss to his forehead, and his lips, which parted softly under hers. "It is good to say it. I love you too, Dav."

"Ahh," he said, on a sigh as he drifted back to sleep. "Tha's goooood."

Carrie let the nurse chivvy her back to bed a few minutes later, but she went to sleep with a smile on her face. Content.

Epilogue

The reporter stood on the sidewalk outside the gallery, twisting the earpiece into a more comfortable place in her ear. Her cameraman was flicking his fingers in the count-down so she stopped fiddling and gave her neat, pressed shirt a last quick adjustment and deliberately widened her smile.

"Three, two, one, live feed." The camera's light blinked green on her indrawn breath.

"We're here outside the Prometheus Gallery tonight, which is hosting the cream of San Francisco's elite. This is the first major showing since the gallery's owner, Carrie McCray, and her new husband, renowned billionaire shipping magnate Davros Gianikopolis returned from Central America where they were held hostage.

"Shortly after their heroic rescue and their return to the United States, Ms. McCray and Mr. Gianikopolis were married in a private ceremony attended only by their closest friends."

The light blinked red, and she continued the voice-over, knowing they would be showing pictures, released selectively to the media, of the happy couple on their wedding day. The bride had been married in a glorious confection of cream-colored silk created by a local designer. The groom, resplendent and handsome in a tuxedo, despite the grievous injuries suffered during his captivity, had beamed with barely suppressed joy.

"Seen here in a photo released after they left for their honeymoon in an undisclosed location, the couple appears to be fully recovered from their ordeal."

The light blinked back to green and she turned slightly to her right, letting her best side show to the camera. She knew the cameraman would be panning wide to get the crowd, and the elegant sign outside Prometheus.

Her busy intern had prepped the area, and was just out of camera range, drawing arriving celebrities and couples over to speak to her on camera as they arrived.

The feed in her ear gave her details to prompt the approaching grouping. "Mrs. Bellweather, I understand you've been a longtime supporter of the Prometheus Gallery."

The society matron did her bit, preening into the camera and giving her an excellent sound bite. Her assistant hustled another couple over, but their comments were gushing and far too lengthy. She moved out of the camera's ideal range as she spotted another local couple. The woman had been in the news about the same time as Carrie McCray, involved somehow in the scandal of the previous year.

Yet, here she was, attending the reopening of the gallery.

"Good evening." The reporter smiled brightly, praying they would talk to her as the cameraman refocused on her and the patrons. "Would you like to say a few words about this evening's event?"

The man avoided her gaze, dropping just slightly behind his wife. The reporter gritted her teeth. The man was gorgeous in a good-camera way with lots of angles and planes to his face, but he wasn't going to talk to her, she could tell. The wife, on the other hand, beamed. This would work, since the woman was succinct and positive about the gallery and the reopening event. Her producer kept urging her to keep them talking, that it was a good clip.

"This is going to be a lovely evening, I can feel it," the woman said, her smile dazzling. It helped that she was visibly pregnant. The delighted glow she exuded would show up well on camera.

"We're so happy to be here. My husband, Gunther, and I"—she smiled over her shoulder at her reluctant husband—"enjoy Prometheus, and are delighted to celebrate this special event."

"It's a lovely event, yes," the reporter prompted. "Have you and Mrs. Gianikopolis compared baby names?" she asked, referencing the society tidbit that Carrie McCray was already obviously pregnant, and probably had been before the wedding.

"Oh—" The woman blushed. "We're not that well acquainted, but of course, I wish her all the best."

"Thank you, Mrs. . . ." The reporter let her fill in the blank space.

The woman smiled into the camera and said, "I'm Mrs. Gunther Kraff," she offered, then smiled. "Caroline Kraff."

"Well, Caroline, thank you for speaking to me. Any words of wisdom for the newly married couple?"

Caroline smiled again, and the reporter hoped the camera was catching the gleam in her eye, and the twinkle of humor. It would make fabulous television.

"Oh, I wouldn't dream of it, but . . ." She glanced once more at her bashful husband, whose head was now ducked a bit.

"But?"

"Well, I'm sure they already know far more than I would about wisdom, but as to advice, they've already followed the advice I'd give."

"And what would that be?"

Caroline Kraff looked at the reporter with a shrewd,

knowing gaze, but the face she turned to the camera was once again that look of innocent, glowing happiness. “Why, when you’ve got a chance at love, take the shot.”

“There you have it,” the reporter said, obeying the signal in her ear to wrap it up. “Thank you, Mrs. Kraff, Mr. Kraff. Enjoy your evening. This is Melanie Stuart, live at the Prometheus Gallery in downtown San Francisco.”

From the balcony, Gates and Ana watched as the attractive pregnant lady and her husband were snagged by the reporter. Gates frowned at the man’s behavior, his avoidance of the camera, but the woman’s obvious pleasure belied any real suspicion.

Until they left the reporter and entered the gallery, that is. He saw the man straighten and sweep the crowd with an assessing gaze.

“Did you see that?” Ana whispered in his ear.

“Yeah,” he muttered, focusing in on the man, watching as Geddey’s men—no longer his team—caught Geddey’s reaction to the sweeping glance, and suggested that someone should get him the guest list and determine just who this was.

“Just like old times,” she said, snickering, remembering how he had told her he knew she wasn’t what she seemed when she too had entered the gallery and given that exact, measured assessment of the teeming crowd.

He laughed as well, never taking his eyes off the couple in question.

A booming laugh distracted him from his quarry and he turned to see Dav and a brilliantly beautiful Carrie coming his way. They looked happier than he’d ever seen either of them.

Ana slid her hand through the crook of his arm and leaned into him. “They look happy, don’t they?”

“They do.”

Dav strolled up, snagging two additional champagne flutes as he came. "You must have champagne, and we must have a toast."

"Absolutely," Gates said. "But first, do you recognize that couple?"

Carrie stepped to the balcony rail as well and looked down. "That's Caroline Yountz Kraff. She married a German software entrepreneur she met through her late husband."

"May he never rest in peace," Ana muttered, having been the target of Yountz's ire prior to his death.

"She looks happy," Dav offered.

"And he looks familiar," Gates replied.

Carrie tapped Gates's shoulder. "No business tonight."

She smiled, and Dav kissed her, and they all agreed. Raising her glass filled with what looked like champagne, she said, "To what should we toast?"

She saw Ana eyeing the glass and said, "Sparkling cider."

"Excellent vintage," was Ana's sly comment.

Dav tucked Carrie against his side and raised his glass as well, facing his best and dearest friends. "To love," he offered.

They each echoed him, "To love."

And drank.

Did you miss Jeanne's other books?
Go back and read them all!

Dark and Dangerous

Sizzling seduction and hair-raising suspense combine in Jeanne Adams's gripping new novel about a woman whose past returns—with a vengeance . . .

Nowhere to Hide

Dana Markham is up against a cold-blooded killer who knows her all too well: Donovan Walker. Wanted for drug trafficking, armed and dangerous—he's also her ex-husband. What she knows about him could land him behind bars forever . . . or put her and her young son in an early grave if Donovan finds them first. Dana's one chance lies with a man she barely knows at all. Tall and darkly sensual, Caine Bradley is an undercover FBI agent who's been posing as Walker's henchman. Compelled to work with Caine to lure her ex out of hiding, Dana must fight against her own raw, urgent needs. But is he who he says he is? Her passionate desire for him could be her salvation—or her greatest mistake . . .

Dark and Deadly

In Jeanne Adams's pulse-pounding thriller, a woman who's lost everything must turn to the man she considers her worst enemy. But he isn't the one who wants her dead . . .

No Escape

Cursed. Bad things happen to men who get close to Victoria Hagan. Now one of them has paid the ultimate price. Her ex-fiancé, Todd, has been found murdered in the very church where he left her at the altar—and Torie is the prime suspect. Her only hope is the last person she wants to see . . .

Ever since he advised his best friend not to marry her and the bride-to-be walked in on the conversation, Paul Jameson has stayed far away from Torie—and resisted their dangerously hot mutual attraction. Still, Paul promised Todd he would take care of Torie. She certainly needs him now . . . almost as much as he wants her. And that's exactly what a killer is counting on . . .

Deadly Little Secrets

In Jeanne Adams's electrifying thriller, a beautiful CIA agent and a billionaire shipping magnate find themselves in a desperate race against time . . .

Hot Pursuit

Security expert Gates Bromley's number one priority is protecting art collector Dav Gianikopolis. But when he joins forces with CIA Agent Ana Burton tracing several pieces of stolen art, Gates is distracted by the leggy brunette who stirs up the raciest thoughts . . .

After botching an operation that cost her colleagues' lives, Ana has been reassigned to cold cases. When news gets out that she's reopened a case involving stolen art and five brutal murders, Ana is almost killed. Seeking comfort in Gates's strong embrace is easy, but surrendering trust to the sexiest man she's ever known isn't—unless Gates can show her that an attraction this hot is worth all the risks. But first he'll have to stop a killer who's bent on keeping the past buried . . .